Thomas Mallon

WATERGATE

Thomas Mallon is the author of eight novels, including *Henry and Clara, Dewey Defeats Truman,* and *Fellow Travelers*. He is a frequent contributor to *The New Yorker, The New York Times Book Review,* and other publications.

www.thomasmallon.com

BOOKS BY THOMAS MALLON

Fiction

Arts and Sciences
Aurora 7
Henry and Clara
Dewey Defeats Truman
Two Moons
Bandbox
Fellow Travelers
Watergate

Nonfiction

Edmund Blunden
A Book of One's Own
Stolen Words
Rockets and Rodeos
In Fact
Mrs. Paine's Garage
Yours Ever

"It's a brilliant presentation, subtle and sympathetic but spiked with satire that captures [Nixon] in all his crippling self-consciousness, his boundless capacity for self-pity and re-invention."
—*The Washington Post*

"Within the framework of the true, Mallon also has to find the plausible, which he has done in satisfying ways. . . . Mallon renders the era, the people and the place in vivid detail." —*Los Angeles Times*

"It is perhaps the unique accomplishment of *Watergate*, the excellent new novel by Thomas Mallon, to depict Nixon not as a moral to a story, a symptom of political pathology, or a walking character flaw, but as a man." —*Washington Monthly*

"Remarkable. . . . The novel's true brilliance rests upon Mallon's ability to weave Watergate's oft-told events into a moral tragedy that feels wholly new." —*The Globe and Mail* (Toronto)

"A pleasurably perverse and darkly comedic thriller. . . . A beguilingly intricate structure." —*The Seattle Times*

"Never less than entertaining. *Watergate* demonstrates how a novelist can peel back layers of personality and motivation that historians must leave undisturbed. . . . *Watergate* is a vivid and witty novel." —*The Wall Street Journal*

"Superbly entertaining fiction. . . . Mallon's insightful novel is a dream realized, not only for Watergate junkies but also for anyone fascinated by politics and human folly." —*Richmond Times-Dispatch*

"Full of telling, vivid detail. . . . Mallon gets each of the characters with perfect pitch." —*The Boston Globe*

"*Watergate*, one of the best novels of the year, is entertaining, profound—and tragic." —*The Charlotte Observer*

WATERGATE

WATERGATE

A NOVEL

Thomas Mallon

VINTAGE BOOKS

A Division of Random House, Inc.

New York

FIRST VINTAGE BOOKS EDITION, JANUARY 2013

Copyright © 2012 by Thomas Mallon

Portions of this work were previously published in somewhat different form in
The American Scholar and *Five Points*.

The Library of Congress has cataloged the Pantheon edition as follows:
Mallon, Thomas.
Watergate / Thomas Mallon.
p. cm.
1. Watergate Affair, 1972–1974—Fiction. 2. Journalists—Fiction.
3. Washington (D.C.)—Fiction. 4. Political fiction. I. Title.
PS3563.A43157W38 2012 813'.54—dc22 2011017393

Vintage ISBN: 978-0-307-47465-0

Book design by M. Kristen Bearse

www.vintagebooks.com

Printed in the United States of America
10 9 8 7 6 5 4 3 2 1

FOR
CHRISTOPHER HITCHENS,
AMERICAN

The Players

Marje Acker: assistant secretary to Rose Mary Woods
Spiro T. Agnew: thirty-ninth vice president of the United States
Carl Albert: speaker of the United States House of Representatives
Joseph Alsop: syndicated newspaper columnist
Stewart Alsop: syndicated newspaper columnist
Susan Mary Alsop: wife of Joseph Alsop
Jack Anderson: syndicated newspaper columnist
Anne Armstrong: counselor to the president
Alfred C. Baldwin: monitor of illegal phone wiretaps at Democratic
    National Committee
Bernard Barker: former CIA operative; White House "plumber";
    Watergate burglar
Carl Bernstein: reporter, *The Washington Post*
William O. Bittman: attorney for E. Howard Hunt
Joan Braden: Washington hostess; wife of Tom Braden
Tom Braden: author and journalist
Ben Bradlee: executive editor, *The Washington Post*
Edward Brooke: U.S. senator (R-MA)
Patrick Buchanan: White House adviser and speechwriter
William F. Buckley, Jr.: conservative author and commentator; editor of
    National Review
J. Fred Buzhardt, Jr.: special White House counsel for Watergate matters
Art Buchwald: newspaper columnist and humorist
Steve Bull: special assistant to the president
George H. W. Bush: U.S. ambassador to the United Nations; chairman,
    Republican National Committee
Don Carnevale: vice president, Harry Winston, Inc.
Rene Carpenter: television personality, former wife of astronaut Scott
    Carpenter
Dwight Chapin: deputy assistant to the president
Anna Chennault: widow of Lieut. Gen. Claire Lee Chennault

The Players

Charles Colson: special counsel to the president

John B. Connally: former governor of Texas and secretary of the treasury; head of "Democrats for Nixon"

Archibald Cox: Watergate special prosecutor, department of justice

Edward Cox: son-in-law of President and Mrs. Nixon

Tricia Nixon Cox: daughter of President and Mrs. Nixon

Richard Darman: aide to Elliot Richardson

Samuel Dash: majority counsel, Senate Watergate Committee

John W. Dean III: White House counsel

Thomas Eagleton: U.S. senator (D-MO); Democratic nominee (briefly) for vice president

James O. Eastland: chairman, Senate Judiciary Committee (D-MS)

David Eisenhower: grandson of President Dwight Eisenhower; son-in-law of President and Mrs. Nixon

Julie Nixon Eisenhower: daughter of President and Mrs. Nixon

Daniel Ellsberg: United States military analyst and antiwar activist; charged in theft of the "Pentagon Papers"

John Ehrlichman: assistant to the president for domestic affairs

Samuel J. Ervin, Jr.: U.S. senator (D-NC); chairman, Senate Select Committee on Presidential Campaign Activities

Lewis Fielding: psychiatrist to Daniel Ellsberg

Betty Ford: wife of Gerald Ford

Gerald Ford: fortieth vice president of the U.S.; thirty-eighth president

Frank Gannon: White House aide

"Tom Garahan": retired trust-and-estates lawyer

Leonard Garment: special consultant to the president; White House counsel

Katharine Graham: publisher of *The Washington Post*

Robert Gray: public relations executive; frequent escort of Rose Mary Woods

Edward Gurney: member, Senate Watergate Committee (R-FL)

Alexander Haig: deputy national security adviser; White House chief of staff (from May 1973)

H. R. Haldeman: White House chief of staff, January 1969–April 1973

Bryce Harlow: counselor to the president

Hubert H. Humphrey: U.S. senator (D-MN); former vice president

Dorothy Hunt: wife of E. Howard Hunt

E. Howard Hunt, consultant to the White House

Leon Jaworski: Watergate special prosecutor, Department of Justice

Lady Bird Johnson: former First Lady of the United States

Lyndon B. Johnson: thirty-sixth president of the United States

Herbert W. Kalmbach: personal attorney of Richard Nixon

Edward M. Kennedy: U.S. senator (D-MA)

Ethel Kennedy: widow of Senator Robert F. Kennedy

Henry Kissinger: national security adviser; secretary of state (from September 1973)

"Clarine Lander": staff member, Democratic National Committee

Fred LaRue: deputy director, Committee for the Re-Election of the President (CRP)

Ike Parsons LaRue: deceased father of Fred LaRue

G. Gordon Liddy: finance counsel, CRP

Alice Roosevelt Longworth: daughter of Theodore Roosevelt; widow of House Speaker Nicholas Longworth

Dr. William Lukash: White House physician

Clark MacGregor: former U.S. congressman (R-MN); chairman, CRP

Robert Mardian: former assistant attorney general

James W. McCord, Jr.: security director, CRP

George S. McGovern: U.S. senator (D-SD); Democratic nominee for president

Janie McLaughlin: housekeeper for Alice Roosevelt Longworth

John Mitchell: former attorney general; director, CRP

Martha Mitchell: wife of John Mitchell

Gail Magruder: wife of Jeb Stuart Magruder

Jeb Stuart Magruder: deputy director, CRP

Pat Nixon: first lady of the United States

Richard Nixon: thirty-seventh president of the United States

Lawrence F. O'Brien: Chairman, Democratic National Committee

Jacqueline Kennedy Onassis: former first lady of the United States

"Billy Pope": political aide to Senator James O. Eastland

Charles "Bebe" Rebozo: businessman, friend of Richard Nixon

Charles Rhyne: attorney for Rose Mary Woods

Elliot Richardson: secretary of the Department of Health, Education, and Welfare; secretary of defense; attorney general

Nelson Rockefeller: governor of New York

William P. Rogers: secretary of state (January 1969–September 1973)

Kermit "Kim" Roosevelt, Jr.: grandson of Theodore Roosevelt; former political action officer, CIA

Manolo Sanchez: valet to Richard Nixon

Diane Sawyer: White House aide
James St. Clair: attorney for Richard Nixon
Earl Silbert: U. S. attorney, District of Columbia
Hugh Sloan: treasurer, CRP
Taft Schreiber: vice president, Music Corporation of America
R. Sargent Shriver: Democratic nominee for vice president
George Shultz: secretary of the treasury
John J. Sirica: chief judge, United States District Court for the District of
    Columbia
John C. Stennis: U.S. senator (D-MS)
Frank Sturgis: Watergate burglar
Joanna Sturm: granddaughter of Alice Roosevelt Longworth
Dr. Walter Tkach: White House physician
Anthony "Tony" Ulasewicz: former New York City police officer; White
    House private detective
Jack Valenti: former aide to Lyndon Johnson; president, Motion Picture
    Association of America
Theodore H. White: author and journalist
Charles Wiggins: U.S. congressman (R-CA)
Edward Bennett Williams: attorney for the Democratic National
    Committee and *The Washington Post*
Rose Mary Woods: personal secretary and executive assistant to the
    president
Bob Woodward: reporter, *The Washington Post*
Robert F. Woodward: American diplomat; former U.S. ambassador to
    Uruguay
Charles Alan Wright: constitutional scholar; attorney for Richard Nixon
Ron Ziegler: White House press secretary

WATERGATE

MAY 22, 1972
9:55 P.M., EDT
WASHINGTON, D.C., AND MOSCOW, U.S.S.R.

Fred LaRue looked out his apartment window at the blinking red light atop the Washington Monument—*on, off, on, off*—and thought about George Wallace's newly recovered ability to wiggle his toes. "First time anybody ever got on page one for doin' *that*," he'd said to the boy who came around the Committee offices this afternoon with the *Star*.

But never mind the toes: Would the governor, shot last week by a kid with short hair, ever get back up on his *feet*? It was doubtful, the doctors still seemed to think.

And it was not to be wished, thought LaRue; not if that meant the governor might get back into the race for the Democratic nomination or, much worse, get set for the kind of third-party run he'd made four years ago.

If Wallace stayed out, lying on some beach and wiggling his toes to his heart's content, then the Old Man should do a wing-tipped cakewalk toward a second term. LaRue couldn't imagine how they'd gotten this lucky, with McGiveup looking like the guy they'd be running against. The "peace" candidate—oh, yeah? When it was Richard Nixon over in Moscow tonight rubbin' noses with the Reds?

LaRue fished a last pinch of tobacco out of his pouch and managed to fill only half the bowl of his pipe. Hell, he thought, putting it down; he'd already puffed himself into a stupor while on the couch, watching that movie. He went back to watching the Monument blink, and to thinking about the gov's tootsies.

If it weren't for George Corley Wallace, Fred LaRue wouldn't even be here in Washington working for the Old Man. God, it had been fun in '68, lining up those radio endorsements from Roy Acuff and Minnie Pearl, doing everything they could to bite into Wallace's southern vote and keep a couple of border states in the Nixon column. "Fred LaRue," he'd been told by Minnie Pearl—very much a lady and very much Mrs. Henry Cannon when she was out of that hat with the dangling price tag—"you've got the sweetest-soundin' voice. We could make you into the next Eddy Arnold."

He laughed every time he thought about it. Hell, he might be skinny like Hank Williams, but he didn't look like anybody you'd want to put on an album cover. Dean, the little fellow in the Counsel's office, had teased him about resembling a basset hound, and he had a point when it came to the ears, but up top Fred LaRue was losing his hair so fast he couldn't support a tag team of fleas.

He looked over to the TV, still waiting for the ten o'clock news to come on. The pictures of the Old Man landing in Russia were supposed to be excellent; at least that was the word that had reached the CRP this afternoon. LaRue sometimes wished he were back inside the White House as an unpaid consultant to the president, even though he'd spent most of his time there working for Mitchell, shuttling between the Justice Department and the southerners on the Hill. But when John decided he needed him, again at no dollars a year, down at the Committee for the Re-Election of the President, he could hardly say no, since it had been John—the campaign manager last time out, too—who'd put him in the White House in the first place.

He had nothing apparent in common with Mitchell, except for their bald heads and pipes, but inside both had the same sort of basic faith in the Old Man, along with a serene skepticism about most everything else.

Mitchell knew how much money he had laid on Goldwater in '64, and then on the Old Man four years later, and naturally enough suspected there was a lot more left than there was. Hell, if Fred LaRue were still as rich as people thought, he would be living on the other side of this crazy, round, Italian-made apartment building, facing the courtyard or the Potomac instead of Virginia Avenue and the blinking old Washington Monument.

God knows there'd been plenty of money to inherit back in '57. "Christ, that's not, you know, is it?" Mitchell had once asked, in this very room, when he saw the elegant bird gun mounted on the wall. Nope, that was not the gun with which Fred LaRue had managed to shoot Daddy instead of a duck; it was the gun old Ike Parsons LaRue, worth thirty million dollars, had been holding when he dropped to the ground during their ill-fated hunting trip.

Daddy had made his money fast, and his son was now losing it slowly. Back home in Mississippi, the oil-and-gas business was starting to sputter out. There were no more big strikes to be made, and the idea that Fred LaRue's being inside the White House would redound to the benefit of I. P. LaRue Oil and Minerals was just that, an idea—one that others, though not Fred LaRue himself, entertained.

He preferred the business of politics to the business of business. He liked the way he got to operate without so much as a business card or a line in the staff directory—same at the Committee as it had been at the White House. If this year he'd pretty much be "giving at the office" instead of from his wallet, the campaign was going to be such a slam dunk that nobody would even notice. Every day McGovern was finding something nice to say on behalf of amnesty or abortion, and all the while the troops kept coming home from Vietnam by the hundred thousand, thanks to the Old Man. The demonstration over at the Pentagon this afternoon had featured the usual moth-eaten old peaceniks, like that ginny priest openly rooting for the Vietcong, but the whole passel of them—he had seen them marching across Memorial Bridge—hadn't required a single canister of tear gas or made it as far up the front page as Wallace's wiggly toes.

The joke, of course, when it came to all these Wallace votes they were about to inherit, was that Mitchell had desegregated ten times more schools than Bobby Kennedy and Katzenbach and Ramsey Clark put together. *Watch what we do, not what we say,* Mitchell liked to whisper into the ears of the party moderates, but folks back home in Mississippi listened to the words, as if they were music. They'd soon fall in line behind the Old Man, whose administration, they scarcely realized, was putting all those colored kids at desks beside their own white offspring.

With Wallace out of the way, there'd be less need for TV and radio spots and everything else down South, including nice old Minnie Pearl. *How-DEEE!* They had the chance for a real blowout, and it was beyond LaRue why they were waiting so much as another week to shift the money they'd planned to spend down home out to California instead.

They ought to make the switch before other operations, like the ones being run by that weirdo Liddy, started laying claim to it.

Project Gemstone, my ass, thought LaRue, who looked up at the clock over the television and wondered if it was too late to call Mitchell at his apartment across the courtyard.

Hell, he'd wait until he saw him at the office in the morning. Martha was so cranked up these days that if he called now she'd probably not only listen in on the extension but burst out with some tirade about "Her," the only name she seemed able to find these days for poor Mrs. Nixon.

God, he'd loved Martha when he'd first met her in '68. She'd felt *familiar*, like the girls he'd known in Jackson and Biloxi, even if she came from all the way over in Arkansas. "Pleased to meet you," he'd said, when Mitchell presented her. "Well, I hope you'll never La*Rue* it, honey," she'd responded, just like that. But she was beyond control now, drinking more than ever, and wearing out John, who let her drink until she passed straight through agitation into something like calm, or until she just passed out, period.

No, he'd wait until morning, when he'd also call his wife and children back home in Mississippi. He decided to skip the ten o'clock news, which was mostly local anyway and would probably lead with whatever colored guy had just killed another one over in southeast Washington. He'd go down to the People's Drugstore instead—below the fancy bridal shop and past the Chinese restaurant and the barbershop and the Safeway and all the other stores that made the Watergate a whole damned world unto itself—and he'd get himself another pouch of tobacco.

"Still nothing?" asked Howard Hunt.

"No, sir, I'm afraid not," replied the Watergate Hotel's desk clerk.

"All right. I thought I'd check."

"We might have increased availability within a few days."

Hunt left without even nodding. *Increased availability.* When had people started talking this way? It irritated him profoundly, if profound irritation wasn't a contradiction in terms. These days he might only be writing his spy novels, but he'd once had a Guggenheim and published a short story in the *New Yorker*, and it offended his ears to hear this sort of abstract claptrap coming out of hotel clerks and thirty-year-old White House special assistants with more status in the administration than he had.

After exiting the hotel, he looked up at the adjacent Watergate office building. Eighteen years ago he'd been overthrowing a government in Guatemala, and here he was now, overmanned and overfinanced for an operation to bug the phone of a party hack.

Barker opened the driver's door of the car, which was idling on Virginia Avenue.

"*No hay lugar en el mesón,* Bernie," said Hunt, getting in behind the wheel. "But I've got a backup plan."

"Any place will be fine, Eduardo," replied Bernard Barker, who always preferred English.

Hunt turned toward the backseat and looked at three of the men he'd just collected at the airport. Two of them were Cubans recruited by Bernie. They merely nodded. He'd heard of Sturgis, the American, but not met him. It was with Barker that he felt well acquainted and *simpático,* going back as they did all the way to Operation Zapata. He hated dragging him into this penny-ante crap, the same way he'd dragged him into the break-in last year in L.A. Now, like then, he'd be deluding Bernie—and himself!—into believing this burglary had some purpose and importance outside of whatever was in Liddy's head, and Colson's.

"Bernie," he said, as he drove the car down Virginia, "this will be a nice little piece of revenge." He pointed to the letters, aglow with moonlight and fluorescence, affixed to the boxy white building beyond the Watergate: JOHN F. KENNEDY MEMORIAL CENTER FOR THE PERFORMING ARTS.

From the backseat, Sturgis followed Hunt's pointing finger before raising a fist and shouting, too loudly for a closed car full of people, "*Brigada Dos Cinco Cero Seis!*"

Barker pursed his lips, needing no further reminder of Kennedy's failure to support Brigade 2506 with adequate arms, air cover, or even a decent place to come ashore. More than a decade had passed since the Bay of Pigs, and even more time than that since Barker had first met Everette Howard Hunt. "Eduardo"—Barker still used the old code name—had been trying to organize a Cuban government-in-exile in Coconut Grove.

"*Coño!*" cried Sturgis from the backseat, in his Americano's Spanish. "*Sólo ocho aviones!*"

"Yes," Barker replied in a soothing near whisper. "We know. Only eight fucking planes." That's all they'd been given—plus a zero hour that fell during darkness instead of light. As Eduardo used to put it, dryly, "They apparently wanted the populace to rise in support of an invasion that wouldn't attract any notice."

The car angled eastward, and Hunt continued his motivational tour. "The architecture gets even worse," he said, pointing to the right. He was indicating, Barker realized, the State Department.

Hunt decided to say nothing more; he was starting to feel guilty about stoking Bernie's long grief and confusion over his adopted country's half-hearted anti-Castroism. He was also trying to conceal the fact that he was slightly lost, unsure how to find Pennsylvania Avenue.

He'd been lost for ten years, really, as unmoored as Bernie since the April of the invasion, his career shot down like the unsupported freedom fighters. It had been the same for anyone in the Agency associated with Operation Zapata. In his own case, what had followed were too many deskbound days at Langley writing Fodor's travel guides for East Bloc tourism, and too many nights at home composing his Peter Ward novels, into which he displaced the derring-do that might have kept filling his own career had there been more than those eight planes in the air.

It had been two years since he left the CIA, and God knew how many more would pass before the Agency let him publish *Give Us This Day*, his impassioned manuscript about the invasion's promise and betrayal. Like Bernie, he had real grievances, ones that burned off stomach lining, not the pseudo-resentments of the preposterous, swaggering Liddy, who was plenty of fun when he told his tall tales amidst the carelessly stacked and more-or-less useless top-secret documents in room 16 of the EOB but who increasingly got on Hunt's nerves. There was a screw loose in the guy, the way he would rush over to the Hunts' house in Potomac to play a just-acquired recording of Hitler seducing some hysterical crowd. His lips were even looser than whatever screw was about to fall out of his head. On the way home from Los Angeles, having accomplished the magnificent feat of messing up a few papers in the office of Ellsberg's psychiatrist, he had gotten half-loaded on the plane and started talking to a stewardess who, under her jaunty cap, looked as if she might be able to put two and two together.

All right, they were on Pennsylvania at last, in sight of the White House, lit up even brighter than the Kennedy Center. One could be sure that, behind the floodlights, Chuck Colson's desk lamp was burning the midnight oil.

"So much light, with the boss not home?" asked Bernie, tightening his lips, perplexed over why the anti-Communist Nixon should be drinking champagne in Moscow with the men who armed and bank-rolled Castro year after year.

"Wheels within wheels," replied Hunt, trying to suggest the intricacy of Nixon's stratagems. "Even tonight, while he makes nice with Brezhnev, there are a lot more than eight planes over Hanoi."

Did he believe it all himself? That Nixon actually knew where things were heading, and remained motivated by the kind of zeal that had sent Bernie's comrades and Howard Hunt's career to their deaths? As far as Hunt could tell, the president spent no more time at the geopolitical chessboard with Kissinger than he did drinking with Colson, who had once said he would run over his own grandmother if it would advance his boss's reelection. During these drinking sessions, Chuck would serve Nixon a new harebrained scheme as if it were just another ice cube or olive. A week ago tonight he had lubricated the president with the idea that they should send him, Hunt, out to the Milwaukee apartment of the kid arrested for shooting Wallace, so that he could plant some left-wing leaflets that would make the boy look like a McGovern acolyte instead of a nut job. "And I'm supposed to accomplish this even though the FBI will have sealed the place off?" he'd had to ask Colson, who even after that couldn't let go of the possibility.

Three years ago, the two of them, Charles Wendell Colson '53 and Everette Howard Hunt '43, had been president and vice president of the Brown Club of Washington, D.C. Then one day, Chuck, knowing about his special skills, aware of his dry dock and frustration, had brought him around to see Ehrlichman. Soon after came Liddy and room 16 and

"Hunt/Liddy Special Project No. 1," which had led them to the utterly beside-the-point contents of that L.A. shrink's filing cabinet. Which Bernie, standing in the shambles of the doctor's office, had unquestioningly photographed.

When Hunt had seen the pictures, he had found himself thinking only that he would like to be on Dr. Fielding's couch, to ask him about the strange waverings and loss of certainty that he'd started to experience from time to time.

"Amigos," said Hunt, "you're here."

The Manger-Hamilton Hotel, at the corner of Fourteenth and K, had seen better days, but at least there was a room waiting for each Cuban. When he'd called here yesterday, after learning that the Watergate had nothing, he'd been told this place hadn't been full since Hoover's funeral almost three weeks ago. And indeed, it looked like the sort of modest spot where sentimental old FBI agents living on fixed incomes in Davenport and Des Moines might book a room in order to come east and say goodbye to their old chief.

Bernie had come to town then, too—to participate, at Hunt and Liddy's request, in a raucous demonstration that would counter the one Ellsberg had planned for the steps of the Capitol while Hoover's corpse cooled in the Rotunda. A little heckling and scuffling turned out to be the only result, but Bernie's trip up from Miami had given Hunt a chance to explain that their *next* job would be bugging Larry O'Brien, a big Kennedy man, postmaster *generalísimo,* now head of the Democrats' national committee. Bernie never asked what they'd be looking for, but Hunt had told him anyway: evidence that money was coming McGovern's way from Havana, out of Fidel's own coffers, which were swollen with expropriations from every exile Bernie knew in Miami.

Hunt now handed him an inch-thick bundle of cash and said he'd be in touch tomorrow. He began the drive home to Potomac, wondering if he himself believed there was the least chance of finding out something so momentous from a lousy tap on O'Brien's phone. If by some stretch of the imagination there *was*—he could feel himself trying to catch Bernie's own wishful train of thought—McGovern would be finished off beyond recognition, and maybe the Marines would be allowed to go in and get rid of Castro once and for all. Credit for the break-in and wiretap could easily be transferred from the White House to the Agency; an illegal act would become an intelligence triumph, and the past decade of his own career would be transformed from a dead end to a mere detour.

As Hunt's car passed 2009 Massachusetts Avenue, the lone occupant of the house's third-floor bedroom, having heard from the television that Nixon might make Brezhnev the gift of a Cadillac, tried to recall what the Czar of Russia had given her for a wedding present in 1906. She remembered Edward VII sending a snuffbox with his face on it; she and Nick had never figured out whether it was intended for the bride or groom or both of them. But the czar? Maybe nothing. It seemed to the still-sharp memory of Alice Roosevelt Longworth that that was right. Father had not long before made peace between the Russians and the Japanese, and the Russians had gotten rather the short end of the big stick. Yes, that was why the Japanese had outdone themselves with *their* present—bolt after bolt of that golden chrysanthemum-patterned silk. Not too different from the United Mine Workers sending that boxcar loaded with coal. Again, all about Father and not about Alice: the miners had still been happy with the way he settled the coal strike in '02.

Pat looked well, thought Mrs. Longworth, gazing over the top of her eyeglasses at the TV. The first lady's hair might be teased a bit too high on her head, but she never got sufficient credit for being pretty—much prettier than Tricia, whom all the newspapers, no matter how they hated Dick, continually described as looking like a fairy princess. With that ridiculous *retroussé* version of Dick's ski-nose? All wrong. And not an interesting word out of her, ever.

Pat Nixon's televised image was gone too quickly for Mrs. Longworth to get a good look at her coat, which might still be cloth but would have come, at the very least, from Elizabeth Arden. Even back in '60, some of Pat's outfits had cost more than Jackie's, not that the press ever had the wit to see it. Mrs. L, as she was resigned to being called, liked both of them, always had; it was Jackie's mother-in-law, the detestable Rose, with that helmet of dyed black hair, who got on her nerves. Six years Alice's junior but forever babbling about how she'd met McKinley, as if he were Moses or Methuselah. Well, Alice Roosevelt had met *Benjamin Harrison,* and didn't feel the need to squawk about it to every reporter who came along.

And those *lamentable* Lilly Pulitzer dresses Rose wore around Palm Beach! Polka-dotted knee-length muumuus that could be shower curtains, for all anyone knew. And which just *hung* against the form. She herself, since the second mastectomy, might be the world's best-known topless octogenarian (her own line, and a good one, too), but a bit of tailoring never hurt, even if it wound up accentuating one's deformity.

Mrs. Longworth now realized that she would be in Florida in just three months for the convention, and that it would be hot. She needed to make a note, if she could find a pencil on the night table, to get a few outfits other than those Lilly Potatosacks to keep her cool.

Well, good for Dick, who for once would arrive in the convention hall as president and not just candidate, and who these days appeared to be accomplishing something. She liked *him,* too. She'd told the newsmen, all through his early days, that *he,* unlike McCarthy, could actually think, sometimes even think big. The thing Dick couldn't do well was *listen,* an odd incapacity in one who curried favor so dutifully, tried so *hard,* at least with her. He was still always sending her books, and he made sure they were serious ones, ever since years ago he'd given her something by that elfin spook Mrs. Lindbergh and she'd told him it had gone straight into the shopping bag of discards for the Junior League sale.

The two men she'd really like to have gotten around her dining room table, together, were Dick and Bobby. Well, too late for that, as it was for most things. Bobby had been even smarter than Dick, and nearly as damaged, but he'd had the ability to approach her without neediness. Awe, yes, and who didn't like that? But he didn't come wanting to *earn* her esteem or affection. As if one could ever earn those things, from anybody; as if they were meted out according to some fair scale of prorated hourly wages that Eleanor had drawn up. (The thought of her distant cousin now made Mrs. Longworth buck out her teeth, as she'd done a thousand times in imitation of her.) No, one was paid esteem and affection according to the whims of the payer, whether one had shown up to work in the vineyard early or late. She was sure Dick knew no more of the Bible than what he got from Billy Graham over some prayer breakfast. Too bad. He might have some small sense of irony if he did; and, having read it, he would at least know enough not to believe in God.

But there was a secret, fifteen years old, that the two of them shared— and the substance of it still made up for a lot of his cartoonable deficiencies, in Alice's mind.

Mrs. Longworth got up to raise the window, and felt certain she could smell the honeysuckle coming up three stories from the garden below. She had a sprig of it on the night table beside the locket containing Father's hair, which she now regarded. She'd often thought she would enjoy having his actual head mounted on the dining room wall, like one of the old elks at Sagamore Hill.

Of *course* the czar had never sent a present. Father had never sent *her* to the *czar*. To Japan, yes; but not to Russia. The closest she'd ever gotten to it were those letters from Willard Straight, on whom she'd had such a nice off-and-on Platonic case, until the flu made off with him after the First War. *You who are fond of the game would love it here,* he'd written her from Moscow as the workers began their revolt, the year before her wedding. (Perhaps, it now occurred to her, the czar had just been too *distracted* to send a present.)

She was sure that Willard's letters were still in that bottom drawer, with the pearls from Cuba and the bracelet from the kaiser, the one whose diamonds had been stolen out of their settings that night a half dozen years ago when she went up to New York for Capote's party and so *stupidly* let the papers know in advance that she'd be out of town.

The television turned its attention to the weather, whose forecast bored Mrs. Longworth more than the weather's actual and never very varied arrival. Yes, she thought, shutting off the set and reaching for her book and letting her mind travel toward Willard Straight: I would have loved Russia in 1905, once the shooting started.

In her room inside the czar's apartments, Pat Nixon, jet-lagged at 4:30 a.m., lay awake and looked toward a crack in the velvet curtains. The White Nights wouldn't really come for another month, and Moscow wasn't Leningrad, but the glow outside had nothing to do with dawn. It was the same strange silvery light that had persisted all night and been shining even when the state dinner ended at ten-thirty. The sky reminded her, oddly enough, of the ones she used to walk beneath in the Bronx on rainy autumn twilights back in the early thirties, looking south toward Manhattan. She'd leave the X-ray machine she'd tended all day and, with her coat pulled tight and never more than a dollar in her pocket, head down Johnson Avenue in search of dinner, often just a slice of apple pie and coffee. She could no longer remember the names of the nuns she'd lived with atop the TB hospital, but could still recall what she would think while walking on nights that looked like this one: Maybe I won't try to get back to California; maybe I'll seek my life right here.

She wondered whether Mrs. Khrushchev, now a widow, still lived in the dacha she and Dick had lunched at back in '59. There was probably no more chance of her having been allowed to keep it than there had been of her being at the dinner tonight. When Pat had raised that second possibility with Kissinger, he'd pompously informed her that it was out of the question, and that she should be grateful for the political progress signified by Nikita Khrushchev's having been merely retired instead of shot.

What a show Mrs. K had made, a dozen years ago, of *not* trying on the hat that Pat and the other ladies had presented her with at a luncheon in Washington, when the Khrushchevs returned the Nixons' visit to Russia. She'd said she would accept the hat only so that back home it could be copied for the masses of Soviet women! *Oh, put it on, dear,* they'd all cajoled, and they eventually did succeed in raising a smile from her plump face. But, no, they never saw her try it on.

The Soviets had certainly never given up any of the swag in *this* room. Pat decided she might as well get up, put on the lights, and give it another look instead of just lying here staring at the curtains and gold-leaf ceiling. But on her way to the mosaic table, the one supporting the beautiful French clock, she stumbled over an extension cord left by Rita, her hairdresser, who'd fought a losing battle with the different voltage until two young men from Kissinger's staff got the dryer going just before they were all due downstairs for the first toasts. Was

Rita—across the courtyard in the block of rooms supposed to be full of ramshackle Communist-era furnishings—getting any more sleep than she was? Poor Bill Rogers wasn't even inside the Kremlin; he'd been put in some hotel a few minutes away, no doubt from Kissinger's continuing need to keep the secretary of state in his place and away from the real action.

It bothered her that Dick encouraged all that, especially if he did it not for some strategic reason but out of resentment left over from their six years in New York, when Bill and Adele would invite the Nixons out to "21" and give the impression—at least to Dick—that the Rogerses were doing *them* a favor. Pat herself had never seen it that way. She remembered those evenings, as well as the law firm's partner dinners from that same all-too-brief time in her life, as being more agreeable than all the political entertainments in the years before and after.

Even Martha, for a while, had been fun.

How Rose Woods would love this room: all the figurines and bibelots, the kind of stuff she filled her little place at the Watergate with, those frilly knockoffs amidst the real little gems she got from Don Carnevale, her very safe escort from Harry Winston.

She heard voices coming from the courtyard below, bouncing up off the paving stones. Dear God, it was—Dick. She parted the curtains and saw him down there in a windbreaker and slacks, walking with Bill Duncan, their favorite Secret Service man, and she thought back to the mad night two years ago when he'd gone to the Lincoln Memorial, at about this hour, with almost nobody but Manolo and some aide of John Ehrlichman's. To talk with the "demonstrators." And a fat lot of credit he'd got for making the effort.

She thought of the people who'd come out to greet them this afternoon, trying to catch a glimpse of the limousine. You could scarcely see them, kept back as they were a block or more from the path of the car, but you could hear them, buzzing and cheering, *interested* in the whole thing, hoping for something to come out of it—whereas back home the only crowds you could gather for politics were the angry, filthy kids and their teachers. Would those same protesters now grudgingly admit that the "warmonger" was really a peacemaker? No, of course not.

She could see Dick now, staying two steps ahead of Duncan, lost in thought until he'd turn around and say something, half from politeness and half from the need to hold forth. And then, after he spoke a couple of sentences, he'd break away and go it alone for another fifty feet, starting the cycle again. For all his need of an audience, he was happier alone. She remembered him just like this on their wedding day, June 21, 1940. She'd looked out the window of the Mission Inn and spotted him pacing the courtyard, a nervous groom, an hour before the ceremony. The birds had been singing in the branches as she stood there in her lace suit from Robinson's department store and watched him without his knowing it. Money had been so much on both their minds: his mother had made the cake; his brother had picked her up and brought her to Riverside to save the cost of a hired car.

Next month, June, would be their anniversary. What would Rose be buying for him to give her? Once this trip was over and the two women had a quiet moment together, she'd have to start dropping hints.

Dick had lately been making all this odd conversation about a "dynasty." David would run for Congress from Pennsylvania; or maybe Julie would. And both Eds, his son-in-law and much younger brother, would find open seats in New York and Washington state. This fantasy was new, another one agitated into life by too much concentration on the Kennedys. She herself never inclined to the long view.

Julie had taken to asking when she would have her portrait for the White House painted. "When I can find the time" was her usual answer, easier than saying what she really thought: that sitting for it in the first term would be bad luck.

She could hear Dick's voice growing fainter. Poor Bill Duncan would be relieved when his boss decided to go back to bed. Maybe she, too, was at last ready for sleep; if she got lucky, she would drift off for a couple of hours before breakfast.

She closed the curtains and undid the long belt of her wrapper, jumping in fright when her hand brushed, and nearly knocked over, a porcelain figure on the largest chest of drawers. No harm done, thank God.

Everything, the whole world, really, was so fragile. Only yesterday there had been that horrible newspaper picture of the man attacking the *Pietà* with a hammer.

She knew from long practice that she could, by sheer force of will, banish such an awful image from her mind. As she closed her eyes, she did just that.

No, he decided, catching sight of another American flag atop the Kremlin; he was not yet ready to quit pacing and go back inside. The yellow walls of the place were coming to life in the dawn's early light, and he could hear the horn of a boat on the river, mixing with the sound of trucks outside the fortress walls. He stopped, turned around, and waited for Duncan to catch up, before telling him, "Napoleon managed to spend one day here before they set fire to the place. Never forget that."

"No, sir," Duncan replied.

Nixon could still not believe that the rug hadn't been pulled out from under the summit. Two weeks ago he'd put the whole thing at risk by mining Haiphong and upping the bombing, and every goddamned editorial writer in the world swore that he was going to get himself disinvited to Moscow—and throw away his chances of reelection to boot. Well, they'd been wrong, and he'd arrived here with a stronger hand than if he'd risked nothing at all.

Looking up at the strange light, he remembered his visit to the Danilovsky Market at this time of day thirteen years ago. Jack Sherwood had been the Secret Service agent, and there'd been plenty for him to worry about, tensions being what they were and no preparations having been made for the appearance. The people in the market had turned out to be friendly, though you would never have known it from the report that ran in *Pravda*. Still, to have made the Soviets' front page even before facing off with Khrushchev in that crappy kitchen: not bad.

It's the work, not the showboating, that matters. For all the good press it got back in the U.S.—that picture of him jabbing his finger toward Khrushchev's chest had nearly made him president—the '59 trip had actually been a frustration, because he had nothing to negotiate and no authority to be doing it.

This time would be different: great things were afoot, and that's why Rogers had to be kept far away and out of the loop, so he didn't raise all the candyass niceties and scruples he'd soaked up from three years inside State. A few months ago, in Shanghai, they hadn't let him know about the big communiqué until he was told to sign it. And then he'd nearly loused everything up with his chickenshit objections about Taiwan!

"Did they feed you all right tonight?" Nixon asked Duncan.

"Oh, yes, sir."

"On that first trip Khrushchev gave us Stalin's favorite fish for lunch. Made a point of saying so, while he and Mikoyan pretended to be fighting over Mrs. Nixon."

Duncan laughed, discreetly, and Nixon remembered—he'd heard it from Ehrlichman—how three years ago Tricia had made this poor guy call the White House from London after Annenberg groped her at a party.

"Mikoyan?" asked Duncan.

"Old-timer," replied Nixon.

He once more walked on ahead, his mind already off to a different place. He was wishing he had Kissinger here, right now, since the two of them couldn't really talk privately anywhere except in the limousine. He couldn't stand, and didn't trust, the goddamned "babbler" device that was supposed to drown out whatever the electronic eavesdroppers might pick up from conversation in the palace apartments.

"Let's go back in," he told Duncan, who noted the local time— 4:51 a.m.—for the log.

"Yes, sir."

"Good night," said Nixon, as they mounted the stairs. It was easier to take them than wait for the elevator, which was probably wired just like the room.

Bug or no bug, Nixon would never be able to sleep unless he made one call, and so the communications man put it through, at 5:05, after Nixon himself reluctantly turned on the babbler.

"You're up late," he said, instinctively shouting the words because of the distance, the way his old man had always used the telephone. He'd had to remind himself not to do it when talking to Armstrong on the moon. As he heard himself now, he hoped he wouldn't wake Pat in the next room, though he imagined the czars hadn't skimped on the plaster.

"Good morning, Mr. President," said Colson. "There are a number of us still here at the White House."

"Good, good. How did things go with Haig's backgrounder?" Kissinger's deputy was supposed to have briefed the Washington press yesterday morning.

"Fine, better than fine, Mr. President. He excluded the *Times*, just as we'd decided after their damned Haiphong stories, and they *still* had to write a positive page-one piece about the trip. Everybody's coverage conveys the impression of a serious, determined, imaginative leader."

"You should hear Brezhnev," Nixon responded. "Serious and determined? Yes. Imaginative? I wouldn't say so. Had to listen to him deliver an opening harangue about the bombing and the mining. But it was pretty much just for show, the way Khrushchev roared on about the 'Captive Nations' resolution by the goddamned Congress back in '59."

This was probably saying too much, babbler or no babbler. Time to rein it in.

"Sir, McGovern's now pulled ahead of Humphrey in both Gallup and Harris. And his delegates are piling up."

"Good, good. How was the Pentagon thing? They had some demonstration planned for today, didn't they?"

"Pathetic. A few hundred, if that."

"Could have taken care of them with your trusty car, huh?"

Colson laughed. "I told Dean I'm saving it to use against the next ones who demonstrate on the Pennsylvania Avenue sidewalk."

Nixon laughed. He wanted to talk about Wallace, too, but knew he should wrap this up. Still, the conversation had done a good job of exciting and relaxing him all at once, the usual Colson cocktail.

"Okay, Chuck. I'll call you later today from the limousine."

"I'll look forward to it, Mr. President."

"Get some sleep in the meantime."

After turning off the babbler, Nixon at last fell into an early-morning dream that found him back in the South Pacific, at "Nick's Hamburger Stand" on Bougainville, his own little operation, where during the war he'd taken a lot of poker winnings off a handful of other naval officers. But something in the dream was wrong; he was winning too much; he had too many chips in front of him. He didn't know how he'd gotten them, but he knew he had to get *rid* of them fast. But *how*? He couldn't figure it out, and so, in this bedroom of the czars, in the middle of the dream, he began to sweat, and finally he groaned—startling the technician in the recording room forty feet below the cobblestones of Red Square.

Part One

———◆———

HIDE

JUNE 17, 1972–APRIL 30, 1973

Chapter One

JUNE 17, 1972
LOS ANGELES, CALIFORNIA

"The president did a wonderful job at the summit," remarked the studio executive, or lawyer, or whoever it was shaking Pat Nixon's hand.

"Oh, thank you!" she replied. "*This* is some summit, too, don't you think?"

She gestured toward the lights of Los Angeles far below Taft Schreiber's mansion in Bel Air and thought of how these days the million blinkings down there stretched all the way to and beyond Whittier, a continuous gold carpet. When she and Dick were kids, Whittier had flickered like a small distant planet, far from the sun of downtown, into which Frank Nixon drove a streetcar every day.

The wife of the man who'd shaken her hand was also now remarking on the Russian summit, the safest topic for any Hollywood liberal who'd come to this fundraiser more from fear of Taft Schreiber and MCA than out of any sudden enthusiasm for Dick. She'd heard one older executive say to his wife, while pointing to the eager-beaver campaign boys knifing into the pâté, "They're pretending it's Helen Gahagan." The wife, young enough to be the husband's daughter, had looked baffled.

Well, that *was* over twenty years ago. But no election provided Pat with sharper—or better—memories. The liberals could say all they wanted that Helen Gahagan had been the martyr to a dirty campaign, but Dick had had her number from the start. She *was* pink, right down to her underwear, and if telling the truth about her voting record in Congress amounted to dirty pool, well, that was too bad. It had been a grand brawl, fought out in the California sunshine while they were still so young. She'd had to carry Julie in her arms when they went to all the new shopping centers in that battered station wagon. Tricia had been just old enough to pass out flyers—including, yes, the "pink sheet," which had the nerve to print the facts about Mrs. Melvyn Douglas on just the right color paper. If Dick had *really* wanted to run a dirty campaign, he could have spread the word that Mrs. Douglas had been having an affair with Lyndon Johnson, something that everyone in Washington, yet no one in California, seemed to know. But Dick didn't go in for that sort of thing—not even against Jack Kennedy. He'd ended the '50 campaign saddled forever with "Tricky Dick" as a nickname, but he'd been the one to go to the Senate.

"We're so thrilled you could be here!"

Oh, golly, the name: a redhead, but which one? Arlene Dahl? Rhonda Fleming? She and Dick had always seen a lot of movies but could never keep those two straight.

"That's so sweet of you to say! But I know you'd all be *more* thrilled if Dr. Kissinger had been able to make it after all!" She winked, a woman-to-woman tribute to Kissinger's supposed charm and magnetism, which Pat couldn't say she'd ever really experienced. Henry had been the administration star promised for this fundraiser by the Committee to Re-Elect; she was aware of herself, a bit painfully, as the second choice, and she hoped it didn't look like a bait-and-switch—Kissinger really did have to attend to something that had come up in the Far East. Still, she wished that the Committee had asked Julie or Tricia (well, Julie) to substitute instead, and that Dick hadn't pushed her so hard to come out here at the last minute.

"We're so happy to have *you*!" said the redhead, maybe even meaning it. Of course the real commotion here tonight was being provided by Martha. By now she was probably a bigger draw than either the first lady *or* the national security advisor, but enough protocol remained in politics that they couldn't make a cabinet wife the official guest of honor—no matter how many times Martha made the evening news. Poor John: there he was, not thirty feet away, his hand gently on his wife's back, trying to keep her from skyrocketing into another burst of hilarity or rage.

"And you look so beautiful in that dress!" said yet another executive's wife, moving up the line behind the redhead.

"Well, look who's talking!" said Pat, with an up-and-down appraisal of the gal's flouncy chiffon outfit. Sleeveless, of course. She herself never had the nerve for it, not even in California in June. She was always getting compliments, or protective cluckings, about how thin she was; well, she might have the waist to wear anything, but not the arms.

The executive's wife wasn't smiling. Her mouth was open in a little "o" of disbelief—shock, even—that the first lady was capable of making a joke. Not even a joke; just a funny figure of speech: *look who's talking*. Good Lord, thought Pat: Was her image (she hated the word) really *that* bad? *That* "plastic"? Well, there was nothing she could do to change it. Every couple of years the press talked about a New Nixon, but that was Dick. She was stuck where she was with the reporters. Especially when it came to clothes. That *beautiful* inaugural gown with the golden jacket! On anyone else it would have been deemed magical, but once she stepped into it, *Women's Wear Daily* pronounced: "schoolteacher's night out." She'd felt so bad for poor Karen Stark, who'd done such a beautiful job designing it. Dick had been furious, and gone on a toot about pansies in the fashion business, which of course had nothing to do with the sharp-clawed lady cats in the fashion *press*.

Actually, they were half right. The dress *was* beautiful, but in some ways the whole past twenty-five years had been a schoolteacher's night out, an improbable recess from what still seemed the real life she'd been settling into as Miss Ryan in the classrooms of Whittier Union High. When she'd made this observation to Dick—as a joke with some truth in it, just to have a laugh and get him off the subject of *Women's Wear Daily*—he'd only gotten madder.

Taft Schreiber was cutting the line. She hadn't yet met the host, and before she could thank him for this lovely party and his generosity to the campaign, he was all over her with flattery of Dick that not even Kissinger could have matched: "When I think of all that the president— one of California's own—has done for the movie industry, I burst with pride as well as the sincerest gratitude. The investment tax credit, the accelerated depreciation allowances—magnificent! But I shouldn't bore you with such technical things."

"Praise of Dick never bores me," said the first lady.

In fact, her curiosity was piqued. With a raised eyebrow she beckoned Connie Stuart, her top aide, to come stand next to her, as Schreiber threw a last bouquet: "Attorney General Mitchell—*former* Attorney

General, I should say—has been particularly splendid. But enough. No more politics. Let me relinquish you to all the people who've come to see you."

She and Connie, now by her side, stepped back from the receiving line for a confidential moment.

"I thought it was just Israel," said Pat, "that made Taft Schreiber such a big supporter. What's John Mitchell done for him? John doesn't run tax policy *or* the Middle East."

"Justice filed an antitrust suit against the TV networks," Connie explained, "to stop them from making their own movies for television. Which means they'll have to keep buying movies from the men here."

Pat, a quick study, nodded and got back to the receiving line. She glanced over at Mitchell, who didn't look happy for a man with such grateful and generous friends. Well, how could he, with Martha berating him in that loud, slicing voice? She sounded like a parrot in a cage. Pat could hear her all the way from over there, scolding the poor man for *being* unhappy.

"John Mitchell!" cawed Martha. "I do not understand why each and every man from the Committee to Re-Elect Mr. President is looking lower than a snake's belly tonight!"

John mumbled and placated and continued to caress the back of his wife's dress. The two of them, even now, Pat had to concede, were a love match. But Martha would be the death of him. And Dick only made things worse by encouraging her with all those give-'em-hell notes and across-the-room thumbs-ups. Instead of clamping down on Martha, the most anyone ever did was try for a little distraction, as John was doing now, pointing out Zsa Zsa Gabor to her.

Even as she watched, Pat could hear herself telling—yet again, automatically—the *Becky Sharp* story she'd already told three times tonight; about how she'd gotten work as an extra on the film during her days at USC, and then been given a single line to read. "But they cut it!" she concluded, once more, with a laugh. "Maybe Chuck," she added, gently touching Charlton Heston's arm, "can ask Governor Reagan where my Screen Actors Guild card is. I'm still waiting for it!"

She'd made the same joke ten minutes ago to John Wayne and his Peruvian wife.

Like most of her memories, the ones involving *Becky Sharp* were something she'd prefer to keep to herself—not that there was anything so private about the story, only that it seemed to lose vividness, be less real to *her*, with every occasion she had to tell it. Each time she described driving over from campus in Ginny Shugart's red Ford, the car grew a little less red, the sunshine above it a little less warm and a little more like CinemaScope. Of course, she never mentioned how she'd hated all the time wasted standing around on the set; how one of the assistant directors had come over to the house one night, drunk, and been tossed out by her brothers. But because she never added any of these details to the recitation, they remained fresher, oddly more satisfying, than the story's rote, pleasant parts.

She saw John Mitchell leaving Martha in the care of that man from Mississippi, the one with the soft, soothing voice whose name she could never remember. He'd been Mitchell's man in the White House, and by now she supposed he'd gone over to the Committee to Re-Elect. She was struck by how patient he was with Martha, who seemed more agitated by the moment.

Six years ago, on the evening they first met, Pat had felt sorry for Martha. It was just after John's law firm had merged with Dick's and his wife was feeling slighted at some University Club function in New York. Pat remembered talking to her softly, as the man from Mississippi was doing now. Martha, responding well that night, had called her "Patty," something she alone in the world continued to do. Like most drunks and flamboyant people, Martha was actually, secretly, shy, whereas Pat knew herself—however unlikely it seemed—to be naturally an extrovert. She held her real self in with discipline, the same way Martha unleashed a false one with drink.

But she had long since lost patience with Martha. It was all too much now, the late-night and early-morning calls—five a.m. tirades to Connie about one thing or another—and the *stupid* comments to the press: how Fulbright needed to be "crucified" and all the rest.

And now Martha was coming straight toward her; the man from Mississippi helpless to stop it. "I'm going to stand beside Patty when Mr. Mitchell speaks!" Martha brayed. "That is, if he can tear himself away from one more hush-hush little huddle back there!"

Oh, no, you're not, thought Pat. Taking Connie by the elbow, she swerved away, as unnoticeably as she could. Together they made their way to a punch bowl. (Better to be photographed with a little crystal cup—*schoolteacher's night out*—than that tumbler of scotch Martha had in her hand.) Martha now looked furious, well and truly snubbed. Still, she would have no choice but to keep silent, at least for a few minutes, since her husband had begun addressing the crowd of contributors.

You be president; I'll be secretary of state. She remembered hearing Dick say this to John, just after the election: evidence of his esteem for Mitchell and a poignant indicator of his own real interests. But right now John looked too exhausted to be even a justice of the peace. He was probably more loaded than Martha, and he was making it through his remarks with the help of a microphone, talking about all the millions of dollars they'd taken in, as if the campaign were for cancer research or the Heart Fund, a money-raising operation that would go on forever. Back in 1960 no one had ever spoken this way. The money was handled by one or two men and went mostly undiscussed even in the press, let alone polite conversation.

It was Reagan's turn now. He had mounted a little box beside the poolside crowd, his skin as smooth and brown as Mitchell's was blotchy. He was making a joke about how he wouldn't be governor today if Lew Wasserman had done a better job getting him parts in movies. Pat threw back her head and laughed and wondered again where all the young men from the campaign kept disappearing to. Martha was right: they'd been scurrying around, nervous and gloomy, all evening. What was going on? What news had they had from Washington? Mitchell himself had once more gone back to the house after finishing his remarks, and the absence of male attention—even the man from Mississippi had vanished—was giving his wife fits.

As Reagan went on talking, Pat wondered how Dick had spent his evening in the Bahamas, at the Abplanalps'. Probably watching a movie. The time difference made it too late to call, but she knew how the conversation would go in any case. She'd mention that Schreiber's house was in Bel Air, and Dick's file-card memory would pop out a recollection of their own brief time here, in '61, between the two defeats. He'd ask if she recalled the day the big fire swept through the neighborhood and he and the fellow helping him write *Six Crises* had gotten up on the roof of their rented house to hose the place down. As he told her this, he'd be silently remembering how by that point he'd already decided to run for governor in '62, something he'd been wrong and she'd been right about. Though neither one of them would mention this now, the conversation would get frosty for a moment or two. No, she thought, smiling: there was no new Nixon.

She hadn't been happy until they'd left Los Angeles and gone to New York, and not really happy until Tom Garahan had come along. And then not really miserable until she'd pushed Tom away. But she wouldn't think about that now; she'd put it out of her mind just as lately she'd been expelling pictures of that boy shooting George Wallace and that madman taking his hammer to the *Pietà*. Still, it was harder to shut out the sensation of happiness, what she'd briefly known with Tom. Best of all, its memory was undulled by the confession of it to anybody, ever. The eight months wearing kerchiefs and dark glasses; the afternoon meetings in movie theaters: there they were, the still-vibrant images and feelings, coming to her, assaulting her will power right now, as Reagan finished speaking.

She needed to get back once more into the receiving line. Shaking another fifty hands would be less of a chore than staying here and being encircled by people who wanted extended conversation. But before she could take a first step forward, she saw the man from Mississippi coming out of the house, no doubt redeputized to look after Mrs. Mitchell. She waved to him, merrily indicated that he should come over; maybe she could delay his getting an earful from Martha about the little snub of a few minutes before.

The man squinted to make sure he was really being summoned. She now remembered the way his weak eyes had kept straining to read the printed handouts at the one meeting she'd ever been at with him; something about the hurricane, back in '69. They'd assigned it to him because he came from Mississippi.

"Hello, Miz Nixon. Fred LaRue."

"Somebody called me 'Miz' about an hour ago, but I'm pretty sure she had it spelled 'M-s-period' in her mind!"

The man smiled and looked at his shoes. "I meant what you call a lady, not a women's-libber."

The soft voice was such a relief from the clipped tones of all the young campaign sharpies who'd come out on the plane. No wonder he was good with Martha.

"I'm remembering that you briefed me about Hurricane Camille. Wasn't that just an awful thing?"

"Yes, ma'am. I imagine it was the worst storm most folks'll ever go through." He looked back at the house, through its glass doors, to the cluster of men still around John Mitchell, before he added: "But you can never be sure."

Chapter Two

JUNE 19, 1972
EXECUTIVE OFFICE BUILDING, WASHINGTON, D.C.

Howard Hunt parked his Pontiac Firebird on Seventeenth Street, across from the EOB and White House. For over an hour he'd been driving around what passed for the capital's downtown—worse than Newark. He was pondering a number of what-might-have-beens, and one of them was automotive. Liddy had run a yellow light Friday evening on his way to the Watergate. If he had mouthed off when he got pulled over—hardly an improbability with Gordon—the cop might have run him in and thereby scuttled the whole operation.

Sixty hours had passed since the botch. Getting out of the Firebird, Hunt looked across Pennsylvania Avenue to number 1701, where the Committee to Re-Elect had its headquarters. He tried to imagine how the news had hit Mitchell and Magruder and all the expense-account boys out in California for that fundraiser. Hunt could have told them that *he* was the one who'd wanted to abort the operation. At a Friday dinner meeting, beforehand, when McCord reported something funny—the disappearance of the masking tape that kept the jimmied door to the DNC unlocked—it was Howard Hunt alone who had said they should scrub the mission. It was Gordon who'd said no, we go ahead, that the tape had more likely been removed by some fastidious mailman than a suspicious security guard. And since Gordon was head of the operation—and needed something to show for his fat quarter-of-a-million-dollar budget—that was that. Bernie and the rest of the boys went in, as planned.

Hunt showed his identification to the EOB guard and took an elevator to the third story, whose big black-and-white floor tiles suggested an infinitely extending chessboard, one whose alternating colors represented not the players' pathways but the players themselves. He himself played for black. The opposition white was monolithic, totalitarian, fixed; but the black squares, his team, hid within themselves an abundance of different colors, all the shades of faction and party whose intramural conflicts could be as deadly as the larger battle. His world, the Free World, was seething with dissent and treachery; he needed to keep his eyes fixed on its black tiles, to detect and avoid all its obscure hues of sickness and appeasement, to steer clear of sinkholes and traps.

He entered room 338, though it was room 214, the room at the Watergate Hotel, that remained on his mind. Saturday had become Sunday, and now Monday, and Bernie and the boys were still in the District jail. Hunt sighed as he lifted the telephone receiver and asked the White House operator to get Mrs. Hunt at her hotel in London. The phone here was more secure than the one at home, and there wasn't much point in worrying about an overseas personal call showing up on the office's monthly printout. He doubted he'd ever be returning to the EOB after today.

Dorothy had just gotten back from an early dinner. She said she was going to stay in tonight: one could have too much theater, even in London. The two children she had with her would go out to a movie by themselves. "No, Howard, they won't slip off to *Oh! Calcutta!* They could have done that in New York."

He tried to get on with what he had to tell her, but he couldn't make himself get to the point. When he finally got near it, all he managed to say was "We had some trouble with the Watergate job."

"Wasn't that a month ago?"

With a deep breath, he launched into a concise, not-quite-complete explanation of how the listening devices they'd installed in May had malfunctioned and been yielding more or less useless information ever since. "So we had to go back in Friday night." He didn't tell Dorothy that they'd attached one of the bugs to the wrong phone. He also didn't tell her that he'd been nervous the moment they arrived, returning to the scene of an inadequately committed crime.

He could hear Dorothy managing her own breath, struggling not to interrupt, as he went through the story of the evening. He told her how McCord's man, Baldwin, had waited and waited at the lookout-and-listening post across the street inside the Howard Johnson's, until he was able to radio word to the Watergate Hotel that the lights had finally gone out in the Democrats' offices. He explained how it was past midnight before the boys went into the office building next door. He and Gordon had stayed behind in the hotel, room 214, watching a late movie, waiting to hear Bernie come in over the radio and say that they'd finished.

"Was Gordon arrested?" asked Dorothy.

Hunt knew she was already worrying about Frances, Liddy's wife, who was always so timid and baffled around her husband's Horst-Wesseling hijinx.

"No, neither one of us." McCord had been the cops' only white-collar capture. Yesterday's *Post* had linked him to the CIA (retired); today's edition had connected him to the Committee to Re-Elect, as its security consultant.

"*They got us!*" He imitated Bernie's voice for Dorothy, explaining how the words had shocked him and Gordon to life once they came over the walkie-talkie. He and Liddy had managed to pack up the hotel room in less than a minute. The last thing he himself snatched up was the wire hanger, a supplementary antenna for the radio, taped to the balcony. He'd then raced across the street with it inside his pants leg, like one of his mother's old washday stretchers. Once inside the Howard Johnson's, he'd helped Baldwin to pack up the listening post.

And that had been just the beginning of a long night, one that wore on through his visit to the pansy lawyer he knew from his job at the PR firm, where he might still be working in full-time peaceful misery had it not been for Colson's offer of exciting opportunities at the White House. The lawyer was a nice enough fellow and a good enough attorney, but he wasn't a criminal lawyer, and that's what they needed—especially the boys. The night's worst moment had come, he now explained to Dorothy, when he'd had to call Miami and tell Clarita, Bernie's wife, that her husband was in the D.C. jail along with the police department's regular nighttime yield of jacked-up dealers and murdering pimps. Her cries had been so anguished and baroque that even Sturgis would not have been able to repeat them *en español.*

When he got home to Potomac, not much before dawn, he had drunk most of a quart of milk. His ulcer had been killing him, just as it was now. He looked over at the safe beside the file cabinet and wished it were a little refrigerator, like the one in room 214.

"Honey," he said to Dorothy, steeling himself. "I had a call from a reporter a little while ago. A fellow named Bob Woodward."

"Bob Woodward! From Montevideo?"

"No, same name."

Robert Woodward, a career prick, had been Eisenhower's last ambassador to Uruguay a dozen years before, when Hunt had been station chief in the capital with an embassy job for his cover. The chief diplomat had disliked the disguised operative from the moment they met. Woodward had known of Hunt's involvement in the Guatemala coup of '54 and didn't want that kind of zealotry kicking over the hors d'oeuvre trays in Montevideo. The ambassador couldn't bring himself to admit that the Uruguayan capital was crawling with Soviet agents, and it galled him that Hunt's local contacts exceeded his own. Woodward had been afraid, in short, that Howard Hunt might actually do his job, and so he'd kicked him home to Washington as soon as he could.

Should he be grateful, or furious, that the reposting had led him to the Bay of Pigs? To this day, even in the fix he now found himself, he didn't really know.

"How did this other Woodward connect you to what happened Friday night?" asked Dorothy. "Howard, you *weren't* arrested, were you?"

"My name and White House phone number were in Bernie's address book."

"Why would Bernie write them there!"

"Well, he did. Now listen, sweetheart, and try not to worry. My name hasn't been in the papers yet—so far it's just McCord—but I expect it will be soon. Maybe even in the papers where you are—"

"Oh, my God!" cried Dorothy.

He knew she didn't need more troubles. Her woes and worries had already, several months ago, sent her to a shrink, who'd then gone and disappeared in a boating accident. Her nerves were so bad that he himself had suggested she get away, take a couple of the kids with her on a vacation to Europe, even though they could hardly afford it—not with the school expenses and the continuing medical bills from the car accident that had blighted the life of one of their daughters. Not when he was paying for the maid in Potomac as well as the horse and the country club. Years ago a deskmate had teased him about all the spending: *Howard, those old OSS guys were living off family money—not their salaries!* But the bills had always stayed high. Even in Montevideo there'd been the Jockey Club.

He now found himself staring at the phone in his hand, unable to remember whether he and Dorothy had said goodbye or been cut off.

He went over to the safe and spun the combination just as he had in the middle of Friday night, when he'd stopped here before rousting the lawyer out of bed. Inside the little vault, behind the State Department cables and the pistol, stood the pile of cash, from which he now took another handful. Should he take the Browning as well? He'd brought it here a few months ago, not for his own protection but to reassure a couple of secretaries who were nervous about a rape that had occurred in the building across the street.

No, he would leave the gun behind. What would be the point in carrying it? Would he really let himself become a fugitive, or resist arrest when the moment came? He wouldn't. After all, on Friday night, once Gordon insisted they go ahead, hadn't he himself told Bernie to make sure he had the White House number, to call him on it once he got home to Miami; *to put it in his book so he wouldn't forget?*

He'd even watched him write it down.

Moreover, hadn't he given Bernie the key to room 214 before the boys went into the office building? And once the radio rasped—*They got us!*—hadn't he, even while grabbing the antenna from the balcony and scooping up everything from the room, left behind on the dresser a check that was waiting to be mailed? *Pay to the Order of Lakewood Country Club, $6.36, E. Howard Hunt.*

Now, back out in the EOB's third-floor corridor, he walked toward the elevator and regarded the black squares hiding all the factional colors of his side. He wondered which part of his own mind was really paymaster to the other. There was a part that had wanted to abort the operation; was there another that had wanted to get caught?

Chapter Three

JUNE 19, 1972, 6 P.M.
APARTMENT OF MR. AND MRS. JOHN MITCHELL,
WATERGATE EAST

"Have one," said John Mitchell. He waved the Mexican lady with the tray of canapés toward John Dean, who sat on a couch with Fred LaRue and Jeb Magruder.

"I'd better not," said Dean, whose stomach had yet to recover from some octopus and pigeon he'd eaten over the weekend in the Philippines. He'd gotten word of the burglary on his way home, while changing planes in San Francisco, and had barely managed to make it into the White House this morning.

"No one should have to go through two Mondays in one week," he told the room.

Magruder's handsome, youthful face showed puzzlement.

"The international dateline," Dean explained.

Robert Mardian, sitting beside Mitchell, snorted over Magruder's ignorance. A Nixon man since the vice-presidential days, he'd lost out on the campaign deputy directorship to this collegiate dope and had had to settle for the vaguely construed post of "political coordinator."

LaRue watched Mitchell light his first pipe of the evening. The two of them had returned from California, without Martha, only an hour ago, but the General—as they still liked to call him four months after he'd left Justice to run the Committee—had decided that the five of them ought to meet here in his curved living room without any delay.

"Where can we stuff them?" he asked. "Liddy and Hunt both."

"Maybe with Howard Hughes? Is he still out in Vegas?" Dean suggested, provoking laughter from everyone but Mardian.

"Fred," asked Mitchell, "do you still own that hotel out there?"

"The Castaways?" LaRue responded, lighting his own pipe. "No, sir. We unloaded that years ago—one hell of a flop. And one more reason I should be back out makin' money instead of workin' for you guys."

Mardian gave him a quizzical look; no one but Mitchell knew exactly what work LaRue did. Magruder patted him on the back. "Maybe we could stash them in one of those houses you own down in Jackson, Fred—the 'Cornpone Compound.'"

LaRue was so benign a figure that even the younger men had no worries teasing him. But he knew the laughter in the room wouldn't last much longer; they'd all soon be looking as miserable as Mardian. For a moment he allowed himself to think of his five children in Jackson; it would probably be weeks before he went down there to see them and Joyce.

Dean supplied the last of the gallows humor: "I see, by the way, that this morning our friends on the High Court ruled that warrants are required for all bugging done in internal-security investigations."

"Too bad they didn't issue that ruling last Friday morning," snapped Mardian, who had lost all patience. "Maybe that would have given those jerks of yours a little pause on Friday *night.*"

Mitchell took two quick puffs on his pipe, as if to say, "Now, now," and then the bedroom phone rang. The General rolled his eyes, and LaRue, knowing who it would be, got up to answer it.

Sure enough, the operator had a collect call from the Newporter Inn in California.

"You've fired Jim McCord! Thrown him to the wolves!"

LaRue took a pause before saying, as soothingly as he could, that they just weren't able to retain as campaign security chief a man who'd broken into the opposition's headquarters. He wondered, as he said it, how Martha had even found out about the firing. Had the *Post's* story already spread to the other coast, even before the evening news broadcasts out there?

"Honey," said Mrs. Mitchell, able to tell what LaRue was thinking, "Helen Thomas can read me the papers whenever she calls. *Or when I call her.* But you get your mind back to Jim McCord now. That man used to drive my little girl to *school.* And you all have *thrown him to the wolves.*"

The Mitchells were each other's second spouse, and people often imagined Marty, their eleven-year-old daughter, to be a grandchild or niece instead of the baby Martha had had with John when she was past

forty. The General's wife regarded it as an honor, not a small humiliation, for McCord to have been asked to chauffeur the girl to school from
time to time. Whether she now saw an injustice to him or to herself
wasn't fully clear.

"Miz Mitchell," said LaRue, trying something that would probably just make things worse. "We're not even sure Jim McCord wasn't
workin' for the other side—that this whole thing wasn't some kind of
trap the Democrats sprang on us."

Martha laughed with sudden exuberance at the possibility, at the
sheer deviousness and fun it seemed to inject into the situation, and
LaRue hoped this new mood would last until he could get her off the
phone.

Before he could think of the next thing to say, she'd hung up.

As he reentered the living room, he heard Magruder saying that
Hugh Sloan, the buttoned-up kid who was the campaign's treasurer,
had come to him today, upset to say the least, with news that the money
found on the burglars could be traced back to the CRP.

Dean said he'd heard the same thing. "And by the way," he added,
"Gordon may not *need* to be stashed away with Howard Hughes. He's
offered to be shot."

"How do we respond to that?" asked Jeb Magruder.

"Tell him things haven't quite come to that."

Understatement was typically lost on Jeb, and when it came to Liddy,
nothing was a laughing matter. "I don't even want to *think* about guns
in connection with that guy," he said. "A while back a couple of us
made a joke about having Jack Anderson bumped off and, Christ, Liddy
thought we were serious."

"You might be interested to know," said Dean, "that he blames you
for Friday night."

Magruder squirmed and pouted. "Oh, swell!"

"To return to the problem of the moment," said Dean, "Ehrlichman
definitely wants to get Hunt out of town."

Mitchell at last spoke. "This whole thing feels like a Chuck Colson
production, doesn't it?"

LaRue knew that he was asking the question rhetorically, just to
indicate a direction he'd like them to start thinking in, the way Dean

had mentioned the dark, absent Ehrlichman to implicate him in what everybody here, even Magruder, understood was already a cover-up. Who knew for sure whether Ehrlichman had said a damned word about Howard Hunt, or whether Colson's fingerprints could be found on the events of Friday night?

Dean decided to answer Mitchell's question. "Colson says no, but he's very touchy on the subject. Liddy does accept responsibility for one thing: picking McCord to do the burglary. He knows he should have hired an outsider, but says that cuts to his budget made that impossible."

The group responded with what LaRue felt certain would be the final laugh of the evening; it was a weak one at that.

"And one last thing," said Dean, who'd clearly been busy today. "There's a safe in Hunt's EOB office. Ehrlichman's put me in charge of getting it open."

"How are you going to manage that?" asked Mardian.

"Somebody from the General Services Administration is coming around with the combination in the next day or two."

"No safecrackers available on the Committee staff?" Mitchell asked Magruder.

Nobody laughed.

LaRue remembered a meeting with Mitchell and Magruder at the end of March, down in Key Biscayne, a couple of houses away from Nixon's. It was there that Mitchell, instead of vetoing it once and for all, had just deferred any decision to fund Liddy's crazy gumshoe plans. They had so much money on hand, and they'd had so many more serious things to discuss, that the proposal had been gently ignored instead of spiked. But of all the guys to take the path of least resistance with: Liddy! That mustachioed nutcase who back in January had stood in front of them all in Mitchell's office at Justice, tapping an easel and talking about prostitutes and wiretaps and knocking guys over the head. Thinking about it now, LaRue winced. Mitchell's mind had already been elsewhere, and it had stayed adrift ever since.

The phone, again. LaRue went into the bedroom to answer it.

No, as it turned out, not Martha; the White House operator trying to track down Magruder.

As Jeb went to the bedroom to take the call, LaRue retook his seat in the living room and noticed a thick file folder on the couch cushion Magruder had vacated. GEMSTONE, said the label: Liddy's James Bond title for his whole array of surveillance and sabotage operations, each stunt named for a different jewel.

While Mitchell discussed the status of fundraising in several states—a business-as-usual interlude, designed perhaps to lower Mardian's blood pressure—LaRue leafed through the file, which bulged with miscellaneous newspaper clippings, photos of McGovern's campaign headquarters across town, and some onionskin copies of what appeared to be the transcripts of telephone conversations picked up by the original bugs the burglars had installed in May:

> DNC Employee: *[inaudible] have to change it from three to four.*
> OUTSIDE TELEPHONE: *Yes, sir, four it is.*
> DNC Employee: *This time we won't take anything off the top.*
> OUTSIDE TELEPHONE: *No, sir. This time no one will even be able to tell.*

LaRue wondered if this exchange had to do with some skimming operation the Democrats had going on with their own meager funds. Then he saw, at the bottom of the page, a notation pertaining to whoever the DNC employee had had on the line. OUTSIDE TELEPHONE (ACC. TO REVERSE DIRECTORY): WATERGATE BARBERSHOP. The whole conversation was about the guy's appointment for a damned haircut.

Alarmingly, the file was crammed with stuff confirming the existence of the surveillance operation that had made this worthless transcript possible. Christ, there was even a bill to the CRP for the listening-post room at the Howard Johnson's.

LaRue closed the folder as Magruder returned to the living room with a big smile on his face.

"Turns out I've got a tennis game tonight," the deputy chairman informed everyone. "With the veep."

Mardian shook his head in renewed disgust over this lucky clown. "I'm surprised it wasn't an invitation to go bowling with the Old Man himself."

Mitchell put down his pipe and picked up his cocktail. "You laugh," he said. "The president called to cheer *me* up this afternoon." He looked at his watch. "He and Bob ought to be getting back to town about now."

Silence descended, as they all contemplated what Haldeman's taking charge of this mess might bring: no doubt a cold wrath that would make Ehrlichman's reaction seem genial.

The phone rang yet again. On his way to get it, LaRue handed the GEMSTONE file to Mitchell. Magruder, in his excitement over an impending singles match with Spiro T. Agnew, didn't notice.

This time it *was* Martha, even more riled up than before.

"Well, honey, is he keepin' his promise?"

"What promise is that, ma'am?"

"To leave politics! What John Mitchell promised me last night in this very room I'm in!"

LaRue took what he hoped would be a calming pause. "I'd have to assume he means after the election, Miz Mitchell."

"And if I try to *redeem* that promise any *earlier,* I suppose that Mr. King, my *bodyguard*—or shall we say my *jailer*—will give me another tranquilizer shot in the rear?"

LaRue said nothing.

"Honey," Mrs. Mitchell continued. "I've given that phone number you're on to Helen Thomas. So you tell the former attorney *general* that he should be expectin' a call anytime now."

LaRue sighed, thinking of the bother he'd soon be going through to change the number once again.

"Well, Mr. LaRuesevelt," Martha said, using one of her many nicknames for him. "You take care of that man of mine until I get back."

"Yes, ma'am."

"You know *why* I want you to do that? You *don't*? Well, I'll tell you. Because when I get back *I'm* going to take care of him but *good*."

She hung up.

LaRue sat on the bed for a moment, silently reviewing the algebra that governed the room on the other side of the wall. Magruder hated Liddy. Mardian hated Magruder. Ehrlichman hated Mitchell. Mitchell hated Colson. And that was all *before* Friday night. He himself was a kind of lotion, a soother, the one most generally trusted because he was the one least thoroughly known. He looked out the window at the swirl-ing green of the Watergate courtyard and wondered what tasks would fall to him in the coming weeks and months. He was good at hiding Mitchell's skeletons, and had managed to keep a giant one of his own hidden for years—a set of bones upon which the whole Cornpone Com-pound rested. He knew he'd soon be covering whatever tracks led from the men in the living room to Hunt and Liddy and McCord. The trick would be covering them without leaving tracks of his own. The reward? One of the benefits he'd always had from politics: the chance—by dis-tracting himself with others' calamities—to forget about his own sin-gular catastrophe.

When he returned to the living room, Mitchell handed him the GEMSTONE folder along with a whispered instruction. There was a lull in the meeting while Magruder put his jacket on and got ready to go. LaRue now followed the younger man into the hallway and handed him the file: "You forgot this."

"Oh, wow," said Magruder. "Thanks, Fred."

"The General suggests that when you get home tonight you have a little fire in your fireplace." LaRue tapped the folder.

"Will do," said Magruder, nodding gratefully as he went off to play tennis.

Chapter Four

JUNE 20, 1972, 5:30 P.M.
HOME OF ALICE ROOSEVELT LONGWORTH,
2009 MASSACHUSETTS AVENUE, WASHINGTON, D.C.

"You look awful!" said Mrs. Longworth.

"Look who's talking," replied Joseph Alsop, forgoing a kiss and sitting himself down beside his second cousin's silver teapot.

Mrs. Longworth laughed. With her head tilted back and mouth open, her long, yellowed teeth looked oddly glamorous, like the ruins of the Acropolis at twilight.

"Mrs. Braden was just leaving, coz."

Startled, Joan Braden picked up her purse. "I guess I am!" she cried, rising to her feet. She shook Alsop's hand. "I'd better get home to my own *homme sérieux*, before he becomes an *homme furieux*."

Alsop frowned. An *homme sérieux* was what he and his brother, Stewart—solid old Truman-Kennedy Democrats—had taken to calling Richard Nixon in their columns, now that all the other old Cold Warriors, including Mrs. Braden's husband, yet another columnist, had hopped aboard McGovern's psychedelic bus.

"Goodbye, dear," said Mrs. Longworth to the much-younger Mrs. Braden. She didn't get up to see her out.

"I can't stand her," said Alsop, once Mrs. Braden was gone. "She's a loudmouth knockoff of Ethel," he added, meaning Bobby Kennedy's widow. "You know how her husband got the money for that paper he used to run out in California? By letting his wife sleep with Nelson Rockefeller, that's how."

"That's hardly news," said Mrs. Longworth. "And if it weren't true, I wouldn't like her as much as I manage to."

"What's she *doing* here?" asked Alsop. "Why isn't she home with her eight children? And what kind of courtesan *has* eight children?"

Joe's problem, Mrs. Longworth knew, involved the one thing that procreation and prostitution had in common: sex itself. Mrs. Braden didn't bother her. Imagine: hatching that brood and still having time—before, during, and after the breeding—to sleep with Rockefeller and, so it was said, with Bobby as well. That might be carrying the Ethel imitation rather far, but when Mrs. Longworth had asked, Mrs. Braden had owned up to it. Alice might have asked her about the Kissinger rumor, too, if the possibility of its being true didn't revolt her in a purely aesthetic way.

Poor Joe, pouring himself a cup of tea and looking as if he'd swallowed a bad clam. He was miserable these days with Susan Mary, and nothing, thought Mrs. Longworth, could be more ridiculous. What was the point of a *mariage blanc* if all the partners did was fight? She'd known Joe was queer as a plaid rabbit from the time he was a boy, and back in '61, unlike everyone else, she had *not* approved of his marrying the widow Patten—as if that could solve everything, or give Joe equal status with all those virile men of Camelot on whom he had his carnal and ideological crushes.

He was twenty-six years her junior and, sitting across from her, looked like a very old man. "So, Joe," she asked, as he took another sip of tea. "When did I last see you?"

"The Gridiron dinner. April."

"That's right. And it was no fun at all, except for crossing the picket line." The club now allowed female guests at its big annual event but still didn't admit women as members. "So stupid of Dick not to go. For the second straight year, too. All because he finds the jokes rough. That's carrying your *homme sérieux* business a bit far."

A thought struck Alice, and pleased her. "He should have said he couldn't go because he was siding with the women. Had his cake and eaten it." She sliced Joe a piece of the delicious chocolate layer cake that sat between them. Her guests were always surprised to find what she served so moist and fresh; they expected Miss Havisham's wedding cake along with the cracked leather cushions and the crumbling taxidermy.

"I just wrote him a contribution for forty-nine dollars," said Alsop. "That's one dollar under the limit of what's got to be reported."

As if, thought Alice, Joe's journalistic integrity, or whatever it's called, was what he really had to worry about—instead of those photographs the Soviets had had in their possession for years, of Joe in his Moscow hotel room in bed with a soldier.

"You know, you really *do* look awful," she told him.

"Nothing's felt right since Mother died."

"Your mother"—Father's niece, and Alice's first cousin—"was a grand gal. She was also eighty-five."

"You're eighty-eight."

"And perfectly willing to be dead. How's Stew?" How foolish that she should find it easier to ask after Joe's brother, dying of leukemia, than to inquire about Susan Mary.

"Not good," said Alsop. "You'll notice I haven't gotten up to mix myself an actual drink. I'm back to playing blood bank this week."

"Easier than donating bone marrow, I suppose."

"You think?" said Alsop, grimacing as he swallowed more tea.

"Poor Stew," said Alice. "What a nuisance." Reflexively, she looked out into the hall, where an old stuffed tiger had lost a paw the last time Stew was here and decided to shake hands with it. "Slice yourself more cake."

Joe declined, and she admired his discipline. What a preposterously fat young man he'd been when he arrived in town in the thirties to cover Franklin and the New Deal. A reporter with a Harvard diploma; silly. She supposed he'd slimmed down to please the boys.

Suddenly, Joanna's voice came up the stairs.

"I'm off, Grandmother!"

"Enjoy yourself, dear!" Alice cried in response. "Try not to be home before midnight!"

"Where's she off to?" asked Alsop. "And why doesn't she come in here to say goodbye? Or, for that matter, hello?"

"She probably thought Mrs. Braden was still in here. For God's sake, Joe, she's twenty-five. I haven't the slightest idea where she's off to."

"Doesn't she eat with you? What, in fact, *are* you going to eat tonight? Does she let you live on cake and tea? Is there a servant left in this whole place?"

"Janie's off for the night. Don't worry. Joanna will come home around one o'clock and bring me a lovely veal chop from Anna Maria's, that little place up on Connecticut Avenue. And it will be *exactly* what I want."

Alsop knew that Alice's routine hadn't varied for decades. She would read through the night, until almost dawn, when she'd mark her place, probably with the bone from the veal chop, and then fall asleep until noon.

"Tell me," he asked. "Are we related to Elliot Richardson? Are *you*, I mean."

"I certainly hope not."

"Elliot *Lee* Richardson? Not one of your Boston Lees?"

"I cannot imagine. I should think that in the forest of Lee family trees I'm fewer branches away from Robert E. or Lorelei."

"I spent half the afternoon with him at HEW. An interview, supposedly, but there was a camera crew traipsing through the office taking 'footage' "—he said it as if the word were new— "for some film they'll show at the convention."

"What possessed him to leave State?" asked Mrs. Longworth. "Even being one of Rogers's undersecretaries has to have been more interesting than sending out welfare checks."

"He left because he was asked to."

"By your *homme sérieux*?"

"Of course," said Alsop. "And this won't be the last job he's given to do. Nixon *needs* him from time to time. Almost the way he needs Ed Brooke." He referred to the Senate's only Negro, a Republican to boot. "Richardson is somebody to put in front of the cameras when they have to show a bit of probity and class—all the Harvard, high Establishment stuff Nixon's usually able to do without."

"You sound as if you're back on the New Frontier, Joe."

"No," said Alsop, loudly putting down his teacup, as if the gesture might reaffirm his new fealty toward the incumbent. "But Nixon's going to require Richardson's type a little more than he thinks." He pointed to a copy of the *Washington Post*. "Kay seems determined to make something serious out of this burglary, doesn't she?"

"Dick's second-story men?" asked Mrs. Longworth. "Don't make me laugh."

"Well, my dear, I wouldn't dismiss it just yet. A CIA connection one day; a link to the White House the next." The *Post* had today run a report of Howard Hunt's involvement.

"I *almost* like Kay," said Mrs. Longworth. "Her mother detested me."

"No, she didn't."

"I'm glad she did. I detest their paper. That copy you're pointing to belongs to Mrs. Braden, not me."

"Ah, of course," said Alsop. He had his own problems with Kay Graham, who had gently let him know that she regarded his column, still running in her pages, as increasingly uncivil and out of touch. But he knew that his ancient cousin was talking about something else.

And she, moreover, knew that he did. Mrs. Longworth would never forgive the *Post* for making it clear, fifteen years earlier, that Joanna's mother, Paulina, had committed suicide by swallowing sixty pills. Except for the *Post*, her only child might have gone out of the world as ambiguously as she'd come into it: recognized as the daughter of Nicholas Longworth, speaker of the House, but the child, in reality, of Senator William Borah, Alice's lover of many years and the one man she'd truly hoped to make president. Paulina's paternity had always, among anyone who counted, been an open secret—which was the best and most civilized kind of secret—and there was no reason her death at the age of thirty-one couldn't have been treated the same way.

Dick had come to the funeral, even agreed to be a pallbearer, just a week after his second inaugural as vice president.

Mrs. Longworth now looked across at Joe, one of Jack Kennedy's spear carriers. These days he liked to present himself as someone who'd made an *intellectual* conversion to Nixon—one *homme sérieux* to another—and liked to regard her own affection for Dick as rote Republicanism, crude. Well, he didn't know the rest of the story, what else Dick had done for her that January, besides carrying Paulina to her grave. The rest of it was very much a *closed* secret, one she would never tell to Joe or anybody else.

There he sat while she cut herself another piece of cake: reading the detestable *Post*, certain that each of her antipathies was more childish than the next, calling on her this afternoon as if *she* were the old lady instead of himself.

She felt the urge to inflict a little pain. "I hear rumors that Susan Mary is going to leave you. Are they true?"

He allowed the newspaper to collapse into his lap, and he crumpled along with it. "I don't think so, but she's threatening to. She's even looked at a place for herself."

"Where?"

"Where else? The Watergate."

The two of them laughed. Her yellow teeth flashed and bit into the cake, and she forgave him.

But she did not forgive Kay.

Chapter Five

JUNE 23, 1972, 3:50 P.M.
THE WHITE HOUSE

"Bob," said Rose Mary Woods, nodding curtly.

She brushed past him on the way back to her office, outside of which Marje Acker and two other secretaries sat at their desks. If one charted the pecking order and included Marje, it was possible to say that the president's secretary had a secretary who had secretaries of her own, which made Rose Mary Woods sound rather grand, but this was not what she had hoped for *at all* when the boss finally reached the White House.

All she'd ever wanted here was the same setup that Ann Whitman, Ike's head girl, had once had. No matter who was serving as chief of staff, Ann remained the gatekeeper, just as Rose herself had been for the vice president. That included barring the door—the incident was now legendary—to the head of the Republican Policy Committee, Senator Bridges of New Hampshire, when he tried to see Nixon during the '60 campaign. "To bother him about nothing," Rose remembered. "I told him no."

For eighteen years, whether they were "in" or "out," that's how it had been. But it had ended once and for all in the elevator of the Waldorf, the morning after the '68 election. Riding down to his press conference, the boss had told her that Haldeman would control all access to him after the inauguration. She'd practically seen stars when he said it, and for the rest of the ride down to the ballroom and the rest of the week after that, she wouldn't say a word to him, refusing to lose her temper and give him the chance to make an awkward little joke about her getting her Irish up. He hated hurting anyone's feelings, least of all hers, and she let him know how bad she felt by her stony, out-of-character silence.

Even so, he never budged from the structure Haldeman had sold him on, a chain of command that made sure he never had to hurt *anyone's* feelings, at least face-to-face. Now, almost four years later, the place was crawling with a whole second generation of admen and junior executives even a decade younger than Bob, all these good-looking dumb-bunnies like Magruder who provided Richard Nixon with a whole new cloud of insulation, like those little Styrofoam peanuts Rose's mail-order knick-knacks came packed in.

They all, of course, had college educations, and knew full well that she had none—no matter that she could correct the grammar and spelling of every one of them. College would have been lovely, but it wasn't in the cards for a girl from Sebring, Ohio, who had to help out at home. As it was, nobody could say she hadn't come a long way.

Over the years there had been plenty of times when she'd had to pull the boss up with her, lift him from some funk and point the way out of whatever jam he was in. And, with the exception of Harry Robbins Haldeman, you wouldn't find anybody along this whole high-and-mighty corridor who didn't think she'd been underutilized for the past three and a half years. Actually, she thought, "underutilized" sounded just like them. What was wrong with "squandered"?

"And what are you looking at?" she asked with mock fierceness, raising a chuckle from one of the subsecretaries who'd just come in and noticed the pickle-puss Miss Woods was displaying.

"Oh, nothing," said the girl, Lorraine, a strawberry blonde like herself. "I somehow thought you might have just run into HRH."

They both grinned at the use of Haldeman's too-perfect initials.

"Get out of here," said Miss Woods, taking a file from the girl and laughing.

At least the folder contained something she could enjoy working on: an invitation list, last-minute additions, for the Polish-Americans' reception they'd be having on Monday in the Blue Room. Such guest lists constituted Rose Mary Woods's chief remaining power, a meager tribute to her memory, smarts, and Rolodex, which over two decades had grown almost to the size of the potters' wheels back at the Royal China Company, her very first employer, in Sebring.

Henry Helstoski? A Democrat from the Jersey House delegation was on the list just because of his name. They could do better than that, she thought, scratching him, ethnic suffix and all, and substituting Charlie Sandman, a Republican from the same delegation who always stuck with the boss, and had plenty of Poles in his district, besides.

Should Agnew be coming? she wondered. Would that seem like penance for the crack he'd made about "Polacks" during the '68 race? Or would his appearance add insult to injury? The whole thing had always seemed ridiculous. None of her Irish relatives had ever called a Pole anything other than a Polack, and they'd never meant anything by it, either.

As she scanned the list, a good line came to her brain—the kind of ad-lib she sometimes passed on to Buchanan or one of the other writers. She put a card into the Selectric and typed it out: *I want you to know that between now and Election Day, you're the only "Poles" we'll be paying any attention to.* She went back and twice underlined "Poles," so the president would remember to pronounce the word strongly enough for people to get the joke. As she put the card into an envelope and marked it for the writers' office, she realized how automatically she now followed HRH's filtration system. In the old days she'd always fed tidbits like this one right to the boss himself.

Resuming work on the list, she could feel a late-afternoon contentment finally coming over her, the kind she used to experience during sleepy days long ago on Capitol Hill, when Pat might come in to help out with the mail and answer the phone: "Senator Nixon's office. Miss Ryan speaking." They'd take a break and gab a little while putting on nail polish, the same pinkish kind she was applying now, since she wouldn't have time to go back to her apartment before Don Carnevale picked her up for an early dinner.

They were going to a new French place tonight: La Chansonette. The *Post* had panned it, and that was good enough for her. The two of them would have a fine time, whatever the food turned out to be like, and at a couple of points in the course of the evening, she'd silently remind herself that she was out with a man who over the years had had Clare Luce and Joan Crawford on his arm. The wives of the junior executives could sneer all they liked about her "confirmed bachelor." As far as she was concerned, Don, a vice president at Harry Winston who'd worked himself up from nothing, was more of a gentleman than the pretty boys they'd married.

At 4:05 she saw the red light that blinked only for calls from the boss. She picked up to hear the voice that for twenty-two years had come to her as often through telephone receivers and Dictabelts as in person.

"Rose, will you bring in that speech about the meat imports?"

"Yes, sir," she said, before hanging up and blowing on her nails. She fluffed her hair, straightened her dress, and started on her way, carrying the typescript through the outer office.

"Ready for your close-up?" asked Lorraine.

"I'll give *you* a close-up," she answered, pretending to swat her with the rolled-up pages. They both knew that this speech, while real enough, was right now wanted as a prop, something she and the president could pretend to go over while David L. Wolper's team shot some film for the little movie that would be shown to the convention two months from now.

She found a half dozen aides rubbernecking in the corridor just outside the Oval Office, and a few more who'd been permitted to stand against its far wall while the president cooperated with the production manager in setting up the next shot.

Dwight Chapin, the best-looking of all the junior executives, smiled and made room for Rose inside the office. John Dean whispered a quick hello and goodbye, vacating a spot for Bob Finch, the boss's old California crony.

The president prepared to sign a document for the cameras. "Anybody you want me to pardon?" he asked, as the paper was moved into place on the blotter. Everyone laughed, and Rose could now see him, emboldened by the joke's success, going into his regular-guy routine. "I'd tell you to shoot me from my good side," he said to the cameraman, "but I'm not sure I have one." More laughter.

The production man nodded deferentially to John Ehrlichman, indicating they'd reached the moment in the script for him to approach the desk for some conversation with the president about revenue sharing and the environment. Ehrlichman chronically griped that the domestic programs he oversaw were ignored by commentators, and even by staffers, who'd rather concentrate on Russia and China and Henry. He could be an even rougher character than HRH, but to Rose's mind his little resentments and occasional flare-ups were genuine. Ehrlichman actually believed in a few things, and if he, too, never deferred to her long history with the president, he at least rejected her on a human basis—he simply didn't like her—whereas Haldeman regarded her as a piece of dust needing to be vacuumed from the transistors.

"I see Rose over there," said the president to the cameraman, between takes of his supposedly unrehearsed chat with Ehrlichman. "She looks great, doesn't she? You know, she and Mrs. Nixon sometimes swap dresses."

Actually, she and Mrs. Nixon hadn't done that in years. But the theme of thrift, embodied in 1952's lifesaving cloth coat, was still honored in Nixon speeches and conversations. "What are you girls?" he asked. "Both size ten?"

"Careful, Mr. President," said the production man. Amidst the general laughter that followed, everyone could detect the sharp cackle of Chuck Colson.

The president reacted to the arrival of his political advisor with a smile, but two seconds after that, Rose saw him signal Chapin, with his eyebrows, that Colson's presence here might not be the best idea. Chuck was continually being urged to lower his public profile, as if he were a kind of mad relative who needed to be kept out of sight. Rose agreed with Ehrlichman and HRH about precious few matters, but she'd bet they felt the same as she did about the break-in at the DNC: the idea for it had to have come from Colson.

Chapin, having gotten the president's message, fabricated a bit of urgent business that caused him to touch the political advisor's elbow and propel him, with a whisper, back into the hall.

It was Rose's moment to stand by the desk and discuss the text of the speech about meat imports. "Wish we had something a little more momentous to show 'em," the president said to her, before the cameraman resumed rolling. "Even so," he added to the film crew, making them feel trusted and important, "I hope you fellows won't leak any of this before it's released next week."

"No, sir."

"Absolutely not."

"Good," said Nixon. "What about zooming in on that?" he suggested, pointing to a page of Rose's typing, which made the words do a zigzag down the page, a system of spacing and capitalization known only to the two of them that indicated just the right speechmaking cadence.

"No one will get it," said Haldeman from several feet away. "It will only confuse people."

"I guess you're right," the president replied, picking up the typescript so that its blank back pages met the eyes of the now-active camera. He tapped the text, made a polite, knowing mutter about a phrase that "could probably go," to which Rose responded, "Yes, you're right."

When her moment ended, she decided to linger by the wall for a bit, and just as she took up her position Kissinger walked in, a genuinely unscheduled arrival. He pretended to regret interrupting and, as the cameraman continued to film, he told the president about his latest, just-completed trip to China.

"Too many banquets," said the national security advisor, patting his stomach.

"How were the dancing girls?" asked Nixon.

"They were all wearing tunics and carrying rifles. You've seen the ballets. It is always like watching the Rockettes invade Normandy."

Nixon made himself laugh, but then told the production man, "Better leave that on the cutting-room floor. And then make sure you sweep up!"

Kissinger seemed to wonder if he'd made a tactical error.

"You know, Roland," the president continued, impressing the cameraman by this use of his name, "Rose back there is a terrific dancer. She's single, too. But be careful. Her brother will have you arrested if you get fresh. He's a sheriff."

Joe Woods hadn't been the sheriff of Cook County, Illinois, for two years, not since he'd left the post to run a losing race for head of the Board of Supervisors. But Joe had been plenty helpful on election night in '68. As the Republican sheriff, he'd been able to delay reports of the count from pro-Nixon suburban precincts. Fortified by his sister's still-fresh memories of 1960, he'd waited and waited, confusing Mayor Daley, who wound up undervoting the Democratic dead and never made up the shortfall. And thus did Richard Daley fail to steal the state a second time from Richard Nixon.

Rose almost found herself wishing they had an opponent tougher than George McGovern, a man for whom Daley didn't even want to turn out the living. (In fact, she and the president would bet their bottom dollars that not only Daley but LBJ himself would be voting for Richard Nixon this November.) What Rose really wanted was a third thrill ride, one last harrowing, protracted hairsbreadth election night, just like '60 and '68. Throughout his whole eight years "in the wilderness," she'd always known that the boss would reach this office. She'd known it even at the most tearful, rock-bottom moment of all, when she was driving her convertible along the Pacific Coast Highway, the morning after they'd lost the governor's race in '62, and over the car radio she heard the horrible "last press conference"—*You won't have Nixon to kick around anymore*—which he'd promised her he wouldn't give.

"Rose," the president now said, as the cameraman set up one more shot. "You'll help Mrs. Nixon with her part of this filming, won't you?"

"Of course."

"You know," he told the crew, "way back when, in California, my wife worked as an extra in the movies."

Out came the stories of *Becky Sharp*, and while they were being told, Rose's mind went to another time and place entirely, to the years in New York, between that morning on the Pacific Coast Highway and the start of the '68 campaign. Pat may have loved that period, but Rose had hated the whole five years. As she sat amongst the Nixons at Thanksgiving or Christmas dinner, she could feel herself waiting for the day when he would get up and once more be *fighting*, and she would be fighting with him, never giving up, just as she hadn't given up when they told her she had less than twelve months to live—a high school girl with cancer! She'd fought it and beat it. And she hadn't given up when Billy, her beautiful, basketball-playing fiancé, went off to the war and was killed. She'd gotten up from her bed of grief, the same way she'd gotten up from the operating table, and come to Washington to start a new life with twenty thousand other government girls.

"You know," the president said, as the production assistant experimented with a slightly more mussed look for the desk, "Rose more or less hired *me*."

It was a story he told more often than the tale of Mrs. Nixon's time on the fringes of RKO.

"Rose was working for the Herter Committee, which was helping to straighten out the Marshall Plan, and I was one of the congressmen on it."

"The only one," she now said, completing the story from across the room, "who filed expense reports that weren't an unholy mess. His were neatly typed and checked out to the penny. I was impressed."

All eyes turned to her as she continued. Though the staff had heard this story many times, every one of them, except for HRH, smiled. Rose paused, waited a beat, and said, "I suspect Mrs. Nixon had a little to do with the perfect typing."

The president tilted his head back and laughed, as if hearing the penultimate line of the story for the first time. He then supplied the kicker: "So when I got to the Senate a couple of years later, Rose decided she could stand running my office."

The laughter might be practiced, but his mood was awfully good, Rose thought. Well, why shouldn't it be? The *news* had been so good these past few months: China and Russia had been just the beginning. Inflation had fallen below three percent, and the Supreme Court's abolition of the death penalty, expected any time now, would be one more millstone to tie around McGovern's skinny neck. What fun it would be to keep forcing him to say he agreed with the ruling.

Her own mood would be better if Bob Haldeman weren't standing just in front of her. He, too, like Ehrlichman next to him, was noticing the boss's genuine high spirits.

"So what *is* it?" Ehrlichman whispered.

"He's relieved to be taking action," Haldeman replied. "Walters is going to call the FBI and tell them CIA wants them to stay the hell away from investigating the burglary thing. National security."

Ehrlichman chuckled.

"Mitchell's idea, actually," said Haldeman.

Now Ehrlichman snorted. "Even he's right once or twice a year." After a pause, he added, casually, "I've told Dean to deep-six the briefcase."

"Briefcase?"

"The one that was in Hunt's safe."

Neither of them worried about Rose's hearing this exchange. They both knew that when it came to things like this—and there were *always* things like this—her instincts were more ruthless than theirs.

She looked at both their collars, appraisingly, and thought: If someone ever told *them* they had less than twelve months to live, they'd crumble.

Chapter Six

JULY 12, 1972, 4:30 P.M.
HOME OF MR. AND MRS. E. HOWARD HUNT,
POTOMAC, MARYLAND

Hunt heard Dorothy's car pull into the driveway. He got up from his desk, covered the half-composed letter in his typewriter, and went downstairs to greet his wife, who had just returned from the Potomac Village Shopping Center.

Her dark complexion could not hide a flush, and she was slightly out of breath, as if she were carrying grocery bags instead of just her black patent-leather purse.

"Well," she said, "I've talked to 'Mr. Rivers.'"

Her husband nodded, welcoming this pseudonymous newcomer to the company of cutouts and code names with whom he'd transacted so much of his life.

"What's he like?" Hunt asked Dorothy, knowing she had made the man's acquaintance only over the shopping-center pay phone that Mr. Rivers had said he would call.

"He's like one of the Dead End Kids."

"Was he faking the voice? 'Dese, dem, and dose'?"

"No," said Dorothy. "The accent was too real, and it never varied. He's a genuine meatball."

Hunt nodded.

"I agreed to be the conduit," she said.

Her husband looked at her admiringly, aware of the pressures she would now be under.

"I've got to get a pad and pencil," said Dorothy, walking toward the kitchen counter. "I'm going to draw up a budget. For us; for Bernie and Clarita; for everybody else."

"I'll get Bernie on board," said Hunt, as if offering to wash the dishes while she dried. "And he can figure out the numbers for the boys."

"If you call him from Potomac Village, try to find a different phone booth from the one I used near Montgomery Ward. It's got no door."

She went off to the kitchen to start calculating the Hunts' share of the payments. Her husband continued looking at her for a few moments, trying to decide whether she was newly energized or ready to crack.

Back upstairs, he resumed drafting the letter he intended to send Chuck Colson, recounting all that had happened in the three weeks since his own name had first appeared in the *Post,* a paper he never read regularly. He would try to avoid any allusions to *The Odyssey* (he doubted Chuck had done as well as he had in classics at Brown), but he'd been peripatetic to say the least.

After leaving Washington on June 19, he'd spent a single night in New York before heading to Los Angeles, where he lay low at the house of his old war buddy, Anthony Jackson. But his presence soon made Jackson nervous, and as the days passed with no word about money or legal representation, Hunt himself had started feeling hopeless. Then, unexpectedly, Liddy—who even *now* wasn't publicly connected to the break-in—had arrived, with cheering assurances that John Mitchell would take care of everyone, even though the administration appeared to be going along with the police investigation. In fact, Hunt could not get over the degree of their cooperation: in more than twenty years, the only element of the government ever to acknowledge his connection to the CIA had turned out to be the White House.

Before June was over, he'd flown to Miami, hoping to see Bernie, who was at last out on bail. But the vans and cameras of the local news stations were all around the Barkers' house, so he'd given up and gotten the next plane back to L.A. As July Fourth approached, weary of imposing on Jackson, he'd gone to Chicago to stay with Dorothy's cousins. It was from there that he'd finally made arrangements with a lawyer, William Bittman, a connection of Jackson's who, conveniently enough, lived and worked here in Potomac.

At that point he'd flown home under a false name and been picked up by Dorothy, who had returned from England. They went straight from the airport to Bittman's office and paid him the first thousand dollars of his retainer with money from the EOB safe. Considerably more, twenty-five grand, soon arrived from somewhere—Mitchell, presum-

ably, if Liddy could be believed. And then "Mr. Rivers" was calling Bittman and asking to speak to "the writer's wife."

Involving Dorothy had been their idea, whoever "they" were; presumably her movements would attract less notice than Hunt's own.
Either way, she was perfectly willing. Today at lunch, as she made herself memorize what she would tell Mr. Rivers over the pay phone, she
had been febrile with purpose and determination.

Through the study's open door, he could now hear her downstairs,
talking to their daughter Kevan, who was on her way back to Smith in
a couple of months. (Would John Mitchell be picking up the tuition,
too? Along with his other daughter's medical bills?) Hunt rose from his
desk and went to listen at the landing, hoping to make certain Dorothy wasn't telling Kevan anything she shouldn't. He also hoped to convince himself that his wife really felt as content with everything as she
claimed to be.

He did not like what he heard. He'd almost rather they be discussing
"Mr. Rivers" than the subject they were on: some pamphlet sent by the
Smith College health services that seemed to be practically an adver-
tisement for the availability of contraception.

His only disagreements with Dorothy involved the grubby new
world in which their children were coming of age. It angered him that
his wife took the same relaxed view of sex and pot that he would expect
from some hip divorcée or social worker. She and Kevan were scandaliz-
ing the Guatemalan maid by reading aloud passages from the pamphlet.

To avoid hearing any more laughter from the whole feminine trio
downstairs, he closed the study door and turned on the portable television near his desk. There was no escape: live from the Democratic
convention that would nominate McGovern tonight, some harridan in
blue jeans was complaining about how the party's platform committee had been insufficiently deferential to "welfare mothers." The term
was proving even more detestable to his ears for the way it somehow
seemed to encompass Dorothy, who'd now be living a life of envelopes
and handouts.

She had stood by him through every secret turn his life had taken
for more than twenty years, even when that meant living over a whorehouse, as they'd done while he was station chief in Mexico City—where

on top of everything else he'd been extortively accused of hit-and-run. They'd met only a couple of years before all that, in Paris, after her French divorce from her first husband, when they were both on the staff of Averell Harriman's Economic Cooperation Administration— the only two non-left-wingers in the Paris office.

He was getting nowhere with this letter in front of him. What he'd really like to do is *call* Colson, but that, of course, was impossible. As he looked at the unusable phone, it, too, seemed one more conveyance toward yesteryear, reminding him of the weeks he'd spent in Vienna, in 1948, while Dorothy remained in Paris. Each time he'd tried to call her, all the taps on the line between the two capitals would siphon the current and sever the connection.

They'd get away from here in a few weeks. Bittman, thank God, had managed to keep him free on bail. In a week or so he'd have to be finger-printed, and give a handwriting sample at the courthouse downtown, but after that there'd be a brief judicial lull, when he and Dorothy could go down to Florida. He pictured it now: fishing off a dock in the Keys with Bernie, neither of them saying much, though Bernie would be say-ing it in English, and he would be saying it in Spanish.

By that point, phone or no phone, Colson should have things fixed for good.

Chapter Seven

JULY 21, 1972, 5:15 P.M.
WATERGATE WEST 310, APARTMENT OF FRED LaRUE

"Tony," LaRue asked softly, "what can I get you?"

"Just a cuppa coffee, Mr. LaRue. Just a cuppa coffee. I'm not stayin' long. You're busy, for one thing." He pointed to LaRue's little oven, whose timer was clicking as his dinner cooked.

"I'm happy to meet you, Tony." LaRue fetched some milk and sugar for his unexpected guest. "I've been hearing from Herb Kalmbach about how enterprising you've been. Still," he added, with as much of his natural politeness as he could, "I didn't really have this in mind." By "this" he meant a personal visit, and he could see that Ulasewicz, rough around the edges but no dope, got his drift.

"You're right, Mr. LaRue. It's irregular. It's not what anybody had in mind."

"So how worrisome is what you're bringing me? We've got worries enough already."

LaRue turned his head, reflexively, in the direction of the Mitchells' apartment far across the complex. The General had resigned as head of the CRP on July 1, pleading personal difficulties, which everyone took to mean Martha. This amounted to more truth than a Washington letter of resignation typically contained, but it was still less than half of it. The Mitchells were mostly in New York these days, but even now LaRue checked in with his old boss every afternoon.

"I'm worried myself, Mr. LaRue," said Ulasewicz.

"So Herb tells me." Kalmbach, the president's personal attorney, was quietly raising money for the burglars and their lawyers. LaRue, through Ulasewicz, had been helping to distribute what was already on hand at the Committee or available inside the White House.

"I told Mr. Kalmbach—more than once, Mr. LaRue—that something's not kosher here."

LaRue wasn't sure if Ulasewicz was Jewish, but he was certainly New

York. You would take him for a guy out of the squad room in *Naked City* even if he hadn't once actually been a cop. The two of them had never met before now, but he knew that Tony had been doing stuff for the White House as far back as Chappaquiddick, nosing around for dirt on Teddy Kennedy. It was more or less inevitable that Ulasewicz would become "Mr. Rivers," shuttling between the money men and "the writer's wife."

"I'm sure you've got another word for it in your part of the country," said Ulasewicz.

LaRue realized that he'd been lost in thought. "I'm sorry. You mean 'kosher'?"

"Let's just say it's not right. Let's just say it don't smell like no magnolias."

LaRue paused, before asking. "Why have you come to me, Tony?"

"Because I can't get through to Mr. Kalmbach. Don't get me wrong, he's a very nice gentleman. But he's the president's lawyer. He's used to dealing with people who sign contracts and even stick by them. This whole thing's a different kettle of fish."

"What specifically is the problem?" asked LaRue.

"I'd say the problem is that this ain't all about legal fees and grocery bills. I'd say this money ain't all for 'humanitarian purposes,' as Mr. Kalmbach likes to say."

"What would you say it's about?"

"I'd say it's blackmail. You can dress it up, but that ain't gonna change it."

"*Quid pro quo?*" LaRue suggested.

"Yeah," said Ulasewicz. "That's the term Mr. Kalmbach uses when he thinks he's being *realistic*. But all that Latin don't manage to call a spade a spade." He hesitated for a moment. "I can tell you who don't mince *any* words."

"Who?"

"The writer's wife."

"Miz Hunt?"

"Yeah, Dorothy. By now we're practically buddies. And let me tell you, Mr. LaRue, this is one tough cookie. This ain't a lady making 'humanitarian' collections for the Community Chest."

"You're sure of that?"

"I'm sure of that. Never even met the lady face-to-face, but I've watched her from a distance, stood by the Eastern Airlines counter at National and seen her take the money from the locker I told her to go to."

"What's she like?"

"Good-looking, tall. Ladylike. Dark skin. Part Sioux Indian, she tells me. We get to ramblin' a little on the phone."

"So how do you know she's so tough?"

"The proof is in the pudding, Mr. LaRue. And there's the pudding." He pointed to the shopping bag on the other side of the coffee table. His host looked at it quizzically.

"I'm no technical genius, Mr. LaRue—though, truth is, the boys you employed for that job next door, including the writer's wife's husband, don't seem to have been, either. In any case, I know how to record a conversation off a pay phone, well enough to pick up what I'm saying into the mouthpiece along with what I'm hearin' out the receiver." He extracted a little rubber-sided microphone from the pocket of his jacket. "It clips on just below your ear, right onto the handset."

LaRue was unsure what to say. Ulasewicz got up, went to the shopping bag, and pulled out a portable tape recorder, no thicker than a book.

"This'll play it for you," he said. "I bought it myself, and I don't even care if Mr. Kalmbach approves the expense. The tape's already sittin' on the spindles."

"You want me to play it now?"

"No, I'm going to leave the whole kit and caboodle with you. I shouldn't be here in the first place. I'm going to leave and let you work things out with Mr. Kalmbach and with Dean."

LaRue was surprised that Ulasewicz even knew John Dean's name. Hearing it made him want to end this meeting even more.

"Well, Tony, I appreciate it."

"You won't like what you hear, but better you should know." Ulasewicz tugged on his narrow-brimmed fedora. "I hope we never meet again, Mr. LaRue. And I trust you'll take that the right way."

"Understood, Tony. Thank you."

They shook hands and he was gone. LaRue sat down, noting that his dinner had ten minutes left to cook. Too little time to return a phone call from one of his teenaged children in Jackson, which was fine: if he put it off long enough, maybe their mother would handle whatever the situation was. He took two sips of his drink, put his glasses on, and wondered if ten minutes would be enough for him to listen to the tape, which had the diameter of a small doughnut.

He plugged in the machine and hit the button. The conversation that came out was startling in its immediacy, as if Tony had begun taping all of a sudden, in the middle of things. The voices seemed to be speaking inside the same room instead of two different phone booths.

—*Mrs. Hunt, you sound like a pit boss. This ain't a casino.*

—*And it isn't some nice legal department inside a charitable foundation.*

—*I've told you, I'm a middleman. I can't negotiate the thing. I leave that to the higher-ups.*

—*Well, I'm not leaving the security of my husband and family to the same men who got him into this.*

—*I don't know who employed him.*

—*Oh yes you do!*

LaRue could hear her snort, while from Tony's end of the conversation there came the clicking sound of quarters being ejected from a bus driver's coin dispenser. They dropped into the pay phone, jangling the conversation into an additional three minutes of life.

—*Every time I talk to you, you're uppin' the ante, Mrs. Hunt. You're now talkin' four hundred and fifty thousand dollars altogether in these five payments you keep harpin' on.*

—*You know why the monthly budget's been multiplied by five.*

—*I'm afraid I do not, Dorothy.*

—*Do the arithmetic. Five months will take us through November, after which, once they're reelected, they'll wash their hands of us.*

—*You think so?*

—*I know so, and so do you. Once we're past November the seventh, we've got no leverage. Until then, I'd say we've got plenty.*

LaRue could hear Ulasewicz emitting a long, low whistle. He himself now pondered what distinction there might be between the terms "quid pro quo" and "blackmail."

—*You'd better get used to these numbers, Mr. Rivers. They don't even include what you're going to be paying Gordon Liddy.*

—*Hold your horses. I haven't even heard that name yet.*

—*You will. He's got a very nice wife who is very very scared. They're coming to our house for dinner on Saturday night, as a matter of fact. She's a schoolteacher, and she's going to lose her job when this comes out. I've already lost mine, along with my medical insurance.*

—*I didn't know you worked, Dorothy.*

There was skepticism in his voice. Mrs. Hunt paused. Another two quarters went into the pay phone.

—*There's a lot you don't know, Tony.*

—*I keep telling you that. You think I've got the power to authorize these big figures you're demanding. I don't. Less than five days ago I gave you forty thousand dollars. You already burned through that?*

—*There are five other men and their families that it's going to. I'm distributing it.*

—*I don't suppose you're getting receipts?*

—*No, not any more than you're getting ones from me. But let me tell you, Tony, you're not aware of the extent of Mr. Barker's problems. You should keep them in mind, even if you don't know what they are.*

—*You're skippin' around, Dorothy. First tell me more about Liddy.*

—*You can make your own arrangements with him.*

—*Are you tryin' to deal him in or deal him out?*

—*That's enough casino metaphors.*

Ulasewicz, uncertain what "metaphors" meant, was silent.

—*Let's talk round numbers, Mr. Rivers. One hundred. There are just about that many days until the election.*

—*I'm gettin' the feeling that you want about a grand a day for yourself. Or would that be just for starters?*

—*Let's talk about the* real *round number, Tony—not one hundred days, or even four hundred and fifty thousand dollars. Let's talk about the thirty years my husband could go away for.*

—*Thirty years is a long time, Dorothy.*

—*Well, there are only those hundred days in which to make sure he doesn't wind up spending those thirty years away from his family.*

Ulasewicz said nothing, and when Mrs. Hunt resumed speaking, LaRue could hear new traces of fear and wistfulness in her voice.

—*When you next talk to your overlords, try to imagine that you're dropping a big uncooked sixteen-pound turkey onto their desks.*

—I don't follow you, Dorothy.

—When I first met Mr. Hunt, I stood in line at the Paris PX for the Thanksgiving turkey he'd picked out and wanted me to cook—even though he knew my oven was too small for it. Once I got the turkey, I deposited it on the desk in his office. He could figure out what to do with it.

—Did he get it cooked?

—Badly. It wound up stinking like sulfur. He forgot to remove its guts.

—The point, Dorothy? Is this another "metaphor"?

—The point is, you don't want me to dump everything I know on somebody else's desk.

—What do you know? And whose desk are we talkin'?

—I know everything that Howard knows. And the desk would be Earl Silbert's.

At this mention of the Assistant U.S. Attorney, LaRue turned off the tape recorder. Tony might be wise in the ways of the precinct house and street, but it seemed clear that he didn't know much about women, or at least the particular category of woman to which Dorothy Hunt belonged. Where Tony heard a tough cookie, LaRue heard a frightened woman pretending to drive the train that was barreling down the track to which she was tied. She was trying in some twisted way to be magnificent, to be Joan of Arc. Whether she wanted to shine in the eyes of her husband or the ones that looked back at her from the mirror, he wasn't sure.

He went over to the window and looked down Virginia Avenue to the sixth-floor terrace of the Watergate Office Building. Even now, whenever he saw the headquarters of the DNC, he had trouble regarding them as the bull's-eye of the mess they were all in. When he looked at them he thought of Clarine Lander. To him, the DNC remained, still and above all, her place of work. Right now it was the voice of Dorothy Hunt bringing Larrie to mind, the way something did most every day.

Fifteen years had passed since he first met her, after the hunting accident, when he walked into the law office in Jackson. He'd come at night, through the back door, scared to death of what jeopardy he might be in, not at all certain some Canadian prosecutor wouldn't soon try to extradite him back to the woodsy scene of what the police had decided was a crime instead of a bad, bad hunting mishap.

He couldn't even remember the name of the lawyer, but he could remember Clarine, looking like Lilli Palmer, sitting behind the secretary's desk, having kept the office open late for his surreptitious appointment with her boss. After a half minute's chat, he'd known she was a girl who wanted to go places, an unusual thing for any girl in Jackson in 1957.

And she had. A couple of years later she wound up in Senator Eastland's office on Capitol Hill. When he himself went up there these days, carrying news of another half dozen southerners appointed to the federal bench, people in the office still talked about Clarine Lander, though she'd been gone from it for nearly ten years—a sultry apostate who'd discovered civil rights and all the problems of the colored, who'd thrown her lot in with Fannie Lou Hamer and Stokely Carmichael and all the Jew carpetbaggers who tried to get themselves seated as the "Mississippi Freedom Democratic Party" at the '64 convention that nominated LBJ.

People in Eastland's office spoke of Larrie as if she were a cross between Tallulah Bankhead and Henry Fonda's daughter, but they always spoke of her warmly, without so much as a shake of the head; a kind of awed mystery trumped any disapproval they might be feeling. "That girl had a voice like smoke, and she was just as hard to get hold of," one old-timer had recently told him, actually grasping a handful of thin air, as if to make one last try.

Looking out the window of Watergate West 310, LaRue's nearsighted squint could discern little more than the curves of the complex's half dozen clustered beehives. Every day now some reporter or prosecutor took a new poke at the place, hoping to rile up another stream of bees that would sting everyone from Mrs. Hunt right up to the Old Man himself. Somewhere on the sixth floor of the office building—for the past three or four years, he'd been told—sat Clarine Lander. How he'd love for her to come to the window right now, even if, wearing his best glasses, he wouldn't be able to see her.

Chapter Eight

AUGUST 21–23, 1972
REPUBLICAN NATIONAL CONVENTION,
MIAMI BEACH, FLORIDA

"If I have to hear that song one more time, I may go join the Yippies in that 'Puke-In,'" whispered Pat Nixon to Ed Cox, one of the two sons-in-law flanking her in the spectators' box.

> *Reachin' out across the sea!*
> *Makin' friends where foes used to be!*
> *Givin' hope to humanity!*
> *More than ever, Nixon now, for you and me!*

Tricia Cox found her mother's reference to the convention's most outrageous protest nearly as disgusting as the protest itself, but Eddie laughed. Both of the boys seemed to "get" Pat better than her own daughters did. Coming into the hall, she and David had caught sight of a banner that some small plane was trailing overhead—and they'd managed to enjoy it, whereas Julie had immediately begun worrying who'd paid for the thing and what Sally Quinn or James Reston might say in tomorrow's papers.

The Miami Beach Convention Center was advertising itself as "Seven Acres of Politics Under One Roof," but on this first night of the GOP's gathering, Pat almost felt she was back at the little movie house in Artesia, in the twenties, on one of those rare Saturday afternoons she was able to go off with Myrtle and Louise Raine to watch a string of one-reelers. With no significant business to transact, the delegates were being kept occupied by one little movie after another—there'd been something on everybody from Alf Landon to Mamie Eisenhower—and each time the lights went down Pat could feel herself nodding off for a minute or two. She'd been doing state delegations and caucuses all morning and afternoon, hopping from the Fontainebleau to the Diplomat to the Doral to shake hands with the Hoosiers, the Lithuanians, the elderly, and the blind.

The air conditioning in the hall seemed to cut out every ten minutes, and the rumored explanation—which Julie insisted could not be true—had it that they were trying to keep whiffs of Mace, being used outside against demonstrators, from drifting through the ventilation system.

But it wasn't going to upset Pat. This was hardly the spring of 1970, when after the Kent State business they were virtually trapped at the White House, sitting inside it with that ring of old metal buses protecting the grounds like a moat, until Dick had finally given up and gone to Camp David. It was there that they gave Julie and David a graduation dinner to make up for the ceremonies they couldn't possibly attend at Smith and Amherst.

No, she thought, this didn't compare. The war, and the dead, were finally tapering off, and the whole country was starting to simmer down. She waved at some of the YVPs—Young Voters for the President—who had been organized into red, white, and blue teams and looked almost like kids from ten years ago. Most of them weren't old enough to have much idea of Jimmy Stewart, but even so, they cheered as he took a place on the podium beside Dole and Jerry Ford and the little rabbi who would later give the opening-night benediction.

A demonstration on her own behalf broke out on cue as Stewart recited the first lady's accomplishments. PAT'S OUR GIRL! said one sign; NO GENERATION GAP HERE! read another. Both signs were hand-painted, but not, one could tell, by the people waving them. They were the campaign's doing, and looked like the self-conscious folk art that people from the NEA were always urging on the White House. She almost preferred the mass-produced NOW MORE THAN EVER banners.

She looked past Eddie and Tricia to Rose Woods, whom she'd seen earlier in the day at the "Women of Achievement" luncheon for all the gals Dick had appointed to office. She mugged a modest *Can-you-believe-all-this* expression, which Rose overruled with a look that said, *You enjoy this; you deserve it.*

"WE WANT PAT! WE WANT PAT!" they kept shouting, until the lights finally went down for the little movie (yet another!) in which she was not an extra but the star, walking on top of the Great Wall of China; waving from a Conestoga wagon in support of grit and volunteerism; being wrapped in a headdress somewhere in Liberia. The several minutes' worth of biography sped by like someone else's life entirely.

The Secret Service agent gave her a gentle signal, and the two of them, in the dark, walked to the podium so that she could be there, arms outstretched in thanks, when the lights came up. The gesture, when she executed it, seemed a bit too Eva Perón, but she'd never heard such cheering, at least not for herself.

"Thank you, thank you," she said, the microphones wildly amplifying the twang that had never left her voice. And still they kept cheering. She thought back to Chicago in '52, to the great surprise of the vice-presidential nomination, when she'd first stood in front of a national convention in that polka-dot dress and planted a great big smacker of a kiss, a real smooch, on Dick's cheek. From the corner of her eye, she'd spotted Eisenhower, their sudden patron, cheerful as a Popsicle and just as cold. He was taking note of the kiss—and not entirely approving, she'd realized.

"WE LOVE PAT! WE LOVE PAT!"

From the moment she'd caught that glimpse of the general, she had stiffened into a twenty-year salute, teaching herself to wave *for* but never quite *at* the crowds and cameras. She'd vowed never to let them see her smoke or cry. For two decades she'd succeeded at the first and faltered only once when it came to the second, on that awful night in '60 when Jack Kennedy had stolen the election and Dick had put them in front of a screaming, anxious crowd of supporters for that not-quite-a-concession speech. *If the present trend continues, Senator Kennedy will be the next president of the United States.* As the tears started coming, she had felt a surge of revulsion that surpassed even Caracas, two years before, when she'd seen the mob start rushing the car. They had done their worst with rocks and fists and spit, and succeeded in breaking the windows, but they'd soon been dispersed, whereas those tears from 1960 were forever still falling, inside every film vault of every television network and on every page of *Life* bound up in a library.

"Thank you! Thank you!" she repeated, just as the teleprompter's screen, complete with exclamation points, urged her to. Jerry Ford handed her a jokey giant gavel, which she pretended to bang. But still they kept cheering: "WE LOVE PAT! WE LOVE PAT!"

"Thank you, Chairman Ford, Senator Dole . . ." The pronunciation of names, as if she were calling the roll at Whittier Union High, had a magical effect. Deciding that lovely Miss Ryan now meant business, the crowd fell into an obedient silence.

She had never been at a podium this high off the ground. She actually felt less like Miss Ryan in front of her classroom than some angel atop the Mormon Tabernacle. She spoke of the "great victory" that lay ahead, and as soon as the phrase left her lips and landed on the crowd, they roared and shook and waved as if she were talking about Judgment Day and the final reward.

In the teleprompter's shiny right-hand square, she caught a reflection of herself brushing back an errant strand of hair. It was a fussy, vain gesture, not at all her style, and as soon as she saw it, she realized she was doing it for Tom. She knew he would be watching her, a thousand miles away and all alone, having a late supper off his widower's TV tray in the library of his apartment, *our place*, above Madison Avenue.

She mustn't think of him now, just as she wouldn't think of the cigarette she was dying to have once she was in the car with tinted windows on her way back to the hotel.

VERMONT, ARIZONA, WYOMING. The lights were such that, as she went on speaking her single page of remarks, she could see only the three state delegations at the front of the hall. In the very first row she now noticed a young man, a Vermonter, who sported a mustache, just like her teasing, funny, hot-tempered father in the handful of photos taken during his mining days, before they'd picked up stakes and left Nevada to have a go at farming in Artesia. Much safer to be thinking of him than Tom as she launched into the last paragraph of this speech, which she was giving on behalf of the number-three male love of her life. Dick had never quite gotten past her father, and he could not get past the more recent memory of Tom, but, with whatever sadness and difficulty, he still made the list.

———

"Oh, so do I!" cried Alice Longworth, two nights later, while pointing to the sign: AMERICA LOVES WHAT THE COLONEL COOKS. "Go get me some, dear." She pushed her granddaughter toward the heaping trays of drumsticks and wings inside Gerald Ford's hospitality suite at the Algiers. The convention's chairman was giving a reception just prior to the president's scheduled renomination and acceptance speech.

As Alice waited for her chicken, Florida's senator Edward Gurney welcomed her to the Sunshine State. With his deep tan and wavy hair, Alice thought he resembled a tennis pro who had just retired to become the hotel gigolo.

"We're honored to have you here, ma'am." He gently shook her white-gloved hand and seemed amazed that she was ambulatory. "How did you travel down?" he asked.

"With my granddaughter and my cousin Mr. Alsop over there." She pointed out Joe, who was chatting up some good-looking lieutenant governor. "We came on one of those planes with the big orange sunburst."

"National Airlines," said Senator Gurney, ready to extol the success of the Florida-based carrier.

"Yes," said Mrs. Longworth. "Marvelous girls. All wearing the most forthright buttons. The one we had in first class had one saying 'I'm Lynn. Fly Me.' I asked who'd flown her *lately*, and she seemed baffled."

"Grandmother, eat your chicken," said Joanna, back with the plate.

"*Marvelous*," said Mrs. Longworth, biting into a drumstick. "Much better than what Rockefeller had over at the Doral."

The suite was decorated with blowups of frames from the Wolper campaign movie: Nixon shaking hands with a soldier in Vietnam; greeting Golda Meir; hugging a little boy wearing short pants and a hearing aid.

Gerald Ford, everyone's host, looked like a happy small-town banker in his blue-plaid suit. He came over to greet Theodore Roosevelt's daughter.

"Mrs. Longworth," he said, taking hold of a gloved hand now stained with the colonel's secret recipe. "Do you remember that we first met at a Republican convention? The one in Philadelphia that nominated Tom Dewey? 'The little man on top of the wedding cake.' "

"I'm afraid I never said that, but *please* continue to give me the credit."

"I remember your telling me back then that you'd be returning to Philadelphia a few weeks later for the Democrats' convention, too."

"I always went to them all. Even in 1912, when there were three."

"Well, I hope you kept away from McGovern's this year. You'd have lost your beauty sleep waiting up for that acceptance speech to start."

A principal theme of conversation among the Republicans was the supreme efficiency of their own convention compared to the Democrats'.

"I should like to lie and say I'd been there—I *love* disarray—but I don't have enough stamina for two conventions anymore. Did you hear the one about the ticket they really should have settled on?"

The opposition party's recent chaos had only ended with the replacement of Senator Eagleton—its original, electroshocked VP nominee—by Kennedy relative Sargent Shriver. No, Congressman Ford said, he hadn't heard.

" 'Kennedy and Eagleton: Waterproof and Shockproof.' Better than 'A Chicken in Every Pot,' don't you think? Have you, by the way, tried the chicken you're serving? *Wonderful.*"

Ford had declared to the convention that "Truth will be our greatest weapon in 1972." Bad strategy, Alice now thought. Dick, after all, was the nominee; one didn't want him playing another man's game.

"Tell me, Jerry," she said, pointing across the room, "which of those two Little Lord Fauntleroys has a better chance, four years from now, of taking the nomination from rough, tough Ted Agnew?" She indicated Elliot Richardson and Senator Charles Percy, who were earnestly conferring. Their look of sleek northern *noblesse oblige* seemed odd in this roomful of delegates whose party was moving ever further south and west, picking up more and more hard-edged high rollers as it went, men who loved Agnew's alliterative scorn for all the pundits and eggheads. Mrs. Longworth looked at Ford, the soul of Main Street moderation, stalled between these arrivistes and those two Brahmins, and waited for him to answer.

"Between you and me, Mrs. L," he responded, reluctantly, "Elliot is the much tougher customer."

"I thought that might be so," she replied.

Ford's wife and Nixon's secretary, each of them carrying a fresh drink, were coming over to say hello. Alice allowed Mrs. Ford to kiss her on the cheek and Rose Woods to relieve her of her empty plate.

"My ears are *not* ready for Miss Merman to sing the national anthem," she said, tapping tonight's program.

"She can certainly belt," acknowledged Rose.

"I believe she's to be released back into the wild after the benediction," mused Alice, as she looked around the room. "Now where is Sammy Davis, Jr.? *I* want a hug." A cringe-inducing photo from yesterday's youth rally, which showed the entertainer embracing the president from behind, was all over the newspapers. "He can grab the same spots on me," said Alice, patting her chest where her breasts used to be. "No impediments." In the brief silence that followed, she asked Rose Woods to take her over to Elliot Richardson.

The president's secretary gave her a doubtful look. Wouldn't she rather be brought to someone besides that pompous Mister Clean whose loyalty was so suspect? Rose still could not get over Richardson's nerve in flying out to San Clemente last summer after he'd failed to get his way on some policy decision concerning that zoo of a department he ran. Like Henry, he was forever hinting he might need to resign and take his indispensable self somewhere else.

But Mrs. Longworth was not to be denied, so Rose dutifully piloted the old lady in Richardson's direction. He had finished talking with Senator Percy and was moving purposefully toward the National Committee's black-affairs man when Alice reached him and dismissed Rose.

"Mrs. Longworth," Richardson said, lowering his six-foot frame and square jaw.

"All your press clippings say Clark Kent, but I'd say the resemblance is more to Dick Tracy. Why don't you complete it by getting some contact lenses?"

"That never occurred to me," said Richardson, laughing.

"You might see the road better."

Richardson looked startled. She *had* read up on him. One or two of his magazine profiles had interrupted their admiration long enough to mention his plethora of reckless-driving arrests and the conviction involving alcohol. The writers generally decided that all this was just the eccentric escape valve of a duty-driven nature, similar to the doodles and watercolors he compulsively turned out. Still, it was unsettling to have her bring it up.

"Yes," said Mrs. Longworth. "I do make studies of things, generally at the local library. When my cousin Mr. Alsop asked if you and I were related, I realized I didn't know *anything* about you if I didn't know *that.*"

"Being related is an honor I would cherish, but alas, I don't believe it's the case. Perhaps very distantly."

He spoke to her, she realized, with the indifferent politeness he'd display to a GS-5 clerk in the elevator at HEW.

"So is it too soon for you to be the next president, after Dick?"

Richardson tried to smile. "The only presidency I've ever been mentioned for was Harvard's, and that was almost twenty years ago. There's a tradition of precociously young college presidents who wind up serving for decades and decades, but I'm afraid the little boomlet for me was quite artificial—a one-man operation, really. Justice Frankfurter, for whom I'd clerked, kept putting my name forward."

"What a lot of jobs you've had since," Mrs. Longworth observed. "Elective, appointive, state, federal. My cousin says you're bound to have plenty more." She could see from Richardson's expression that her conversation was provoking the nervousness she always enjoyed inducing in a listener, especially one so assured of his own rectitude. "One shouldn't, however, have too much ambition without a clear plan, don't you think?" she concluded.

"Well," said Richardson, "I'm happy to go wherever I can be of use."

She made no effort to hide how the answer bored her; immediately she went off on another tack.

"Which of us do you think had it worse?" she asked.

"I don't understand."

"My mother died giving birth to *me.* Your mother died giving birth to your younger brother. I was made to feel *guilty,* but you must have felt *angry*—at your brother. Which feeling do you suppose is the harder to bear?"

Richardson smiled thinly. The word "impertinence" was actually rising to his lips, but one could no more deploy it against this famous crone than against some Negro picketing the department for higher benefits.

"My brothers and I," he said with forbearance, "were raised by a very fine woman who agreed to take us on."

Yes, thought Alice, the housekeeper who beat you. She spent the next moment or two wondering how she herself might have turned out with treatment like that instead of the gentle ministrations of Auntie Bye.

"We do have one thing in common," she said at last, causing Richardson, from his great height, to regard her wide-brimmed hat as if it were a fortune-teller's turban.

"We both dislike doctors," she explained, knowing that Richardson had declined to extend a six-generation family string of them. "We both knew, early on, what they're capable of—what they did, or failed to do, for our mothers. After that, you wouldn't *be* one, and I won't even *see* one, at least for years at a time."

Joe Alsop came hurrying over, realizing that Richardson—whom Alice suspected he had a little crush on—might be needing rescue. He also needed to inform them of some logistical fuss. "Those drum majorettes," he explained, "are going to lead people out to their cars. It's time everyone was getting to the hall."

Richardson smiled and gratefully peeled away.

"Mark my words: that man hates Dick," Alice warned Alsop. "I guarantee it. He'd like to give the whole *world* a beating."

Joe looked at her dismissively, urging her forward toward one of the baton-carrying girls now trying to conga-line the guests out the door. GET TO KNOW A NIXONETTE, said the large bright button the girl was wearing.

"Someone will be flying *her* before the night's out," Alice said to Joe.

The president, punctual to the second, begins making his way to the podium, moving between all the agents and advance men talking into their radios. He can swear that there are tears in his eyes: Has all this talk of his "last convention" and "last campaign" gotten even to *him*? No. He can't stop thinking that the Republican Party remains the world's largest and laziest Rotary Club; if he can't get them to nominate Connally four years from now, he'd just as soon see a whole different party with a new name take the GOP's place.

He'd still love to kick Agnew to the curb and run with Connally this year, but it has been apparent for months that all the Chevy dealers and country-club lawyers who still dominate things at the local level won't accept a Democratic convert for the number-two spot. Nor will the party's new fire-breathers let go of their hero Spiro without a lot of grumbling. So, a week before the Watergate thing, he'd made Mitchell give Agnew the word that he could stay.

The president wipes his right eye. No, it isn't nostalgia causing the tears; it's the goddamned Vietnam Veterans Against the War, who even now are only blocks away on Collins Avenue, provoking the cops into firing the occasional canister of gas. He's seen the news clips; half of them seem to be in wheelchairs, which he bets they need about as much as he does. Colson doubts that most of them have even been in the army, let alone over to Vietnam. If the Secret Service had let them get any closer as he came into the hall, he'd have flashed them the "V" sign, which drives them nuts whenever he uses it in the old Churchillian sense of victory instead of peace.

What really changes the world, he's been telling Henry and Haldeman all summer, is Tory men with liberal ideas. Churchill had been one of those, and so is he. That's what took him to Peking and Moscow, and that's what will propel him through the whole second term.

He is already focused months beyond this moment, so much so that he barely hears the cheering for Agnew's lousy introduction of him, barely realizes it when he is already a page into his own speech. He has forsaken the teleprompter's crawl for Rose's typewritten text with its cues about cadences. He's already paid tribute to the platform and to Pat and is now telling all the newly enfranchised eighteen-year-olds: "Years from now I want you to look back and be able to say that your first vote was one of the best votes you ever cast in your life."

If he'd been able, in '32, to cast a vote at the age of nineteen, he'd have cast it for Roosevelt. He'd thought about admitting that tonight, putting it into this speech, but decided it would get too much play in the coverage that followed. He'll save it, make it a good story for his memoirs, which five years from now he'll be contentedly composing, his feet up, a long yellow pad on his lap, the tape recordings from the Oval Office bringing it all back to memory and life.

Hunt listened to Nixon's speech on the TV in his study. Its reminder that "people on welfare in America would be rich in most of the nations of the world today" pleased his ears. He also liked the president's refusal to consider McGovern's precious amnesty for draft dodgers. "The real heroes," said Nixon, pausing a moment before the predicate, "are two and a half million young Americans who chose to serve their country rather than desert it!" Hunt turned up the volume, wanting to get into the spirit of things, to feel that he was actually in Miami—as he could so easily have been, if things had gone otherwise.

He and Dorothy had gotten home six days ago, after a week in the Keys spent fishing with Bernie and waiting for a reply to the letter he'd finally sent Colson at the beginning of August. Sitting on the dock down there, regarding his fishing rod and line, he'd imagined the four of them—Clarita and Dorothy, too—setting off for Central America by boat, or having one of the *brigadistas* fly them into Nicaragua, where Somoza would almost certainly grant protection and a home.

Then a message from Colson's secretary had reached them, with instructions for Dorothy to call in from yet another pay phone, which they found by the side of US 1. Colson assured her that they would all be taken care of, that the commitment would be kept. However short it might be on specifics, the pledge had reassured both Dorothy and himself, at least for a while—long enough for him to take a breath and concentrate on things like the deposition he would soon have to give for the Democrats' civil suit over the burglary. That he was scheduled to give it before Edward Bennett Williams, owner of the Redskins and darling of the *Washington Post*, made the prospect troublesome; he couldn't imagine Bittman being a match for him.

In the last day or two the vagueness of Colson's promise had started to gnaw at him, along with Mr. Rivers's clear hints that Dorothy's demands were excessive. She and "Tony" were engaged in a continuing test of wills, and his wife feared losing it. At the same time, she appeared intent on going for broke. She was urging her husband to call Colson again, to pressure him so that she in turn could press for larger sums and an extended series of payments, could get more and more, as much as possible, before the election. How, after all, did these men in the White House expect him to make a living from now on? Did they want him shopping a book proposal? He didn't even need to write the book; just circulating the pitch would guarantee spillage of the story's best beans in the press.

Hunt wondered how long Dorothy's adrenalized energy would last. She'd been up on the ladder cleaning gutters, all over the garden pulling every weed; when would she lapse back into the despondency of springtime? To distract himself from the question, he lifted up the big pink seashell he'd brought home from the Keys and put it to his ear, the sound from its empty heart growing louder, until a particular bit of Nixon's oration startled him back to life:

"Let one thing be clearly understood in this election campaign. The American people will not tolerate any attempt by our enemies to interfere in the cherished right of the American voter to make his own decision with regard to what is best for America without outside intervention."

He hoped Bernie was listening, and was understanding the remark exactly the way he himself was taking it. The audience in the convention hall and throughout the country might think Nixon was imagining a North Vietnamese trick—maybe a prisoner release designed to help McGovern—but he knew, and Bernie would, too, that the president was talking about Castro's money going to the DNC, the very thing they could have established if they'd had a little more time inside the offices before the cops showed up. Nixon was giving the burglars a signal that what they had attempted was important, and that, yes, they would be taken care of—even after the election.

As he listened to the televised cheering from Miami, he decided—once and for all, he told himself—that the commitment Colson had spoken of was real, and that Mr. Rivers's complaints were no more than the insubordinate grousings of a messenger boy who didn't know the real story.

That was what he wanted to believe. But the way his mind had been turning and working of late, he knew he might believe something quite different an hour from now.

"Dorothy!" Hunt called down the stairs, wanting to enjoy and prolong his certainty. He wished in fact that he had turned on one of his study's several small tape recorders before Nixon had said what he said. But he remembered it word for word, and he needed to share it with his wife. He called her name once more and added, *"Buenas noticias!"*

Fred LaRue, sitting on a spare folding chair with his state delegation, read no special meaning into the Old Man's warning about foreign interference in the election, but he did experience a moment of satisfaction over the presidential promise to keep appointing tough-on-crime judges—a pledge that surely wouldn't hurt his own dealings with southerners on the Hill.

LaRue looked over at the big vertical state standard—MISSISSIPPI—and imagined Clarine Lander trying to seize its equivalent for the liberal insurgents at the Democrats' Atlantic City gathering, back in '64. He'd still been trying to get over Larrie that summer, when he went to his own first convention, all the way out in San Francisco. When Rocky came to the Cow Palace's podium, all the mad-for-Goldwater delegates had had a ferocious go at their nemesis, screaming, "You lousy lover! You lousy lover!" to this fantastically rich governor who'd just divorced his wife to marry his mistress. LaRue had joined in the shouting, and even if his own yells were scarcely louder than another man's murmurs, he'd been shocked to hear them come out of his mouth. What he felt toward Rockefeller wasn't so much anger as identification and envy. By Mississippi standards, Fred LaRue was a very rich man, but he had not been able to spirit Larrie away from her own life and into his.

Tonight, eight years later, Rockefeller had actually put the Old Man's name in nomination, making their long rivalry seem very far back indeed. Which made the time of Clarine Lander seem long ago, too. None of the men he was here in Miami with had been part of his life in the years when she drove all his thoughts.

Mardian, Dean, Magruder, and Colson—looking god-awful in his Bermuda shorts each afternoon—were all here, but at no point tonight had he spotted a one of them on the convention floor. Even by day, instead of being anywhere near the activities of the ethnic "heritage groups" and special-interest caucuses, they could be found by the pool at the Doral, ordering drinks and talking about the effort to keep a lid on Watergate.

They were now all pretty sure they'd done that. Magruder, after hours of coaching by Dean, had lied his way through a second grand-jury appearance only last week, and two days later had gotten word that his name would *not* be among those being charged when the indictments came down, probably in the middle of September.

The agreed-upon story, that it had all been Liddy's harebrained idea, and that no one else had any clue, seemed to be taking hold not only in the minds of the prosecutors but in the heads of half the guys peddling it from the White House and Committee to Re-Elect. The youngest of them, so eager for promotion, were lining up to testify to all kinds of stuff they knew nothing about; they just asked for a script. And once they recited it, they more or less believed it.

The night Magruder got his good news, the two of them had gotten plastered. Jeb, experiencing a sentimental moment, had looked him in the eye and said, "You know, Fred, we're not covering up a burglary; we're safeguarding world peace." To which he himself could only reply, "Jebbie, you're going to have one blue-ribbon motherfucker of a hangover in the morning."

If Magruder knew how the burglary had actually come about, who ordered it, he'd never told him. And maybe, of course, he *didn't* know. Not knowing the exact truth was another thing that made the lying easier; it created the possibility that some of what one told the investigators just might *be* true, like the stopped clock that's right twice a day.

"I thought he was the best man for the job four years ago. I think he is the best man for the job today. And I am not going to change my mind tomorrow!"

The president had gotten to the point where he was talking about Agnew, and his jab at the Eagleton fiasco had everybody on their feet for what must be the twentieth time. LaRue was standing with them, but this mention of "the best man for the job" and the supposed constancy of Nixon's affection made him think of the man who was no longer at the head of the Committee to Re-Elect, and nowhere to be found here in Miami.

He imagined that Mitchell was watching the speech on a couch in his apartment at the Watergate, where he and Martha were still marooned, though she'd begun looking at places for them back in New York. Martha never liked missing a shindig, and to be away from this one because her husband's presence had been deemed too toxic would surely not be improving her mood.

Up on the podium Nixon gets ready to end the speech the way he ended his televised address in Russia three months back, quoting the diary of the twelve-year-old girl whose whole family was killed in the siege of Leningrad during the war:

"All are dead. Only Tanya is left."

He waits for a second, at the pause marked in Rose's typing. Then he goes on: "Let us think of Tanya, and of the other Tanyas, and their brothers and sisters everywhere in Russia, in China, as we proudly meet our responsibilities for leadership in the world . . .

Brezhnev told him that the diary passages had brought tears to his eyes when he heard Nixon read them. And right now Nixon wonders if the cameras are close enough in to see that his own eyes are damp. Whether this is from the words, or from another trace of gas that has gotten through the goddamned ventilation ducts, he honestly doesn't know.

Chapter Nine

SEPTEMBER 15, 1972, 8:15 P.M.
POTOMAC RIVER, NEAR MOUNT VERNON, VIRGINIA,
ABOARD THE *SEQUOIA*

"I talked to Connally this morning."

Nixon's words brought a sudden end to several moments of revery that Pat Buchanan and Alexander Haig had been enjoying in their cushioned chairs on the starboard side of the presidential yacht. The eyes of the two aides stopped following the *Sequoia*'s gentle wake and met the president's gaze.

"I told him I don't want Teddy Kennedy sweeping up the Democrats' smithereens after November seventh. There's plenty of opportunity to be found in defeat—nobody knows that better than I do—and I don't want Kennedy looking like some elder statesman they should turn to in their time of need."

Buchanan let loose his whinnying laugh. "It'd be a lot easier for Connally to influence the matter if he were really still a Democrat."

Nixon was unamused by Connally's still-ambiguous status. Disappointed even now at having to keep Agnew on the ticket, he wished that his former Treasury secretary were already fully inside the Republican tent. He thought him wasted running his "Democrats for Nixon" sideshow, even if that operation did succeed in humiliating the opposition every few days, whenever some big labor leader or old Johnson appointee agreed to put on a press conference for the purpose of declaring that no amount of party loyalty could make him vote for George McGovern. Connally now privately swore that LBJ himself—a nonperson at his party's own convention—*did* intend to vote for his Republican successor.

The sudden darkening of the president's mood was noted a few deck chairs away by Rose Woods. But she knew the boss had had too good a day for any grimness to last, and that he was pleased to have General Haig for company tonight instead of Kissinger. Henry's deputy was brisk, funny, and given to quoting Shakespeare; older and less brass-knuckled than Buchanan, but just as full of pep. When the boss tried to relax, he didn't need Henry underlining his every offhand insight with some guttural profundity or toadying compliment. Rose liked to do an imitation of Kissinger's pompous low growl for the girls in the office; she'd talk about "decdonic shifts in de geobolidical bicture." The shift she'd really like to see was *Teu*tonic, a double whammy that would move Henry out of the White House and over to State and send Halde-man all the way back to California.

Yes, it was not impossible that HRH might decide he was feeling worn out as the second term got under way. But what then? The man had no particular credentials and no interest in policy and no desire for social advancement, so there was no clear reward that Richard Nixon could give him—no judgeship, cabinet post, ambassador's job. But maybe that wouldn't matter. HRH was a strange enough bird that Rose could imag-ine him going right back to his ad agency in Los Angeles, as if nothing had happened since 1968.

She was happy about his absence tonight, the same way the boss was happy about Henry's. She had allowed herself a third glass of white wine along with the Dover sole. The album with "Georgia on My Mind" was again softly playing. Ray Charles had been in the Oval Office for a photo op this morning, and the first time the song came on tonight Buchanan had predicted how friendly and massive the presi-dent's reception would be when he and Pat campaigned next month in Atlanta.

Rose felt the breeze on her cheek and caught sight of some shoreline cyclists starting to pedal a bit harder, trying to make it home before dark. She didn't want the day to end, and felt sorry that Mount Vernon's familiar cupola had come into view.

The *Sequoia* offered its usual salute to the first president: Nixon always had a navy bugler play taps when they reached this point. But tonight he seemed surprised by the gesture, jumping in his seat when the first note sounded. When the sad little tune was over, he hurried to make a casual remark, trying to deflect attention from his startlement.

"Did you hear that bastard Shriver called me a 'psychiatric case'?"

General Haig replied that the Democrats' veep-replacement nominee was "something infinitely more pathetic."

"What's that?" asked Buchanan.

"A brother-in-law," said Haig.

Buchanan whinnied again, and Rose suppressed a laugh, lest they know she was listening closely. The boss managed a smile and indicated that it was time to transfer to the little landing craft that would take them to the helicopter waiting on the Mount Vernon lawn. He disembarked with his arm around Julie, who'd been sitting by herself doing needlework.

When they reached the helicopter, Rose looked wistfully back at the *Sequoia*. She never knew when it might disappear; the president had decided it was outmoded and probably riddled with listening devices, despite numerous security sweeps. He'd recently told Dean—the administration's new can-do white-haired boy—to acquire photos and blueprints of the best possible replacement yachts, and to investigate the regulations under which their current owners could legally be approached to make a public-spirited donation of them. As soon as the election was over, an open competition to do so would become its own little regatta, Rose imagined.

Aboard the helicopter, she strapped herself into a seat opposite the boss.

"Your cold doesn't sound so bad," she said.

Nixon pointed to Dr. Lukash a row away and said, loud enough for him to hear the compliment, "He knocked it right out of me." Then, more softly, for only Rose to hear, he added, "I'm afraid Pat's earache isn't any better."

You couldn't say he really missed her, thought Rose. But even so, the first lady's presence here tonight would have made him feel fully armored and more comfortable.

Nixon pointed to General Haig. "Al did some nice stroking of the Taiwanese ambassador when we had him in today. Poor bastards," said the president. "But things are now the way they've got to be."

"They haven't got a Chinaman's chance," said the conservative Buchanan, with a laugh, though the Peking trip had tested the limits of his ideological flexibility.

"I'll tell you the really important conversation I had today," said

Nixon. "A little talk with Haldeman and Dean. Now that these indictments have finally come down, we're gonna get these goddamned Democrats. I promise you, once we're past November seventh, we're going
to use the IRS against all of them, Edward Bennett Williams included."
When no one higher than the burglars was charged this afternoon,
the Democrats' civil suit had become the worst remaining Watergate
annoyance.

"Mr. President," said Buchanan, "what you've got to worry about is
the *real* chilling effect of this whole scandal. If we let the Democrats
criminalize what's nothing but ordinary politics, the people on our side
are going to be too scared to operate. They're going to go around acting
like the League of Women Voters."

Nixon nodded. "Exactly right. The point is they *should* be finding
out stuff like the connections between Larry O'Brien and Hughes.
There are a lot better ways of doing that than breaking into the stupid committee headquarters, but damn it, we *still* ought to be pursuing
that, even after November seventh if need be."

"The information can be a gift to your successors," said Buchanan.
"A little something you put in the bank for them."

Everyone laughed. Unlike Henry, Buchanan understood how to
encourage the boss without flattery and fawning. "Billy Graham says
you're becoming a father figure, like Ike," the speechwriter was now
saying. "I got that from Haldeman—and told him I didn't think you
were *that* mean." He winked at Rose just before the rotors started up
and the nine-minute flight to the South Lawn got under way.

She recalled how nice it had been last month when Don Carnevale
chartered that seaplane so the two of them could skip one of the convention's afternoon sessions for a low, scenic excursion over the Florida
Keys. Now, in the still-not-full darkness, as the helicopter flew parallel
to the Roosevelt Bridge, Rose looked down at the monuments to Jefferson and Lincoln and wondered what would be standing there two
or three generations from now commemorating Richard Nixon. He'd
already earned a bridge, at the very least, she thought; and if the next
four years turned out anything like the past six months, it was hardly
foolish to think he might have his own marble temple on the Mall
someday.

They landed at 8:52, and Rose could sense that the boss was itch-ing to call Colson before he even had his seatbelt off. He put his arm around Julie for just a second while people made their goodbyes. As he departed, there were even a couple of hear-hears, acknowledgment that what Attorney General Kleindienst called the most thorough federal investigation of any crime since the JFK killing had reached its essential conclusion and they could get on with the business of crushing McGovern once and for all.

At 9:09 in the Lincoln Sitting Room, with his Irish setter at his feet, Nixon asked the White House operator to get hold of Colson.

"Well, we got through it," the president said, as soon as his special counsel came on the line.

"Free and clear," said Colson, laughing. "Just like Willy Loman."

"Well," said Nixon. "There are still those damned hearings in the House that Patman's trying to hold."

"Jerry Ford can put the kibosh on those. If every Republican refuses to participate, they won't get off the ground."

Nixon wished that Colson would somehow fess up to the whole thing without *exactly* fessing up—that is, admit he had set the burglary in motion; admit it clearly but obliquely, without burdening the president with explicit knowledge that would be dangerous for him to have, information that might yet, someday, necessitate perjury, if only in some other far-off civil suit. What he wanted most was to know that Mitchell was not responsible, and that these investigations—if they turned out *not* to be really over—wouldn't claim the friend to whom he owed so much. No, he supposed he didn't truly believe that today's chickenshit indictments would be the end of things, but he'd be able to sleep a little better if he knew Mitchell was in the clear.

"I was worried they'd get Magruder" was all he said for a moment.

Colson laughed. "Jeb will just be mad he wasn't out on the *Sequoia* with you. He's like a doll without batteries when he's not wearing his White House cuff links."

"You heard from your friend Hunt?" Nixon asked, casually.

"No, not a word," said Colson, without specifying the time frame his answer was supposed to cover. If the president meant since the indictments came down this morning, or since last week, then the answer was true.

"Mitchell won't be in town much longer," said Nixon. "He's alone right now, in fact. Martha's gone up to New York to live in a hotel until this apartment she's found is ready for them. And I suppose until they can get past whatever co-op board they've got to go through. God-damned Fifth Avenue liberals! The man was the attorney general of the United States, for Christ's sake."

Colson said nothing.

"I'll be seeing both of them—Martha, too—at this fundraiser in New York, week after next, after I'm back from Connally's ranch. If she behaves herself at this thing, and the press gets some good pictures, sees she's still on board, that'll make things easier for everybody, especially John."

"Your new buddy Ray Charles going to play for this fundraiser?"

Nixon had to remind himself that Colson couldn't stand Mitchell. There was no way he'd be drawn into discussing him just to assuage the boss's concern about his old friend. So the president decided to let it go, for tonight and forever. He would choose to believe that it really *was* over, and that—from the sheer force of his will, and the power of Dr. Peale's positive thinking—it would stay over. He poured himself another finger of 100 Pipers, rattled the ice cubes in his glass, and sank into philosophy, as the music from the boat came back into his mind.

"Which do you think is tougher in this world?" he asked. "To be blind or to be black?"

"These days? Oh, to be blind, definitely," said Colson.

Nixon would not have agreed, but having forgotten his own question, he said nothing.

Chapter Ten

SEPTEMBER 19, 1972
EOB; U.S. DISTRICT COURTHOUSE;
SENATE OFFICE BUILDING; WATERGATE WEST

Fred LaRue straightened his tie, hoping its Rhodesian-flag crests would be a welcome touch at a meeting on his schedule later this afternoon. Nothing, alas, could brighten the meeting about to start in John Dean's office.

Herb Kalmbach, waiting with LaRue for Dean to open his door, nervously crossed and uncrossed his legs on the two-seater couch by the secretary's desk.

"By the way," said Herb. "Tony Ulasewicz says hello."

"Tell him the same," said LaRue, who the other night had finally thrown away the tape recording of Dorothy Hunt and "Mr. Rivers."

"Guys," said Dean, opening the door and adjusting his tortoiseshell glasses. "Come on in."

Kalmbach wasted no time once they sat down. "Here," he said, pushing a manila envelope across Dean's desk. "Twenty thousand dollars."

"Jesus," said Dean.

"Yeah," agreed Kalmbach. "As Tony would say, 'That's a lot of cabbage.'"

LaRue asked, softly, "Herb, are you all right? I've been wondering, ever since I talked to Tony." *I already told Mr. Kalmbach—more than once, Mr. LaRue—that something's not kosher here.*

"No," said Kalmbach, his voice strained from months of tension and the certainty that his news would displease Dean. "I want out."

LaRue's poor eyesight could barely distinguish Dean from half a dozen young men over at the Committee, and his hearing wasn't much better, but he had no trouble perceiving that Herb's strangulated message was final.

"I'm sorry to hear it," he murmured.

"I'm sorry, too," said Dean, less tolerantly. "To say the least."

The news felt personal to LaRue. Almost twelve weeks had passed since he first met with Herb to organize the cover-up payments. He'd developed a liking for the president's refined, low-key lawyer and by now thought of him as a kind of partner in the small business they were running. They joked about being the Bradford Brothers, since each used that coded surname when leaving messages for the other. LaRue had come to understand Tony Ulasewicz's protectiveness toward Kalmbach, who would never survive prison if things came to that. And they might. The men in the White House and over at the Committee were so happy about those who'd *not* been indicted that they were starting to forget about the unpredictable characters who *had*.

What about LaRue himself? If everything fell apart, could he survive prison? He fiddled with the Rhodesian tie and for a second or two wondered if he would hold up the way his father had, coming out of the clink with a smile on his face after doing a few years for bank fraud, picking up right where he'd left off as a wildcatter and going on to make his biggest score ever—becoming truly rich as an ex-con.

"There appears to be enough money for a while," said Dean, somewhat ridiculously, thought LaRue, as if he were Irene Dunne talking about Mama's bank account.

"I'm worn out," pleaded Kalmbach, who had already helped to raise and distribute—to or through the Hunts—two hundred and twenty thousand dollars. "The FBI is calling me, and my nerves are shot," he said, addressing Dean. "I only got into this because Ehrlichman told me it was all right. My Barbara and I have been friends with John and Jeannie for years. I could hardly say no to him. But I don't see any end to this." He paused before adding, "I'm sorry to leave Fred holding the bag."

"Almost literally," said LaRue, who knew he'd end up being called the cover-up's "bagman" if any of this ever came out. While he didn't like to think of the Bradford Brothers turning into a one-man operation, he meant the two words as a gentle joke that might relax Herb. There was certainly no relaxing Dean, who sucked hard on a Winston and said nothing.

"Here's my accounting," said Herb, handing Dean a slip of paper the size of an index card. Dean shook his head to indicate there was no need of that from a man of Kalmbach's integrity; he handed the paper to LaRue, who then reached for Dean's ashtray. With the lighter he carried for his pipe, LaRue set fire to the column of figures, and the three men watched "Bradford Brothers" go out of business in a little plume of smoke.

Once out on Pennsylvania Avenue, LaRue decided he would walk to his next appointment, on Capitol Hill. It was a hot day, but not Mississippi hot, and his old linen suit would keep him comfortable on a long eastward stroll past the Justice Department and the Archives. When he neared the corner of Constitution Avenue he saw a cluster of reporters racing over a lawn to the front doors of the U.S. District Courthouse.

Hunt and Liddy and the Cubans, having at last been arraigned, were coming out and heading toward cars, leaving their lawyers to face the microphones. LaRue moved just close enough to the action to get a look at Bittman, whose legal services were costing so much.

Though past forty, the attorney still had the build of the linebacker he'd once been. He was explaining to the reporters that Hunt was now ten thousand dollars lighter—the price of bail. He also expressed dismay that John Sirica, the court's chief judge, had decided to assign the Watergate trial to himself. LaRue could see the newspeople turning their heads and craning their necks, hoping that Liddy, who had lately established himself as the case's star oddball, might somehow come back into view and make himself available.

LaRue's concentration remained on Bittman. Could this onetime prosecutor who'd sent Jimmy Hoffa and Bobby Baker to prison keep Howard Hunt out of it? There was a grudge-match element to the whole tangled situation: Edward Bennett Williams, representing the Democrats in their civil suit, had been Baker's lawyer; he lived across the street from Bittman, and by all accounts detested the man who'd beat him in that earlier case. Swell, LaRue had thought upon finding this out—as if regular political passions hadn't risen high enough without adding a personal pissing contest!

No, the prosecutors hadn't gotten to Jeb, and Kleindienst was assuring everybody there was no way the burglars could be tried before the election, but LaRue, resigned to trouble by nature and experience, saw plenty of it ahead. He resumed his walk and in another ten minutes reached his destination on the Hill.

He was quickly made to feel more at home in Senator Eastland's outer office than he'd been in Dean's inner one.

"Hi, there, Mr. LaRue," said the pretty girl at the desk. "He says he'll be with you in two or three little old minutes."

LaRue smiled. Eastland had finally let the Judiciary Committee he chaired hire one or two blacks, but his own staff remained lily-white. As the girl busied herself with some typing, LaRue paced a little and looked at the familiar items on the wall. He'd been coming here from the White House for the whole four years, bringing hurricane relief funds and then sympathetic judicial nominees. The latter job had been easier when Mitchell was the General; now Haldeman gave him his marching orders up the Hill toward this office decorated with two signed photos of Ian Smith and a small-scale model of a Titan missile, which—Eastland liked to point out—could be made more cheaply now that Nixon had lifted the chrome boycott against the white Rhodesian government. The domestic roots of the senator's foreign policy could be found in the framed yellowing text of a speech he'd given back home seventeen years ago: "On May 17, 1954, the Constitution of the United States was destroyed because of the Supreme Court's decision. You are not obliged to obey the decisions of any court which are plainly fraudulent."

LaRue's personal connection to Eastland could be found in an object hanging from the ceiling: a big blue marlin that the senator had caught way out in the Gulf with LaRue's father one summer during the mid-1950s, around the time the Constitution was getting destroyed and shortly after Ike LaRue had gotten out of jail.

"Freddie!" cried Eastland, his round face preceded through the doorway by the cigar between his lips. "You lookin' at that fine old fish? I don't think Ike ever landed a bigger one in the precious little time he had left to him, God rest his soul. Come on in and sit down. You here with the name of another appointment as good as Charlie Clark? He's bringin' the Fifth Circuit back to somethin' like sanity, if I do say so myself. That was our finest hour, Freddie, our finest hour!" Eastland was chuckling over the memory of how he'd been able to ram the conservative Clark's nomination through the Senate on a day when one of the Vietnam "Moratorium" protests had taken most of the liberals out of town to address campus rallies back home.

"I'm not here with a nomination, Senator, but I've got some good news nonetheless. Bob Haldeman tells me that the president is urging his daughter to endorse you when she campaigns for her father next week in Mississippi. The Committee can make the arrangements if you're interested."

"Which daughter is that?"

"Tricia."

"Pretty as a princess," said Eastland with a smile. "Why don't you have her come right through Sunflower County and speak her piece to my home folks?"

"I'm sure she'll be happy to go wherever you think best," said LaRue, who still couldn't get over how Eastland, after thirty years in the Senate, now found himself in a tight race. Nixon was so far out in front of McGovern that he was pulling the senator's unknown Republican opponent up with him. The voters needed some indirect reminders—short of an actual presidential endorsement—that Richard Nixon would be just fine having Jim Eastland, the Democrat, stay right where he was in the Senate. They didn't want the Judiciary chairmanship slipping into the hands of some northern left-winger, as it might if Eastland lost, did they? So the White House and the Committee had been finding little ways to help him, such as not letting his Republican foe join the rest of the GOP Senate hopefuls on the podium in Miami. And now they would have Tricia say she just couldn't help pulling for Senator Eastland, Democrat though he might be, given all the support he'd been giving her daddy these past four years.

"Well, Freddie, I truly appreciate it. I can use all the help I can get. After all, I'm still really just a planter, not a politician. Always been better at countin' soybeans than votes."

LaRue laughed. Eastland clung to his five thousand acres the way he'd been clinging to the committee chairmanship for fifteen years. His parliamentary skills were lately getting him one Charlie Clark after another, and finally getting the White House, after its own early stumbles with Supreme Court nominees, a justice like Rehnquist.

"Yes, Freddie," said the senator, as if reading LaRue's mind. "We don't win 'em all, but we have fun even with the ones we go losin'. Best losin' battle I ever fought was just a few years before your time here, trying to keep the NAACP's own nigger lawyer off the highest court in the land." He shook his head, disbelieving even now that the ascension of Thurgood Marshall had come to pass. "Stood shoulder to shoulder with Sam Ervin on that one. Good man in a clutch, none better." He smiled and sighed. "Well, if your Miss Tricia don't stave off *my* losin', I'm gonna get back to the full-time cultivatin' of soybeans and cotton down in Sunflower County."

"Oh, we've got some victories up ahead," said LaRue. "And I don't mean just the president's."

"You mean on busin'? Oh, yes, we're gonna win that one sweetly and completely. Give the northerners a taste of their own medicine and you'll see how quickly they withdraw that particular 'remedy' to their 'de facto segregation'—which is just another name for human nature, isn't it, Freddie? People wantin' to live and get schooled among their own kind?"

LaRue wondered if a hymn to Rhodesia might be in the offing, but then saw Eastland reaching into his drawer.

"Almost forgot to give you this," said the senator, handing him an envelope. "It's from Betty Boyd. I've already seen it. She had to be out of the office today and told me to be sure I gave it to you when you stopped by."

As LaRue opened the envelope, Eastland told him what he was looking at.

"Betty had lunch with fiery old Clarine Lander about a month ago. They took some snaps of themselves outside the restaurant and Betty wanted to give you one of 'em. She tells me you were always a little sweet on Clarine, that you knew her back home." He allowed himself a knowing chuckle.

LaRue regarded the photograph and immediately saw not its cheerful Polaroid image but his own mental picture of Larrie, one fall night a dozen years ago, lying naked by his side, a bottle of bourbon between them, in room 205 at the old Gulf Hills Dude Ranch that he'd owned with his brother. The picture in his head started to move: the breeze rustled the curtains; Larrie reapplied her lipstick. But it was a hard picture to keep in focus. Larrie had been gone for years, and the dude ranch had burned down last Christmas.

"I must say," Eastland declared, "Clarine's no less pretty for all the questionable company she's been keepin' these last years."

"You'll have to thank Betty for this," said LaRue, putting the picture in his pocket.

"And *you'll* have to thank the president for suggestin' such a nice gesture to his little girl." The senator looked at a button that had lit up on his phone. "Well, I'd best be gettin' to the floor for a vote." He rose from his chair and shook LaRue's hand. "Freddie, you get back here soon with another good judge for me, you hear?"

"Yes, sir," said LaRue.

Eastland walked him to the door, gave him a wink and patted the jacket pocket into which he'd seen him put the picture—as if to tell LaRue that his little romantic secret involving Clarine Lander was safe with Senator James Oliver Eastland.

What the senator did not know, and what LaRue never forgot, was how Clarine Lander remained the keeper of a much bigger secret, remained the one person in the world who could tell him what had really happened, fifteen years before, in the Canadian duck blind where Ike LaRue met his death.

LaRue took a cab back to Foggy Bottom. There were no more Tuesday-night dinners at the Mitchells' apartment, as there'd been in what he already thought of as "happier days." So inside Watergate West 310, his own place, he began heating some leftovers for dinner, wondering as he did if there'd been any truly happy days since the long-ago ones he'd stolen with Larrie.

He heard an unexpected knock. With the first of the day's meetings still on his mind, he felt a momentary fear that this might be Ulasewicz. But he opened the door to find Mrs. Anna Chennault, another Watergate resident, the beautiful still-young Chinese widow of the American general whose "Flying Tigers" had fought the Japs for Chiang Kai-shek. Mrs. Chennault had continued to champion Taiwan in all the years since her husband's death, but even after the president's trip to Red China, she remained an ardent supporter of Richard Nixon. She was an important fundraiser and back channel and, by one or two accounts—which LaRue didn't believe—the only woman who had ever made the president stray from Pat. LaRue himself had met her several times at the Mitchells'.

"I won't come in," she said quickly, batting a fine pair of false eyelashes. "But I wanted to give you this for the Committee. I hear you have some special needs, and this comes from some grateful foreign nationals who are not permitted to contribute by check."

She handed him an envelope, the third one he'd seen today, and then waved to a man halfway down the hall, asking him to please hold the elevator. She dashed off as if she'd just dropped by to return a cup of sugar.

As his dinner cooked, LaRue spread the envelope's contents on his coffee table. He counted thirty thousand dollars in cash.

Chapter Eleven

OCTOBER 4, 1972
WALDORF-ASTORIA HOTEL, NEW YORK CITY

Pat Nixon looked out the hotel window eighteen floors above Park Avenue. It was ridiculous for the campaign to be shelling out for this suite of rooms in which she'd spend less than an hour before the event downstairs and a late-evening flight back to Washington. But there was apparently money to burn, so she let herself stop thinking about it, kicked off her shoes, and called Connie Stuart in the room they'd taken for *her.*

"Can you get hold of Julie for me?" the first lady asked. "And tell her I'm thinking that maybe tomorrow afternoon we could take that same walk we took a week ago? On that little island near the Teddy Roosevelt Bridge?"

Mrs. Stuart said she'd track Julie down.

"Thanks, Connie. I'll be ready here whenever they come for me."

The little island in the Potomac was, in most ways, a good bet. The drive from the White House, in a regular car with just two agents, took only five minutes, and the trail, once you got there, was as pretty as any at Camp David. Almost no one would be around, and the agents stayed far enough behind that she and Julie could have an actual non-whispered conversation. And yet, last week the two of them had never quite relaxed. The Watergate complex, on the east side of the river, had glowered like some enemy fortress, and Julie had not been able to stop talking about how the campaign's headquarters in Phoenix had burned to the ground. (In what little had been reported, the blaze was said to be "suspicious." As Rose had said the other day: "Gee, you think so?")

Well, maybe this time she and Julie could look west instead of east, and rise above things. A walk outdoors would still be better than sitting in the Solarium yet again, or going down to the basement bowling alley, where she was beginning to find the speckled red ball too heavy for her arthritic—*slightly* arthritic—right hand.

She noticed a basket of fruit and flowers on the table and thought she ought to read the card. The envelope was marked with a little green-and-gold harp, symbol of the American Irish Historical Society, the organization honoring her tonight. The flowers were lovely out-of-season ones, and they took her mind back more than thirty years to the May basket in which Dick had hidden her engagement ring.

She extracted the note, expecting to find greetings from the Society's president, Mr. Joseph T. P. Sullivan—as always, she'd done her homework—but she discovered something quite different. She recognized the handwriting as much as the names:

VICTORIA—I'LL BE AT TABLE 28—ROGER

"Oh my," she said, the twang in her voice suddenly exaggerated, the way it got when she became tired or elated. Her right hand was also trembling, as if she'd just bowled several frames.

"Oh my," she said again, sitting down on the bed and looking out the window toward the part of Manhattan where the two of them had met six years ago. It had been a fall day like this one, early afternoon, when walking home from Elizabeth Arden she had stopped in a Schrafft's on Madison Avenue.

Dick had been in the Midwest, speaking for congressional candidates, nine of them on one trip, collecting the IOUs that would get him nominated two years later—doing what he'd sworn he wouldn't do, if only because it was supposed to be impossible. After the loss in California, the single greatest appeal of New York had been Dick's assurance that no comeback could be mounted from here because the state party was so firmly in Rockefeller's grip. A candidate, after all, needed a home-state base, and Nelson wasn't about to cede his. But as it turned out, all those dozens of candidates he campaigned for in '64 and '66 *became* Dick's base, made him a new sort of stateless candidate.

And so, in their way, they'd brought Tom into her life.

That fall Tricia had been at Finch and Julie at Smith, and she herself had relished having so many hours alone—until for the first time ever she found herself with too little to do. She actually began watching a soap opera, *Dark Shadows*, late in the afternoons.

Victoria. Roger.

She would go out in the mornings by herself, and she never wore dark glasses. In New York she wasn't often recognized, and when it did happen she was almost always let alone. That day she'd had a big kerchief on, protecting her just-tinted hair, and so she was all the more startled when the Puerto Rican waitress in Schrafft's brought her a dessert she hadn't ordered and said, "The gentleman said to tell you that he's an independent but that everybody likes apple pie."

For some reason she hadn't felt edgy, as she usually did when approached by even the nicest of strangers. She'd started to laugh, and to look around for whoever had sent the pie; she smiled when he nodded at her. She took him in right away, thanks to twenty years' practice with quick introductions and size-ups: a few years older than herself; Irish, of the laciest-curtained sort. As she would learn in the next hour and over the coming months, he was a widower, an early-retired trust-and-estates lawyer with plenty of money who lent his efforts to so many boards and organizations that she now realized she'd never known the American Irish Historical Society was one of them.

It was the mischief in his eyes, the kind her father used to have after the first drink but not the second, that made her wave and then beckon him to her table. Before she knew it silver-haired Tom Garahan had sat down and they were talking, for two hours, until she joked that it would soon be time for her to go home and watch *Dark Shadows*.

Which is how they became Victoria and Roger, pet-named for two characters on the program.

All that fall, and during the winter and spring that followed, they would meet on a corner of Park Avenue at whatever time they'd arrange when she called him. If they went to the Frick, and someone did recognize her, people would assume he was a docent; if someone came over while they were in a restaurant having lunch, she would introduce him as one of her Ryan cousins, or a valued old contributor to the California campaigns who was here in the East on a visit. When she went to his apartment on Madison, she *did* wear dark glasses, and identified herself to the doorman as Miss Ryan, as if she were still answering the telephone in Dick's Senate office.

She always got home well before Dick did, and always carried a shopping bag from Rizzoli or Bergdorf's to show where she'd supposedly been.

And then the summer of '67 had arrived, and there was no more denying what would soon be upon her. For three weeks she tried to delay giving Dick the answer—*Yes, you can run*—that she knew all along she'd be giving in the end. She went out to California to stay with her old pal Helene Drown, pretending for a last little stretch that things might stay the way they were. And then she'd come home and said yes. She gave up Tom, whose merry and hurt way of letting her go made her love herself for the first time in her life.

They had not seen each other or spoken since. But here he would be at table 28. She willed her heart to slow down, telling herself the two hours ahead would be easier than the hailstorm at Yellowstone or the wind in Billings, both experienced in recent weeks. The campaign had her lightly scheduled, mostly making stops in safe states, but even here in New York Dick seemed to be way ahead.

She heard the knock, and then Connie's voice saying "We're ready." The agents and the advance man took them downstairs to a little spot outside the ballroom where they had a chair for her to sit on while being photographed.

"I'm glad you don't get to see my bony knees," she said, adjusting the floor-length hem of her emerald-green dress. One gal with a camera laughed—the photographers were always nicer than the writers—and protested that she looked great.

The reporters had been told "no questions," but of course that didn't stop them.

"Mrs. Nixon, do you have any response to the protesters outside? Several of them have signs saying 'Irish Blood on Nixon's Hands.' They're referring to American military cooperation with Great Britain."

"I haven't seen them, so I really can't comment."

Actually, she'd seen them through the tinted windows of the car, and heard them even up on the eighteenth floor. She'd thought that "Irish blood" was a nice change from Vietnamese.

"Do you have any reaction to the latest Watergate developments involving—"

"Only that I think it's all been blown out of proportion." She'd noticed that they no longer used the word "caper"; it was now a "scandal" or at least an "affair," or just the word by itself. Connie was reminding them about "no questions," and the female reporter who'd asked about

Watergate actually tsked and shook her head. Pat kept smiling. Alice Longworth had once told her that Mrs. Harding used to keep a fat red notebook for the recording of every slight; but didn't one remember them all, without writing them down?

Mr. Sullivan said it was time for them to go into the ballroom. As she stood up, she could feel the Lexington Avenue subway line rumbling beneath her feet, and she got a kick out of realizing what it was. She had *loved* the subway back here in the thirties, and had ridden it again, dozens of times, each one a lark, with the man who would be at table 28.

The ballroom contained nine hundred guests, and the flowers on the dais weren't nearly so pretty as the ones Roger had managed to get to Victoria. She had the card in her clutch purse and was glad to realize that the lights, just like at the convention, prevented her from seeing beyond the first row of tables.

The program listed her as Patricia Ryan Nixon, and the lieutenant governor of New York was now extolling her as "this gracious woman of Irish lineage," all of which somehow only made her think of her German mother, and of the names she herself had dropped along the way, not just Catherine but Thelma, which she knew—thanks to Rose—Haldeman sometimes called her behind her back. She'd kept things as simple as possible with the girls, given them easy names that sounded like nicknames, and no middle names for either of them. She was counting on them to be more public during the second term, to take over a lot of the things she was doing now. Julie was better prepared and less lazy than her sister, but if both of them helped she might really be able to recede into the kind of privacy Mrs. Truman and Mamie had had.

"Thank you, thank you," she heard herself say a few minutes later, while holding up the crystal plate they gave her. Her remarks were no longer than the ones she'd delivered at the convention, and in less than a minute she was back in her seat, eating dinner, chatting with Mr. Sullivan, forcing herself not to look beyond the dais, now that they'd dimmed the lights a bit. As the coffee came, Carmel Quinn and a trio of Irish girls began singing. She wondered if one of them might surprise everyone with a shout of protest over the Irish or Vietnamese blood, take your pick, on Dick's hands. You never knew. Last January, one of the Ray Conniff Singers, not exactly the Rolling Stones, had done just that in the East Room.

They had a short after-dinner receiving line for her to work, and that would be it. In twenty minutes she would be back on the plane, sitting down with the Taylor Caldwell novel right where she'd left it in the cabin.

Would he come through the line? Two of the first dozen hands she shook belonged to men wearing the little gold pin that signified their gift of at least a thousand dollars to the campaign. A couple of nuns now approached, an old-fashioned pair like the ones she remembered from the Bronx, not the habitless girls of today, all big on abortion and against the war.

As the line moved and shortened she felt her heart beginning to pound—whether from relief or disappointment she couldn't be sure.

"What a beautiful green your dress is!"

"Thank you! I couldn't have worn anything else. Not tonight—not to this!"

Like the queen, she always wore bright colors, never black, though she didn't do it to help the people in crowds struggling for a glimpse of her. It had started with the trousseau for her Mexican honeymoon. She did it for Dick, who'd seen nothing but those awful black Quaker dresses growing up. His mother had *still* been in them the summer she died, only five years ago, the same summer she herself had had to give up Tom.

And there he was, right in front of her: a pair of blue eyes instead of brown ones; a jaw that was firm instead of jowled. Not Dick, but Tom, with his slight, good-natured Irish paunch, a man not forcing himself to eat cottage cheese for lunch.

"Thomas Garahan," he said, extending his hand with a big grin.

She smiled and gave the Secret Service man the usual signal, a gently cocked head, to indicate the need for a private word with the person coming through the line. There was always someone special, often recently bereaved, and the agent would take them to a nearby little room that had been secured for this purpose, while Connie told the next people in line that Mrs. Nixon would be back in just a minute.

"Victoria."

"Roger."

They didn't embrace, just sat down on the kind of tufted bench you found in a powder room. By themselves for the first time in five years, they looked at each other.

"I keep thinking I deserve only half of that crystal platter," she said. "You know, my German mother."

"It'd still be big enough to hold a piece of pie."

She laughed, thinking there was nothing in their words or expressions that couldn't have been exchanged in the receiving line.

"Well," he said. "I held out for as long as I could. Then a couple of months ago I decided I was going to throw caution to the winds."

"Oh?" she asked. "What made you do that?"

"That gesture you made down in Miami. Brushing back some phantom hair that wasn't even out of place. You never do that unless you know I'm looking."

She laughed, remembering how this used to thrill her—hearing a man apply his shrewdness to her psychology instead of to a realignment of the nuclear superpowers.

"I was hoping for a blush," said Tom. "I'm not wrong, am I?"

"You watched the convention?"

"Of course I did. I watch every piece of film the evening news runs of you. You should tell Agnew to let up on the network guys a little. They've shown some very pretty pictures of you out West."

Now she was blushing and avoiding his gaze. "Kids okay?" she asked.

"The finest of fettle. Both married off, same as yours. Saw you dancing at Tricia's wedding, too. I would have cut in if I'd been there."

She laughed. "He really is the worst dancer, isn't he?"

"I took a vow, you'll remember, never to criticize him. But Herbert Hoover could cut a better rug."

After a moment, she asked, "You want to hear about holding out?"

"Tell me."

"I've twice written notes to Rose Woods saying 'Put Mr. Thomas Garahan of New York City on this or that invitation list'—Boy Scouts, cancer, one or another of your good works. Nobody would have thought twice about your being there." She paused. "And I almost sent them to her."

"But you didn't."

"I didn't."

"Good. Whenever I was with you, I hated seeing a third person in the room, let alone three hundred of them."

She thought that she would give anything for it to be five years ago, noontime on a weekday, the two of them sitting over plates of spaghetti at Gino's.

She touched his hand and looked down at her lap. "I've got to get back out there."

He stood up, took both her hands, and gently brought her to her feet.

She laughed as soon as she noticed his thousand-dollar-donor pin.

"Kiddo," he said, "the things I do for you." He added, softly, "But I promise I won't pull anything like this again."

"Thank you," she whispered.

"I won't need to next time."

"Oh?"

"You'll be the one who does."

Chapter Twelve

OCTOBER 10, 1972, 8:30 A.M.
STATE DINING ROOM, THE WHITE HOUSE

"Tea, please," said Elliot Richardson to the waiter coming around with coffee.

Clark MacGregor, the former congressman who'd replaced Mitchell as CRP chairman, was giving a long-winded update on the campaign to an assembly of Cabinet secretaries, senators, House members, and "surrogates"—speakers, some of them Cabinet wives, who would keep stumping the country for the next four weeks. The event was more a rally than a serious strategy session; many of those in the room had not seen one another since the convention in Miami. While MacGregor remarked upon the health of the campaign's budget in Ohio and Indiana, Richardson waved to Jerry Ford and a cluster of House Republicans. Trapped between Kleindienst and George Shultz, he guessed that he was even more bored than they.

A glance over at Ehrlichman showed the president's domestic advisor to be hard at the doodling habit he shared with the HEW secretary. It was about all they had in common. Richardson now recalled the day last fall when Ehrlichman had had him over to the West Wing to suggest broadly that Nixon would be considering him for the vacant Supreme Court seat—which soon enough went to Rehnquist. The conversation had been designed to ensure that, while he hoped and waited for the seat, he wouldn't offer congressional liberals any concessions on the administration's welfare-reform bill, which even Richardson would have admitted was surprisingly liberal to begin with.

MacGregor now remarked that things looked very good in Kentucky.

At least this wasn't a meeting of the Cabinet. During those, Richardson wore himself out trying to find the sweet spot between grandstanding and too-evident boredom. He almost missed the presence of Mitchell, who used to give Nixon a discreet signal, no more than the shake of a wattle, when the president began to ramble. Even so, Richardson could never forgive the former attorney general for joining Nixon and Agnew in what he regarded as a three-way humiliation of him a couple of summers ago. Just after he'd left State for HEW, he'd had to listen to each of them, right there in the Cabinet Room, insisting that the South be let down easy when it came to desegregating the schools—as if he'd started flooding the region with carpetbagging bureaucrats!

Henry, with his Cabinet rank if no Cabinet position, would have witnessed the spectacle had he not been traveling that day, just as he was absent from this morning's moribund show. Was he in Paris or Saigon? Perhaps even Hanoi? Richardson knew they were struggling to get Thieu to accept a settlement, and that a handful of men in this room, the ones working on it, were divided about whether it would be better to get a deal before the election or after. The latter school of thought held that an announcement of peace just before the country went to the polls would look phony. "So what's your point?" snorted those from the opposing school. Richardson wondered which school Nixon himself belonged to.

The president finally stepped up to the microphone to shouts of "Four more years!" While others roared the campaign slogan, Richardson just murmured the words, with enough of a smile that a distant lip-reader might think he was joining in for real.

After a few tortured football metaphors, Nixon began assaulting the *Washington Post*'s recent story of how some kid named Segretti, a pal of young Mr. Chapin in the West Wing, had been hired to perform some pranks, "dirty tricks," against the Democrats running in the primaries last winter.

"Yes," said Nixon, mocking the *Post*'s connection of Segretti and Chapin as fellow USC almuni, "it sounds like a grand conspiracy to me. I'm wondering if they've questioned O. J. Simpson about it." He got a big laugh with that—and an even bigger one with what followed: "Come to think of it, Mrs. Nixon went to USC as well."

The president now emphasized how there had been, in contrast to the Truman and Johnson years, "no *personal* corruption in this administration," his stress on the adjective creating an unfortunate suggestion that there had been every other kind. He ended his pep talk by promising that the election would represent "the last burp of the

Eastern Establishment." This of course got a tremendous cry of approval, but Richardson refrained from applauding. He locked eyes for a moment with Bill Rogers, his old boss at State, who seemed to be thinking the same thing: the Establishment doesn't burp, even when dying.

The long pointless session was at last over, and the troops began a slow shuffle through the too-few exits. Richardson found himself standing next to Ehrlichman, like two schoolboys frustrated by the lunch line at Milton Academy.

"You know, Elliot, just yesterday the Old Man was telling me that every Cabinet ought to have at least one future president in it."

Richardson pretended to smile. "I wonder who he believes that would be now that Connally is gone."

"Oh, I think he meant you, Elliot. He said this just the other day, satisfied that we were filling the bill."

"Well, there's no sweeter smell than the perfume of flattery." He wasn't going to fall for it a second time from Ehrlichman.

"The president intended no flattery, believe me. There was only 'fear and loathing' in his voice, as our countercultural friends like to say."

The remark was a serious insult, not the towel snap it might have been if uttered by, say, Mitchell. Ehrlichman knew that all the job switching and musical chairs bound to take place after the election would be a mere warm-up to the jockeying to succeed Nixon himself. Richardson maintained his smile but fixed his gaze on the narrow backs of the two Haldeman flunkies who were shuffling forward an inch or two ahead of him.

"Dean thinks he's going to be an ambassador," said one to the other.

"I know. When you pass his office you can hear him playing how-to-learn-French tapes."

"If he has to stay here, he's supposed to become the new Colson."

"Where does that leave the old Colson?"

"Same as before—with Nixon reporting to him."

As the two of them laughed, the bottleneck still showed no sign of clearing. Richardson turned his head and saw Rose Woods, who'd actively detested him since his uninvited visit to San Clemente last summer, when he'd actually succeeded in getting her boss to change his mind about something.

Rose, too, was listening to the Haldeman boys, the kind who were dispatched as spies even to White House parties. The morning after, some poor dress-uniformed Marine on the social staff would be terrified to get a memo reprimanding him for something inappropriate he'd been overheard to say while waltzing with a secretary from the Costa Rican embassy.

As the line finally began moving, Rose fell into step beside nice quiet Fred LaRue. Before they could say hello, Colson and Magruder cut in front of them, much to her annoyance—though Magruder, whom Colson regarded as unqualified to run a candy store, let alone a campaign, had no choice in the matter. Colson was squeezing his elbow, propelling him, insisting the press needed to know that McGovern had recently insulted Katharine Graham. "They asked him about what Mitchell said"—that the *Post*'s publisher had better keep out of Watergate lest she get her tit caught in a wringer—"and McGovern, for once taking off his preacher's collar, responded by saying, 'Having seen her figure, I don't think there's much danger of that.'"

Rose asked LaRue, who looked awfully low, if *he'd* heard that.

LaRue didn't want to comment on a sexual remark, even if the lady had brought it up herself. He replied in a whisper: "You know, Mitchell says that Colson's constituency consists of the president's worst instincts."

Rose bristled for a moment—long enough to make clear she didn't think the president *had* any bad instincts—but then she laughed. She knew that Colson's ability to absorb hours of the boss's ventings made HRH's life easier; the provision of such a service was reason enough for her to dislike Colson too. The line was moving fast now, and the only other word she heard out of Colson's mouth was "Hunt," before she strode ahead of him toward the West Wing.

Back at her desk she found a stamped, sealed envelope with a cobweb of black handwriting and a return address that she recognized. Alice Longworth was one of the few people—Mamie was another—whose letters didn't have to go through "the system," so long as there was somebody in the mailroom sharp-eyed enough to spot them. Haldeman wasn't interested in Mrs. L, but the letter's evasion of his maw still pleased Rose, as if it were a secret message flung over the battlements without the castle's ogre having noticed.

She set it aside for a moment to look at a folder that interested HRH very much, one marked "Oslo," containing a plan of action to be implemented should the president win the Nobel Peace Prize. If he secured the Vietnam deal on top of China and Russia, how, Rose wondered, could he *not* get it? Inside the file were variant schedules: one had the boss visiting a few allied capitals before picking up the prize; another had him doing that afterwards. She and Dwight Chapin and someone politically reliable at State (a rare bird) were rigging up the itineraries amidst Haldeman's constant warnings against letting any of this get into the press, where it would be made to look like some active effort to get Nixon the award.

All of Rose's current worries seemed to be of this second-level, can't-win-for-losing kind. Among them was the fear that next month's victory would be diluted by everyone's saying it reflected only McGovern's incompetence and represented no tribute to Richard Nixon.

She wouldn't think about that now. Don Carnevale, in town from New York, was taking her to lunch today, and her overnight bag, packed and standing in the corner, was ready for an unusual midweek trip to Camp David. She would love to be taking a beau up with her—separate cabins, of course—though she doubted the wisdom of pushing her luck, or testing Don's ardor, beyond lunch or dinner.

Though it was only October, she suspected that Mrs. L might be writing in regard to one of the Christmas parties. TR's daughter was welcome at any or all of them, and it would be like her to tell the White House in advance what dates she could *not* make, so that the schedule could dance to her tune. Rose slit open the thick old envelope—the stationery must be forty years old—and prepared to get a kick out of whatever Mrs. Longworth had to say. She'd heard how the old girl had confounded Miss Priss Richardson in Miami; maybe she'd be giving it to him again on paper.

What Rose found instead was something quite different, cause for a bit of *first*-level worry. But she'd gotten only halfway through the letter when Marje Acker came in and gave her the passenger manifest for tonight's helicopter ride to Camp David.

"Cheer up," said Marje. "You'll be sitting next to Julie, not Tricia."

Chapter Thirteen

OCTOBER 23–24, 1972, 11:30 P.M.–12:45 A.M.
OVAL OFFICE AND LINCOLN SITTING ROOM

Nixon's leg was bothering him. He'd been on and off planes and in and out of limousines the whole day—a long one of campaigning—and it wasn't over yet. As the helicopter landed on the South Lawn, he could see that the lights in the West Wing had been left on, as he'd instructed. While Pat headed upstairs to the residence, he made his way to Woodrow Wilson's old desk in the Oval Office.

He'd had the desk taken out of mothballs at the beginning of his term, determined to outdo the president of his early childhood in rearranging the world. And then Safire told him the goddamned thing had belonged to *Henry* Wilson, one of Grant's vice presidents. Well, so be it. He continued to tell himself that he was sitting just where Woodrow Wilson had remade the map. He would do the same, but he would do it with toughness instead of preaching, and he would do it alone, without a League of Nations or even the goddamned United States Congress, which Wilson had let break him in body and spirit. If necessary, he would do it without even Kissinger, whom he could now hear somewhere down the hall, joking with the female assistant he'd brought with him.

As Nixon looked at his watch and waited, he thought some more about Wilson, whom even Alice Longworth, for all the squawking she'd done against the League, hadn't really hated. She'd once admitted that she hated only Wilson's sanctimony, along with the way he'd more or less stolen the idea of the League from her father. Wilson, she swore, had grown a long beard in his last, paralyzed years, and slept with it over the covers instead of under—an image that now brought to Nixon's mind a picture of crazy Howard Hughes in his Las Vegas hotel, or wherever he'd gone since.

The president shook his leg and stomped it a few times on the carpet, hoping his present discomfort wasn't a flare-up of that long-ago god-damned phlebitis. He made a vow to swim and walk each day during the second term, so that he wouldn't wind up having a stroke like Wilson or Kennedy's old man. Even so, he'd rather drive himself toward something like that than content himself with a presidency like the one conducted by Eisenhower, still the laziest white man he'd ever seen. It was probably easier to get Hughes out of bed in the morning.

How happy he'd have been if Hunt's gang of idiots had managed to get inside the DNC without getting caught and had somehow found Hughes's connection to Larry O'Brien. Well, maybe they'd find it yet, in some other place, during the second term—which was likely to be over before Kissinger got his ass in here.

"Mr. President," the national security advisor, feigning breathlessness, said at last upon entering the office. "Pocantico Hills is really something, no?"

Nixon snorted, to make clear he had not been overly impressed by Rockefeller's baronial lair, where he'd been having dinner five hours ago. "Ziegler told me he spotted two fireplaces inside the indoor tennis court."

Hesitating between fealty toward his former patron and his current one, Kissinger said nothing, and Nixon decided to let the silence hang in the air for a few seconds. While it rested there, he pondered how he had almost liked Nelson tonight. Their long rivalry, with himself now triumphant, had at last been put to rest. Rockefeller had seemed to say as much, with his champagne toast about the honor Nixon had done the house as the first president to step inside it. During dessert Nixon had watched Rose Woods sitting next to Ann Whitman, once Ike's secretary and now Nelson's, and had thought about the peculiarities of fate.

It was Kissinger who had asked to meet at this late hour, and while Nixon daydreamed for another few seconds, the national security advisor tried getting down to business. "Mr. President, it is urgent that we conclude the agreement before the election."

Nixon sighed. He and Haig, Kissinger's own deputy, thought otherwise. He was weary of this discussion, tired of hashing the thing out after every temporary development in Paris or Saigon or Hanoi. But mostly he was worn out from the day of barnstorming. He and Pat had motorcaded through Westchester, sticking their heads out the limousine's roof every ten minutes like cuckoos in a clock, and after the dinner at Rockefeller's he'd talked himself hoarse to five thousand people in some coliseum on Long Island.

Kissinger said nothing more.

"It'll look awfully fishy, Henry. I'm telling you that for the dozenth time. For Chrissakes, in '68 we had Julie and David hold off their wedding until after the election because we thought it would look as if we were trolling for votes from old ladies. By comparison, *this* goddamned thing—"

"It's not just politics, Mr. President. The North Vietnamese have more incentives to make concessions now instead of later. They may change their minds and decide to keep fighting after the election."

"Henry, even *they* know we've already won this election. Which means they know we're not going to try and convert a bunch of McGovern's voters by going soft. And I'm not going to dent the big majority we can roll up by pulling some jackass stunt that will turn people off."

Kissinger grumbled. "Well, there are *other* problems that may give you this delay you want. Thieu would not budge all day today, in cable after cable. He thinks the proposed 'National Council of Reconciliation' will turn into a coalition government."

Nixon snorted. "If they're lucky!" He added, more somberly, "It's really not much of an agreement, is it?"

The president knew that one way or another, within several years, the Communists would be in Saigon. But if by that point he'd achieved the big realignments he wanted, especially with China, it wouldn't matter. The whole goddamned, tormenting Vietnam War would be as forgotten as the Spanish-American one.

He didn't wait for Kissinger's silent rumination to become a spoken reply. He replaced his first question with a second, more specific, one. "You honestly think those North Vietnamese units will 'wither away' if they're left in the South?"

"Yes," Kissinger said, with such force it was clear he had yet to convince himself. "They will not be able to get reinforcements or supplies."

"It's a nice dream, Henry. Keep selling it to Thieu."

"You know," said Kissinger, with respect to the South Vietnamese president, "he's been encouraged to remain stubborn by what Julie said." A reporter had tricked the president's daughter into declaring that she would be willing to die for the Saigon regime if asked, just like any boy being drafted.

Tenderly, Nixon offered his analyis of this particular: "I think that's her way of saying she'd die for me." He paused for a moment and then toughened up his voice: "Henry, once this agreement comes through, either before the election or after, not even King Timahoe is going to be dying for Thieu."

Kissinger, who needed a moment to remember that Nixon was referring to his dog, knew that the president was reaching the point—*he* was, too—where he hated the South Vietnamese even more than the North.

"Let's call it a night," said Nixon.

It was past twelve when the president reached the Lincoln Sitting Room in the residence; not too late to call Colson, who would still be up at home.

"This Baldwin character has been talking about you," said Nixon, without even a hello once his advisor came on the line. "According to the damned paper."

Colson dismissed what the burglars' listening-post operator was rumored to be saying to the prosecutors. "The *Post* is playing up my name because they want to give Justice a basis for calling me to testify at the trial. They figure once I'm on the stand the government can go to town with all kinds of questions about all kinds of things, which will give the paper a chance to follow up with all kinds of crazy stories."

"Yeah," said Nixon.

"I think they're in for a big disappointment," Colson continued. He then paused—not to think, but so that his next remark would be a separate unit, its message of reassurance underlined. "I'm going to talk to Hunt after the election. I'm going to find him something to do—a job he'll know he can count on keeping even if he has to spend a few months in jail. If he feels secure, this whole thing really *will* go away before the inauguration. For all of us."

The mention of jobs made Nixon think about all the firing and shuffling he intended to do after the election. He pictured himself down in Key Biscayne, happily attending to the task, a clipboard in hand and his feet on a hassock; he only hoped he wasn't tempting fate with such comfortable imagining of the near future. He'd been oddly worried about his safety all afternoon, as if part of himself believed he wouldn't be allowed to see the coming landslide—not on top of Russia, China, and the winding-down of Vietnam. Rose had recently passed him an astrological warning from Jeane Dixon, who had once claimed to see Kennedy's end coming. Ridiculous, of course, but he allowed the anxiety some oblique expression in what he next said to Colson: "I was worried about Pat today, every time we put our heads up through the roof of the car. I was surprised the Secret Service allowed it."

Colson responded quickly: "If—God forbid—something *had* happened, the press would have made it seem less bad than Segretti's having a dozen pizzas delivered to Muskie's headquarters."

Satisfied by a renewed feeling of ill-treatment, the president concluded the call.

But he felt too tired to sleep, and so he reached into the drawer of the end table, where Rose always put papers that required extra-personal attention, the sort of items he liked to ponder during his regular late nights in this room. Among them he spotted Alice Longworth's letter, which had been in the drawer, opened but unread, for a couple of weeks. Exhausted as he was, he decided he might as well attend to the tall black handwriting now.

Dear Dick,

Surely you remember old man Meyer, Kay Graham's father, who died in '59. Years and years before that, before you ever came to town, he said to me, "You say more things with more finality and less foundation than anyone I know"—a remark I found hilarious.

You'll note he didn't say I was *wrong*, and I don't think I'm wrong about what follows. Not long ago Kay told my cousin Joe: "I hate him"—meaning, of course, you—"and I'm going to do all I can to defeat him." Joe cannot of course write or even "leak" this remark for the obvious reason that Kay's awful paper still pays his bills. But I urge you to think of what it means. Once McGovern is finished off, all of his supporters will be like fleas who've lost their dog. Their mournfulness will motivate them. And they will wage war against you by other means.

I suspect that the boys at Kay's paper know a bit more than they've already printed, but they don't know something *I* do— something I shall wait to pass on until I have the chance to see you in person—probably just after the fleas have started jumping off the hound's carcass.

In the meantime, send my greetings to Pat and to the girls.

Alice

The president guessed that what she had to impart wasn't so much fresh information as her shrewd assessment of different persons' motives. It would be all worth listening to, but it was hard to tell— Mrs. L being such a creature of whim—what degree of urgency really attached to this preview. She herself said it could wait until after the election, so he would not press for anything now. Still, he wouldn't forget to ask once he saw her.

He went over to the writing table, where he would answer her, fountain pen for fountain pen. Unscrewing the cap of his old Waterman, he looked out the window, toward the south, at the winking Washington Monument, and wondered: Would he have made it here without Mrs. L? Maybe not—not if she hadn't told him to fight all the Stassens and Herters trying to get Eisenhower to drop him in '56. He thought back to the January after all that, when she'd come by herself to the house on Tilden Street, just hours after they'd all been at Rock Creek Cemetery burying that odd, stuttering daughter. Paulina: only days before she'd been alive, with her own little girl on Twenty-eighth Street, crazy with religion and still mourning that queer drunk of a husband she'd had.

Nixon remembered Mrs. L making it clear, once she arrived at the house, that she wanted to talk only to him, not Pat. Mrs. L, however ashamed she might be over her failure as a mother, was implacably convinced that the death had been an accident—no matter the *Post*'s report about the girl's having swallowed a bottle of pills. He and Bill Bullitt had gone to see the insurance company, which because of the newspaper story wouldn't pay out. When, after a little persuading, they did agree to pay, Mrs. L demanded that the *Post* retract their story. Which of course they did not.

Odd, thought Nixon—looking back from the window to the blotter and writing the date at the top of the page—how coldly rational the old lady could be about everything but this. She'd always regarded the little task he performed with Bullitt—let alone what he'd convinced her of that night on Tilden Street—as heroic. She'd spent the last fifteen years making things up to the *grand*daughter, redeeming the cruel botch of an upbringing she'd given her own child.

Dear Mrs. L—

I wasn't too far from Oyster Bay tonight, and I noticed that nearly half the crowd in the Long Island auditorium were Italians, who would all have been voting for Truman twenty-five years ago— before they moved out to the suburbs from Brooklyn, I suppose. I think we're now going to have them on our side for a generation, maybe more.

I appreciate your word to the wise about Mrs. Graham and the *Post*. The paper's coverage of Pat and the girls, when it's covered them at all, has been a disgrace, nothing but mockery. And let me tell you this: my man Colson has some interesting ideas about what to do with Mrs. G's TV licenses once the election is behind us.

I know, as you do and your father did, that all victories are temporary, but we'll soon be celebrating together—not just the election but a peace agreement. So keep the television on over the next couple of weeks—even if you've got to tune in to a station the *Post* owns!

Pat and I have talked about having a little dinner party upstairs in the Residence sometime in December. Rose will be in touch about it, and we'll hope you can make it. Once you get here, please let me under the brim of your hat so that we can put our heads together over that piece of intelligence you mention.

Affectionately,
Dick

He addressed the envelope and put it on the table from which it would be picked up and sent on its way in the middle of the night. Then, heading to his bedroom, the long day over at last, he found himself wondering: What if she *had* meant an actual, specific piece of intelligence—and not just her opinion of things?

But what could she really know? And when could she have come to know it?

Chapter Fourteen

NOVEMBER 7, 1972; ELECTION DAY

Pat Nixon turned around to wave through the car's rear window. The cluster of poll workers and teachers outside Concordia Elementary began receding as the presidential limousine pulled away. The Nixons had just cast their votes, at 7:10 a.m., too early for any children to be at the school—a small miscalculation that would deny the campaign some warm, last-minute imagery from San Clemente. But Pat now realized she would never again have to worry about such a thing. Over the next four years there would be plenty of hands left to shake, but not one of them would belong to a voter she was trying to sell on Dick Nixon.

They were heading back to the house for a couple of hours; a flight from El Toro would take them to Washington in time for dinner. For the moment Dick was as quiet as herself, looking out at the Pacific and thinking. But after a minute he pointed toward Red Beach and told her, "When I was swimming out there yesterday, I realized the tide was farther out than I'd ever seen it."

Pat lit a cigarette and began humming "Ebb Tide."

"Think it was a bad omen?" the president asked.

She playfully swatted his hand. "You're acting like Lincoln, pal. Seeing signs and symbols everywhere."

Dr. Hutschnecker, her husband's intermittent psychiatrist, had long ago told him that dreams were not portents, that they were always about the past and never the future. Dick could usually remain persuaded of this, and on occasion, at the breakfast table, would even sift through one of his dreams like a set of election returns, breaking down the details as if they were precinct reports. His talk of dreams with Hutschnecker was the only part of his sessions with the headshrinker that he ever revealed to her, and she wished he wouldn't share even them. They seemed to invite the reciprocation of some intimacy that was beyond her to give.

She now pointed to the sandstone cliffs and the giant peace symbol that early in the administration had been painted onto one ridge near the house. The lines of the circle and arrow were faded now, barely discernible, and she took their disappearance to mean not that peace was fading—it was still "at hand," in Kissinger's phrase—but that the war itself, especially the one at home, was at last going away.

As the car reached the driveway of La Casa Pacifica, Pat couldn't help telling herself, for all its seeming self-indulgence, that peace was at hand for her, too. The girls would be coming to the fore; Martha was gone from Washington; for all she cared, the photographers could catch her smoking now.

"Let yourself relish it, Dick," she said, patting his hand.

It was 10:30 a.m. in the East when Howard Hunt, returning from the polls, pulled into his driveway in Potomac, Maryland. He had feared that the firehouse where he voted might be staked out by photographers on the prowl for "irony." As it turned out, the TV stations and papers had lacked the cleverness or manpower to send anybody, but early this morning Hunt had decided he would run whatever gauntlet he had to, since this could be the last election in which he exercised his franchise for quite some time. If the trial went badly, he would be stripped of his civil rights—in the strict, old-fashioned sense of that term.

He had voted for Nixon and Agnew, feeling no enthusiasm for the ticket's junior partner, who'd been as crooked as any other Maryland governor. Sustained by the belief that Colson would yet come through, Hunt had summoned up a small degree of gusto for Nixon himself.

Dorothy did not share the feeling. Recent payments to "the writer's wife" had been pitifully meager. After the Cubans got their cut, barely enough remained to meet the mortgage, let alone Kevan's tuition at Smith. Dorothy's summertime fervor, that adrenal emergency, had been replaced by alternating bouts of anger and depression.

He would spend the rest of the day working on *The Berlin Ending*. He was about twenty thousand words from finishing the novel, though he'd yet to figure out a way to wind up the plot. After ascending the stairs to his study, he opened the door to his wife's bedroom just widely enough to find her still under the covers, still asleep in her nightgown.

"Mr. Secretary," said the voice coming through the intercom. "Mrs. Richardson called a little while ago. She could only get car service at nine-thirty tonight—earlier than you both wanted, I know. She asks that you figure on having dinner together a little before you'd planned."

"Thank you," said Elliot Richardson, whose frown would have been imperceptible to his assistant even if she were in the same room. He had let his after-hours government driver take Election Day off, forgetting that, with the thousands of people heading to one party or another, private cars would be at a premium tonight. He wanted to arrive at the Shoreham with Anne just before Nixon accepted victory, no sooner, and one of the CRP's precision drill teams had assured cabinet secretaries that that would happen a few minutes after midnight.

Nine-thirty. Oh my. Richardson did not believe he could stand being in that hotel, amidst the madding crowd, for more than two hours. But if he suggested to Anne that they take their own car, she'd insist that she drive or that he not drink, neither of which possibilities he approved. He would need a stiff one to get through ten minutes of just Nixon himself, and more than that to bear two hours of all the delighted-with-themselves little Magruders—let alone Sammy Davis, Jr., and Sinatra, whose presences at the Shoreham were promised in this morning's *Post.*

"I'll call Mrs. Richardson in a bit," he at last replied through the intercom. As soon as he released its lever, he made a decision: he and Anne would not go at all. They would stay home and he would complete one of his bird watercolors, part of the series he was doing from photographs. For all he knew, impolitic absence, a refusal to kiss the presidential derrière up on the dais of the Shoreham, would actually improve his standing with Nixon.

The half-finished watercolor was not exactly the study of a soaring hawk. Richardson had gotten it into his head that all the highest-level appointees would be expected to supply the chieftain with a little gift commemorating the reelection, something to match the tie clasp or cuff links that would no doubt be coming their way from the president, and toward that end he had begun creating a customized tribute, a painting of a prothonotary warbler, the little yellow-chested, blue-gray-winged creature that long ago had allowed Congressman Richard Nixon to connect Alger Hiss to Whittaker Chambers. The warblers that nested by the Potomac would now be heading south for the winter. Did they, Richardson wondered somewhat preposterously, hate themselves for always coming back to Washington?

"You want my *thoughts*?" Rose Woods asked Theodore H. White.

"Yes," the author said. "What you're feeling on this day of days."

"I'm feeling," said Rose, "that I'd better get the president's speech typed." The clocks aboard Air Force One had been set forward to eastern time, and even so said only two p.m. It was hardly yet urgent for Rose to push the boss's brief victory remarks through her IBM, and she realized that her reply to White had come out harsher than it needed to. Still, she couldn't help herself. She'd read his book about the '60 campaign and knew that he'd later cooked up the whole Camelot label with Jackie Kennedy; she didn't see why they had to let him on the plane. But history, of course, trumped everything with the boss, and having White here to write about an imminent landslide was a way for Richard Nixon to further outrun Jack Kennedy, twelve years minus one day after he'd lost to him.

White smiled and began to move away.

"Maybe later?" said Rose, trying to sound conciliatory.

The president was in the plane's open area, alternately chatting and dozing in a seat beside Haldeman, two away from Kissinger. "Peace is at hand," Rose muttered to herself, thinking she would believe it when she saw it. As of now, Henry still had two doves in the bush and *nothing* in his hand. There was no sign of Pat, who must be asleep in her private cabin. Rose had hoped for an invitation to dine with the family tonight, upstairs in the residence, but *que será será*. Nothing was going to dampen her spirits. As it was, she had an invitation to Alice Longworth's election-night party, and as soon as the boss was through at the Shoreham she was going to make a beeline over to Dupont Circle. She'd make sure to have one or two belts beforehand, because the old lady served very little booze. Mrs. Longworth liked the conversation sharp, and Rose hoped she could oblige.

———

At 8:44 p.m., when the networks called McGovern's home state of South Dakota for Richard Nixon, the president's head snapped backwards and he let out a sharp cry.

"I'm very sorry," said Dr. Chase, who was nonetheless satisfied that the temporary cap he'd just put on one of Nixon's front teeth would hold. "I'd avoid apples until we can get something more permanent for you—but champagne and strawberries ought to be fine." He smiled politely at his preoccupied patient and began gathering up the implements he'd brought along on this unexpected call to the White House's basement dispensary.

The original cap, which had been put on Nixon's tooth the year he came to Congress, had fallen off during dinner—the only bad, or even inconvenient, occurrence of the day. The whole family had been together for supper—David had gotten home from the Mediterranean, without any strings being pulled, a little earlier than expected—and during the meal Pat had let her husband take calls from Colson and Haldeman without any objection. And why not? Each one brought more good news than the last.

Chapin entered the dispensary as Nixon swigged some Listerine.

"Mr. President, somebody will come up to the residence to make you up at eleven twenty-five, just before the drive to the Shoreham."

They were expecting five thousand people there; he had gotten the speech down to two minutes.

"Fine," he told Chapin, who nodded and left.

He felt an odd desire to go upstairs and find the old cap, which had disappeared into the carpet. It seemed like some telltale clue he had left behind, and he felt, despite the replacement, somehow incomplete without it. Well, a cap wasn't even a tooth, but it had to indicate *something*. And if it wasn't a portent, it wasn't about the past, either. He'd be too embarrassed to bring it up with Hutschnecker and by the time he saw him again would probably have forgotten all about it. Meanwhile, he could feel a dull pushing sensation where the old real tooth met the new false one; he decided he would let it take his mind off the pain in his leg.

But he couldn't take his mind off the letdown he was feeling. Rose was having to fight it, too; he could tell that when he saw her getting off the plane at Andrews. Only Pat seemed genuinely happy. He tried for a moment to think of the election as a gift to her—it meant, after all, no more politics. But he didn't suppose there was much logic in giving thanks to politics for putting an end to itself; sort of like thanking God for sparing some people in the earthquake He'd just caused. Why not just dispense with the quake to begin with?

But it was not 1947, and he could not stop the life that he himself had set in motion. He went upstairs to look for the artificial tooth through which he'd spoken his first words in Congress.

There had been so much good news so early that the CRP team in charge of the Shoreham's ballroom looked worried about maintaining what their memos called "a suitable level of enthusiasm" until the president arrived. The Nixonettes continued to twirl their batons every time another state was called, and every so often someone would roar "FUCK MASSACHUSETTS!" to diminishing bursts of laughter, as the Bay State remained the only one in the opposition column. McGovern's concession speech had already been booed, along with Shriver's, the latter providing a special pleasure, given all the Kennedys up onscreen with him.

Fred LaRue milled about, nodding hello and sipping his drink and relighting his pipe. He saw Ziegler hug Chapin and Kleindienst kiss Bebe Rebozo, but there wasn't anything loud or down-home about these encounters. The whole thing felt less like a celebration with your battle-field buddies than some faraway military victory won with long-range missiles.

LaRue looked at his watch and realized he might have to miss the big moment. The stage was already filling—there was Clark MacGregor and his wife; the Agnew daughters; now Tricia and her husband—but he had no choice except to fight his way out of the ballroom, murmuring "'Scuse me, please, 'scuse me" a hundred times, as he swam against a crowd pressing closer to the action.

He at last made it upstairs to a quiet stretch of carpeted corridor that ran between some empty meeting rooms. He stopped in front of a particular pay phone and pretended to consult his address book while waiting for it to ring. That happened, as agreed upon in advance, precisely at midnight.

"Yes, ma'am," he said, picking up the receiver.

"You've gotten five-hundred-plus electoral votes," said the voice on the line.

"It looks that way, ma'am."

"You must have a great many people to thank."

"Indeed," said LaRue.

"Tell me, Mr. Friend-of-Mr.-Rivers, how much have you budgeted for canapés at all those inaugural balls?"

LaRue did not lose patience but tried to convey a smidgen of sternness by using the caller's name. "I can't say I really know, Miz Hunt."

"I'll bet you it's more than is being spent to sustain the defendants' families until the trial."

"I hope it won't be too much longer before the trial gets under way."

"It will probably start right around the time of that inauguration," said Dorothy Hunt.

"So they're sayin'," said LaRue.

"You know, the same things that could have lost an election can cripple a presidency."

The fearsome bluntness reminded him of Clarine Lander. Appalled, and a little thrilled, he had nothing to say for a moment.

"I'm looking at the little calendar I keep in my purse," said Mrs. Hunt. "I've circled December eighth on it."

LaRue still said nothing.

"It's an important day. I'll be making a trip to Chicago. A trip with its own special requirements."

"Special requirements," said LaRue.

"That's right. Ones you're going to supply, and which you'll be hearing about closer to the time. Meanwhile, let me remind you that there's a payment due a week from today."

LaRue acknowledged the last point and mentioned the figure. Mrs. Hunt snorted at the sum. "Do you ever talk to the president?" she asked.

"No, ma'am."

"Do you ever talk to those who do?"

"Yes, I suppose so." He hadn't had the heart to call Mitchell tonight, or the stomach to talk to Martha, who would likely have picked up.

"Well, tell those people to recall how Mr. Nixon not long ago relaxed some of the wage-and-price controls that he himself put on the economy."

"Yes, ma'am."

"Tell them that controls are about to be lifted altogether for several key employees."

LaRue hesitated, then said, "I've made a note of what you just told me."

"Tell them there's a reliable forecast of a surge in inflation. It should arrive in early December."

LaRue felt a rumble and then a roar beneath his feet. The whole floor was throbbing, and the pulsations were driving up through his legs. Richard Nixon had taken the stage in the Regency Ballroom, and Mrs. Hunt had hung up the phone.

Most of Mrs. Longworth's guests were Democrats, and a few of them groaned when Nixon concluded his brief victory speech on her black-and-white television. But such opposition didn't keep Joe Alsop from raising a glass to the triumph of his *"homme sérieux."*

"Joe," called Alice from her seat on the couch. "*You* remember 1916, don't you?"

"I was six years old," answered Alsop, "but if you're talking about election night 1916, yes, I do remember it."

"I was just telling Mrs. Braden how nothing compares to it—not '48, not 1960—and certainly not *this*." She pointed to the television, and signaled with a snap of her fingers for the live coverage to be extinguished. "We didn't really have an election *night* in 1916. It went on for *days*, while we all waited to see how California had turned out—just *clinging* to the hope that Professor Wilson had been knocked back to Princeton from Pennsylvania Avenue."

A street fiddler from Dupont Circle, whom Alice knew from her errands in the neighborhood, had been asked to provide the evening's entertainment. He now struck up a plaintive Scottish air while her granddaughter's friends, off in a corner, did some marijuana-fueled imitations of Nixon's tormented body language. The whole second floor sported only one red-white-and-blue decoration, an old piece of bunting hung from the jaws of the decaying tiger.

Alice felt glad that Dick had won so big. But along with regrets about the lack of suspense, she was experiencing a keen awareness that Joe had been right at the beginning of the summer, and that Richard Nixon's troubles were just getting started.

"Charles Evans Hughes was the only Supreme Court justice ever to run for president," Joe was now informing Joan Braden, with a touch of condescension.

"Perhaps the next Democrat to become president can give the chief justice's job to McGovern," Alice mused. "He can do a little 'legislating from the bench,' and we'll get amnesty, acid, and abortion after all."

As she spoke, she kept an eye on Stew, who really did look like death.

Lyndon Johnson's elder daughter now approached, with her good-looking young husband. What *is* his name, wondered Alice, who had even been to their wedding. She accepted a box of chocolates from Lynda Bird, her favorites from a specialty shop over in Alexandria. So delighted was she by the gift that she neglected to say thanks before rising from the couch to put a note on the box—*DON'T LET ANYONE ELSE EAT THESE.* She sent it down the dumbwaiter to Janie in the kitchen.

On her way back to the couch, she saw Bob Taft, the grandson of her father's fat protégé-turned-nemesis, now himself a senator from Ohio, chatting with Strom Thurmond's beauty-queen bride. Thurgood Marshall, eager not to be drawn into that conversation, greeted Alice instead, taking her hand and admiring her Spiro Agnew watch, which had the vice president dressed up like Mickey Mouse and telling the time with little gloved hands. "I told Dick," she explained, tapping Agnew's image, "'*promise* me you'll always have this one travel on the same plane with you, in case there's an accident.'"

When Rose Woods arrived, she was offered the most watery cocktail she'd ever tasted. A lot of the crowd here wasn't really her cup of tea, she soon realized, and the room was too small for dancing. Ever eager to get out on the floor, she wondered if she shouldn't have stayed at the Shoreham instead—though the hot ticket over there was the party in Agnew's suite, and she hadn't been invited.

She said hello to her hostess. "You'll be seeing the president and Pat next month?" she asked, helping the old lady resettle herself on the couch.

"Yes," said Alice, looking up with a suddenly businesslike stare. Rose wanted to ask about the letter to the boss that she'd opened last month, and Mrs. L. was sly enough to see this.

"Kim!" cried Alice. "My nephew," she explained to Rose, as Kermit Roosevelt, Jr., thin and balding and in his fifties, wearing old-fashioned tortoiseshell glasses, approached the couch and introduced himself to Richard Nixon's secretary.

"Please give the president my congratulations," he added.

"I know he'll be glad to get them," said Rose. "I'm sure you must know him yourself."

"I've *met* him, yes," said Roosevelt, in an accent just like Joe Alsop's. "But *know* him? Not really."

"I'll tell you which White House man Kim *does* know," said Alice. "Or I should say *former* White House man. That's your Mr. Hunt."

"Alice, for Christ's sake," said Alsop, who'd been listening to this.

Kermit Roosevelt looked around the room, as if to decide whether he was among friends, and cautiously explained his aunt's remark to Miss Woods: "I met Mr. Hunt in Cairo some years ago when we both worked for the same outfit. I learned some very interesting things about him as we tried getting Mr. Nasser to help out poor old King Zog of Albania. It's rather a long story." He said this as if speaking of somebody's complicated business reverses, giving assurances he wouldn't bore you with the details.

Rose remained all ears, but Joe Alsop was trying to nudge his relative out of this conversation, asking Kermit Roosevelt if he wouldn't enjoy saying hello to Stew over there near the television. On top of that, a new guest had just entered the room. Alice rose from the couch yet again. "Play something Asiatic," she said to the fiddler, as Bob McNamara came over to greet her.

The Secret Service logs would note that the president had spent twenty-four minutes inside the Shoreham. His real victory celebration took place afterwards, between one and three a.m., in the company of Bob Haldeman and Chuck Colson, inside his hideaway office at the EOB.

Nixon and Colson drank cocktails, while Haldeman sipped a Christian Scientist's Coca-Cola. Together the three men pored over some wire-service returns from Illinois, usually a cliff-hanging state for Nixon but tonight not even close. "*Everything* played well in Peoria," said Haldeman, meaning the whole tumultuous past four years.

Nixon sorted through congratulatory messages and returned phone calls from Rockefeller and Frank Rizzo, Philadelphia's tough-cop mayor, who made Agnew look like Elliot Richardson, according to Ehrlichman. When Haldeman reminded them of this line, Nixon asked, "Was Richardson on the platform at the hotel?"

"Didn't see him," said Colson.

"Probably at some goddamned private party in Georgetown," the president groused.

"Rocky and Rizzo," said Colson, marveling at the combination. "Like Scylla and Charybdis."

Haldeman and the president did not respond to the allusion. Colson himself, who only half-knew what the phrase meant, realized he'd picked it up from Hunt.

"I have Senator Humphrey," the White House operator said to Nixon. Why, he wondered, had he bothered to return Hubert's call at 1:30 a.m.? From genuine affection? To rub it in? To enjoy the contrast between tonight and four years ago? Actually, he felt far too sharply that the squeaker of '68 had it all over tonight's landslide.

Humphrey burbled some congratulations upon his former foe's historic victory. Nixon reminded him that he, too, could still make it to the presidency—look how old Churchill had been—and felt a curious envy as he said it.

The bacon and eggs ordered from the White House kitchen at last arrived, on a cart wheeled in by the normally early-to-bed Manolo Sanchez. This gesture from his personal valet touched Nixon more than anything had tonight. In fact, the only way to banish an audible catch in his voice was to start in again on candyassed Richardson. "Can you believe that guy?" he asked Colson.

The call he really wanted to make—and needed to be alone for—was the one to Mitchell. He'd put it off until tomorrow, by which time he might convince himself that his old partner really wanted to hear from him. Meanwhile he flipped through the sheaf of phone messages once again: no, nothing from John.

"Well, there's no pretending the House results are anything but lousy," said the president. "You watch what they write tomorrow. 'Big landslide, no coattails.'"

"Which means," said Haldeman, "that the next four years aren't going to be much easier than the past four."

Nixon nodded, still wondering why he seemed determined to feel so bad. His mind went once more to Woodrow Wilson, who'd never gotten over feeling like a fraud, even when he was being cheered in the streets of Paris. He looked down at the plate of eggs and felt his appetite waning. Dr. Tkach had been telling him there might actually be something to this research linking heart attacks and high cholesterol. Christ, imagine keeling over like Eisenhower, with goddamned Agnew waiting to take over.

By three o'clock the president had returned to the residence to listen to his old LP of *Victory at Sea*, just the way he'd done four years ago at this hour. For a moment, he felt his spirits rally and his energy surge, as if he were pulling far ahead of the convoy of smaller boats that had helped get him here. As the music rose and he closed his eyes, he decided that, yes, tomorrow morning he would tell every last one of them—from Chapin to Ehrlichman to Rogers—that he wanted their resignations.

Chapter Fifteen

NOVEMBER 20, 1972, 12:10 P.M.
CAMP DAVID, MARYLAND

"Dick, don't you remember the Checkers speech, the stoning in South America, your defeats in 1960 and 1962? I was the only one who didn't turn her back on you. Doesn't that count for something?"

"It does, Pat . . . I assure you we will take a close look at your record before we make any definite decision."

Reading the *Post* was usually a grim job, but today Pat Nixon laughed out loud over Art Buchwald's column.

A lot of the serious commentators had found the president's post-election request for everybody's resignation absurd, since staff turnover would probably end up being about the same as in most second terms. Still, the chance of having one's letter of resignation accepted was real enough to have created, these past two weeks, a peculiar atmosphere at the top of the administration, an air made stranger by the feeling that the president had somehow himself resigned. Almost all his meetings were taking place in Key Biscayne or at Camp David; his absences from the White House seemed to contradict the determination with which he had fought to extend his lease on the address.

Pat was delighted to be away from the Mansion, and especially to be at Camp David, where everything, not just reading the *Post*, seemed easier. She'd once, during the vice-presidential years, spotted a black rat snake on the grounds, but on most trips she was untroubled by so much as a mosquito or a fly. She had all of today to herself, and sitting before the mirror, getting ready for a solitary lunchtime hike along the mountain trails, she decided to forgo even her usual splash of Arpège, so that nothing would interfere with the crisp piney scents she was looking forward to.

Instead of reaching for the atomizer, she opened a drawer and took out a pair of scissors. Buchwald didn't run in any of the New York papers, did he? Not in the *Times*, she felt sure. So she clipped the column and put it into a plain envelope, which she addressed herself, feeling a small silly thrill as she wrote Tom's old apartment number. That was it: no note, and certainly no return address. But he would recognize the handwriting on the envelope, and he would laugh.

This was the only time she would let herself do something like this.

To this day she kept a book of stamps in her purse—a housewifely habit that Rose teased her about. Eisenhower's eight-cent face seemed slightly accusing as she brought him to her lips; FDR, who had gone away with the six-cent denomination last year, might have smiled, she thought, with a certain conspiratorial mischief.

She gave the envelope to a navy steward as soon as she stepped out of Aspen Lodge to begin her walk. Steam rose off the heated pool that had been built above the bomb shelter, but the thin plumes looked more soothing than sinister. Looking over to Laurel Lodge, she could see Bob Haldeman and Elliot Richardson standing on the porch, waiting to lunch with Dick. They both waved to her as she set off.

Nixon was finishing up with Ehrlichman and UN ambassador George Bush, telling the latter that he would be replacing Bob Dole as head of the Republican National Committee. Within the administration Bush and Richardson were often viewed as a set of twins: Ivy League scions; young war heroes; good heads of slicked-down hair. But Bush was too gosh-oh-golly and eager-to-please, an overage version of the Magruder crowd, and that's why he was being kept in sales positions—the UN, the National Committee—rather than moved to the more substantial ones that kept coming his twin's way.

Richardson would not have minded another year at HEW, where his administrative reforms had begun to rouse the agency from its paraplegia. But he could hardly say no to the Pentagon, and only ten minutes ago Haldeman had told him that's what he was getting. Of the two top prizes, he would actually have preferred State, which he supposed would go to Connally once they finally dislodged Rogers. But Defense did have a nice counterintuitive aspect; it wasn't what people would be expecting for him.

He hoped there might be a Bloody Mary with lunch, something to warm him halfway back up to the internal temperature he'd enjoyed during five postelection days of swimming and rum in the Virgin Islands. At the moment, outside Laurel Lodge, he was having to blow on his hands to keep off the chill.

Haldeman spoke for the first time since offering him the job on the walk over here. "He probably forgot to thank you for the bird picture. But I know he liked it."

"Ah, good," replied Richardson, who suspected the watercolor had already been dispatched to the presidential gifts department at the Archives, or to one of the bathrooms at San Clemente.

The two men were at last ushered into Laurel, where Nixon, in a sport coat, greeted Richardson with a smile but no handshake. "You know, Rose is a Catholic," he said, pointing toward the Dogwood cabin, where his secretary usually stayed, "and she tells me we ought to get a little machine for the roof here, something that would send up a puff of white smoke, like they do for a new pope, whenever one of you fellows takes one of the big jobs."

Pleased by the mild laughter he got in response, the president added, "We ought to tell that to Balzano, Colson's liaison to the 'ethnics.' The Catholics would love it. They're with us now, and we're going to keep them." He paused. "So, have we got ourselves a new secretary of defense?"

The question was directed more to Haldeman than Richardson.

"Yes, we do," answered the chief of staff.

"Good," said Nixon, without much enthusiasm.

The steward brought in lunch; Richardson noticed only coffee and water on the trolley.

"I'm greatly honored, sir," he told the president.

"I want to hold the announcement—and I mean it, no leaks—for about a week. Maybe by then we'll finally get the damned peace settlement wrapped up. When we present you to the press, I'd like their questions to be about what comes *after* Vietnam, instead of all about whether Congress is going to cut off funds for the goddamned war." He continued musing: "The press are always trapped in the past. Like their asking Ziegler if all the personnel shake-ups have anything to do with

Watergate. I mean, for Christ's sake. The only way we're going to get hold of and squeeze the career bureaucracy—which is ninety percent Democrats, in every department—is to reorganize the whole political layer on top of it. Things are no different at the Pentagon. Christ, Elliot, some of these generals have more screwed-up ideas than your sociologists over at HEW. I'm counting on you to cut their budgets without losing the Joint Chiefs' support for SALT."

"I'll do my best," said Richardson, before biting into his tuna sandwich. "I've bested the brass once before," he added, with a self-deprecating laugh. "The only way I could make it into the army was by memorizing the eye chart."

Nixon didn't want to hear about Richardson's Normandy heroics or Bronze Star. He moved quickly to politics. "Well, you'll be running the armed forces of the Free World while Agnew handles the bicentennial festivities." He laughed, to underline how favorably he was positioning Richardson against the vice president for 1976.

Haldeman did not smile, and Richardson could tell what his expression was trying to convey to the president: *The sale has already been made; he's taken the job; why give him these illusions of special favor when you don't need to?*

But Nixon continued to talk, as if trying to make Richardson, never an insider, feel part of things. "I had a difficult meeting with Rogers a few days ago," he said. "It's going to be harder to change things over there than anywhere else—though our biggest headache at the moment is your friend Kissinger. Jesus Christ, the credit-grabbing. Did you see the interview he gave to that Italian gal?"

Richardson smiled and nodded.

"Anything you can do about that?" asked Nixon.

The president knew that Kissinger would be pleased by Richardson's shift to the Pentagon. The two men had gotten along fine when Richardson spent the first sixteen months of the administration as an undersecretary at State, the man Henry preferred dealing with to Rogers. "Kissinger needs to understand," Nixon went on, "that the whole operation looks weak unless the man at the top gets the praise for what's going right. I don't say this out of any personal ego at all, and I'm not the slightest bit thin-skinned, as you know. The fact is, Henry hasn't got a lot to brag about right now, not if he can't bring Thieu around. Haig is back over in Paris—maybe *he* can get Henry focused. But I'll tell you one thing in complete frankness. I'm hours away from cabling him and threatening the North Vietnamese with a resumption of military action. And if I do it, they won't just get bombed back to the Stone Age, to quote our old friend LeMay. They'll get bombed off the face of the goddamned Earth. I have had it with every bit of their delays and chickenshit."

Richardson tried somehow to indicate and to hide, all at once, that he was aghast. He wanted Nixon to see he thought this a terrible idea, both morally and politically—they'd just won a landslide by declaring that peace was at hand—but he also wished Nixon to see him subordinating his own feelings for the good of the team in a manful, disciplined way. He would not be a dissenting prima donna, and he would not pee all over the carpet with enthusiastic assent, the way Bush would.

He nodded again, silently recalling how Kissinger had remarked to him on the pointless butchery of the president's call for mass resignations. He decided he would change the subject.

"I saw Mrs. Nixon before coming in. She looks wonderful."

Nixon's smile clicked into place. "I'm hoping they'll make her grand marshal of the Rose Parade this year. Did you tell Ehrlichman to get on that?" he asked Haldeman.

Richardson allowed himself to doodle while the president went on to talk about Pasadena and USC football. Glancing occasionally at Haldeman, Richardson wondered whether the chief of staff himself might not, perhaps by choice, be on the way out. There had been speculation, of a decidedly guarded kind.

The conversation meandered for ten or fifteen minutes more, until Haldeman mentioned that George Shultz would soon be coming in. Richardson took his cue to start back to the helipad, where he would be lifted away from Camp David just as he'd descended on it, without having to go through the gate and be spotted by reporters at the end of the one road leading in and out of the compound.

"I need to phone Colson," said the president, once he and Haldeman were alone.

"Let me make the call," said the chief of staff. "Before you get into anything else with him, I'd like him to play you a tape he made of a call he had, about a week ago, from Howard Hunt. Dean played a copy of it for me and Ehrlichman up here the other day."

"You want me to listen to it?" asked Nixon.

"Yeah. You'll hear Colson making a taped record of his own noninvolvement with Watergate—it's quite a performance. He *gave* Dean a Dictabelt of it. He's very pleased with himself. But I'd like you to really pay attention to what *Hunt* says."

Haldeman dialed the White House and had Colson play the Dictabelt. It was soon audible over the speakerphone in Laurel Lodge.

On the tape, amidst expressions of sympathy toward Hunt, Colson could be heard asking for the continuation of his own blameless ignorance: "*I don't want to get in the position of knowing something that I don't now know for the reason that I want to be perfectly free to help you . . . people around here know I didn't have anything to do with it.*"

Hunt, for all his apparent friendliness ("*congratulations on your victory*"), made several sharp points: "*There's a great deal of financial expense here that is not being covered. What we've been getting has been coming in minor dribs and drabs . . . this thing must not break apart for foolish reasons . . . we're protecting the guys who were really responsible. Now that's of course a continuing requirement, but at the same time, this is a two-way street . . . surely the cheapest commodity available is money.*"

Once the Dictabelt finished ("*Give my love to Dorothy, will you, Howard?*"), Haldeman told Colson that the president would call him back in a few minutes.

Nixon had been entertained by Colson's caginess, the way he'd betrayed discomfort only when Hunt observed that Mitchell might already have lied to investigators. What the president mostly seemed to hear were Colson's reassurances that everything would turn out fine, along with Hunt's agreement that the president's reelection was cause for thanking God.

Haldeman, on the other hand, had been worried by the tape as soon as he first listened to it. Money was hardly the cheapest commodity, whatever Hunt might say: after he and Ehrlichman had heard the recording, they'd sent Dean to New York to get Mitchell to raise more cash.

The possibility that all of this could go on for years, whether the burglars were found guilty or not, seemed to strike Nixon as just one more element of the approaching second term, a matter perhaps requiring some reorganization, but nothing one should expect to see disappear, any more than the State Department and Pentagon might themselves vanish.

"I waited to have Colson play this for you until a day when you'd be having meetings here in Laurel," explained Haldeman. "Because Aspen, you may remember, has been wired same as the White House since May. I didn't want a tape recorder over there to pick up your listening to Colson's tape."

Nixon nodded and paced a little before saying anything. "You know what those tapes are going to show years from now?"

Haldeman waited for the president to answer his own question.

"That I ran the goddamned show when it came to Russia and China and, for that matter, Vietnam. Not Henry."

"Yes, but—," said Haldeman.

"You know, we need to have the navy guys get this lodge wired, too."

Chapter Sixteen

DECEMBER 8, 1972, 12:05 P.M.
NATIONAL AIRPORT, WASHINGTON, D.C.

"Sweetheart, I still don't have an ending," confessed Howard Hunt, as he turned into the airport parking lot. "Which is more of a problem than it otherwise might be, given that the novel is called *The Berlin Ending*."

"Let the bad guys win," advised Dorothy, while she tightened one of her earrings.

"The bad guys aren't *supposed* to win in this genre."

That, of course, was what he wrote now, what the publishing trade called "genre fiction," cartoon versions of the serious stuff he used to write in the days of his Guggenheim Fellowship. Somehow, at some point, if he survived legally and financially, he would get back to being an honest-to-God literary man.

"Well," said Dorothy, as her husband searched for a parking space, "try bringing a little verisimilitude to that genre." She checked her lipstick in the mirror of her compact. "In fact, Papa, when I get home, if I flip to the last pages and see the good guy getting the girl and saving the Free World, I won't type the rest of the manuscript."

Hunt laughed, but his mind was even more troubled than it had been in June. A month had now passed since he'd heard Colson covering his ass during their postelection phone call, making him realize that the White House wanted to wash its hands of him and Bernie and the rest of the boys. Ever since, try as he might to focus on next month's trial, his thoughts had been as circular and blocked as his literary labors.

As he continued to look for a parking space, Dorothy opened her purse and playfully fanned a packet of hundred-dollar bills that she extracted. The ten grand here came not from "Mr. Rivers" but their own savings, and when she got to Chicago she would give it to her cousin's husband. Hal Carlstead had promised that in exchange for this stake

Howard would derive good income from a Holiday Inn near the city. Moreover, once the trial finished, the whole family could regroup in the Midwest and Howard could go to work for Hal, who'd told him, "Heck, Holiday Inn gave *John Glenn* a new start when he came back down to Earth."

But Dorothy well knew that ten thousand dollars wouldn't take care of the mortgage or her daughter's medical bills, or even payments on the Pontiac. The White House would have to cover all that.

And in a few minutes she would know whether or not they had. If the news was good, she would keep it from Howard for a few days, until she could get back from Chicago and enjoy the surprise on his face.

She put the ten thousand dollars back into her purse and took out her plane ticket.

"Milady," said Howard, noticing its first-class stamp.

Dorothy laughed. "Papa, you said I could, just this once." The first-class fare had been only thirty dollars more than coach. "And when I'm back, you're going to take me to the Potomack for popovers and Bloody Marys."

Hunt smiled, guiltily. He ought to be making this trip himself, but the terms of his bail wouldn't allow him to travel that far out of Washington. The other day Dorothy had asked him to appeal to the court for permission to take the family to Key West for Christmas, and he'd had to tell her that Sirica would never consent, particularly if it looked like he was trying to consort with Bernie down there. Besides, he'd added, they couldn't afford it. To which Dorothy had oddly, serenely, replied, "I think you'll find that we can."

Hunt at last found a space near the aging white terminal. His wife kissed him goodbye and said, "Remember, no happy endings."

"All right," he replied.

LaRue sat in a chair across from the Eastern Shuttle counter, reading the paper and waiting for his rendezvous. Watergate had lately been absent from the *Post,* but the paper was beginning to fill up with the administration's darker, related secrets, some of which LaRue had found out from Liddy a few days after the break-in. A White House secretary, he now read, was admitting the existence of the leak-plugging "Plumbers."

Its most important member may have been the writer, whose wife LaRue was supposed to meet, for the first time, ten minutes from now.

The only good news to reach him this week had come from East-land, who'd confided that Mike Mansfield, the majority leader, wanted Sam Ervin heading whatever committee the Senate Democrats formed to investigate the break-in. An old, unenergetic southerner who lacked any particular animus toward Nixon, Ervin smiled upon the conserva-tive judicial appointments LaRue had been shepherding up to the Hill through Eastland. He wouldn't dig too deep.

Sitting in the row of fake leather chairs, LaRue watched a plane take off. He would be happy to stay here all day, just puffing his pipe and gazing. Only the tight grip he kept on a Hecht's shopping bag gave away his lack of calm. Inside the bag was a single envelope filled with two hundred and eighty thousand dollars, a pile of White House cash in nontraceable, nonsequential bills that Haldeman's boy Gor-don Strachan had cobbled together and delivered to LaRue's Water-gate apartment about ten days ago. LaRue had taken care to wear rubber gloves when receiving the money and when packing it up this morning.

Lord knew where they'd be able to get any more. Even the flushest contributors now wanted to know why a White House that had just won a landslide reelection, thanks to a campaign operation that had fin-ished up well in the black, needed more of their money. LaRue had been scouring his brain for the names of people who might not ask too many questions. There was Tom Pappas up in Boston, but—Christ, LaRue had hoped to be doing oil business with Tom before too long, not dragging him into this briar patch.

He wanted out, the way Kalmbach had wanted out back in Septem-ber. Just the other day Dean, who never seemed the worse for wear, had told him he looked like a zombie. But he would not leave Mitchell in the lurch.

And there she was, the writer's wife, entering his peripheral vision five minutes ahead of schedule, and most definitely looking like she was not to be denied. Her phone calls—made, LaRue felt pretty sure, without the writer's knowledge—had put fear into them all, and his first actual sighting of her confirmed Tony Ulasewicz's assessment of her good looks: dark skin; high, sort-of Indian cheekbones; a coat that matched her dress; and the exact, identifying hat she'd promised to be wearing. Everything together suggested an older, more pained version of Clarine Lander.

LaRue nodded, and she nodded back. He stood up and walked to a spot that would be out of anyone's earshot. She followed him.

"Miz Hunt," he said, once they got there.

"The 'friend of Mr. Rivers,' I presume," she replied.

" 'The writer's wife,' I take it," he added, with a little bow, trying to lighten the mood. But she wouldn't crack a smile or feed him another line. So he said, "You're early," hoping it came out as a compliment and not a scolding.

"My husband drives fast," she replied, evenly.

LaRue pulled a big yellow envelope from the Hecht's bag and unwound the string on its clasp. He opened it wide enough so that Mrs. Hunt could see the top stack of rubber-banded bills it contained. "Two hundred and eighty thousand dollars," he said.

"That's not a Missouri bankroll?" she asked.

"I'm not familiar with the term."

"How do I know there's not just a bunch of newspaper under that one layer of bills?"

"I've stuck to the deal we made," he assured her.

"Yes, the deal we've made—for now." She took the envelope.

"For now," he agreed, thinking of all that lay ahead, and sighing.

Mrs. Hunt held the envelope and gestured with it toward a row of lockers. The sign above them said 24 HOURS/75 CENTS. "I'm afraid I don't have any change. Would you mind?"

LaRue replied with a look of astonishment.

"I'll be back soon enough," she explained. "And I'd rather not be carrying this around Chicago for three days."

Without protest, LaRue rented a locker from the man at the counter and took the receipt for $2.25. He wondered why Dorothy had this need to keep him off balance. Did exhibit have the same need with the writer himself? She could, after all, have told her husband to wait in the car for this package—but only if she'd told him in the first place that she was about to pick up all this cash.

LaRue helped her put the whole Hecht's bag, with the envelope, into the locker. The two of them looked like a couple trying to lighten their load before a day of sightseeing in the nation's capital. For good measure, Mrs. Hunt removed a jade brooch from her dress and put it in the bag with the money. "I've got enough jewelry on without this, I think."

LaRue noted the locker number—J20—and stored it in his head; who knew what game she was playing and whether he might need it? He handed her the little key, which she put inside a large cameo-covered locket she was wearing. Then both of them walked off toward the boarding gate for United Airlines Flight 553.

They proceeded with no sound but the click of her high heels, until LaRue, whose life had been transformed by insurance, pointed to the kiosk where it was sold. "Five dollars?" he asked. "For two hundred and fifty thousand dollars' worth of coverage?" He put the question to her with a grin that tried to combine hucksterism and black humor—anything that might make their encounter feel the least bit friendly.

"If the plane crashes," she replied, without any smile, "I'll still be thirty grand behind."

LaRue gave up and turned his gaze toward the ground as they resumed walking to the gate. After a few more steps, however, she stopped, and with the smallest hint of a thaw said, "You're right. It's only good sense." She opened her purse and took out her wallet, without letting him see her own ten-thousand-dollar stack of bills. She nodded goodbye and made her way back to the insurance kiosk, on her own.

Sixty other people were flying to Chicago with Dorothy, and from her seat in first class she noticed a couple of them reading about Howard and the Plumbers in this morning's *Washington Post*. Forgoing any conversation with her seatmate, she fiddled with her diamond solitaire, which had come from Howard's mother, and which she'd worn through all the years of their marriage. Today she was also sporting a charm bracelet, with little dangling boys' and girls' heads, one for each of her children, as well as a few carved nuggets representing some of Howard's old postings: Mount Fuji for their days in Japan; the Fountain of the Athletes in

Montevideo for their too-brief time in Uruguay. Would there soon be a charm for the Windy City?

She completed a tactile inventory of her jewelry by fingering the big cameo locket hiding the key. She thought of the money that would be waiting for her back in Washington along with the little jade brooch she'd left behind. She had already decided how to divide it up, and she would not tell Howard the figures. The Hunts would keep one hundred and eighty thousand dollars for themselves; they had risked and lost more than anyone else, and if any of the Cubans, even Bernie and Clarita, complained—*tough*. Getting this money had been Dorothy's doing, and its distribution would be her decision. She had been managing things for months and might have to manage them for years beyond the trial.

Ever since talking to Colson, her husband had worried about being followed. Chuck had suggested as much over the phone, and after their conversation Howard had begun to assume that anyone he saw lurking was a low-level agent from Langley and not just some reporter from the *Post*. His old employer, he now felt sure, was keeping tabs on him. For all she knew, he was right; the possibility had started her worrying about McCord, Liddy's choice to perform the wiretapping, another retired CIA man whose scattershot résumé, a series of implausible covers, gave Dorothy the creeps. His whole manner never added up— part preacher, part village idiot, part eccentric professor.

The plane was coming in through a peculiar mid-afternoon fog. Dorothy checked her watch, already set to central time, and saw that it was 2:26 p.m.; outside the window it looked more like night. She searched for lights and shapes below, hoping to feel a tug from them, a sensation that she was being drawn in by her new home. She twisted the diamond ring and reviewed her resolves: she would make the deal with her cousin's husband; she and Howard would get past the trial; with the money in the locker they would get past the bills. And compensation from the White House—"compensation" was exactly the right word—wouldn't stop even then.

All summer she'd assumed that Howard's leverage would end with Nixon's reelection. But as November approached she had realized the timidity of her reasoning. Nixon might be done with the voters, but not necessarily with the courts, or even Congress. Her few moments of conversation with LaRue on election night—*I've made a note of what you just told me*—had convinced her that she was right to start thinking bigger. She had been able to sense the power she held from the nervousness in his voice at the other end of the phone line.

She closed her eyes now and rested her head against the back of the seat, enjoying the descent toward a new world and life, where she and her husband would be secretly rewarded for all the dangers they'd endured these past twenty years. Dealing with Mr. Rivers and LaRue might be an odd way to collect at last, but collect she would. As the plane drew closer to its destination, she felt almost as she had on that morning more than twenty years ago when she and Howard, laughing in their white convertible, pulled away for the last time from that awful Mexican apartment over the whorehouse.

Now, finally, they were above the airport, and getting close to the ground. She could see a nearby schoolyard full of children and had time to wonder how the teachers got anything done with what must be the constant jet noise. But the question was driven from her mind by a more urgent one: *Where was the runway?* The plane made a sudden, sickening turn, as if the pilot were afraid of the schoolchildren and needed to flee them. Seconds later it was over the rooftops of some houses, barely clearing them in its last moments of flight. In her own last seconds of consciousness—amidst an explosion of blue and orange flames that fused her locket forever shut—Dorothy realized that she was in someone's living room.

At first LaRue thought it was film of a riot: the noise and the Chicago Fire Department hoses brought '68 to mind. But then the TV announcer explained that this had been United Airlines Flight 553.

There was no mention of Mrs. Howard Hunt, only of a Negro congressman who had also been on the plane.

As it sank in, nausea and dread took possession of LaRue, as if he might be listening to the description of an "accident" that was really something else. He looked toward the telephone, certain that Mitchell or Magruder or Dean would now call him. But they didn't, and as he continued staring at the silent phone, amidst the noise of the early-evening news, the smell of his pipe began to sicken him. He took it out of his mouth and whacked its contents into an ashtray, then put his head between his knees, as if he were getting airsick on a plane that was still aloft. His mind went to all the things he didn't fully know or understand: to Liddy, to the CIA, to whatever dark sludge the Plumbers may have been working to keep inside the administration's pipes.

He got himself a glass of water, then poured it down the drain without taking a sip. The sight of a bourbon bottle on the kitchen counter made him vomit into the sink. With enormous effort he picked up his keys, shut off the television, and went down to the garage.

Planes coming into National flew so low over the Watergate that the huge, swirling complex might as well be those little houses in Chicago. He never really got used to it, and now, as he made the five-minute drive to the airport, the noise of the low-flying jets pulled him out of his skin. Once at National, he sat in the parking lot for ten minutes, composing himself, watching the news crews and their vans, there to film the family members of passengers who'd been on United 553. LaRue himself could spot them running into the terminal to demand any available seat to Chicago.

At last he got out of the car and entered the building, trying to look calm as he approached the locker-rentals counter. He told the attendant that he was Harry Johnson and that this morning he'd put his things in J20; he remembered the number because he'd gotten married to his wife, Joanne, twenty years ago this month. And he was damned if he hadn't gone and lost the key sometime later in the day.

While he spun this tale, he thanked God that he had been the one to pay for the locker and to get a receipt; he just prayed that the alias he was remembering had been what he'd actually used this morning.

The attendant didn't even bother checking one slip of paper against the other. He just reached up to the pegboard and took down a duplicate key to number J20. "Happens all the time," he said.

LaRue retrieved Dorothy Hunt's jade brooch and the two hundred and eighty thousand dollars—"one helluva lot of cabbage," Tony Ulasewicz would have said. He then exited one door of the terminal, while Howard Hunt, his face as white as his raincoat, entered through another.

Chapter Seventeen

DECEMBER 18, 1972, 6:10 P.M.
WEST WING, THE WHITE HOUSE

Rose Woods revised the invitation list for the last of the holiday parties, a New Year's week reception. She decided to add a few names from far down the staff roster of the National Security Council. It might be their final shot at a White House shindig, since rumors of Kissinger's resignation were swirling. Six days ago the peace talks had collapsed, and Henry had come home empty-handed to a president who told him to stop being brilliant and start being effective. Rose had heard the remark with her own ears.

Along with the invitations, she had on her desk, courtesy of Dwight Chapin, a memo titled "Four Truman Death Hypotheticals": scheduling scenarios for each of the next several weeks, during any of which Harry Truman might die. It was the fashion for everyone to admire Truman now—there were people here in the White House who saw the same toughness and tenacity in both him and Richard Nixon—but to Rose the foul-mouthed thirty-third president remained a nasty character, the same breed of cat as Helen Gahagan Douglas and Stevenson and all the rest.

Six weeks after the election, a damper had fallen over the White House, and nobody seemed able to remove it. The president, when he was around at all, couldn't keep from limping, though he made an agonized effort to hide this from reporters. The doctors had concluded that the problem wasn't his old phlebitis but a bone in his foot that he'd splintered months ago during a spill at Camp David—where he continued to spend most of his time. Having lost any remaining patience with the enemy, the president had yesterday—high time, too, thought Rose—begun carpet-bombing North Vietnam. Within hours everyone in the Mansion and EOB had started hearing the loud, slow thump of a bass drum in Lafayette Park, somebody's idea of a protest against the assault, performed by a steady relay of long-haired demonstrators. It was beyond Rose's comprehension how they remained immune to arrest. Her own nerves had started to shred, and she knew that Pat would never be able to sleep with it going on.

Rose felt relieved not to be working on the inaugural. Magruder was in charge of it, and the whole operation had moved out to Fort McNair. In fact, she'd seen Mr. Junior Executive only once since the election, when he'd breezed through the West Wing, tan as a coconut from ten days in the Bahamas, telling everybody about the two hundred thousand "honorary invitations"—whatever the hell *that* meant—his committee was sending out.

As she went about keeping the Christmas-party list to a manageable number, Rose took a certain comfort in how even Magruder seemed infected by the current gloom. It now looked as if during the second term he might have to settle for running the bicentennial under Agnew, since all the undersecretary jobs he hankered for required Senate confirmation. Nobody was going to send Magruder's name—or Dean's, or Chapin's—up to the Hill for any of those positions, not when hearings would allow the Democrats to ask any Watergate question they liked.

All of a sudden HRH was darkening her door.

"Did you authorize flowers for Mrs. Hunt's funeral?"

"I did," Rose replied, stiffly.

"Why?"

"Because Howard Hunt had been a White House employee, that's why. It's what we do when there's a death in anyone's family."

Dorothy Hunt had been buried out in Potomac, not far from her house. The *Post* had tailed the funeral procession and reported in its smartass way that one of the vehicles carried a "Re-Elect the President" bumper sticker. And now here was Haldeman telling her that the paper had just followed up with a call about the White House's little floral tribute, which would probably get a snide mention in their next Watergate story.

"You should deviate from the usual procedures when there are special circumstances," said Haldeman.

"I thought the circumstances were *very* special in this instance. The man's wife burned up in a plane crash."

Haldeman turned and left her office. Rose went back to the invitation list, so angry she thought she might burst a blood vessel. The root cause of her feeling was not Mrs. Hunt's death but Don Carnevale's. He had passed away two weeks before, at the age of sixty-three, from a heart attack he suffered behind his desk at Harry Winston in New York. Had there been flowers or a word of sympathy for *her*? Only from Pat and the girls, a little bouquet delivered to her apartment, its card commemorating "Uncle Don," who'd overseen the design of Julie's and Tricia's wedding rings. According to the *Post*, Don had "remained a bachelor." The picture they ran with the obituary showed him dancing with "the president's secretary, Miss Rose Mary Woods," and Bob Haldeman had surely seen it. But not one daisy had appeared on her desk. Maybe HRH thought the "usual procedures" required her to order flowers for herself.

Rose closed her eyes and rubbed her temples and thought about how rotten the past few weeks had been. She wished that, instead of those bogus assassination warnings, Jeane Dixon had provided advance word of the actual calamities that had been in store; and yet, what good would knowing have done?

Then, all at once, at the sound of an old lady's voice, her eyelids sprang open. It was Mrs. Longworth, who had decided to saunter through the West Wing on her way to dinner in the Residence. "I thought I would check on how the place is looking!" she informed the Marine escorting her. "My father had it built, you know. Just like the Panama Canal."

There were twelve people at two tables, six around each. They'd put Alice between the president and Julie, and more or less across from Kissinger and Anne Armstrong, the wealthy Vassar-educated rancher's wife who was the president's newest advisor, with Cabinet rank. Admiral Moorer, chairman of the Joint Chiefs, had looked scared of Mrs. L when introduced to her during cocktails, and he'd been glad to find himself assigned to the other table, over which Mrs. Nixon presided.

As dessert started coming around, people shifted a little, and Pat squeezed an extra chair for herself between Dick and Mrs. L, who had been their first dinner guest in the Residence, along with J. Edgar Hoover, back in '69. The first lady smiled at the steward when he remembered to bring Alice tea with brown sugar instead of coffee.

"Well," said the president, "this is a lot more fun than the dinner we had for the Cabinet two nights ago!"

Pat tapped Alice's skeletal left arm and said, so that everyone could hear, "I'll bet Mrs. Armstrong wishes you'd been at that one, to give her a little feminine support."

From what Alice could see, Mrs. Armstrong didn't require any.

"Mrs. L," asked the president, "how long have you lived in Washington?"

"Seventy-one years and three months," she replied. "I keep waiting to see if I like it."

"Do you think you can convince Julie and David to stay? I'm trying to fix up something for her on the East Wing staff."

"*Daddy*," said the president's daughter.

"But then what would you do with Sugarfoot?" asked Alice, startling the table with her use of the Secret Service's code name for Tricia Nixon Cox. "Or is it *Mister* Sugarfoot you have plans for? Putting him on your legal team perhaps?"

Nixon could see that Mrs. L was revving up for some playful conversation about Watergate, so he decided to get out in front of her on the subject. "You know," he said, stealing a joke of Kissinger's, "if McGovern had given a few more speeches about the scandal, he would have made people *like* wiretapping."

The ensuing laughter included Kissinger's, and when it ended, Nixon added, quietly, "You'll see. We'll come out of this just fine, the way we did with the Hiss case."

"Yes," said Alice, "but you were the *investigator* on that one."

Nixon pretended to laugh. "It'll end in victory is all I meant." He then made a sharp change of subject. "We're having all the inaugural balls inside government buildings next month, Mrs. L. No hotels, except for the kids' thing at the Sheraton Park. It'll be a lot cheaper and we can entertain a lot more people. I just hope it can hold a candle to 1905." He flashed her what he hoped looked like a flattering smile.

"The only inaugural ball of my father's that I can remember is the impromptu one my brothers and I had when McKinley was shot and killed. We danced a jig upon realizing that we, and, incidentally, Father, were now going to the White House."

Pat burst out laughing. Mrs. Armstrong shook her head and pretended to be scandalized. "Children," she said.

Alice quickly corrected her: "The others were children. I was seventeen. My pleasure was quite adult." She looked around for a moment and realized that they were dining in what had once been her bedroom.

The president returned to the subject of his inauguration. "The parade's going to be shorter. We're going to tighten the distance between the bands and floats." Everyone except Alice nodded politely. She was stupefyingly bored and remained so until a sound penetrated the silence at the table and made her break into a huge grin. "I *hear* it!" she cried. "They mentioned it on the television!" As the others watched, she started tapping the tablecloth with her knife, matching the drumbeat from Lafayette Park.

Pat looked down into her coffee cup. The current atmosphere, unexpectedly, was beginning to resemble the spring of '70, when that ring of empty buses had seemed all there was to protect them here. The military's prediction of heavy plane losses over North Vietnam was proving true. If the bombing operation kept going, there would soon be, along with all the cries about civilian casualties, accusations that Dick was only adding to the number of POWs rather than forcing the release of those already held. Even so, he'd told her he was prepared to have them fly five thousand sorties if that's what it took to break the North Vietnamese once and for all.

"Haig is over in Saigon, pressuring Thieu," he said now, trying to remind everyone that he had to deal with the South's intransigence as well as the North's. He looked straight at Alice, hoping she would stop the business with her knife. He ignored Kissinger, though his remark seemed to imply that Henry ought to be in Vietnam with his deputy, doing the heavy lifting instead of sitting here stuffing his face with Christmas cookies. Nixon's reflexes were urging him toward a joke about Hanukkah, but Mrs. Longworth spoke before he could make it.

"You are *not* to worry," she said, "about all the noise down the street." After observing a general perplexity, she clarified her pronouncement. "Not *across* the street. Not the drum. *Down* the street: the Congress, at the other end of Pennsylvania Avenue."

Honestly, she sometimes felt as if she were talking to a fish tank.

"They're already yelling their heads off," Nixon acknowledged. "But I'm *not* worried about them. I've got worse problems even closer to home." He finally looked at Kissinger, whose phone calls to and from the press he'd been monitoring ever since the Italian interview. The president laughed. "Henry says it may not be so bad if the North Vietnamese think I'm crazy. What do *you* all think?"

Alice brightened considerably, as if a parlor game had just begun. "Are we talking about your actual craziness or their perception of it?"

"I don't care if that's what they believe," said Nixon, with a measure of the same delight in mental gymnastics. "And I especially don't care if the Russians and Chinese think it. Let 'em. They can push the North Vietnamese into a settlement before they *all* have a wider war on their hands."

Kissinger retreated into conversation with Mrs. Armstrong and Julie, while Pat, getting good and depressed over the war's new life, returned to the other table to take care of Admiral Moorer and his wife. She hoped that Howard K. Smith, the ABC anchor who was also there, hadn't been hearing any of this.

With everyone else otherwise engaged, Nixon now had Mrs. L to himself, and he began explaining to her how in the coming days, down at Key Biscayne, he hoped to be photographed on the beach looking as if he didn't have a care in the world. "That'll infuriate the Democrats, but it'll dismay the North Vietnamese and Thieu—and that's what's important."

"An *homme frivole*," said Alice. "If only on the surface."

He didn't know exactly what she meant, but understood she was playing on the Alsops' term for him.

"How is Stew?" he asked.

"Drinking Joe's blood," replied Alice. "And it's pretty thin gruel. Now, listen: I want to talk to you about a different one of my relatives. My nephew Kermit. We call him Kim. You've met him."

"Several times."

"Well, he knows your Mr. Hunt from days gone by."

Only now did Nixon remember the letter she'd sent back in October. "Is he sure he's *our* Mr. Hunt and not theirs?" he asked. The burglary had been such a fuck-up that the president had wondered, more than once, about the possibility of double agentry.

"I'm afraid he *is* your Mr. Hunt. It's wishful thinking to believe otherwise."

Nixon nodded.

"Kim's story involves King Zog!" She loved just saying the name. "Do you remember him? He looked a bit like Paul Muni. He was the president of Albania before he made himself king, sometime in the late twenties—long after my time."

"A president who became a king. Something I can look forward to?" asked Nixon, grinning.

Alice gave him a scolding look. One did not gain a reputation for wit by swinging at the easy pitches. If Dick really was an *homme sérieux*, this would be a good moment to focus on what she was trying to tell him. "They attempted Zog's assassination on fifty-five separate occasions," she said sternly. "One time he even shot back."

It was Nixon's turn to grow impatient. He wanted her to get back to Hunt, whom he'd been concerned about since the plane crash. Colson thought he was the type who might become unhinged.

"Kim knew Hunt in Cairo," Mrs. Longworth explained, "during a period in the fifties when Nasser was preparing to give exiled old Zog the boot. Farouk had been kind to him, and that was reason enough for Nasser to be otherwise. It fell to Kim and Hunt to plead the case for his being able to stay. In the event they failed, there was a place waiting for Zog on Long Island. Muttontown! You know, when we lived at Sagamore Hil—"

Nixon knew Mrs. L well enough to understand that, with a story of this nature, she would be grateful if he brought her back to the point. "What was Hunt's exact part in all this?"

"Forgery!" cried Alice. "He concocted some cables showing why the Israelis hated Zog for one reason or another—thinking that, in Nasser's mind, the Jews' *dis*like of Zog would trump Farouk's approval of him, and that Zog would thereby get to stay in Egypt."

"Didn't do the trick?" asked Nixon.

"No," said Alice. "And when he got thrown out, Zog wound up going to France instead of Muttontown. But the episode convinced my nephew that Mr. Hunt can be very creative, and that he has a tendency to start believing in his own fantastical ruses."

She could see Nixon's eyes moving. The president was remembering the cables that Hunt had been forging in order to pin the Diem assassination on Kennedy. Dean had found them in that damned safe.

Alice continued: "Kim says that his and Mr. Hunt's former employer, the Central Intelligence Agency, is rather worried about being tarnished if its name gets bandied about at the burglars' trial."

Nixon hesitated. He would love to be able to tell her about his and Haldeman's own attempt to use the Agency in this matter. Days after the break-in they'd passed word to the CIA that it needed to shut down the FBI's Watergate investigation, on the grounds that a serious probe might open up the whole Bay of Pigs thing, given the history of Hunt and his Cuban cronies. The ploy had been a good one—it might have made the whole goddamned thing go away—but after a moment's worth of cooperation, Helms, who was slippery even for a spy, had balked.

"The point is," said Alice, who had been watching Nixon resist the temptation to spill these beans into her lap, "the OSS—sorry, CIA, I'm dating myself—were worried that Hunt might try something foolish even *before* his wife died in that crash. That's why I wrote to you last month. His superiors gave him a long leash for many years, let him write his books and so forth, but he was judged an odd duck even by that collection of very odd ducks. Indeed, to hear Kim tell it, Mr. Hunt is odder than Kim himself, and that's saying plenty. Their former colleagues are currently agitated by one element of Mr. Hunt's mentality that they've been very aware of from years of observation. A very dangerous and rather unusual facet."

"What's that?" asked Nixon.

"He loved his wife. Inordinately, I would say." She paused, before adding, "Don't be surprised if some new 'document' turns up and changes this little Watergate calamity into something even worse."

Alice decided to let the president chew on this.

Her chief exasperation was with herself. She'd scoffed at the prankish burglary back in June, but had adjusted her thinking since. She wondered if Dick had adjusted his. She looked over toward Kissinger, still chatting up Mrs. Armstrong, and decided that, after ignoring him all evening, she ought to say at least something. She beckoned him to lean across the table, and when he was within whispering distance, she asked, in a voice no lower than her usual one: "Tell me, Dr. Kissinger, did you and Rockefeller ever trade impressions of what it was like to sleep with Mrs. Braden?"

Chapter Eighteen

JANUARY 18, 1973
KQED-TV, SAN FRANCISCO, CALIFORNIA

Howard Hunt explained, in flat tones, that "critical commitments made by high officials of the United States government" had simply not been kept.

William F. Buckley, Jr., responded with a quizzical grin, as if wondering whether his guest might be thinking of something other than the subject at hand. Hunt was not on *Firing Line* to discuss Watergate; the subject was U.S. policy toward Cuba, and he was appearing together with the exile Mario Lazo. Both of them were explaining the Bay of Pigs.

It was decent of Bill—that bright boy Hunt had supervised in the Agency more than twenty years ago—to fly him out to San Francisco for the taping, if only to take his mind off Dorothy and try to ease the terrible depression that all Hunt's friends knew he had fallen into. Even the small appearance fee would be helpful, but the invitation to be on the program was also Bill's way of reminding people that Howard Hunt had had a career before Watergate, that he had done important and honorable things with his life. The court's permission for him to make this trip, while he was between conviction and sentencing, seemed to validate that idea.

Buckley raised his eyebrows—a signal for Hunt to lift his voice above a murmur as he finished detailing the CIA's long-ago efforts against Castro.

Like Buckley, Mario Lazo seemed determined to help Hunt out, venturing as far into Watergate as the other man's legal situation would allow. Specifically, he managed to work in a suggestion that Castro's regime had been funneling money to the Democratic Party, the reason for the break-in that Hunt had given Bernie and the boys eight months ago.

As Buckley tried to keep the discussion from spilling over the boundaries that had been agreed to, he also kept his eye on Hunt, whose dazed lack of animation was worrying him. The host began to wonder whether the invitation, however well-intentioned, had been a good idea. Hunt looked like a convalescent who'd been severely overtaxed by an outing he'd been asked to make much too early.

When the taping ended, there was no time for the two of them to have even a drink. The terms of the court's permission required Hunt to return to his hotel immediately, pick up his suitcase and head straight back to the airport for a flight to D.C. As he left the studio, he managed only a quick thanks to Bill, for having him on the program and for agreeing to serve as executor of Dorothy's estate. Hunt's new status as a convicted felon prohibited him from a good many civic activities, including suing United Airlines on his dead wife's behalf.

An hour later, as the rains came down and he waited for a cab under the Palace Hotel marquee, a reporter recognized him and asked, as always, what he had to say for himself—and whether he could reveal anything about anyone higher up. Hunt was almost too exhausted to get the usual words out, but he finally succeeded: "Anything I may have done I did for what I believed to be the best interests of my country."

Once aloft, in the skies over the Rockies, he started thinking about the plane trips he'd made six weeks before, between Washington and Chicago. He recalled landing at Midway while smoke from United 553 still rose over the wreckage and the runway. And he remembered his trip to the Cook County morgue, his hope against hope that Dorothy's first-class seat at the front of the plane—*Papa, you said I could, just this once*—might have allowed her to survive with the dozen or two on board who were believed to have made it.

In the morgue's linoleum corridor he had sketched the jewelry she'd left the house with, thinking that if worse came to worst she could be identified by any of the items she'd worn: his mother's diamond ring, the cameo locket, the charm bracelet, the jade brooch. As it turned out, the solitaire had been looted from Dorothy's finger by some crooked fireman or medical technician. The jade brooch was gone, too. But the locket, fused shut by the fire, served to confirm that one of the blackened bodies was his wife's. He had thrown it away once its work was done, but had decided to keep the equally grotesque bracelet, its charms melted just enough to render the sexes of his children indistinguishable.

At the moment he slipped the bracelet into his pocket, he had decided to plead guilty. What was the point in fighting?

His depression had deepened in the weeks before Christmas, but the government's lawyers had insisted he was well enough to endure all the trial's preliminaries and proceedings. Even so, he kept expecting his body to drop to the ground the way Dorothy's plane had dropped from the sky. He'd known even before the crash that there was no real chance of acquittal. When he and his lawyer had been allowed to examine the contents of his White House safe, already available to the prosecutor, he could see that his Hermès notebooks had conveniently gone missing. Without their jottings about the Watergate operation, there would be no chance for anyone to see the break-in for what it had been. The same U.S. Attorney's office that had callously publicized his CIA career— violating the strict secrecy that kept every operative alive—was now even trying to strip him of his Agency pension.

At the trial, just eight days ago, the Italian judge, probably mobbed-up, had allowed him to enter his guilty plea only after the government got to lay out its case, so that it would appear he'd decided to cave only upon feeling the crushing weight of the prosecution's arguments.

Now, flying eastward, Hunt sipped a glass of milk for his ulcer and thought about the jury with whom he might have taken his chances— most of its members old and black and filled with a lifetime of grievance. No, there had been no point in doing anything but what he'd done. Liddy, delighting in his own mute defiance, would no doubt end up serving whatever maximum time the Wop could dish out.

Maybe, when his own sentencing took place some weeks from now, he would get off easy, as a reward for knuckling under to the judge. Perhaps, by some miracle, he'd come away with only probation. But either way, from within jail or without, in order to pay for all his life's obligations and extravagances, he would have to keep playing the game that Dorothy had played so much better.

After landing at National, he walked through the terminal building, full of those coming to town to see Richard Nixon be inaugurated one last time, thirty-six hours from now. His own mind continued to project itself backwards, forty or so days, to the December afternoon he had rushed here in his car after trying to silence the sobs of his nine-year-old son.

He had at the present moment no more desire to return to his house than he'd felt after his trip to Chicago and the morgue; or after the funeral; or after the family's miserable Christmas in Florida (Sirica's one mercy); or after the shamefaced *mea culpa* in the same judge's courtroom.

He forced himself to retrieve his car from the long-term lot and make the trip home. As the windshield wipers scraped and ticked, he pondered the odd or atrocious behavior of so many people over the past several weeks, conduct that had made the time seem all the more hurtful and unreal. Colson had sent a letter of sympathy rather than show up for the funeral. McCord, looking rumpled and mismatched, had appeared at the house after the rites, with nothing but the holy Agency on his mind and lips, as if he feared its besmirching by Watergate more than he feared going to prison.

Hunt's own mind still sometimes went back to McCord's peculiar absence at crucial moments on the night of the break-in. Had he been doing the bidding of someone else entirely? Dorothy had always had her suspicions. Then, and now, he seemed to be reading a different script from the one that Hunt and Liddy and Bernie were.

Whatever the case, James McCord was now the key to things. During the last hour of his just-completed flight, sipping his milk and fighting his mental fog, Hunt had begun to craft a plan, a kind of nuclear option that he could put into play if the White House—after one last squeeze he intended to apply—should let him go to jail without a prior, massive infusion of cash.

He hung up his raincoat in the sepulchral house and went into his study to concoct a document. Unlike most forgeries in his career, this letter would be composed over his own signature, and rather than back-dated it would be written from a time still several weeks away. And if it was ever sent at all, it would not be sent to the addressee.

Hunt began to type:

Dear Bill,

Much time has now passed since the *Firing Line* taping, and I again want to thank you for both the opportunity to appear and for the much greater—indeed profound—kindness of agreeing to serve as my children's legal guardian should I enter prison, as now seems likely.

Many rumors reach my ears. The latest and most sickening (and I'm afraid most reliable) indicates that the White House will soon try to suggest—slyly and deniably—that the CIA brought down the plane on which Dorothy died, because she was somehow getting ready to talk about the agency's involvement in the burglary.

The Administration will first try to implicate McCord, saying that he was acting at the behest of the agency during the break-in— and that the rest of us were somehow doing his bidding rather than the other way around.

Then, with whatever evidence it can fabricate, the WH will try to use even the plane crash in order to shift blame for Watergate over to the agency I proudly supervised you in more than twenty years ago.

If any of this fiction reaches your ears while I am in jail, I urge you not to give it any credence—just as I ask you not to come visit me, however much your Christian impulses push you in that direction. Please, instead, allow my children to visit *you* from time to time during my absence, so that they may have the benefit of your kindness and counsel as well as a sense of the caliber of man with whom their father associated for most—if, alas, not all—of his career.

With the highest possible regard,
Howard

If his last approach to the White House failed, he would get this letter into the hands of James McCord, not Bill Buckley. He would secretly drop it off at McCord's Rockville home, along with a forged cover note in which an unidentified CIA agent would claim to have found the letter—addressed to Buckley, stamped but not postmarked—in Hunt's own roadside mailbox, awaiting pickup by the next mailman to make his rounds.

McCord, awaiting his own sentencing, would be in a bind. Upon reading the letter, he would feel compelled to strike out against the White House, and yet he would be unwilling to implicate the Agency even in so small a thing as the surveillance of Hunt and a theft from his mail-box. And so, McCord would be left with only the truth for a weapon: he would tell Sirica that higher-ups *had* ordered the break-in and cov-ered it up. The judge's lust for punishment would then be directed at the White House, and Hunt's own desire for revenge against that faithless entity would be satisfied—without his even having to appear disloyal.

Bone tired once more, he sealed the letter and placed it inside his desk, wondering if he would ever put it into McCord's possession. He wondered, too, whether the White House *had* had a hand in bringing down Dorothy's plane. He no longer knew what to think, did not even understand some of his own actions on the night of the break-in—such as how he'd left behind that check made out to his country club for $6.36. He had *intended* to mail it before he and Liddy had gone to their room at the Watergate Hotel; but he had somehow forgotten to, and then, by leaving it behind—deliberately?—he'd linked himself to the operation as surely as if he'd plastered his fingerprints all over Larry O'Brien's telephone.

Now he looked blankly at the manuscript Dorothy had never fin-ished typing. Its bottom pages, with their unhappy ending written in a Christmas daze, remained in his own handwriting, as did a few of the pages at the top of the stack. He reached for them now, looking first at the dedication, with its arithmetic of heartbreak:

TO MY BELOVED WIFE, DOROTHY
TWENTY-THREE YEARS, THREE MONTHS AND ONE DAY

He then turned to the epigraph he had chosen from Jean Galtier-Boissière:

It is in the political agent's interest to betray all parties who use him and to work for them all at the same time, so that he may move freely and penetrate everywhere.

Then he replaced the title page—*The Berlin Ending*—atop the manu-script and picked up Dorothy's scorched charm bracelet from the candy dish in which he kept it. He jingled it like a pocketful of change, closed his eyes, and began one of the Transcendental Meditation exercises he had been teaching himself—from a book his daughter had left lying around when she was home for the holidays. Always a quick study, he had mastered the steps with ease. He followed them now, amazed at their efficacy, until he felt himself penetrate a cloud of unknowing.

Chapter Nineteen

JANUARY 20, 1973; INAUGURATION DAY
THE NATIONAL MALL, WASHINGTON, D.C.

The Old Man's amplified voice traveled on a raw twenty-five-mile-per-hour wind: *We shall answer to God, to history, and to our conscience for the way in which we use these years.*

LaRue stood beneath the West Front of the Capitol, on the other side of the building from the president, and thought that it was not a morning fit for new beginnings. The weather was awful, fifteen degrees colder than what had been promised, and the climate within the White House remained even chillier. Having pled guilty, Hunt was making everyone nervous over what he might say next on television, whether to Bill Buckley or somebody else. Meanwhile Liddy and McCord, refusing to cut a deal, continued to drag out the burglary trial. God knew what dangers still lay in that. How the hell would Magruder handle himself on the stand when he testified three days from now? Was he really smart enough to lie his way through a cross-examination?

Clapping his gloved but still-freezing hands together, LaRue guessed that the platform on the other side of the Capitol was dotted with space heaters. Well, on this side, it was just too goddamned cold to keep standing around listening to the loudspeakers. So to warm himself up he began walking westward toward the Mall. Before long he was running into tens of thousands of demonstrators giving antiwar protest one last long-haired college try.

"NIXON YOU LIAR—WHERE'S THE CEASE-FIRE?" one bunch of them kept shouting. Another bunch, dressed up like Grim Reapers with black robes and scythes, passed by on LaRue's right, a sort of minstrel show in reverse, their whiteface makeup peeking out from under their black hoods.

And, Christ, there was Bella Abzug, at her own microphone, bellowing like a cement mixer. He stopped to listen to the snarl coming from under her wide-brimmed hat. While he stamped his feet and rubbed his hands some more, he saw that a few of the boys close by her were keeping warm without any problem, thanks to a couple of flags they'd just torn from the poles around the Washington Monument and were now burning inside oil drums. One of the Grim Reapers offered up his black robe to keep the blaze going.

LaRue thought nothing in this town could shock him anymore, but as he watched the flags go up in flames, he noticed that the Park police weren't making the feeblest move to stop it. For all he knew they had orders from Ehrlichman to stand aside and not let the arrest numbers get too embarrassingly high. Even so, it was hard for LaRue to contain his disgust, and after twenty minutes of wandering the Mall he turned northeast, toward Pennsylvania Avenue, where he thought he'd join the crowd waiting for the parade.

He discovered it to be one deep, if that, for long stretches. The sparseness embarrassed him and he changed his mind. With his White House pass he managed to go around the unnecessary sawhorses, cross Pennsylvania, and head toward his favorite breakfast place, an old waffle shop opposite Ford's Theatre. Once inside, he sat and ate a stack of pancakes served by a tired old Negro lady. Up on the Hill the Old Man would now be suffering through lunch with a congressional leadership that was forced to host him between the speech and the parade. The Democrats controlled the guest list and menu, so maybe Bella would hightail it back from burning the flag and propose some nasty toast before she put on the feedbag.

LaRue had thought about staying inside his apartment, but the day's milestone nature had made him anxious: once the TV stations started their inaugural coverage, he kept half-expecting Gordon Strachan or Mrs. Chennault to come by with another bagful of money that would require him to re-don his rubber gloves. He would be better off out of the capital altogether, down in Jackson with his wife, who had no interest in coming up for the inaugural balls. But he needed to stick around; nobody knew what he and Dean and the rest of them might have to improvise next.

Martha would be making the rounds of them, because Nixon had indicated he wanted Mitchell on the scene—not too conspicuously, but enough to show that the man who'd done more than anyone else to make him president was still a figure of honor within the administration, someone whose move to New York didn't mean he'd been thrown overboard. Toward that end, Mitchell was now being cast as a kind of bald, pot-bellied Duke of Windsor, a fellow who'd given up Washington for the sake of his irrepressible wife, a complicated woman who loved him beyond the social whirl, and whom he adored beyond whatever power he might have kept accumulating down in Washington.

For stretches, Martha was able to make herself believe this fiction. She had been in good spirits over Christmas, vacationing with Mitchell at Bebe's place in Key Biscayne, telling anybody within earshot she didn't give a who-happy about politics now that she'd gotten her husband away from all that. Yes, she'd do her duty and come to the inauguration, but she'd wear all the same outfits she'd worn back in '69 and then scamper right back to New York City, where people, she insisted, understood her a lot better than they did in poky old D.C. That place was all now part of her past, she said, and maybe she was right; just yesterday, when a group of college students got a glimpse of her outside the F Street Club, they'd cheered her with a kind of startled nostalgia.

And yet this morning Mitchell had told LaRue that Martha was in a tizzy because it appeared no seats had been reserved for the former attorney general and his wife on the parade reviewing stand. When Mitchell told her that places *had* in fact been reserved—and that he himself had declined them, figuring one appearance at an inaugural ball to be enough showing of the flag—she'd refused to believe him. Nonetheless, both John and Martha—he placid, she fuming—would be watching the parade from a window high above Pennsylvania Avenue, inside the Washington offices of what had once been Nixon, Mudge, Rose, Guthrie, Alexander & Mitchell.

With no real celebrating throngs to impede him, LaRue now left the waffle shop and walked to the corner of Pennsylvania and Fourteenth. He took up a spectator's position once he heard the first motorcycles begin their slow, roaring way from the Capitol to the White House. The raw wind had not let up, and he could hear the chattering teeth of a nice woman next to him, a mother from the suburbs who'd brought her two small kids to see the parade, just the kind of voter, multiplied by many millions, who'd given the Old Man his landslide. As the limousine approached, its flags flapping, LaRue waited for the president's upper body to poke through the canopy, which sure enough it soon did, allowing Nixon to make that strange, faggy version of Churchill's "V," his frozen fingers limply wagging high above his head. Mrs. Nixon stood up, too, squeezing herself into the tight rectangle of space that had been opened by the limousine's sliding roof. The first couple looked as if they were caught in a vise, ready to be crushed by the retractable panels.

"Hi!" shouted the mother's children, only a few seconds before some college kids in windbreakers began to chant: "NIXON IS A RACIST SWINE! MAKE HIM SIGN ON THE DOTTED LINE!" LaRue now realized that their sporty windbreakers were protective coloring. Still chanting, the protesters pressed against a sawhorse, hurling pebbles and fruit at the limo. Secret Service agents trotting beside the car clearly wanted the Nixons to sit down, but the president kept waving his fingers, and Mrs. Nixon, setting her jaw a little more firmly, smiled past the demonstrators toward some nonexistent second row of parade watchers who must have been, in her imagination, more friendly.

Several minutes later, after a break inside the White House to freshen up, Pat took her place behind the bulletproof glass of the reviewing stand, next to an empty seat still reserved for Alice Longworth. They'd all been hoping, as late as this morning, that she might be well enough to come, but Connie Stuart had gotten a call from Mrs. L's doctor, who said her flu remained pretty bad; she just couldn't be exposed to the weather, not at eighty-eight.

So, with Tricia on one side of her and nobody on the other, Pat waved to some passing baton twirlers from West Virginia. The trumpeters alongside them would have drowned out the bass drum in Lafayette Park, had parade regulations not already allowed the police to clear away whatever drummer had this afternoon's shift.

Pat could feel the cold air freezing the Aqua Net spray that all morning had managed to hold her hatless hairdo in place against the wind, even when she'd stuck her head through the open roof of the car. She wasn't going to let a few pebbles and pieces of fruit force her back into her seat. Once they reached the White House driveway, she'd told Dick, who didn't laugh, that "all this ecology and back-to-nature stuff must be catching on. Four years ago they threw coins." The noise they'd made striking the limousine had caused her to remember a joyous cry she'd heard her mother let out one morning when she found a nickel while sweeping the miner's shack.

She had long ago learned to find sympathetic faces in whatever crowd she was gliding by or plunging into. There had even been some in Caracas as the spit and stones rained down, simple people even more astonished to find themselves watching a parade than she was to find herself in one.

A military unit playing a Sousa march now came into view. Dick was back on his feet, hand over heart, and she knew he'd want her to stand, too. So she did, just as the unit's flags and shouldered rifles passed. She noticed a press photographer across the street adjusting his lens to get the exact shot she knew he wanted: one of the whole family, looking like stiff little pinheads behind bulletproof glass and a passing forest of bayonets.

A few feet from the first lady, Nixon looked at the fife pressed to one soldier's frozen lips and thought about how much he'd like to shove it up Thieu's Oriental ass. Five minutes before getting into the limo to go to the Capitol, there'd come word that the South Vietnamese president finally seemed ready to say yes to the agreement—now that he'd gotten a rhetorical pounding from Goldwater and a few others that almost equaled what the B-52s had dropped on the North. Christ, he would *never* forgive him for holding things up, for forcing him to give this tentative, chickenshit, peace-is-sort-of-at-hand inaugural address that even Ray Price's high-toned pen couldn't save. Then again, maybe Thieu deserved some grudging spoonful of admiration for toughness, for holding out as long as he had against this deal that would eventually see his miserable little country sewn back into a single stringbean controlled by the North. If he preferred fighting on to cushy exile, you could hardly knock him. Still, whenever they saw each other again, he would be hard-pressed to shake the man's hand if there wasn't a camera around.

Toughness would be their own order of the day, for the next four years, and especially the next four months, however long it took the goddamned Senate to get through their Watergate hearings. He'd take his inspiration from Eugene Ormandy, his favorite conductor, up there on the podium last night after telling a bunch of his left-wing musicians they could look for jobs with another orchestra if they refused to sit their asses down and play an inaugural concert for the man who'd just been reelected president.

Right now, as the umpteenth state float passed by, Nixon could feel a chill go straight through him. He closed the lapels of his topcoat, determined not to catch his death like William Henry Harrison. He wished the whole damned day were over and he was alone in the Lincoln Sitting Room, feet up, drink in hand, talking to Colson, though these days even *he* tended to bring more trouble than consolation. All these hints about clemency for his pal Hunt: without it, Colson argued, astronomical sums of money would be required to keep him quiet. But for the moment clemency was a nonstarter, a PR impossibility, and if it came up again tonight, Nixon would cut the conversation short and hit the sack.

Jesus, thought the president, looking through the frozen glass at a man with a small magnifying scope up to his eye and a finger on what looked to be a trigger. After a moment's fright, he realized it was only Haldeman shooting one of his home movies. He waved at him to come join them for a bit; Pat and the girls could each scoot down a seat toward the one left empty by Mrs. L.

"He's driving me crazy," the president whispered to his chief of staff, once he got within the enclosure. He gestured with a tilt of his head toward Agnew, who was on his feet, clapping too loudly and enjoying himself too much while some Ohio National Guard unit marched past. "We ought to let him take his goddamned Middle East trip if he wants to. Yeah, it'll build him up, but it'll at least get him out of our hair."

Haldeman nodded, trying to decide whether he was actually supposed to set this in motion, or if the remark was just the usual letting off of steam. A brass band was soon deafening them with "Anchors Aweigh," and Nixon was back on his feet, his eyes peculiarly focused on the corner of Fourteenth Street, far from the reviewing stand but still visible. "You see that?" he asked Haldeman, pointing to some protesters who appeared to be chanting. "If you drown it out, it goes away—as if it were never even there."

The brass instruments blasted: *Here's wishing you a happy voyage home!*

"Are you talking about the Johnson idea?" asked Haldeman.

Nixon nodded. He and Haldeman had been discussing this elegant long shot off and on all month. It went like this: They could find out from Cartha DeLoach—an old Hoover loyalist who still talked to Mitchell—just who at the FBI had bugged the Nixon campaign plane, at LBJ's direction, in '68. Then they could privately insist that this abuse be made part of the Senate's investigation into "presidential campaign practices"—thereby evening the score and confirming the already common-enough public sentiment that *they all do it and so what?* Maybe Johnson, sure to hear about it, would ask the Democrats on the committee to back off, and maybe—as a favor to a dying man—they would. And then maybe the whole thing would fade into nothingness.

The only problem was that Johnson, dying or not, *already* seemed to have gotten wind of what they were thinking; he'd sent a signal that they'd better not try to bring up that business about the plane, not if they didn't want *him* talking about how Mrs. Chennault had helped out during the '68 race by trying to sink the peace negotiations, telling the South Vietnamese to quit the talks until Nixon could be elected and get them better terms. Apparently, LBJ was down there in Texas—pouring Jack Daniel's on his cornflakes and letting his hair get longer than Howard Hughes's—using his last breaths to say that he might still come out and accuse Nixon of treason, the way he could have in '68 before Hubert went down for the count.

The brass band had marched out of view, replaced by twenty piccolo players from New Hampshire. Nixon took advantage of the lower decibel level to ask his chief of staff whether there'd been any new word from Austin on Johnson's physical condition.

The president could see himself reflected in Haldeman's blue eyes. Embarrassed to look as if he were pushing too hard, taking advantage of the near-dead, he added, "I just want to make sure we're quick out of the box doing everything we can for Lady Bird as soon as, you know . . ."

"Yeah."

Oh, what was the point of dissembling? "I don't know if it would be worth it or not to play the plane card once he's gone," said Nixon, hoping Haldeman might have a thought on this point. The chief of staff, now watching some trampolinists perform on a moving float without breaking their necks, replied with only a circumspect shrug.

Nixon gave the athletes a big smile and the OK sign, and he thought of the gymnasts he'd seen in China. "Well, we've all got to be more cheerful, that's for sure," he told Haldeman. "There's been too much death." He'd been weirdly affected by Truman's passing a few weeks ago. "In fact, I want to give a party," he suddenly declared. "Something in the State Dining Room. Cocktails for every Democrat in the House and Senate who stuck with us on the war."

Haldeman nodded, recognizing this for a real order and ready to get on it.

"Who knows when we'll need them again?" asked Nixon.

Rose hid behind the dinosaur inside the Smithsonian's natural history museum. She was trying to avoid Jeb Magruder and his pretty wife and their whole brood of Pepsodent-fresh kiddies, who ought to be in bed, she thought, inaugural ball or no inaugural ball—even one organized by their father.

Charlie Wiggins, the California congressman, was providing her with additional cover, laughing over her tale of how the president had called last night, while she was getting ready for the Kennedy Center concert, to complain that a line from the last draft of his speech seemed to be missing. Could she help him find it? " 'Not unless you want to come over here and zip me up,' I told him. He seemed to think about it for a second, too—until I reminded him that I live in the Watergate!"

Wiggins was enjoying the story, but Rose herself had been miffed last night. Honest to God, what did he expect? She'd been half-prepared to hear him ask that she spend the weekend taking care of his eighty-year-old aunt Jane, the one who'd taught him piano back in Whittier and had come to Washington for the ceremonies.

Telling the tale through a second glass of champagne was beginning to make her feel better; in fact, all at once she felt a flush of well-being.

Truth be told, she'd never been prouder of Richard Nixon, even if he sometimes irritated her the way a husband might. Her one wish right now was that Wiggins would ask her to dance—she really missed Don at a moment like this—but the congressman was getting the high sign from his wife.

And Jesus, Mary, and Joseph, here were the Magruders, coming round the dinosaur. Well, the wife was even prettier than Rose had imagined—sort of like a runner-up for Miss America—and it was hard not to like the kids, who seemed bored and well-behaved as they got introduced to "Miss Woods." But Junior remained insufferable. She supposed she should congratulate him on the whole inaugural shebang, but couldn't bring herself to.

"You don't look any older than you did in '60," she said, after resisting his kiss of her cheek a little too evidently. "I remember you from when the campaign passed through Kansas City. What were you doing? Selling women's stockings?"

"Paper products."

"Jeb's thinking about running for California secretary of state!" the overexcited missus chimed in. Rose could tell from hubby's expression that this particular cat wasn't supposed to be out of the bag.

"Really?" asked Rose. "It's a shame Charlie Wiggins's wife snatched him away. He might be able to help you out there."

"I'm making a trip to talk to Reagan and to Bob Finch," said Magruder. "We'll see."

"You do keep a busy schedule," said Rose, hoping he took it for a dig at his impending appearance in Sirica's courtroom, where he'd no doubt have to swear he'd never given Liddy an order to commit the burglary. She already knew that nothing was going to come of this California idea; she'd heard that HRH was planning to rescue him with some job in the Commerce Department.

The wife broke the silence. "Well, Rose, I hope we'll see you at the White House church service in the morning. We're so thrilled to be going!"

"I went to five o'clock mass this afternoon so I can sleep in tomorrow." She said it as casually as she could, to leave the impression she saw the president too regularly for such an invitation to mean anything.

Rose's eyes scoured the room, hoping to catch sight of Ed Brooke, the best dancer she'd ever met in Washington. He liked to joke with her that some stereotypes were true, but there was nothing jazzy and jivey about him. All his moves were out of Fred Astaire and Vernon Castle—sophisticated and sleek; just the way he spoke. Could she ever use him now!

An enormous roar from the crowd finally put her conversation with the Magruders out of its misery. They waved goodbye to Rose while the source of the excitement, Martha Mitchell, entered the big room. After hugging Kissinger and some astronaut just back from the Moon, she began signing autographs, while the light of a hundred Instamatic flash cubes bounced off the silver tinsel hanging from the ceiling. "Honey," Martha cried to a big bald businessman, "you can snap me next to the dinosaur—so long as you don't ask which of us is older!"

Once boredom overcame her, as it always did within minutes, she began a push for the main ballroom. The crowd made way for Martha, dragging Kissinger into her wake. He followed along until he came to the VIP boxes, which overhung the ballroom from a height no greater than the upper berths on a train.

Elliot Richardson stood in one of them, telling a reporter that he'd tried to do a bit of jitterbugging right where he was rather than venture into the mob scene below. "Still, it's rather nice that the people here get a chance to see the faces that belong to all those names they're always seeing in the newspaper."

"How should I identify you?" the reporter asked. "With HEW, or as secretary of defense designate?" The confirmation hearings for all the new and repositioned Nixon nominees had gotten a little backed up.

"The latter, I should think," said Richardson, leaning over to talk to Kissinger, several feet below. He'd seen him yesterday, too, during the "Heritage Groups" reception over at the Corcoran, where Henry had told him, as a hundred ethnics swirled around his tall Brahmin presence, "At last you know what the Jewish quota at Harvard felt like."

Richardson bid goodbye to the reporter and pointed to a little doorway that could bring the national security advisor up into the box. A moment later Henry was at his side, first bemoaning how he had to return to Paris in the morning and then confessing his latest anxieties.

"He's been talking to Haldeman about the disposition of my papers. Who's entitled to what when the time comes."

"Posterity is just around the corner," mused Richardson.

"Do you think he still has confidence in me?"

Richardson's reply was lost in a sudden new cacophony, when the ballroom's two orchestras, supposed to be alternating, struck up different numbers at the same time. Kissinger and Richardson watched Ehrlichman dance with his daughter to the competing strains of "Picnic" and "Moon River" until another great roar from the crowd made everyone, even Martha Mitchell, look toward one of the doorways.

A false alarm: it was Agnew who'd just arrived, not the president.

"A heartbeat away," said Richardson.

"And about fifteen IQ points," replied Kissinger.

Alice Longworth was falling asleep with the television on. The station had been showing film of the parade, the announcer remarking on Dick's unusually happy expression and then pointing out the empty seat in the front row that had been reserved for none other than herself.

As her fever persisted, thought and dream began to merge, making her believe she was actually *at* the parade and that it was 1957, Dick's second inaugural as vice president. The little Nixon girls were shrinking from her while Pat whispered to them that they shouldn't be afraid of the old lady.

Old? Why, Alice had been only seventy-two that morning, with her own daughter much on her mind: poor Paulina, alone on Twenty-eighth Street, a drunk's young widow now drinking herself through despair. The dream of '57 ran on—past the overdose and the body's discovery to Dick's shouldering of the coffin; past her coming to his study on Tilden Street, clutching the detestable *Post* article with its reference to the empty bottle of sleeping pills.

This dream, like the fever, came and went for two more days, during which Alice sometimes thought Joanna, her granddaughter, was really Paulina passing in and out of the room.

And then, on the twenty-third, the fever at last broke. The flu and the dream went with it, and she was lucid once more, back in the here and now of 1973. As Janie fed her broth, Joanna came in with news that the first lady was on the telephone. Both housekeeper and granddaughter expressed doubt that she was well enough to take the call, but Alice overruled them: "Don't give me those *looks*. I know which first lady it is. I know it's not Mrs. Taft, and I know it's not Eleanor. It's Pat. Tell her to hold the line while you bring me the phone."

They did as they were instructed.

"You were beginning to give us a scare!" said Mrs. Nixon.

"Not to worry. I'm paper thin, but I've decided to stick around for another year or two."

"Well, that's the best news yet," Pat declared. After a pause, she added, "What a combination of the sad and wonderful we've had while you were under the weather!"

"I haven't heard any of it. Give me the sad stuff first," said Alice, realizing that Pat might well have a different idea than she about what was sad and what was happy.

"I'm sorry to tell you that Lyndon Johnson died last night." Pat said it slowly, thinking to cushion any shock.

"I imagine there'll be loud grief in the animal kingdom," responded Alice. "Will they be putting him in the Rotunda?"

"I'm not sure yet." Pat imagined that even Johnson's corpse might still attract pickets, but offering such an observation seemed rude, so she settled for saying, "It would be such a long trip for Lady Bird."

"You said there was good news, too."

"Yes!" cried the first lady. "And it's brand new. Dick's going on television tonight to make the announcement. Henry Kissinger is on his way back from Paris with the agreement."

Alice remained silent.

"The war is over," Pat explained. "Isn't it marvelous?"

Perfectly aware of which war she spoke, Alice nonetheless thought back to the Paris Treaty of 1898, which had settled the Spanish-American War; and to the Versailles treaty after that; and then to her half brother, Ted Jr., dropping dead of a heart attack after hitting the beach at Normandy when he was fifty-six.

She sighed in a way that alarmed Janie and Joanna. She shut her eyes and waited a moment, still lost in thought, until she at last told Pat: "I want you to enjoy it, dear."

Chapter Twenty

FEBRUARY 23, 1973, 9:00 P.M.
1030 FIFTH AVENUE, NEW YORK CITY

"Mr. LaRue is downstairs," the doorman announced.

The reply coming through the telephone was loud enough for the arriving guest to hear. "Send him up!" cried Martha Mitchell. "And tell him not to mind the elevator lookin' like a horse stall!"

To LaRue's confusion, the elevator car did contain a considerable litter of hay and straw—as well as the mayor of New York City, John V. Lindsay, wearing a tuxedo. "Didn't have time to change," he said to LaRue with his movie-star smile.

"There's a little ole *square dance* goin' on two flights up," explained Martha, as she took LaRue's topcoat. "A birthday party for Mr. *Teddy Kennedy.*"

Martha rarely engaged in lengthy exposition, but allowed that the senator's sister and brother-in-law, Jean and Stephen Smith, lived in the building. From the open living room window of the Mitchells' apartment, LaRue could hear an old-fashioned square-dance caller speaking commands into a microphone: "Bow to your partner!"

"Just don't *drown* her!" shouted Martha, to the unseen guest of honor, who was turning forty-one. Down below on the Fifth Avenue sidewalk, near the building's canvas canopy, a handful of tabloid photographers and TV cameras were hoping to catch late arrivals.

"That poor little wife of his, Joansie, is travelin' out West, so I wonder who they've got lined up to be Mr. Teddy Bear's *birthday present* tonight."

LaRue just smiled.

"Sit down, honey," Martha ordered. "Mr. Mitchell's on the phone." She mixed LaRue a drink. "I understand that Miss Triciabelle and Mr. Eddie Coxman are about to move smack into my neighborhood. Right down Eighty-fourth Street, from what I hear."

LaRue wondered if this development amounted to cachet or competition; either way, he was sure Martha found it nowhere near as exciting as having Jackie Onassis just one block away.

"So, honey," she said, settling herself next to him. "Is Mr. President doin' any work at all?"

"He's mostly scramblin' to figure out how he can sell Congress on givin' reconstruction aid to North Vietnam." LaRue laughed softly at the thought of how only two months ago everybody in the White House had been worried about funds for the war being cut off.

"You always *love* the one you *hurt*," said Martha, conclusively. The only topic she wanted to pursue right now was Richard Nixon's sudden new social life in Washington. The president and first lady had, in recent days, been photographed dining out at Trader Vic's, visiting Alice Longworth in advance of her eighty-ninth birthday, and going to the theater with Tricia to see Debbie Reynolds in a musical whose wholesomeness was above reproach.

LaRue smiled. "It's kinda like the 'peace dividend.' Or normalcy. He's showin' that, with the war over, even he's allowed to enjoy himself. I doubt it'll last long."

"The man I see in these pictures is *not* havin' a good time," said Martha. "We are dealin' with a most irregular Joe here." She was back at the window, leaning out and giving the photographers a chance to catch on. "No *Vertigo* for me!" she suddenly cried, pulling herself back in. "Neither the condition *nor* the movie, which is what Mr. President and old Thelma are gonna be watching at Camp David tonight. That comes straight from Mr. President himself, I'll have you know. He told Mr. Mitchell so when they talked an hour ago. Oh, yes, Mr. President still calls when he *wants* something. Tell me, are you and Mr. Mitchell still tryin' to raise money to keep everybody quiet and protect him?"

"I'm hopin' that'll come to an end soon," said LaRue.

Martha snorted. "One way or the other!" She was back at the window yet again. "Oh my! Look at the mop of curls on little John-John! Do *not* tell me that boy doesn't belong to Mr. Agnelli. He's not pink and pasty enough to be a real Kennedy." She returned to the couch and her drink, exclaiming, "I just love it here! Aside from everything else, it's *safer*. John Stennis ought to get himself out of Washington, D.C., and back home before some other colored mugger finishes him off."

Mississippi's aging junior senator, a wizened stalwart who would never catch up to James O. Eastland in seniority, remained at Walter Reed, recovering from gunshot wounds sustained in a robbery that had taken place on his front lawn.

"He's doin' pretty well, from what I hear," said LaRue.

Martha suddenly remembered that gunshots, like cancer, gave her the willies.

"Mr. Mitchell!" she shouted in the direction of the bedroom. "Freddy LaRooster is here!"

She liked to tease him about old amatory exploits. She imagined they weren't very great, but kept poking in hopes of a revelation or two. Certainly he had never told her about Clarine Lander.

"How *does* Mr. President get everybody to keep workin' for him without pay?" she asked, pointing toward the bedroom where her husband was still transacting Richard Nixon's business. "Everybody's half in and half out, still at it, even when they've got no more title and no more office. There's my husband, and now there's Cole Slaw."

Chuck Colson had returned to private law practice, but he was still an official, if unsalaried, consultant to the president. Nixon could continue to get his advice and, if need be, still claim executive privilege for him.

"There he is!" cried Martha, as Mitchell at last emerged from the bedroom. His appearance, only five weeks after the inauguration, shocked LaRue. His hands were shaking and two gin blossoms had burst across his nose. His silvery whiskers matched the hair curling over his collar. It also looked as if this might be the second day for the shirt he had on.

Martha strode back to the window. LaRue noticed that her right hand was twirling a little red-checkered scarf she'd picked up from a table.

"Come on in," said Mitchell, as if the bedroom were an office. "Bring your drink."

LaRue noticed newspapers and legal pads, as well as the phone, lying all over the unmade bed. Mitchell lay back down on it, propping himself against the headboard.

"I talked to the president a couple of hours ago," he said.

"So I hear," said LaRue. "He's supposed to be watchin' a movie about now. You should be doin' the same on a Friday night."

Mitchell, whose mind was never completely off his wife, replied, "You know, she wants to go upstairs to that party."

"Yes," said LaRue, who'd seen the red-checkered kerchief. "But tell me the latest."

Mitchell took out a pad with some notes. He pointed to the telephone. "If you listen to him," he said, meaning the president, "you'd think it was all in the past. I could barely get him to discuss our little troubles. He'd rather talk about our new North Vietnamese friends."

LaRue laughed softly. "Next thing you know we'll be raisin' money to pay off McGovern's campaign debt."

Mitchell looked at the notepad, pausing before he made a suggestion. "Maybe clemency for Hunt is not so outlandish. We'd take tremendous heat for a few days, but we could slip it into a bunch of other amnesties and pardons. Not for the draft dodgers," he hastened to explain, knowing LaRue's feelings on that subject, "but, say, for some GIs with Lieutenant Calley's kind of problems."

LaRue managed no more than a skeptical nod. If it would keep himself out of trouble, the Old Man probably *would* pardon the draft dodgers, same as he went to Red China without a by-your-leave to the Formosans. It sometimes felt to LaRue that there were no deal-breakers anymore, no about-faces that weren't beyond the pale. If the subsidy paid better than the crop, why plant?

"John, I don't know about clemency for Hunt. It'll intensify the investigation."

"You're probably right," said Mitchell. "There's only one way to really fix this thing, and I'm afraid you're looking at him."

LaRue shook his head in protest.

"I can tell he wants me to come forward and take the blame," said Mitchell. "Colson wants me to do it, too, and so does Haldeman. Just step up to some microphone and say I ordered the break-in. The Democrats will think they've solved that mystery where even the trial couldn't. And they'll lose interest in our little cover-up, because it will have failed."

"There's only one problem with that," said LaRue.

Mitchell nodded. "The small fact that I never ordered the break-in."

"I know you didn't," said LaRue.

"Who did?" asked Mitchell.

"I don't know."

"Neither do I. I'd say it was Magruder. And so would Liddy, I'm pretty sure, if he decided to talk instead of playing the tough guy." The lead defendant at the burglars' trial had winked theatrically at Jeb when his despised former boss at CRP entered the courtroom to testify, not very forthrightly, last month. Liddy had wound up being convicted along with McCord, and could expect the longest prison term of all once the judge sentenced everybody, including Hunt and the Cubans, a few weeks from now.

"But why would Magruder even think to bug the DNC?" asked Mitchell. "Why would it even be on his mind?"

"It makes no sense," said LaRue. "And Jeb's not going to admit anything to you, or to me, any more than he's going to admit it to a jury. Not with four kids who could wind up seeing their daddy go to jail."

After a pause, Mitchell said, "I'm not sure I'm ready to do it."

LaRue looked at his blotchy face and supine posture and thought he didn't look ready to do anything.

"Aside from everything else," Mitchell continued, "she'll kill me if I agree to be the fall guy." He pointed toward the living room.

"Hell," said LaRue, "I'll kill you, too."

He wondered, when he caught himself using that expression, if his partner in conversation might be thinking, *And that's more than a figure of speech to him.* But Mitchell looked at him and said nothing. LaRue was, he supposed, being "paranoid"—that word the Old Man's enemies loved to toss around. But this momentary fear, just a second or two of social awkwardness, stemmed from a genuine terror, his unquenchable dread that the shooting in the duck blind, years ago, had been something other than an accident; a catastrophe brewed by drink and dark, deliberate impulse.

Mitchell had said no more than "hell of a thing" when he first heard about the incident from LaRue, during some otherwise casual talk of their childhoods. By that point LaRue had already come to understand that Mitchell didn't especially care what a man's secret was, so long as he could keep it; but LaRue was keeping a secret he didn't fully know himself. The whole truth of what had happened up in Canada was probably knowable even now—and had been so for fifteen years—but there was sufficient trouble in this room without straying toward an old mystery that no prosecutor was pursuing.

Mitchell at last spoke. "The only thing to do right now is keep a lid on it and get ready for the Senate hearings. The president did manage to see Howard Baker the other day."

LaRue frowned. He didn't think the investigative committee's ranking Republican—Everett Dirksen's son-in-law or not—was likely to provide much protection.

"The president's strategy," said Mitchell, "is to look as if we're cooperating even while we claim executive privilege for everybody down to the janitor. And, oh yeah," he remembered to add, "the president says we're supposed to draw everyone's attention to 'the good things.'"

LaRue smiled. "Colson says the return of the POWs equals one thousand Watergates."

"If that's his idea of math," said Mitchell, "I'm glad he isn't running NASA."

The president's hopes for joyful distraction were getting him involved with every detail of the prisoners' release: checking to see that all the wives had orchids to wear as their men got off the planes; picking just the right entertainers—cornball was okay, but not too ancient— for the welcome-home evening at the White House. LaRue had heard how the Old Man choked up, nearly sobbed, the other day when talking to what he now called his "peace cabinet" about the staunch Nolde family, whose father had been the last American to die in the war.

"Speaking of Colson," said Mitchell, lifting his glass from its place on his chest. "*He* thinks we might be able to get away with clemency for Hunt if we just hold off on it until the holidays. Make it a merciful gesture."

LaRue laughed. "Mercy: the president's Christmas specialty. We can drop it on Hunt from a B-52."

"But it'd be too late," Mitchell said with a sigh. "This Hunt character is likely to blow long before that. Which is why our friend Dean says you and I have got to get busy raising more money right away."

LaRue nodded, depressed that they'd arrived at the matter he'd come to New York to discuss. As it was, Mitchell seemed eager to avoid it for just a little longer by citing more of Nixon's own avoidance behaviors. "You know, he's been telling Haldeman to see about getting King Timahoe bred."

LaRue laughed at the thought of a canine dynasty. "Easier than finding congressional seats for the sons-in-law."

"He also wants Ray Price to see if they can't change the procedures for compiling each year's volume of presidential speeches; he'd like to see his off-the-cuff remarks and toasts get printed, too. And," said Mitchell, pouring himself what LaRue hoped would be a last drink, "he wants Bebe to take charge of sprucing up the White House bowling alley." He added, more forgivingly, "I suppose everybody needs to get away from this nightmare, even if it's only down to the basement to roll gutter balls. They say Kissinger's already made three trips to the zoo to see the pandas."

LaRue watched Mitchell's bald crown slip a little further down the headboard. There seemed no more time to waste. "John, word is that Hunt doesn't feel any of his legal fees should come out of what he's received. He thinks all of it—and it's more than a small fortune—should go to 'living expenses.' I don't think there's a chance in hell we can raise enough money to satisfy him."

LaRue had never told anyone, not even Mitchell, about his rendezvous with Dorothy Hunt on the day of the plane crash. But he had by now disbursed to Hunt's attorney nearly all the money that had sat for those hours in the airport locker. And each night he still struggled to push from his mind the thought that there'd been a connection between the cover-up and the crash.

He now found himself wondering whether not just Mitchell but all the Mitchell men—including Jeb and himself—would soon be cut loose. But there was no time for speculation. He needed to get Mitchell focused on Hunt and the money. If that's where things came apart, they were all goners.

From the living room came a sudden happy shriek, followed by an equally loud cry of disappointment. "Oh, GODDAMN and GLORIOSKI!"

Martha came to the bedroom door to explain: "I thought it was Jackie down below. But it's just some big old bouffant copycat."

"Take her upstairs," Mitchell gently urged LaRue, once Martha returned to the living room. "To the Kennedy party. They'll love having her, trust me. She'll be more fun than a girl coming out of a cake—even for Teddy."

LaRue appeared hesitant.

"Don't worry," said Mitchell. "I'll be here when you get back."

Martha insisted that crashing the party was the farthest thing from her mind, but LaRue had no trouble getting her up to the Smiths' apartment. In fact, while putting the checkered kerchief around her neck, she suggested they take the two flights of stairs, lest the surprise of her entrance be blunted by an elevator ride shared with other guests.

LaRue felt as if he were entering the party with a live cheetah; there were gasps all around when they came in. He saw no sign of the birthday boy, but Patricia Lawford, Kennedy's sister, came straight over, accompanied by what LaRue took to be some good-looking fag in leather boots. John Lindsay, who'd kept his black tie but added a cowboy hat, also approached Martha to introduce himself.

She smiled with a mouth so wide open you could have put an apple in it. "*I* did *not* have to become a Democrat in order to get in here!" she shouted, extending her hand to the mayor, whose switch from the Republicans last year had done his pursuit of the presidency no good at all.

A waiter bowed slightly to Mrs. Mitchell and offered her a bottle of Lone Star beer, the theme party's designated beverage, but she refused it. "Martha wants a nice tall Dewar's, honey—lots of ice, no water."

Stephen Smith came over to tell her she was most welcome, and one of Ethel Kennedy's kids began snapping pictures. Martha draped her arm over anyone who wanted to pose with her, and LaRue began getting nervous.

She pulled him down onto a couch and pointed, with her drink, to a gaggle of miniskirted young women. "The boiler-room girls?"

LaRue wasn't sure what she meant.

"The ones who were up on Chappa-Q-tip, or whatever it's called. I'll tell you one thing, honey. If this Supreme Court had come to its senses a little earlier, the guest of honor, wherever he may be, would still have a *future*."

"How so?" LaRue responded.

"*Abortion*, honey," Martha explained. "It's been legal for the last month, or have you only been payin' attention to the *earth*-shattering matter of who picked the lock on the Democrats' clubhouse?"

LaRue had learned never to use the word "logic" when seeking clarification from Mrs. Mitchell; it inflamed her. So he asked instead for the "connection" between abortion and Edward Kennedy.

"You don't think that drowned girl wasn't pregnant? Well, I'm tellin' you that she *was*, and that we're movin' toward a world where that won't any longer be such a big ole catastrophe. But that was *not* true three years ago. Tell me, Freddy LaRooster: Did you ever pay for one of those operations? Or fa-*cil*-i-tate one?" She drew out the last word, as if mocking the jargon of Magruder and the junior executives.

"Miz Mitchell, I've got five children," said LaRue.

Martha hooted, and swirled the ice cubes in her drink. "That proves *nothin'*," she declared. "Though I suppose I do take your point, honey."

LaRue silently remembered Larrie coming to see him, one night in 1961, a few months after their last time together at the resort property. Over a cup of coffee at a restaurant in Jackson she asked for what she said was "the only thing I'll *ever* ask you for. A plane ticket to Los Angeles. Round-trip. Open-ended." He'd gone and got one for her and asked no questions; she wouldn't have answered them, anyway. Six months later she was back in town, briefly, before her permanent departure for Washington, D.C. He'd often wondered, then and later, whether she'd gotten rid of a baby, or given birth to one, out in California.

Martha detested quiet, and here he was creating some. He looked out into the room, worried that her novelty might already have worn off for the Kennedys. He didn't want this party to turn into one of her defeats, the kind of crash landing whose debris John Mitchell would be forced to sort through.

Fortunately, that guy who'd joined the Detroit Lions for a year in order to write a book about it was coming toward her.

"I'm George Plimpton," he said, in a voice that sounded too much like Elliot Richardson's for LaRue's taste. "I'd like to meet you, and so would Lee Radziwill."

Martha lit up and offered Plimpton her hand. While he shook it, she managed to whisper to LaRue, "It's a little like bein' offered Princess

Margaret instead of the queen, but hell's hooley, she *is* a princess, *supposedly*." To Plimpton, she cried, "Take me to her, Georgie boy!"

LaRue knew he shouldn't leave, but Plimpton seemed enough of a gent that she'd be safe with him for a while—maybe long enough for LaRue himself to get back downstairs and conduct his business with Mitchell. Then he could come back up, escort her home, and head over to his hotel room, having concluded this whole sorry business trip.

"I'll be *fine*," said Martha. "You go check on Mr. Moral Obligation Bond," she instructed, mocking her husband with mention of the fiscal instrument he had invented before Richard Nixon took over their lives.

LaRue left the Smiths' apartment after the two bodyguards at the door promised to let him back in.

Reentering the Mitchells' place proved slightly difficult: no one answered his repeated knockings before he realized that the door was unlocked.

"John?" he called, venturing into the dim rooms. The only response was a faint snore—more of a wheeze, thought LaRue, as he got closer to it. He went into the bedroom and saw Mitchell asleep with the cocktail glass on his chest. He moved it to the night table and took off Mitchell's shoes: wing-tips, just like the Old Man's. He covered him with an afghan and put out the light.

Back in the living room, LaRue sat by himself for a few moments in the near dark. He looked out the window that was still open from Martha's rubbernecking and saw a plane fly by in the winter darkness. He thought of Dorothy Hunt and listened once more to Mitchell's labored breathing.

Chapter Twenty-One

MARCH 21–23, 1973

WEST WING OF THE WHITE HOUSE; WATERGATE APARTMENT
OF FRED LARUE; CELLBLOCK 1, DISTRICT OF COLUMBIA JAIL

"It hurts my sacroiliac just to look at her," Rose whispered to Lorraine
while the two women stood near a door of the Oval Office. It was almost
lunchtime, and the president was greeting the Soviet women gymnasts.
Little Olga Korbut, whose pretzeled form and grimace had become
famous during last summer's Olympics, had given Nixon flowers.

Hoping she wouldn't be heard over the applause, Lorraine asked Rose,
"Are these girls even old enough to get their period?"

"Probably not," answered the president's secretary. "They cheat at
arms control; why not cheat at this?"

"*Dasvidaniya!*" said Nixon, who marched out of the office while the
girls were still clapping. He gently tapped Rose's elbow, indicating that
he needed a word. The gesture had a furtive, emergency quality, making her wonder if, say, the Israelis had just dropped the bomb on Cairo.

"Let me ask you something," said the president. "We may have a
need for substantial cash for a, uh, personal purpose. Do you know how
much is around?"

The question knocked her off balance, as did the drained, waxen quality of his face, which she was seeing close up for the first time today.
The boss hadn't looked this bad since that awful week during the '60
campaign when he'd slammed his knee on a car door and wound up in
the hospital with an infection.

"I don't know," she answered nervously. "I would have to look. I'd
have to get into the safe."

The president gave her a consoling pat on the arm and walked off to
his next meeting, knowing she'd have a look, and an exact count, before
the afternoon was through.

Rose knew that he had cleared his calendar to spend much of the
morning, before the gymnasts, with John Dean. The president's counsel

had been scurrying around the West Wing these past couple of days, contributing to Rose's sense that things had taken a swift, terrible turn. Watergate stories were piling up in the *Post* once more, and the president had been projecting a false and fragile gaiety. Everything was off-kilter: somebody had picked last Saturday night, St. Patrick's Day, to have Merle Haggard come sing his country songs at the White House, and the president had burst into the East Room, late, wearing a clownish green tie he'd gotten off Freddy, the old man who ran the elevator. He had looked glazed and keyed-up all at once, as if he were stumbling through one of those dreams where you find yourself onstage without any drawers.

On the way back to her office, Rose nudged Steve Bull, one of the president's youngest assistants: "Let me know when he goes over to the EOB."

Bull nodded, promising that he'd get word to her. For part of every day, Nixon chose to work inside the vast stone hive of offices next door, where he'd spent much of his vice presidency. Today, however abnormal the atmosphere, was unlikely to be an exception.

Rose ate a sandwich at her desk and thought about how little she'd been out to dinner, let alone lunch, since the second term—so different from what they'd expected!—had gotten under way. She missed Don but wouldn't let herself get blue now. She slapped the crumbs from her hands and returned her attention to a set of thank-you letters. They were going out to the musicians who'd performed here a couple of weeks ago with Sammy Davis, Jr.—who, come to think of it, wouldn't have made any less sense on St. Patrick's Day than Merle Haggard had. There was also a packet of materials to be assembled for tomorrow's Oval Office meeting of the Commission on Marijuana and Drug Abuse—what she and the girls kept calling "the pot party."

She was still working on that at 1:21 p.m., when Steve Bull called to say the president was crossing the driveway and heading to his EOB hideaway.

A minute later she was in the Oval Office. She closed its doors and hit the button on the machine inside the Wilson desk, listening impatiently to the high-pitched squeak of the reels as they rewound the president's morning. Yard after yard of tape took her back from the girl gymnasts—*Dasvidaniya!*—to the soft-footed ten o'clock entrance of John Dean. At this point, once she located it, Rose let the tape run forward, keeping its volume low enough not to draw anyone's attention. There really wasn't much need for caution: she frequently came in here by herself to organize things, a right of access even HRH had never dared to question.

While she listened, she pitied whoever would be stuck transcribing these things a few years from now. She had always hated working with Dictabelts, but at least they involved somebody's deliberate, steady effort to make each word audible—not the picking up of all the murmurs and asides that this machine strove to catch. The conversation she now heard was full of stammerings and pauses; the voice-activated equipment had often stopped and restarted while recording it, as if struggling to stay alert.

With his peppy sports car and platinum second wife, young John Dean was less insipid than the rest of the Magruder-style junior executives, but Rose had no particular affection for him, and whatever she did have quickly vanished as she listened to him speechifying on this hours-old tape:

We have a cancer—within, close to the presidency, that's growing. It's growing daily. It's compounding. It grows geometrically now because it compounds itself . . . and there is no assurance—

The president cut him off:

That it won't bust.

She knew better than most that the only thing to do with cancer was cut it out. She could remember perfectly the sense of lightness and relief she'd awoken with on that long-ago morning when she came out of the ether feeling as if some horrible twin had at last been severed from her. But on this tape all she heard was irresolution, a lot of clucking but still a willingness to coddle the cancer, to feed it further. Dean spoke from what she realized had been a lot of rehearsal:

Hunt is now demanding another seventy to a hundred thousand dollars for his own personal expenses; another fifty thousand dollars to pay his attorney's fees; a hundred and twenty-some thousand dollars. Wants it, wanted it, by close of business yesterday. Because he says he's going to be sentenced on Friday and needs to get his financial affairs in order . . . Mrs. Hunt was the savviest woman in the world. She had the whole picture . . . This is his blackmail. He says, "I will bring John Ehrlichman down to his knees and put him in jail. I have done enough seamy things for him that he'll never survive it."

Rose's ears perked up further. She allowed herself to feel a momentary thrill at this mention of Ehrlichman, thinking that a threat against Haldeman might immediately follow. But the next voice was the president's—

What's that? On Ellsberg?

—to which Dean responded:

Ellsberg, and apparently some other things.

She didn't know anything about Ellsberg or whatever else Dean referred to; her alarm came from realizing that the boss did. Instinct made her reach for her pad, but it wasn't there, so she opened one of the desk drawers, took out some stationery, and began making a shorthand transcription from the point at which the two men started talking turkey:

RN: *How much money do you need?*
JD: *I would say these people are going to cost, uh, a million dollars over the next, uh, two years.*
RN: *We could get that.*
JD: *Uh-huh.*
RN: *I mean, you could get the money. Let's say—*
JD: *Well, I think that we're going—*
RN: *What I mean is, you could, you could get a million dollars. And you could get it in cash. I, I know where it could be gotten.*
JD: *Uh-huh.*

RN: *I mean, it's not easy, but it could be done. But, uh, the question is who the hell would handle it?*
JD: *Well, Mitchell's got one person doing it who I'm not sure is—*
RN: *Who is that?*
JD: *He's got Fred LaRue doing it.*

She was taking the words down faster than they could utter them, and when she heard Nixon ask, *Don't you, just looking at the immediate problem, don't you have to handle Hunt's financial situation?*, she wondered if his bashful tone reflected not just his usual dislike of giving any order that implied criticism—in this case, of Dean's apparent reluctance to do what had to be done—but also a strained awareness that he himself might at this moment be committing a crime.

She now understood the sick look of his skin at lunchtime, understood that this was way beyond the spring of '70, when all that stood between them and the incensed mob was that ring of empty buses.

Shaken, she returned to her office and the pot-party list. The words ringing in her ear were not the muffled ones on the tape, but what the president had said to her at noon: *We may have a need for substantial cash.*

She couldn't bring herself to move until it was past three o'clock. Only then did she go to the little room with the safe and reach in for the money, some of it in neatly banded stacks, some of it in wadded fistfuls. It took her a half hour to count up nearly a hundred thousand dollars, her coral nail polish flashing against the bills, over and over, before she put them into three manila envelopes, interoffice mailers whose string ties she looped as tightly as she could.

The envelopes sat on her desk for the next hour and a half, beside the letters to Sammy Davis's band. If she passed the money on, would *she* be committing a crime? Would the lack of a specific instruction to have done so make her *less* guilty—or more? All her instincts spoke of the danger and foolishness of what she was about to do, but if this was the boss's chosen course, she wasn't going to second-guess him. She would do what had to be done, demonstrating even more loyalty and initiative than the great degrees of both already attributed to her. She would take this step even if it lowered her to the level of the Chicago ballot-box stuffers, the ones who'd prevailed in '60 and then been thwarted by her brother Joe eight years later.

The action would put her heroically far out on a limb, farther out than HRH, whom she'd heard the boss trying to protect on the tape. Looking through the loose pages of shorthand, she found the part about the burglary itself:

> JD: *I had no knowledge that they were going to do this.*
> RN: *Bob didn't either.*

At five-thirty she called the Committee for the Re-Election of the President, which remained in business across the street, dealing mostly with subpoenas these days. She asked for Mr. LaRue and was told he had already gone home. With no hesitation now, she grabbed her coat— still sporting its St. Patrick's Day pin—and swept through the outer office, the three heavy envelopes held against her chest like a schoolgirl's books. "I've got to go check on a neighbor," she told Lorraine and Marje.

She knew that LaRue lived in her own building, Watergate West. After parking her car, she walked over to the clamshell canopy, said hello to the doorman, and got the apartment number from him. She found LaRue cooking steaks for two gentlemen seated at his kitchen table. He was clearly startled by her arrival; after opening the door, he tipped his glasses down from his high forehead and onto his nose.

"Miz Woods," he said. He was one of the few on staff who didn't first-name her.

A tilt of Rose's head indicated that she would be more comfortable talking out in the hall.

"Millican, keep those steaks from burning," called LaRue, still not losing the softness of his voice. He stepped out of the apartment and guided Rose toward two club chairs by the elevator.

"A couple of friends," he explained. "One's an old business associate who's in town. The other's . . . working on something more current."

"Would it involve Howard Hunt?" Rose asked, struck by how she sounded like Dorothy Kilgallen playing *What's My Line?*

"Yes," said LaRue, unable to hide his surprise. Rose could see him wondering if she might have been sent here by Richard Nixon himself. She stared at him, waiting for more information.

"I've talked to John Dean and John Mitchell," LaRue said, finally. "Mr. Millican, one of the fellows in there, will make a delivery to Hunt's lawyer tonight, out in Potomac."

"It's not too late?" Rose asked.

"I hope not," LaRue murmured. "The sentencing's Friday."

"Do you have what you need?"

"Barely."

Rose thrust the envelopes toward him. "You can add this to it."

The glance they exchanged came not from a quiz show but the last reel of a movie—the kind where you knew that the explosive device would, very soon, either be disarmed or go off.

. . . there is no assurance—
That it won't bust.

"I'd better get back to the stove," said LaRue, nodding his thanks.

Forty-eight hours later, Howard Hunt swatted a cockroach as it approached the piece of orange rind he'd carelessly left on his bunk in cellblock No. 1 of the District of Columbia Jail. Having earlier today been given a provisional sentence of thirty-five years—his cooperation with the grand jury and Ervin Committee might get it reduced—he now found himself wondering whether he would ever again see the gray business suit he had donned when he got up this morning.

Before leaving the house for Judge Sirica's courtroom, he conducted a solemn conversation with his children. While he was gone, for however long, they must understand that they would not lack for fathers: a whole battery of strong men, from the Bay of Pigs' Manuel Artime to Bill Buckley, stood willing to assist in their protection and upbringing.

He had arrived at the courthouse somehow still hoping to get away with probation. But, hedging his bets, he'd brought along a shaving kit and extra underwear, all of which had been seized with the gray suit. A few hours after sentencing he had been sent to block No. 4, the last of the defendants to arrive there from court. Liddy had greeted him warmly—"Welcome, amigo!"—and remarked admiringly, as if they were in the locker room at a men's club, on the weight he'd lost. Bernie, in a tender act of respect, had already made up a bunk for him.

Then, inexplicably, without having committed any infraction, he'd been sent far below ground into this disciplinary hellhole. He'd tried stopping his ears and nostrils with wet toilet paper, but the plugs were proving useless against the belfry-like din and the smell of vomit. The blare of four televisions, each tuned to a different station, made a screaming soup of sound that was eventually pierced by a radio, closer than any of the TVs. A newscaster informed listeners that the president had gone for the weekend to Key Biscayne.

Back to where it all began, thought Hunt. Exactly one week less than a year ago, *somebody*—and it could only be John Mitchell himself—had approved Gordon's quarter-million-dollar budget.

"You really know the Big Dick?" asked an unshaven transvestite, strolling past Hunt's cell in denim overalls that had been cut down to make hot pants.

Hunt closed his eyes and didn't answer. Amidst the cacophony, he realized that, for the first time since Dorothy's death, he couldn't hear planes flying overhead. He was too far below ground, with too many stone layers of bedlam between him and the sky. There was no way to call out into the world: the dimes he'd sewn into the extra under-wear he'd brought were gone, too, confiscated, joined with Dorothy's diamond ring in some cosmic closet full of petty officialdom's lootings.

His lawyer, Bittman, had delivered the money to him yesterday morning—just past the deadline he himself had set. The envelope had been forty-five thousand short of what he'd demanded, as if to show they were still trying to exert some control over him. But he had never really expected full compliance—not the way they had let Dorothy down all last year. Which is why four days ago *he'd* jumped his own deadline for bringing John Ehrlichman—and who knew who else—to his knees.

He'd driven out to McCord's mailbox in Rockville on Monday night and left the phony letter to Bill Buckley (*"Many rumors reach my ears . . ."*). The effect had been precisely as hoped: McCord immediately wrote his own letter to Sirica, the one read in court today, absolving the Company and placing blame for the burglary high up within the administration: *"There was political pressure applied to the defendants to plead guilty and remain silent . . . Others involved in the operation were not identified . . . The Watergate operation was not a CIA operation."* Without naming those who had committed it, McCord insisted that perjury had taken place—an assertion that, once read in court, provoked a comic scramble of reporters toward pay phones.

Most of the newsmen never made it back to hear Hunt's own plea for leniency, which he'd insisted to Bittman on writing himself: *"For twenty-six years I served my country honorably and with devotion . . . Had I not lost my employment because of Watergate involvement, my wife would not have sought investment security for our family in Chicago, and four children would not be without a mother. For the last nine months I have suffered an ever-deepening consciousness of guilt. I pray that this court and the American people can accept my statement today that my motives were not evil. The real victims of the Watergate conspiracy, Your Honor, are, as it has turned out, the conspirators themselves."*

Typing this last rhetorical flourish had given him a familiar pleasure, the sort he had when writing his novels, and it seemed to him now, however real his love for Dorothy remained, that he had at last fallen into one of those books. Earlier this afternoon, he'd begun a meditation exercise up in cellblock No. 4, and gotten a what-the-hell-is-that look from Liddy. But right now he was feeling the need to do it again, no matter what catcalls might ensue once he got into the proper position.

He sat on the floor and imagined all tension and responsibility dissipating from his body, falling off his shoulders and out of his hands.

Whatever he tells the grand jury will not matter. He knows that they will now get all the information without him. The reporters, who this morning had leapt like birds from a rooftop at the crack of a rifle, will get to it even before the prosecutors. Everything will now fall to the ground without him.

And yet: he had been the one to ensure that the trail would lead back to the White House—not just by the trick he'd played on McCord, but by what he'd done on the night they were caught. With the clarity of mind that meditation provides, he can now see himself back in room 214 of the Watergate Hotel, can hear Bernie's voice—*They got us!*—coming over the radio. He can see himself racing out of the room, spotting the check on the bureau, the one waiting to be mailed—*Pay to the Order of Lakewood Country Club, $6.36, E. Howard Hunt*. And he can now, at last, for the first time, remember the split second in which he *decided* to leave it there, like a fingerprint or a shell casing.

A part of him had always wanted to take up citizenship in some other place entirely, in a life not his own, and now the doorway to that place seemed to be right here in the gathering dark, just beyond the bars, where the quizzical eyes of the jail's calico cat were looking straight at him—sympathetically, he thought.

Chapter Twenty-Two

APRIL 14, 1973
WASHINGTON HILTON HOTEL

"I'll have you back home and in bed by ten-thirty. It's a promise," said Richard Nixon to his wife.

Their limousine pulled away from the White House grounds at 8:58 p.m., and Pat smiled. "This is an awful lot of hair and makeup for ninety minutes."

"You look beautiful," the president responded. "Julie thought so, too. Of course, it'll be wasted on this crowd."

"Fina even took in the waist, half an inch."

Nixon looked out the window as the car proceeded up Connecticut Avenue toward the annual banquet of the White House Correspondents' Association. Had Pat ever been this thin? he wondered. The last few weeks' headlines—MCCORD: HUSH MONEY CAME FROM HUNT'S WIFE . . . MITCHELL GOT TRANSCRIPTS OF "BUG" RESULTS . . . CONSTITUENTS CLAMOR TO CONGRESS ABOUT WATERGATE REVELATIONS—had taken a bad toll. The papers always called her "skinny," whereas of course Paley's wife and Jackie got described as "marvelously thin." Soon they would say she was sick.

"You know," he said, "you looked awfully pretty in that blue-and-white dress this afternoon." He'd come out to greet the tour group she was leading—the black mayor of Washington and some local civic-improvement types—through the White House gardens.

Pat looked up from the novel she had open under the limousine's yellow ceiling light. She smiled. "Did you know I put that little bed of snapdragons in myself? They're *blazing*." She snapped the book shut on Dick's hand, in playful imitation of the flower's blossoms.

The Nixons' arrival at the dinner had been worked out for 9:05 p.m., so that they could avoid being present when the correspondents conferred an award on the two *Post* metro reporters, the ones who'd refused to let go of the Watergate story before McCord's letter tore everything open.

The car phone rang. It was Ziegler, who had to face these press clowns every day. "They're through with the *Post* guys," he reported from the Hilton.

"Good," said Nixon. "Then I won't tell the driver to slow down. But I'll tell *you* that this is the last year we do this goddamned event."

"Yes, sir," said Ziegler, who knew the president had made the same vow two years ago. "I should warn you that the atmosphere here is rough. Sirica is a guest at one of the tables, and the emcee earlier made a point of 'introducing' some of our guys to him—saying they'd no doubt be getting better acquainted soon."

The president did not laugh. "I'm assuming Mrs. Nixon will be sitting on my right. Who's on my left?"

"I am, sir."

"Good. Is Dean there?"

"No."

"Okay. See you in a couple of minutes."

The president put down the phone and Pat clicked off the reading light. After a moment's hesitation, she spoke: "Rose says that Martha reached her on the phone this afternoon."

"Did she?"

"Yes. And that last night she was ranting and raving to one of the girls on the switchboard."

"What did she want today?" asked Nixon.

"Supposedly to find out when John would be coming home. I'm sure she really just wanted to find out whether you'd seen him in person."

Pat and her husband often employed indirection with each other as a matter of considerateness, a method for softening bad news or criticism. Nixon knew that this casual-sounding mention of Mitchell's afternoon visit to the White House—and his own avoidance of a face-to-face meeting—was really meant to scold. But he felt guilty enough already.

The whole thing had bust. Since the meeting with Dean on March 21, they'd stopped trying to cover up the burglary. They were now trying to cover up the cover-up, and it was by no means certain that Dean remained part of the effort. Magruder was believed to have spent most of today, a Saturday, with the prosecutors. God knew what else he was saying, but for sure he was fingering Dean and Mitchell for being present when Liddy first proposed his crazy ideas in Mitchell's office at Justice.

Only this morning, but once and for all, Haldeman and Ehrlichman had decided that Mitchell had to take the rap—had to step forward and claim responsibility for everything that had happened, so that it could all disappear in the orgy of self-congratulation the press would throw themselves for having caught such a big fish.

But when Ehrlichman put the proposition to Mitchell, the answer was a polite, emphatic no. However depressed and seedy he'd gotten, he wasn't going to be bamboozled. He didn't come down from New York, on the shuttle, until after lunch, and he'd probably gotten home to Martha, as she knew he would, before dinnertime.

This may have been everyone's last chance, and it was gone.

The president resumed speaking to his wife when the limousine turned into the driveway of the Hilton. "I let Ehrlichman talk to him. Not very successfully."

"Did you consider seeing him yourself?"

"I couldn't do it. And besides—"

The rest of his sentence disappeared in a burst of flashbulbs.

The hotel's International Ballroom was a vast underground and airless modern space; it gave Nixon the feeling that he was in steerage on some giant spaceship. A small band played "Hail to the Chief" as he and Pat made their way down a head table many times longer than the one for the Last Supper. He said hello to Rogers and Richardson and to Cap Weinberger, the Reagan man they now had at HEW.

Ted Knap, the fellow from Scripps Howard about to become the association's president, welcomed the first couple with a please-dig-in gesture toward the dessert now being served. At the direction of the White House, a bowl of consommé, rather than strawberry shortcake, had been set in front of Nixon, who believed *he* never got credit for remaining trim in a town where half the men, by the time they turned forty, were shaped like bowling pins; Ehrlichman was a good example.

No, Pat was just "skinny," and he himself got mocked for eating cottage cheese with ketchup.

Sweets had ruined his teeth, not his torso. Today had started with yet another visit to Dr. Chase on Eighteenth Street, to deal with some rot underneath a lower-right crown. He and the dentist both put the blame on his three years' worth of nickel breakfasts while at Duke: a Milky Way bar, economical and energizing, every morning he awoke inside Whippoorwill Manor, the off-campus dump he'd shared with a bunch of other law students.

Did he need a criminal lawyer now? Someone other than Dean, who these last three weeks had felt less like his counsel than a mole? Sure as shooting, he would follow Magruder to the prosecutors and make a deal, if he hadn't already.

The president looked at the three *Washington Post* tables just below the dais—a whole little government-in-exile presided over by Bradlee, Jack Kennedy's fellow cocksman; the two of them had fornicated their way into middle age like Harvard boys still panting outside the burlesque stage door in Boston.

He also caught sight of Mrs. Longworth, sitting with her cousin Alsop at a table slightly farther back. He rose from his chair and made a courtly bow, remembering all of a sudden her Christmastime warnings about Hunt. He realized he'd never followed up on them, but how, in any case, would that have been possible? And what damage could Hunt have done by forgery, beyond what he'd accomplished with plain and simple blackmail?

"They'll be ready for you in about five minutes," said Ziegler.

Nixon nodded. "Did Mitchell's little trip down here make it onto the wires?"

Ziegler laughed. "I heard he wound up sitting next to Daniel Schorr on the shuttle back to New York. Needless to say, he didn't reveal anything."

"Old Stone Face," said Nixon, alarmed by the surge of affection that speaking Mitchell's nickname brought. But, goddammit, how could John have let the bugging idea continue beyond that preposterous meeting in the DOJ? It was goddamn Martha's fault, driving the man further toward distraction every year. He thanked God for Pat, who was graciously nodding to some butch gal from the Philadelphia *Bulletin* as she took another tiny forkful of cake.

"You know," he said, leaning toward her on his right, "it wouldn't have done any good anyway. Mitchell taking the blame, I mean."

"Why?" she asked, not even needing to whisper in the ballroom's din.

Nixon sighed. "Connally says, if people are told Mitchell knew, then they'll believe Nixon knew. Because the two of them are too close for it to have been otherwise."

"And it will be the same with Haldeman, Dick. His going won't satisfy these people either. They're coming for *you*."

She might have said *us*, to make him feel less alone, but she couldn't bring herself to do it. Besides, the starker the message the better.

Ted Knap began his introduction of the president. Nixon, pushing away his bowl of soup, spoke softly to Ziegler. "I'm thinking about a Warren Commission kind of thing. Put both Ervin and Sirica on it. Let them compete to see who can leak the most and get the biggest fawning headlines."

"An interesting thought," Ziegler whispered, hoarsely.

"Liddy is the key to this, you know. If I could be seen pressuring him, maybe even going to the D.C. jail, telling him to *talk*—well, then it would be the *president* cracking the case."

Hiss was on the boss's mind yet again, thought Ziegler, who prayed for Knap to finish. He realized that a visit to the District of Columbia Jail was no more beyond possibility than 1970's middle-of-the-night trip to the Lincoln Memorial.

To the press secretary's relief, Knap picked up a sterling-silver globe, a copy of one made in eighteenth-century Williamsburg, and prepared to bestow it upon the president in recognition of the past year's foreign-policy triumphs. The object, held aloft, received polite applause, which diminished to something even milder when Nixon rose to accept it.

"I can't give up Haldeman," the president whispered to Pat before walking to the lectern. "He's the only one who can handle Kissinger."

The first lady shook her head, imperceptibly, masking her disbelief while she applauded her husband and smiled toward the fifth and sixth rows of tables.

As he took possession of the globe and posed for pictures with Knap,

Nixon felt his anger rise against the sick, disproportionate thinking of the crowd that was giving him this gift. The actual globe could fall apart at any time, but moments ago this throng in front of him had no doubt whistled and hollered for the *Post* boys, all for saving the world from what was—truthfully—a third-rate burglary.

"President Knap, distinguished guests, and friends: It is a privilege to be here at the White House Correspondents' dinner. I suppose I should say it is an *executive* privilege."

Now that he had the bastards laughing, he would snooker them with a little solemnity: "In the past several months, two men who appeared at these annual dinners on a total of twelve separate occasions have passed away, and President Knap, with your permission I think it would be appropriate this evening for everyone to rise in a moment of silence in memory of Presidents Harry S. Truman and Lyndon Baines Johnson."

As everyone stood, he stole a glance at Pat, knowing he hadn't gotten through to her with what he'd said about Haldeman.

But it was time to get back to being a good sport. He offered the reseated crowd a little tribute to Ziegler's patience and loyalty, setting up a joke that Buchanan had written. "I must say that you've really worked him over, ladies and gentlemen. This morning he came into the office a little early, and I said, 'What time is it, Ron?' And he said, 'Could I put that on background?'"

Time to steer things back to seriousness, to the big themes of "a lasting peace abroad and prosperity at home," phrasing he could by now roll out with the rote ease of "We hold these truths to be self-evident."

He kept things short, got them to stand and clap for the four returned POWs in the ballroom, and ended by flattering them with what they'd believe to be a quotation from one of their own: "Now that the burden of our nation's longest war has at long last been lifted, I am coming to realize the truth of what David Lawrence, a charter member of this group fifty-nine years ago, said to me not long before his recent passing: "'There is only one more difficult task than being president of this country when we are waging war, and that is to be president of the nation when it is waging peace.'"

Stepping away from the lectern, he found himself smiling, genuinely amused to have put them into the position of not knowing whether they were applauding him or Lawrence; as a result, they couldn't decide how far up to set the thermostat of their approval. Christ, he'd have to see half of them again tomorrow morning, the ones who were here from out of town, when they sat their fat asses down in the East Room for the worship service. What ever possessed Ziegler to think *that* invitation would be helpful?

"First-rate, perfect," said Richardson, as the president returned to his seat on the dais.

Puffect, he pronounced it, irritating Nixon.

"Did you like the Lawrence quotation?" the president asked his new defense secretary.

"It hit exactly the right note," answered Richardson.

"I made it up."

Nixon took his wife's hand, and the crowd stood up as the two of them got ready to depart. He said good night to Rogers, who told the president about a cheap shot the emcee had taken against Agnew, before adding one of his own, calling the vice president "your insurance policy."

"Well, that policy may have to be canceled," Nixon responded. "Haldeman's found out that our friend from Maryland has a few problems of his own that are being investigated."

Rogers looked puzzled.

"Not Watergate," said Nixon. "Something else entirely." He rubbed his thumb against his index and middle fingers to indicate money.

Rogers's mouth opened slightly as he relinquished the president, who snapped off a salute to the POWs.

The tablecloths looked like hundreds of whitecaps, but Nixon forced himself to step down into the sea of guests, far enough to kiss Mrs. L's hand and shake Joe Alsop's. He gave the writer's elbow a small appreciative squeeze, thanks for his not having sat at one of the *Post* tables, even though Mrs. Graham's paper remained the flagship purveyor of his column. Nixon felt particularly grateful for Alsop's having recently written that the media should think twice about turning Richard Nixon, the only president they had, into a cripple on the world's dangerous stage.

"How's Stew?" Nixon asked the columnist.

"He's got his ups and downs, Mr. President. He was at the Gridiron last month and feeling just fine. But he wasn't strong enough to come out tonight."

"Just like Harold," said Nixon, baffling Alsop with this reference to his own brother's long illness. "It went on for ten years."

Alice Longworth, accepting a peck on the cheek from the first lady, experienced her own moment of confusion. It was Joe's mention of the Gridiron dinner—weren't they there *now*? But if they were, where was the Marine Band? And where were the white ties?

She emerged from the daze within seconds, realizing with her usual detachment that some piece of arterial plaque must have clogged things in her noggin before getting flushed out of the way. She was perfectly lucid once more: she was at the *other* dinner, the one for the correspondents' association, and there was Dick, receding toward the exit with his hand nowhere near the small of his wife's back, as it ought to be.

She noted Pat's exceptional thinness, though she herself had weighed only ninety-two and one-half pounds the last time she'd been forced onto a scale. She might be making it to ninety-three tonight, if they'd served her one of Anna Maria's veal chops instead of this chicken that had choked to death on its own paprika.

"He's got to give another Checkers speech," said Joe, watching the president disappear.

"What's he going to say?" asked Alice. "That he's keeping Haldeman the way he allowed the girls to keep the dog?"

Elliot Richardson, having greeted the *Boston Globe* table, now approached Alsop and said hello. Alice listened with exasperation to their brief, maloccluded exchange, wondering why so many people in her own dying social class continued to speak in that maddening double-slur of alcohol and lockjaw.

"Mrs. Longworth," said Richardson, reluctantly. "How lovely to see you. So much has happened since Miami."

"I have never been to Miami," she said, provoking his retreat.

She sat down, and tugged on her cousin's jacket to make him sit with her. "Joe, you need to update your advice."

"What advice do you mean?"

"The advice you gave in that column supporting Dick, the one putting political hijinx like Watergate into *perspective*."

"You make perspective sound like spinach."

"You referred to that forged letter from the British ambassador during the campaign of 1888. Cleveland and Harrison. Whom do you think you're writing for? *Me?*"

"I thought you didn't read the *Post*."

"I don't. My granddaughter does."

"And her copy fell open on your breakfast tray."

"I don't eat breakfast. No, Joanna read me that column, and your conclusion was wrong, wrong, wrong."

"How so?"

"You say the press are trying to cripple Dick."

"And so they are."

"They are *not*," Alice said firmly, as the vast room around them began to empty itself. "They are trying to kill him."

Chapter Twenty-Three

APRIL 16, 1973, 8:40 A.M.
4800 BLOCK OF FORT SUMNER DRIVE, BETHESDA, MARYLAND

"The Gillespies have been aces," declared Jeb Magruder, in praise of his neighbors. Fred LaRue had been allowed to pull into that family's driveway, undetected by reporters staking out the Magruder house down the street, and Jeb, who'd been drinking coffee in the Gillespies' kitchen almost since dawn, was now able to slip into the passenger seat of LaRue's Chrysler. The older man had called late last night, asking for this talk.

A few weeks ago, after McCord's letter to Sirica went off like a cluster bomb, Jeb had been the one needing an ear, since he and everyone else knew that the perjury referred to in the letter was his own. He had shown up at Watergate West a couple of times to discuss developments and to express hope that things might—if Liddy didn't talk— still somehow hold together.

But two days ago he himself had finally spilled things to the U.S. Attorneys, and now he was hearing LaRue say, in his soft, undramatic way: "I saw Dean on Friday. I told him I'm going to the prosecutors."

Somehow the words still came as a shock, and during the long pause that followed, Magruder snuck a glance out the Chrysler's rear window. In the street he saw a thick black cable belonging to one of the TV news outfits. It looked like a snake that had escaped from the Woodley Park Zoo.

"Jeb," said LaRue, "I love John Mitchell. And it's damn near going to kill me to talk about him. But if I let this go any later, it's going to be worse for me and just about everybody, maybe even for him."

Magruder nodded. "I met with Mitchell a week after McCord's letter. He gave me two pieces of advice. The first was to get a lawyer, and the second was to not tell the lawyer the truth."

LaRue smiled, even as his head sank a little.

"You know," Magruder continued, "I gave some thought to suicide." He conveyed this revelation in the same tone with which he might once have informed LaRue that he'd considered and rejected a direct-mail campaign for the CRP's Kentucky operation. "The circumstances didn't really make it appropriate."

It was the possibility of Mitchell's suicide that remained much on LaRue's mind, and he didn't like hearing talk of that act from Jeb, in whose case it would seem plain stupid.

"I also thought about skipping the country," Magruder added. "I even had my assistant at Commerce research extradition treaties—who we've got them with and who we don't." He shook his head. "It was too complicated. And I decided I couldn't do it to the kids, even if I managed to get them out with me and Gail."

It all sounded fantastical to LaRue, who had come here this morning to discuss the legal realities in front of them. "I just hired Fred Vinson, Jr., to be my lawyer," he told Jeb. "You old enough to remember his daddy? Truman's chief justice?"

Magruder shook his head. The name sounded only vaguely familiar. "You know," he said again, appearing to be off in his own world, "I really loved that Commerce job. It was supposed to be a waiting room for me until things cleared up and I looked confirmable again, but I think I had my happiest six weeks in Washington there."

"Things are not going to clear up, Jeb."

"Oh, I know that now. And here's a funny thing: once you start telling him the truth, you'll *like* Earl Silbert. He's a stand-up guy. On Saturday, when I finally let everything out, I ended up apologizing to him for having lied so long."

LaRue felt his own mind beginning to wander as Jeb meandered along all these tangents. He remembered being in the CRP office last spring, trying to settle an argument between Jeb and Liddy, almost having to separate them physically. Why hadn't he told Jeb to fire Liddy then and there? And down at Key Biscayne, when they got to the Gemstone memo in the stack of things to be considered, why hadn't he told Mitchell in no uncertain terms to get rid of the goddamned idea, along with goddamned Liddy, once and for all? Mitchell had said, "We don't have to decide that now," and they had let it go, allowed things to drift—until they'd all washed up where they were now.

LaRue's best guess remained that Liddy had decided to go into the DNC all on his own, but to this day he had never asked Jeb how *he* thought the thing had actually happened. He wasn't going to ask him now, either, not when it was so dangerous for anyone to know more than he already did.

He volunteered some gossip instead: "Mitchell says the Old Man wouldn't see him in person on Saturday. Since then he's even stopped taking his calls."

"When did you talk to Mitchell?" asked Magruder.

"Last night."

"I haven't spoken to him since I went to Silbert with, you know, the truth. I wanted to call him this weekend, but I was scared Martha would pick up."

LaRue snorted. "Mitchell says the reporters are sendin' her flowers and fruit baskets every half hour, tryin' to get her to come downstairs and do interviews."

A scream penetrated the rolled-up windows of the Chrysler.

"You get away from my child!" shrieked Magruder's pretty, well-brought-up wife. "If you have something to say, you come to *me*! Don't you *ever* come near my children!"

Both men turned in their seats, and LaRue saw Gail Magruder in the middle of the road, shoving a blonde he recognized as Lesley Stahl from CBS. The Magruders' boy, Whitney, was soon free to continue walking to school.

"Shit," said Jeb, "I ought to be out there."

"She looks like she's handling it pretty well on her own," observed LaRue. He wondered, though, how she would do when the reporters were gone and Jeb, along with himself and the rest of them, was off in prison.

An hour later LaRue was downtown, sitting on his usual stool in the waffle shop across from Ford's Theatre, eating a second breakfast and trying to stir himself toward action. Even after a third cup of coffee, he lingered, and once he left the little eatery he strolled along the streets by the National Archives, becoming curious about whether his rubber gloves and Tony Ulasewicz's coin dispenser might achieve eternal rest in that building.

It was ten minutes past noon when he called Fred Vinson, Jr., at his office several blocks away, and another half hour went by before the two of them were sitting in front of a team of shirtsleeved lawyers headed by Earl Silbert, who looked like one of those Jews hauled before HUAC twenty years before, with glasses thicker and goofier than LaRue's own.

"So, Mr. LaRue, you've decided you may have something you need to tell us."

"Yes," he murmured. Sensing that Silbert *was* a stand-up guy, he felt glad that, unlike Jeb, he didn't have any courtroom perjury to apologize for. He cleared his throat and began responding to questions on several particular subjects:

About being out in California, for the fundraising gala, on the morning after the burglary: "I told Mr. Mitchell about the call Magruder had just gotten from Liddy. That was the one where Liddy said Jeb had better get to a secure phone at the nearby NASA base. I told Liddy I thought a pay phone would be okay."

About the meeting two days after the burglary, in the former attorney general's apartment: "Mr. Mitchell thought—we all did—that this sounded like one of Colson's shows." To LaRue's way of thinking, it still did, but there had never been that much to connect Colson to it.

About his own meeting with Liddy, a day after that, in his own Watergate West apartment: "Yes, he mentioned the other attempted burglary, the one of Mr. Ellsberg's psychiatrist."

About how, on June 29, he'd devised a set of code names with the president's personal attorney: "Mr. Kalmbach told me this would be a highly secret operation. He said we needed to conduct our business over pay phones, and that we'd both call ourselves Bradford."

And, finally, *about Key Biscayne on March 30, 1972:* "Magruder handed a paper to Mitchell. Mitchell read it and asked me what I thought about it, and I told him it wasn't worth the risk. To the best of my recollection, Mitchell responded by saying something like, 'Well, we don't have to decide this right now.'"

The questioning went on for hours. Every so often a new shirtsleeved lawyer would come into the room and take the place of another. Eventually, LaRue stopped looking over to Vinson before answering each question. His attorney just kept nodding, indicating that he should keep talking, should let them pump him like some old oil well that might still have another thousand gallons pooled at the bottom. LaRue realized he had entered the backwards, flip-sided world of plea bargaining, where the more you confessed to, the less you'd wind up being guilty of.

Through a window on the office's west side, he watched the sun descend, and he heard Silbert ask, "Mr. LaRue, will you be prepared to testify that during a telephone conversation on March the twenty-first Mr. Mitchell instructed you to meet all or most of Mr. Hunt's demands?"

LaRue gave the only acceptable answer, yes, and as he did he began to cry. Lowering his head and closing his eyes, he put himself, yet again, back in that living room in Key Biscayne. He wondered if Mitchell had kept the plan alive, and he had protested it so feebly, because deep down, in what his wife sometimes called the subconscious, both had known it was the kind of thing that might appeal to the Old Man.

Or had it appealed to something in themselves? To the memory of that afternoon early in the first term, when they'd stood on the DOJ balcony with Martha and looked down at the demonstrators carrying their North Vietnamese flags? The two of them had laughed when Martha called the protesters "the very liberal Communists," but they had also wanted to spray them with machine-gun fire. Three years later, had Liddy's array of plots and sabotage operations simply appealed to the bit of Liddy in all of them? The part that longed to pulverize every McGovernite who thought those kids with the flags were okay?

Or was it just the love of the game, the excitement of the foxhole, that had made him spend most of the last few years up here instead of at home with Joyce in Mississippi, tending to his businesses and the lives of his kids? The swirling bowls of the Watergate and the checkerboard floors of the EOB had been an alternative to all that, a chosen displacement from it and from everything that had happened years ago—first in the Canadian woods, and then at Gulf Hills.

After today this strange city would no longer be a choice; it would be a jurisdiction, one he could leave only temporarily, whenever the shirtsleeved men across the table deemed that permissible. He looked at them now, aware that he had told them the truth this afternoon, and aware that, by doing so, he'd likely invited a much older truth—a half-

known and catastrophic one—to break out of the mental compartment
where he tried to keep it stowed.

By 6:45 LaRue was having a drink on the balcony at Watergate West,
looking down Virginia Avenue toward the Washington Monument,
whose sky-high pair of little red lights had not yet begun their nighttime winking. April was more than half gone, but the cherry blossoms
lingered on the air, and Washington seemed, as it often and oddly had
to LaRue, the most pleasant city on earth.

He had called Mitchell, not ten minutes ago, to tell him where he'd
been this afternoon. "I'm sorry, boss," he'd added, after one of his long
pauses.

"You have to do what you have to do," Mitchell had answered, with
no hint of surprise, between puffs on his pipe.

"I'm still sorry."

And he always would be, whether the two of them ever spoke again
or just nodded at each other inside all the committee rooms and court-
houses now awaiting them.

The phone rang. He hoped for a second that it might be Mitchell with
something more to say, or even Martha ready to scald his ears off. *Is
this Mr. Freddy LaRuthless? Mr. Freddy LaTruth?*

But it was only the doorman. "I have a message for you, Mr. LaRue.
It doesn't seem to be signed, but it must have been put on the desk here
a few minutes ago, while I was on my break. Whoever left it is waiting
for you at one of the umbrella tables down in the shopping plaza."

"No name?"

"No, sir."

LaRue felt a wave of dread. Was someone down there who knew he'd
been with Silbert? Somebody waiting to punch him in the nose? Maybe
even shoot him?

If he had a pistol here, instead of just Daddy's bird gun mounted on
the wall, he might take it with him. But when he could at last bring
himself to leave the apartment, the only defense he brought along was
the self-deception that he was really just going downstairs for a pouch
of tobacco, and to see whether the barber shop might be open this late.

He wondered how he would recognize the person, before realizing that hardly mattered. Whoever was there would recognize him. Maybe it would be McCord, still out on bail? Dean? Somebody who'd regard the conversation's Watergate location as a bit of coincidental black humor? Or would have reasoned that a conspiratorial rendezvous here would be a matter of hiding in plain sight—a case of the purloined letter?

Once in the shopping plaza, LaRue found no one at the tables except a woman with most of her back to him, and two Chinese boys from the restaurant who were having an early dinner before making their deliveries throughout the complex. The woman had long black hair that fell between her shoulders. She was smoking a cigarette and drawing the panels of her cardigan sweater a little closer, as if, despite the evening's balminess, the weather wasn't as warm as the kind to which she was most accustomed. LaRue allowed himself to gaze at her shoulders for a moment before deciding that the summons here had been a hoax. He set off to the drugstore to get some tobacco after all.

But the woman in the sweater seemed somehow to recognize his footfall. She turned around in her chair under the big picnic umbrella.

At that point he saw Clarine Lander motion for him to come sit down beside her.

Chapter Twenty-Four

APRIL 28, 1973, 8:30 P.M.
CAMP DAVID, MARYLAND

"Your family loves you," said Rose.

"I suppose they do," Nixon replied.

The navy steward poured some California wine and then retreated to a discreet distance, leaving the two of them to their shrimp scampi.

Last night, the boss had made a spur-of-the-moment decision to come up here—and had shanghaied her along—after a grueling day-trip to Mississippi, where he'd dedicated a new naval air center to John Stennis, who was once more up and around. Rose knew the pillars of the temple were coming down, as in those old biblical movies, and she knew that the president didn't want his family around during what could only be an awful weekend. This morning, Saturday, she'd found out that Pat and the girls had stayed awake most of Friday night, before deciding to send Tricia, visiting the White House from New York, up here to Camp David. She'd surprised her father at lunchtime, prior to a meeting he had with Bill Rogers, whose reputation for probity appeared to be giving him new value within the ruined administration.

Rose had never liked Tricia as much as Julie (no one did), but she had to give her credit. She'd arrived in a no-nonsense, acting-her-age outfit and took up no more than fifteen minutes of her father's time, telling him that his family would support him no matter what he decided. Rose did have to wonder if she'd worked in a brief, special pitch to get rid of Ehrlichman, with whom she'd clashed long ago, and who regarded Tricia as a nasty piece of candy stuck between two teeth.

But there was no time to dwell on such things. Since getting here Thursday, Rose had been telling herself they *could* still fight their way out of this, just as they had with the Fund, when Eisenhower dangled the boss over a cliff and a few days later hauled him back in.

"Reverend Peale called," she said, as she sliced a shrimp in half. "Around five."

Nixon, enough at ease with her to mop up the sauce on his plate with a piece of bread, nodded. "I haven't been able to return it."

"The power of positive thinking." Rose quoted the pastor's famous title with a slow emphasis, as if to declare: *That's all you need to survive.*

In the silence that followed, she thought about the March 21 tape, imagining what might be on the hundreds of others made at the Wilson desk. She wanted to tell the president, before the steward brought them their plates of sorbet, that all those tapes needed to be destroyed, immediately. But she couldn't bring herself to speak: it was presumptuous, and right now the boss's ego was more fragile than the bubbles sparkling in the wine.

She had questioned him only once—months before the break-in—about the relentless production of tape. He had mumbled something about "historical importance" and she'd said nothing more. All right, maybe these tapes would just end up locked in some library vault, but she still couldn't imagine sending them even that far out into history. It would be like mailing someone a page from her steno pad instead of a typed letter. Maybe the retired president did want them only for help in writing his memoirs. But would he really destroy them afterwards? She doubted it. In truth, she hadn't thought the matter through any further than he had, because she never wanted to think about turning sixty years old out there in San Clemente, working with him on those memoirs away from everybody else and every other place she knew.

"You know, Rose, domestically this country can run itself."

"Oh, I agree."

"But somebody has got to run the rest of things. We should have started bombing North Vietnam two weeks ago. Christ, the cease-fire violations! You should see the satellite pictures: the Ho Chi Minh Trail looks like the San Bernardino Freeway. The amount of supplies and weapons they're sending south is unbelievable—and you can thank John Dean for that. If we send one plane into the air, the Democrats will scream their heads off that it's a plan to distract everyone from 'Nixon's Watergate troubles.'"

"Then," said Rose, "I suppose the North Vietnamese can also *blame* John Dean for not getting their reconstruction aid from Congress. Those louses on the Hill are determined not to support you on *anything.*"

Nixon laughed. "You know, I thought I'd be feeling guilty when I met with Thieu out in San Clemente the other week. I mean, I *know* they got the short end of the agreement. As it turned out, I barely had time to talk to the son of a bitch, let alone feel bad for him. Sorry," he added, as the steward set dessert in front of them.

Rose smiled. He always apologized for these slips into profanity, when they both knew her own speech could be more salty than his.

Eating his sorbet, the president returned to the catastrophes at hand. "Haldeman wants me to put Rogers in as attorney general. Kleindienst certainly can't keep the job; he'll be lucky if he doesn't get indicted with Mitchell." When Rose offered no reply, he pushed the dessert away. "I keep thinking of Arthur," he said, with a studied softness. "Two days before he passed away. 'If I should die before I wake, I pray Thee, Lord, my soul to take.' He recited it in my mother's arms."

Rose had often seen him self-pitying—he was entitled!—but this reference to the dead *younger* brother instead of to Harold, the dead older one, alarmed her. She couldn't remember him being this maudlin, even at the end of '62.

"You need to destroy John Dean," she said. "And you need to get rid of those tapes."

She was eager to get into that practical, emergency mode where she functioned best. Holding her dessert spoon, she could feel the itch to grab paper and pencil and start making a list of all the phones and desks that had been wired back in '71 and now needed to be disconnected.

The president, not waiting for the steward, poured himself some more wine. "What about Bob?" he asked.

She bit her tongue and called upon her will power, deciding that she would not indulge herself. She would recommend only what was best for the man in front of her. "If you get rid of everybody, then the whole pack is guilty—and you look guilty, too. But if you make John Dean out for a liar, everybody else may end up okay." None of them knew what that fragile-looking little operator had been saying to the prosecutors since he'd gone to them two weeks ago.

"There's only one good reason *not* to get rid of everyone," said Nixon. "Let me hear it."

"Because it'd still be too little too late."

The following afternoon, Sunday, he fired them anyway—both Haldeman and Ehrlichman, in that order, after summoning them to Camp David by helicopter.

While he was still with the latter, Rose met HRH on the path near Witch Hazel Cottage. He was carrying Mary Baker Eddy's Christian Science book, which she supposed was like the Bible to people of his persuasion. She was trying mightily, and failing, to feel sorry for him. She didn't know what to say, and she left it to him to speak instead.

"Rose, I obviously won't be in anymore, but he's going to talk from the Oval tomorrow at nine p.m." He paused, uncertainly, before adding: "He's exhausted and on edge."

She felt her jaw clench. She didn't need Bob Haldeman to tell her Richard Nixon's moods.

"Tomorrow night," he continued, "I would instruct the switchboard not to put through any calls after the speech. The calls will all be supportive, but they'll crank him up further, and he's likely to say something indiscreet that will find its way into the papers."

Yes, thought Rose. You *would* instruct the switchboard, if you were still the chief of staff. But you're not. She wanted to ask who his replacement would be but even now wouldn't risk looking inconsequential by admitting she didn't know.

She could see him reading the hard look on her face, taking it to mean she would keep the switchboard uninstructed and that calls would keep going through.

"Bob, I wish you well," she said at last.

"Thanks, Rose. The same to you."

No embrace, no handshake. He just walked away with Mrs. Eddy. *We have a cancer—within, close to the presidency.* Did he think they could cure it without a doctor? Get rid of it with prayers to Mrs. Eddy's version of Christ? The cancer wasn't even the most pressing danger. There was a blood clot—John Dean—racing toward the boss's brain.

She watched Haldeman recede. No, she was not enjoying this moment that she'd imagined so often and in so many ways; his comeuppance was too small a piece of the general calamity. Turning around, she walked toward Aspen Lodge, wondering how much more "exhausted and on edge" the boss would be after getting rid of Ehrlichman, too.

Ron Ziegler was on the porch. She liked him. He ought to be just another Magruder-style junior executive—he'd even started his work life at Disneyland—but there was a soul, she thought, behind the hooded eyes. As soon as she got up the steps, he put a gentle hand on her shoulder. She'd been to a hundred Irish funerals in her life, and she half-expected him to say, "I'm sorry for your troubles."

She'd been, as a matter of fact, to a wake in Pittsburgh only two weeks ago, and had learned, when she got back to Washington, that Dean had tried to track her down while she was gone—in order to set up a last appointment with the president without having to go through HRH. At that moment she had known there really was no more administration; the team was scrambling off the field in a dozen different directions, leaving Richard Nixon by himself.

"Is Ray Price around?" she now asked Ziegler.

"Yeah. They're going to start work on the speech before dinner."

"I'm not sure that's a good idea."

"It isn't," said Ziegler. "The boss doesn't have the strength."

"He'll get it back," said Rose. "But not tonight."

After a pause, Ziegler told her that Kleindienst had been fired, too.

"Who's the new AG?" she asked.

"I'm not sure. I'm not sure the president knows yet."

Rose chewed a corner of her lip and pretended to look at the ship's model on a table across the room. She'd been hoping to hear that Rogers had been named. Now she had a sick feeling as to why she'd seen Elliot Richardson strolling the grounds an hour or so ago. She'd assumed he was here on some couldn't-wait Defense Department matter, but that seemed unlikely now.

A minute later, she and Ziegler were surprised to see the president emerge, alone, from the lodge's main room. Tears ran down his face, and they realized that Ehrlichman had already gone out the back door.

"You know what he said?" asked Nixon. "He wanted me to tell him how to explain all this to his children. I couldn't think of an answer."

"You don't have to," Rose snapped. "That's not your job. You need to go on being president, dealing with North Vietnam and Russia, not John Ehrlichman's kids."

"Rose is right, Mr. President," said Ziegler.

At this particular moment Nixon's self-pity was a mere overlay, a kind of plastic transparency protecting the authentic anguish visible beneath. His hurt almost glowed, and it rendered Rose and Ziegler speechless.

"I told him I'd hoped I wouldn't wake up today," the president continued.

Rose looked at him, wanting to strangle the ghost of little Arthur, which she could sense hovering around. She took a single reflexive step forward, as if she were the corner man in a boxing match, about to lean in and slap the fight back into her boss.

Nixon turned away from her. He sighed and shrugged his shoulders, affecting a sudden indifference. "I may tell Ray to put a line in the speech that says I'm resigning, too."

All at once Rose felt remotely hopeful. His theatricality had taken over; he was *playing* to her and Ron. Maybe he could still find the wherewithal to play to Congress and the country.

Chapter Twenty-Five

APRIL 30, 1973, 7:40 P.M.

WHITE HOUSE SOLARIUM

Pat Nixon stubbed out a cigarette before picking up a phone she was certain had no tape recorder attached to it.

"Operator," she said, "this is Mrs. Nixon. Please get me Mr. Thomas A. Garahan in New York." She gave the Madison Avenue address and hung up, and as she waited for the connection to be made, she pictured Tom behind the tray table in his study, drinking a second cup of coffee after having eaten his dinner with Cronkite.

She glanced at the clock: there were only eighty minutes until Dick went on the air, and he still wasn't back from Camp David.

The phone rang. "I have Mr. Garahan in New York," said the operator.

"Thank you." Pat listened for the civilized click that assured her there was no one listening in, that for the next several minutes her conversation with Tom would only shine as a small red light amidst all the switches and wires downstairs.

"I want to tell you what I've been thinking of," she said to him. She was alarmed by the strain she could hear in her own voice.

"Tell me," he said, gently.

"I'm remembering a day late in '68. A few weeks after the election. We were going from New York to Key Biscayne, and Johnson gave us Air Force One for the trip. We got on it together for the first time. And you know what he did? Dick?"

"Tell me."

"He picked me up by the waist and spun me around. Twice. He hadn't done that when we got the house in Whittier or even the one on Tilden Street, just a couple of miles from here. But that plane. *That* was carrying me over a threshold he could appreciate."

She didn't have to ask if Tom was listening; she knew his silence indicated patience, a willingness for her to tell this story at her own pace. And she didn't have to worry that he was hearing anything in it but a tormented affection for her husband.

"We thought we were alone," she continued. "Later I found out that Ron Ziegler was near the back of the cabin and had seen the whole thing." Her eyes were still dry, but she didn't know for how much longer.

"I haven't been myself since Easter," she said, briskly, straightening her shoulders. "The most horrible weekend we ever spent in Florida. I couldn't make myself open the newspapers. Julie's down there now, giving a speech to the Girl Scouts. She won't be back here for this one tonight. I'm sorry; I'm rambling."

"Ramble."

"I can't. I've got to go. I can hear the helicopter coming toward the lawn."

Suddenly Tom Garahan roared with Irish laughter—over this absurdly grandiose version of the *Oh-my-God-he's-home-early* moment that each of them had seen a hundred times at the movies. Pat herself couldn't keep from smiling.

"Back in October," she said, "you told me that I'd be the one coming to you next time. A month or so later I told myself that sending the little Art Buchwald column didn't count."

"It didn't."

"But I guess this does, and so I guess you were right."

"My being right doesn't matter. But I can tell you what does, Victoria. What matters is that much, much worse is yet to come. I suppose you still don't risk offending Agnew by watching the network news, but the reporters on it are so worked up you'd think it was D-Day."

"Yes," she said. "Their liberation is in store."

"Find a way to get up here."

She said nothing, just hung up, hoping he would think that the rotors had drowned out her reply.

Three hours later, Rose handed the president one of the messages the switchboard had sent up to the Lincoln Sitting Room, where she and Steve Bull were fielding things.

MR. HALDEMAN CALLED.

She wondered if HRH was testing the system, trying to find out whether his suggestion had been heeded. Well, she would get his message to the president—and thereby let him know that his advice had been rejected. She'd been through dozens of televised speeches with Richard Nixon and knew he needed phoned-in accolades the way an outfield needs chatter. "Crank him up," indeed. Let the cranking begin—and plenty of it!

Nixon took the slip of paper and waited for Rose to return to the mahogany work table across the room. At his spoken instruction, the White House operator immediately reached Haldeman at his home.

"I hope I didn't let you down," the president said to the chief of staff he'd just dismissed on national television.

"No, sir," said Haldeman, his voice neutral as ever. "You got your points across, and you're right where you ought to be. You did what you had to do, and now it's time to move on."

Nixon had never doubted that Haldeman would act the good soldier, but he was moved nonetheless. He took a large swallow of 100 Pipers and said, "I'm never going to discuss this goddamn son-of-a-bitching Watergate thing again. Never, never, never, never. Don't you agree?"

"Yes, sir," said Haldeman, with the kind of brisk nine a.m. energy Nixon knew he would soon be missing.

"Interesting thing, Bob. The only Cabinet member who's called, and this is fifty minutes after the thing is over, is Cap Weinberger, bless his soul. All the rest, you know, are waiting to see what the polls show." He took another swallow of his drink. "Goddamn strong Cabinet, isn't it?"

"Well, you should check, sir. The board may be operating under the instruction that it's not supposed to put all the calls through tonight."

"No, no," said Nixon, sensing some rare bit of confusion in Haldeman. "They know how to get through. They know, believe me, they know." He could hear the sing-song slur in his own voice and made an effort to speak more crisply. "You're a strong man, Bob, goddammit, and I love you, so *keep the faith*. You're going to *win* this son of a bitch."

"Yes, sir."

He waited a few moments.

"I don't suppose you could call around and get any reactions to the speech and call me back, like the old days? Would you mind?"

"I don't think I can, Mr. President. I'm in an odd spot here—"

"Of course, of course. I agree. Don't call a goddamned soul. The hell with it. God bless you, boy. I love you, as you know. Like my brother. Keep the faith."

He hung up the phone. He was getting drunk, and he knew it. Christ: *Keep the faith?* Where had that come from? Adam Clayton Powell? He pushed the empty glass across the table and vowed to pull himself together, as if the red eye of the camera were coming on again, and would stay on until he was in bed with the lights out.

You're going to win this son of a bitch. "You're" instead of "we're." He'd been talking about Haldeman's legal jeopardy, as if none remained for himself. And *Like my brother*—had he meant Arthur or Harold? He wasn't sure which, but it was one of those two—the dead ones to which he was bonded, not the two that were living.

Another conversation now came back to his mind. *We have a cancer—within, close to the presidency.*

It was never cancer that scared him; only tuberculosis could do that. There was no *shame* in cancer, but TB? It was something that came from the squalor of tenements, or, in the case of the Nixon brothers—he couldn't prove it, but he believed it even now—the goddamned unpasteurized milk his crackpot old man had insisted they drink.

Was it possible his presidency might not be dying of cancer, but be sick with TB? Harold had gone on for ten years with it, his own nursing paid for by the nursing his mother gave to those four tubercular boys in Arizona. They had all died, one by one, but Harold survived through that whole time—besieged, rallying, then beset even worse—until the end came, suddenly, three days after Roosevelt moved into this house. Could *he* be in for such a siege, long and scarifying but something he could weather until he walked out of here in '77?

Rose put another message onto the table. "You'd probably better attend to this one. Your new attorney general."

He nodded. "Like a goddamned revolving door up there yesterday afternoon." He said it cheerfully, to buck Rose up and placate what he knew was her dislike for Richardson. He, too, would have preferred

Rogers in the job. But if he sent Rogers's name up to the Senate, all the left-wingers would get the chance to do an autopsy on the whole Vietnam thing, with endless questions about Rogers's four years at State. He needed somebody over at Justice *now*, and Richardson was what they had available. "Revolving door" was no exaggeration: yesterday he'd barely had time to can Kleindienst—who'd known too much from day one—before he found Richardson sitting down next to him, ready to say yes to Kleindienst's job. He'd later heard that the two of them had gone back to Washington on the same helicopter.

"Thank you for calling back," said Richardson, once he was on the line. "I thought your speech was really great, top drawer."

"You're very kind to say that."

"Your finest hour."

"Well, I want you to know that you can always get through to me directly, Elliot. I want you to know that. You can always get through."

"Thank you, Mr. President. I was very moved and touched by what you said about me. I won't let you down." Richardson went on to explain that while the president had been speaking, he'd been hosting a party for some military aides about to depart the Pentagon. Most of the Joint Chiefs were at his house; they'd actually been watching together— "and I don't think I've ever been with a group of people who were more moved by an occasion like this."

"Really?" asked Nixon, wondering exactly when there'd been an occasion like this before. "Well, as you know, Elliot, it came from the heart." He sighed, and waved for Manolo to refill his drink. "You're my man, and by God, Elliot, I'll back you up to the hilt."

"I understand that, I do. And really, I won't let you down, Mr. President."

"Oh, I know that, I know that. That's why I named you!" He heard himself nearly giggling as he said it, and held up his thumb and index finger, squeezed together, to indicate that Manolo should make it a small one. Normally, a little slurring wouldn't matter with Richardson, who tended to be half in the bag by seven o'clock, but tonight he seemed peculiarly alert. Maybe the Joint Chiefs had drunk up all his booze and left him dry. "That's why I named you," Nixon repeated, as if the real reason weren't that Richardson's Harvard sanctimony guaranteed quick confirmation.

"I think I can do it right, Mr. President. I really do."

"Of course you can. Of course you can." He paused. "Elliot, the one thing they're going to be hitting you on is the special prosecutor. But I'm not sure you need one. I'm not sure you shouldn't say, once you get over there, that *you've* assumed responsibility for the prosecution." There was no response. "But whatever you want. Good God, if you want to exhume Charles Evans Hughes, just *do* it, I don't mind."

He heard a general burst of laughter from Richardson's living room. Had one of the Joint Chiefs just told a dirty joke? Or was he himself perhaps on speakerphone?

"I'll think about it some," Richardson said.

"Do what you want and I'll back you to the hilt. Get to the bottom of this son of a bitch. Do your job, my boy. It may take you all the way." He knew, after he spoke it, that this last sentence was the only one the two of them both believed, and that right now both were receiving a mental picture of the Capitol steps, upon which Warren Burger, one snowy, sunny morning less than four years away, was swearing in President Elliot Richardson.

"Thank you for calling, Elliot. And give my best to your lovely wife."

What was her name again? Did Rose have it written on the back of the phone message, the sort of reminder she often put there? He should have checked, but it didn't matter now. The call was over, and Richardson could go back to yukking it up with the Joint Chiefs, who—yes, thanks to Dean—wouldn't be losing any sleep having to wait up for any B-52s to return from runs over the Ho Chi Minh Trail.

"Rose," he called across the room. "No more calls."

"Yes, sir."

He had the strange sense, not unpleasant, of a new beginning, of something unknown. He wanted to be by himself here, to put on the *Victory at Sea* records, as if he really believed what he'd told Haldeman, that he'd never have to discuss Watergate again. Deep down, of course, he knew better, which is why, amidst this odd feeling of possibility, he couldn't banish from his mind all the thoughts he'd been having of Harold and Arthur, named like him for the kings of England.

Mother. The idea that Quakers were peaceful! Pacifist, yes, but *turbulent*, with that sense of God always rumbling up from inside them. People only knew the movie Quakers, thanks in part to his cousin

Jessamyn West, who'd written all that *Friendly Persuasion* crap. That was what they'd seen, that and Grace Kelly, the Quaker wife in *High Noon*, sick of the guns before they even went off.

He got out of his chair and headed upstairs to the Solarium, without telling Rose or Bull just where he was going or if he'd be back. Through one of that room's huge half-moon windows, he looked out toward the Washington Monument, before sitting down at the piano and starting to play one of the hundred or so pieces of music he still had by heart. He didn't so much as murmur the song's lyrics, but he heard himself singing them, in his head: *Do not forsake me, oh, my darlin'*. He knew that he was singing not to his mother, or to Pat, whom he'd still not seen since Friday night, but to that odd, invisible part of himself, the darkest and the weakest, which he would now have to rely on as if it were another person altogether.

Part Two

—✦—

SEEK

MAY 18, 1973–SEPTEMBER 8, 1974

Chapter Twenty-Six

MAY 18, 1973, 6:35 P.M.
WATERGATE WEST 310

Fred LaRue was lighting his pipe on the balcony when Clarine Lander tapped her very large sapphire ring against its sliding glass door.

LaRue couldn't understand why she still wore the ring now that she'd separated from her second husband, but Clarine's summons was so urgent—three more hard taps of the sapphire—that there was no time to think about the matter. The glass would soon be scratched if he didn't get back inside.

"You need to see this," said Clarine, her voice much calmer than her signal had been. She gestured toward the television.

Martha Mitchell filled the screen. Her hair was in a wild ponytail, an instant's gathering of yellow straw, and her sunglasses half-covered a face she'd not bothered to make up. She stood, LaRue realized, by the Fifth Avenue sidewalk canopy he'd looked down onto two months before.

"Who do you think Mr. Mitchell has been *protecting*?" Martha shouted at the reporters. "*Mr. President*, that's who! Mr. Mitchell and I went to Washington to *help* this country. We didn't make one *iota* of profit from anything! Where do you think all this *originated*? Do you think my husband is that *stupid*?" The breathlessness of the tirade, spreading out over the whole NBC network, allowed no moment for reporters to answer the questions she was pelting them with.

"You can place *all* the blame right where it belongs—on *Mr. President* and his White House!"

"Dear God," murmured LaRue.

Clarine, lying once more on the bed where they'd spent most of the afternoon, lit a cigarette and laughed her low, growling laugh.

"Is this live?" LaRue asked her.

" 'Live'? She's the only one in your whole criminal caboodle who *is*. I just love her to death."

LaRue imagined Mitchell, ten stories above his wife, listening help-lessly as she reached her crescendo: "My husband tells me that if any-thing happens to the president this country will fall apart. Well, it would be a darned sight better for Mr. President to *resign* than for him to get *impeached*!"

LaRue's chin sank to his chest. "Turn it off, Larrie." He walked back to the sliding glass door. Out on the balcony again, he looked in the direction of John and Martha's old apartment, where he'd so often headed for dinner at just this time of evening.

Mitchell had to be past his limit now. No amount of leftover love for his crazy belle could let him stand for this, unless he'd slipped far-ther down into the bottle than Martha herself. And why shouldn't he? Eight days ago he'd been indicted for something that didn't even cover Watergate: his supposed attempt to block an investigation into the two hundred thousand dollars that weird Bob Vesco, from whatever country he was hiding out in, had contributed to the Old Man.

"I'm going to make you a drink," Clarine called.

LaRue came back inside and watched her move from the unmade bed to the little kitchen bar. As she plunged some tongs into the ice bucket, he regarded the black hair falling past her shoulders, almost halfway toward the skirt she'd just put back on; the garment was so short it could scarcely be called a skirt at all. He made himself remember the way she'd looked fifteen years ago at her receptionist's desk in Jackson, with a cardigan sweater over her shirtwaist dress. He felt himself aroused by the tangle of the old memory and the present sight.

She was here every few evenings, and sometimes, like today, for the morning and afternoon as well. She appeared to be her own law at the DNC, which had recently departed the Watergate for cheaper premises across town: the burglars had made the complex so famous that rents were being jacked up for all the offices and retailers. As it was, Clarine would soon be leaving the National Committee altogether. The McGovernites who'd led the party to defeat were being replaced by moderate types not at all to her liking. So she would be "going away"— her words—saying goodbye to her job and the District as she'd said goodbye to her second husband. She didn't say where she was going, and LaRue had yet to ask her destination, fearing such a simple question might put a match to the atmosphere inside the apartment, which for the past four weeks he'd been breathing like pure oxygen.

If he didn't have a morning appointment with his lawyer or the prosecutors, and if Clarine weren't still here, he'd head off to the CRP, where even now, however ridiculously, he remained on the staff roster. He'd putter around with what those in the office called, even more ridiculously, "loose ends," as if they were on top of instead of beneath things. From time to time he'd even have to deal with the Democrats' civil suit, flipping through documents that contained the name of Clarine Lander on lists of employees whose rights had been violated by the burglars.

As Larrie now threw lime wedges into the cocktails, LaRue thought of all the things that might have set Martha off today. On top of the Vesco indictment, there had been this morning's Ervin Committee testimony by Jim McCord, a man she had liked. There was also the deposition Martha had just finished giving in the civil suit.

"She'd been drying out a couple of weeks ago," LaRue explained to Clarine as they both sat down. "But she went right back to pills and all the rest the day she got home."

"Well," said Clarine, poking at her lime wedge with a long, clear-polished fingernail, "one more piece of the world's now gone officially upside down. Martha is out of love with 'Mr. President.'" She drank the first full inch of her gin and tonic. "I'll tell you what's also seriously upside down. This whole investigation. As soon as you boys started turnin' yourselves in, all those overeducated sleuths got so enthralled by the cover-up that they stopped investigating the crime itself. By which I mean what went on down there." She pointed vaguely in the direction of the Democrats' old offices. "They seem to have lost interest in why your pals broke in there in the first place."

She appeared to be starting a serious conversation, maybe the one she'd come to have with him on April 16, under the umbrella. But twenty minutes after she reentered his existence they'd wound up here in bed, alive to things that had happened eleven years, not eleven months, before. And now that she at last seemed ready to rekindle the initial conversation, he felt like a green piece of wood that couldn't take the flame.

"Martha's right about money," he said. "Money may have been my whole part in it, but you can't name me one other political scandal where nobody had money as his motive, at least at the start." He was practically quoting a column, by one of the Alsop brothers, from which he'd taken comfort.

"That makes you boys worse, not better," said Clarine, annoyed that the lime wedge was now too far down the glass to be stabbed with her fingernail. "You-all were interested in nothin' but power. In tyranny." Forgoing the lime, she picked up a Subpoena Duces Tecum—the prosecutors' latest request for documents—from the coffee table. She played with it absently, as if it were a coaster. Then, seeing LaRue's hangdog expression, she looked at him more sympathetically.

"Hound," she finally asked, using an old nickname, "do you remember the envelope?"

"I do," said LaRue, who knew she wasn't talking about any of the hush money he had spent the past year collecting and distributing. She was talking about the envelope that had come to the law office in Jackson fifteen years ago, the one containing a report from the Canadian investigators on what had happened in the duck blind where Daddy died. As soon as she'd shown him the unopened envelope, twenty-two-year-old Larrie had written "MOOT" straight across it. Money had already been paid to a person who'd been able to get things called off, and the secret report had been sent merely on what today would be called "an FYI basis." They'd even returned Daddy's bird gun, now mounted on the wall not ten feet away! He and Larrie, already involved, had never opened the envelope, preferring not to know whatever forensic truths it contained. But they had decided she would keep it. Possessing it gave her a kind of power over him, one that both of them enjoyed her having. She became the guardian of his most awful secret, without either one of them knowing exactly what it was.

LaRue now tried to smile. "One day early last year I was up in Eastland's office and your old friend Betty Boyd started joking about 'Clarine's mementos'—all the photographs and Cracker Jack prizes, all the 'little boxes and envelopes' you kept stuffed in your bottom drawer back when you worked with her."

He looked at Clarine, and she looked back at him. "Yes, it was there.

With all those other things." She had never kept it in any of the homes she'd shared with a man.

"The trinkets and tokens of my successors," said LaRue.

Clarine laughed and sipped, and then just looked with mild interest toward the glass door.

LaRue had for weeks been piecing together her last decade, assembling a timeline as if he were one of the prosecutors, albeit without subpoena power or even the right to ask questions. He knew that after bolting Eastland's office for the Mississippi Freedom Democrats, she'd gone to work for SNCC, staying until the blacks more or less threw out the whites from the organization. She'd even had a black boyfriend during this period between her two husbands, one a lawyer and the other a professor, both of them Jews—all of this before '69, when she came to the DNC. By that point Humphrey had lost to the Old Man and she could foresee the rise of the party's lefties.

As he sat here now and watched her heart-shaped face—its widow's peak dipping and rising ever so slightly as she munched a peanut—LaRue thought of all the times he thought he'd seen her these last few years: in a wire-service photo of some May Day protest against the war; in a wide-angle TV shot of the floor demonstration for McGovern in Miami; and in the distance, with his own eyes, as he watched a gaggle of women's libbers tote a bedsheet banner past the EOB.

"You never did open it, did you?" he asked. "The envelope."

"No, I didn't."

He now felt certain that this was what she'd come to talk about last month. At the moment he could see the same look she'd had in April, under the umbrella. She was edging up to the subject, as if newly urged toward it by Martha's crazy performance, and as if his old secret might somehow be connected to Watergate itself. But now that she looked ready to speak, he feared her words would put a sudden end to the past month's idyll.

Over the past four weeks, in the midst of all else, he had told Larrie much of what he'd done in connection with the cover-up, notwithstanding his occasional suspicion that she'd planted herself here as an agent of the DNC. But what would be the point of that—or of his being reticent? The prosecutors already knew the lion's share of what he'd told her. In return, of course, she had told him approximately nothing, about herself or anything else. But he liked the imbalance, the way it added to the power she retained through holding on to that envelope.

He looked now at her big sapphire ring, knowing he would never have her fully or for long, wondering if a Jewish doctor would be next.

On impulse, he went over to the top desk drawer and pulled out Dorothy Hunt's jade pin. The airport encounter was the only thing he had told to Clarine but *not* the prosecutors. And now he felt the urge to place this piece of jewelry, a macabre tribute, atop his revelation.

"Hunt's wife put this in the locker with the money. She said she felt overdressed. Like I told you, she was trying to rattle me and I couldn't make her out. Is it worth a lot?" He handed the pin to Clarine.

"Maybe more than you think," she said.

"Keep it."

Clarine looked more thoughtful than startled. "Why not give it to the prosecutors?" she asked. "Isn't it evidence?"

"There's enough evidence already," said LaRue, even more softly than usual. He thought he could continue to keep the airport meeting from Silbert's men: all the money in the locker had eventually found its way to the burglars, so there seemed no need for the prosecutors to find out about its brief layover. There was also, of course, no practical reason why LaRue, having told them everything else, shouldn't tell them about this as well. But some piece of him rebelled against being written into the story of Dorothy Hunt's incineration.

"I suppose this really belongs to Howard Hunt," said Clarine, declining to put on the jade pin. She just fingered it, the way she had the subpoena, while LaRue once again tried to reassure himself that not even Dorothy's husband knew of the meeting at National.

"Maybe it's only fair that you have it," said Clarine. "Because I think he may have something of yours." She put the pin on the coffee table.

LaRue laughed. "You mean all the money I funneled his way? Big lot o' good it wound up doing anybody."

"I don't mean the money."

LaRue blinked a couple of times and exhaled. He realized she had finally gotten to whatever she'd come here about last month.

"I don't have the envelope anymore," said Clarine.

He didn't reply.

"After your pals got caught," she continued, "everyone at the office beavered away looking for anything that might be missing. Almost nothing was, except from me. And I wasn't going to tell them what it was."

"The envelope?" asked LaRue, with the same nauseated sensation he'd had upon hearing of the plane crash.

"Yes."

"Why do you think they took it?"

She laughed. "What did those peabrains expect to hear when they tapped Larry O'Brien's telephone? That he prefers the Caesar salad at Duke Ziebert's to what he can get at the Sans Souci? Who *knows* why they took it?" She paused. "I'll tell you what I think happened, Hound. If you listened to McCord's testimony this morning, you know that Hunt was never on the DNC premises, not the first time they went in or the second. Well, maybe the Cuban who was photographing things in my desk saw this big ol' envelope marked MOOT and decided it looked too thick to photograph page by page, but too interesting not to show to Big Chief Spy, Señor Hunt, back in his hotel room next door. And maybe Señor Hunt, having written one too many of his novels, thought MOOT sounded like a code name for something, and so he put the envelope in his pocket, thinking he'd look at it later, when things were a little less frantic."

"So where do you think it is now?" asked LaRue, automatically, as if talking about something to which he had no personal connection.

"I have no idea," said Clarine. "Someplace as unlikely as an airport locker?" She reached for Dorothy's pin and began to twirl it between her index and middle fingers.

LaRue wondered if the envelope might be in the prosecutor's office, ready to be thrust toward him at some crucial moment he hadn't figured on. Or maybe it had been in Hunt's White House safe—before going up in flames in Pat Gray's fireplace, when the hapless interim FBI director fulfilled Ehrlichman's wish to get rid of the safe's contents. Could it even have been in the little pile of stuff Mitchell asked Jeb to burn just three nights after the burglary? Perhaps he himself had failed to notice the envelope amidst those transcripts and memos that

Jeb almost left behind when he rushed off from Mitchell's apartment to play tennis with Agnew.

Or maybe it was still intact, in Hunt's own desk out in Potomac, the contents waiting for their new owner to return from prison.

"Do you know how much I detest 'Mr. President'?" asked Clarine.

"I think I do."

"No, you don't. There were moments, like Cambodia and Kent State, when I thought I might *open* that envelope and see what the Canadians had had to say all those years ago about your daddy's mishap. If it were bad, I reasoned, well, Jack Anderson might be interested in knowing what manner of man Mr. President had on his staff. Might be interested in runnin' an item that would put one little dent, just a BB's worth, in the presidential hide. Hound, I'd have been willing to ruin your life just to make Mr. President endure one uncomfortable page-twelve story."

LaRue didn't flinch. He himself had thought about something like that happening. He hadn't been able to relieve his mind of the thought that the envelope's contents might be worth a small something to the Old Man's enemies, enough to let them wreck his own life as heedlessly as Larrie claimed she'd been willing to do.

"If you felt that way, why'd you come here?" He almost said "back" instead of "here." Staring, he pressed for an answer. "Why'd you come here last month?"

"Because I heard you'd just been to the prosecutor. We hear everything in the office."

"And?"

"I came to warn you. I decided I didn't want you to get any more than you deserve."

She looked at the coffee table, lost for a moment in these second thoughts. After lighting another cigarette, she fastened Dorothy Hunt's pin to a ruffle on her blouse.

Chapter Twenty-Seven

MAY 25, 1973
THE WHITE HOUSE AND KEY BISCAYNE, FLORIDA

"Ignore the scandal, think of the country!" said General Haig, playfully tapping the shoulder of a new West Wing typist Rose was introducing him to.

The president's secretary was crazy about the new chief of staff, and she now invited him to step into her office for a few minutes prior to the eleven a.m. Cabinet meeting. The boss was running a bit late in any case, taping a Memorial Day message for whatever radio stations in the South and Midwest would bother to play it.

Rose poured Haig some coffee. Neither of them had had anything like enough sleep last night, but for once the reason was joyous. The welcome-home dinner for the POWs had brought a thousand guests to the White House, and a handful of couples continued dancing until a quarter to five in the morning. The smell of a dozen extra corsages—bought for the men's wives and mothers with the Nixons' own money—still filled Rose's office. As Haig shook some Cremora into his coffee, she looked out the window to see whether the sun was at last drying off the South Lawn. Yesterday's rains had made a soggy mess, but the enormous white tent had held up beautifully. She could spot a few sling-back shoes that the younger women had abandoned to muddy revelry in the wee hours. Pointing to a couple of soldiers dismantling one of the army field kitchens, she asked, "Does that make you nostalgic for the battlefield, Al?"

Haig shook his head. "No, but Rose, I must tell you: during the entire battle of Ap Gu, I never had a cup of coffee as bad as this one."

She roared, thrilled again to have this funny, manly, Shakespeare-quoting replacement for HRH on the premises. A Catholic, too—with a priest for a brother!—instead of one more Christian Scientist.

"Do you know," she asked, full of wonder at the fact, "that I danced

with a man last night who'd also been a POW during *World War Two*?"
The officer may not have had Don Carnevale's smooth moves, and she'd
had to relinquish him soon enough to his wife, but a few minutes with
him had given her a wonderful feeling, as if this were her basketball-
playing Billy somehow come back to life and they were celebrating victory in the big, real war of long ago instead of stalemate in this grubby
eight-year business that had just ended.

"There was another guy who'd been penned up in Korea," said Haig.
Rose shook her head, amazed.

"You know," said the new chief of staff, trying to sound wistful and
reluctant, "it's not a good idea for a military man to have this job I'm
now in."

"Oh yes it is!" Rose responded, happy to say just what he wanted
her to. "You're *exactly* what we need right now. Tough. Organized.
Upbeat." All of which didn't include the wonderful fringe benefits he
brought along, like the spectacle of Henry's having to report to a former
member of his own staff. "So you're here 'for the duration'!" exclaimed
Rose. "Until we 'win this son of a bitch,' if I may quote the boss. Here,"
she added, rummaging behind the corsages to retrieve a plaque the president had been given last night. "Take this in with you to the meeting."

Those weak sisters in the Cabinet could do with seeing how *brave*
men appreciated their commander in chief. TO OUR LEADER—OUR
COMRADE—RICHARD THE LION-HEARTED. Every last POW and every
one of their wives knew that only Richard Nixon's guts had freed them.
One fellow had even told Rose that the Christmas bombs sounded like
the voice of his mother calling him home for supper.

"Put this thing right in the middle of the table," said Rose.

"Yes, sir," Haig replied.

God, she loved this guy! As he left the room and the two of them
went back to the new, grinding war that devoured every day, she realized that she was counting on him, not the boss, to get them out of it
alive.

When the president entered the Cabinet Room and saw the assembled
members admiring the plaque, he felt a moment of vexation. Last night

he had thrilled to its eerie fulfillment of his mother's royal choice for his name—but he now feared the object would trump the item he himself had brought to the meeting.

He took his seat at the middle of the long table, giving a protocol-driven nod to Agnew and then winking, more warmly, at Cap Weinberger. He paused a moment before speaking.

"Most of you know what a night we just had. I can say without question that it was the most gratifying evening I have ever spent in my long public life." A bit too stentorian, he decided. He would lighten the tone, and smile: "I gave instructions that the orchestra should keep playing as long as anybody remained on the dance floor. As some of you know, I've always been very liberal when it comes to dancing. I managed to loosen up the Quakers at Whittier College on that issue when I was student-body president forty years ago."

No, that was *too* light, given what he had in his hand. When the laughter ended, he took things back down a notch: "I'm holding something I thought you all might be interested to see, a present from Lieutenant Colonel John Dramesi, one of the POWs, who was here with his mother from Blackwood, New Jersey." He held up a handkerchief onto which the imprisoned officer had secretly embroidered a small American flag. "The blue threads came from an old sweater, and he got the red ones from a pair of underwear. He managed to hide the flag from the North Vietnamese while he was making it, and managed to sneak it out with him when he was released." Nixon handed Bill Rogers the little piece of cloth, as if it were one of the letters from world leaders that he sometimes passed around the table. "I think it's important to remember that while some young Americans were burning their country's flag, there were others still willing to risk torture and death so that they could have a flag to salute."

The men around the table were gravely respectful as the handkerchief made its way from hand to hand. Two or three bowed their heads when it reached them, and Connally—back among them as a special advisor, having at last switched parties in the GOP's hour of maximum need—exercised his talent for the theatrical and snapped off a salute.

Nixon pushed his chair back from the table. He wasn't in the mood to talk about the bankrupt Penn Central or the price of gasoline. Nor did he feel like yielding the floor to Kissinger for a long sonorous description of all the national security advisor was doing to prepare for Brezhnev's Washington visit.

Actually, he realized, he could use Henry to keep the focus on last night's triumph.

"Did you see all the grateful kisses and hugs Dr. Kissinger got from the wives and girlfriends last night? I think he got kissed by a couple of the men, too."

Kissinger knew that any reciprocation of levity was, in this instance, out of the question. In responding, he even injected a quaver into his guttural growl. "I have never been more moved in my life, Mr. President."

"You may have noticed," said Nixon, his eyes on some bookshelf high above the group, "that there was no head table last night. The greatest honor that could come to me, I thought, would be dining with all of our guests. You know," he said, lightening things up again, and wishing he could be gone from *this* table, "the whole thing was really Sammy Davis's idea. He was here a couple of months ago and he suggested a big entertainment for the men as soon as they were up to it. Pat loved the idea, but said 'no girlie shows.' I mean, from the start we knew that Bob Hope would be the ideal emcee, but the occasion seemed too special for a USO kind of thing. Even so, did you see Joey Heatherton there last night? God bless her. And I'll bet Henry wasn't the only one to notice the *Playboy* gal that one of the guys brought as a date."

"There's a picture of her in the *Post* this morning," said George Shultz.

"The *Post* isn't *all* bad," added Weinberger.

After a few seconds of laughter, the men seemed to remember that the appointment of Mrs. Armstrong with cabinet rank had added a woman to the room. They quickly reined in the locker-room talk, and the president changed the subject. "So, Elliot, is it hard to remember where you're supposed to sit?"

Richardson was still in the defense secretary's chair, but an hour from now he would be sworn in to the attorney general's job—his third cabinet position in six months.

"It's only a difference of subject matter," he replied, repeating a line Nixon had heard him give to the newspapers, which quoted it as if Richardson were goddamned Noël Coward.

"Well, we know you'll do a first-rate job. After all, you've already managed to do something—twice—that I've never accomplished." Pause for a beat, the way Hope had taught him to, long ago. "Carry Massachusetts!"

Everyone laughed and then at last got ready to drone through the agenda, fully aware they were working for a president who didn't believe in cabinet government to begin with, and who, before Watergate began to swallow him, had been intent on combining their domains into three or four super-departments. In less than an hour the meeting was over, with only three of the secretaries having uttered a word.

"Gentlemen, lady," said Nixon, rising from the table. "A pleasure, as always." He left the room alone.

Those remaining milled about for a minute or two, relieved to be no longer getting on the boss's nerves. They exchanged stories about last night or, more quietly, swapped the few bits of inside information they'd been getting from Republican staffers on the Ervin Committee. Senator Baker, the ranking minority member, was so eager not to appear the president's man that only a trickle of leakage had been coming from the GOP side. "I think you need a new set of Plumbers," Connally was telling Shultz. "This time to *loosen* the faucets."

Haig was supposed to escort Richardson to the Oval Office for a short meeting with Nixon before the swearing-in. The chief of staff had never liked Elliot, not since the first days of the administration, when they were both vying for Kissinger's favor. But only for the last three weeks had Haig actively detested him, after discovering on his first day in the White House that Attorney General *designate* Richardson—before his confirmation hearings, let alone a vote!—had taken it upon himself to okay the placement of FBI agents outside the offices of the just-fired Haldeman and Ehrlichman. The Old Man had nearly died of apoplexy when he came in the morning after his speech and saw his ex-aides' papers being guarded. He'd even shoved one of the poor guys on the detail. Haig, furious himself, had managed to get the G-men out of the West Wing, but when Nixon learned of Richardson's role in the matter, the president had been curiously passive, so cowed by circumstance that he acted as if Elliot were just doing his job, no matter that the job wasn't yet his to do.

"I thought that little flag was marvelous," Richardson now murmured to Haig, struggling for small talk as they walked the colonnade to the Oval Office. "The plaque, too."

"He got another little token of esteem from one of the POWs—a card he's carrying in his breast pocket."

"Oh?" said Richardson.

"Yeah," said Haig. "A handwritten note that says 'Don't Let the Bastards Get You Down.'"

Richardson allowed himself an amused chuckle, as if, Haig thought, he were appreciating a clever locution from the lower orders.

"Elliot?" he asked, as the Marine opened the door to the office.

"Yes?"

"Why don't you try not being one of the bastards?"

As he took his position at the front of the East Room—to warm applause from even the press—Richardson looked around for James O. Eastland, who a couple of weeks before had convulsed his colleagues with laughter when he asked his first question at the confirmation hearing: "Mr. Richardson, have you ever heard of the Watergate affair?"

Too bad Eastland didn't seem to be here today. Greeting him might put one more layer of gloss on Richardson's reputation for exhibiting respect to just about anybody, and a reference to that comic moment in the hearing might ease the tension of this swearing-in. The president had issued an aggressive statement on Watergate only three days ago. It contained seven denials, six of which Richardson suspected were mendacious in the extreme. When Ziegler had gone to the press room after the statement's release, he'd been nearly eaten alive.

Now, while hearing the president describe him as "a man of character, one of the finest men ever to be named attorney general," Richardson caught the eye of Ted Kennedy, whose presence today, a home-state courtesy, clearly displeased Nixon. Nevertheless, the president looked straight at the senator, opened his rictus of a grin, and repeated his joke about not carrying Massachusetts.

Chief Justice Burger extended a robed arm and directed the nominee and his wife to their places. Richardson could not help but wish that Anne had shed five pounds in advance of all this, or at least worn a darker color for the occasion. But as Burger recited the oath's repeat-after-me clause, the new attorney general found his thoughts turning to the biggest ham in the whole drama. Sam Ervin, not present here today, was nonetheless threatening to steal what from this point on ought to be Richardson's show. The only matter that had disrupted the confirmation lovefest was the senator's insistence upon being able to grant witnesses before his Watergate committee whatever immunity he saw fit—thus increasing the chance that Ervin would get to the bottom of things before Richardson himself.

The applause following his "so help me God" lasted longer than it would take Richardson to deliver the three sentences of remarks he had prepared. While the clapping subsided, he looked at Agnew's high, shiny forehead and decided that as soon as he got over to DOJ he would find out what was up with any investigations into the VP, whose transgressions were still rumored to be much simpler and more old-fashioned—a matter of kickbacks and cash—than anything to do with Watergate.

". . . in order to do a job worthy of my predecessors, as well as the American people."

He stepped back from the lectern to the most sustained applause yet, and exchanged nods with Nixon.

Do your job, my boy. It may take you all the way.

The president returned to the microphone for a single moment to make a joke that sounded like the work of Buchanan: "There'll now be a reception in honor of the new attorney general down the hall in the State Dining Room, and I hope all those who do not have any matters pending before the courts will be able to attend."

The ensuing laughter was fairly robust, and Nixon deadpanned his way through it, practicing show business, thought Richardson, the way he must once have tried playing football: via earnest application of the playbook, without any brawn or natural talent.

Could it actually be the rotors of the helicopter he was now hearing? Would Nixon be departing for his latest Florida sojourn without even clinking glasses? One could hardly expect him to stick around for Archie Cox's swearing-in as special prosecutor this afternoon, but skipping the reception for his own new AG? That appeared to be the case. Only halfway down the hall to the dining room, the president had stopped at the staircase, and his traveling companions—among them Haig and Miss Woods—seemed to have quit the scene. Incredible: their boss was descending the first stair-step to the floor below, from which he would exit to the helicopter.

Nixon paused only when Kennedy's extended hand entered his vision.

"Ted," he said, turning around as if pleased.

"Mr. President," said Kennedy, who pointed to Richardson beside him. "I'm afraid Elliot will be putting up with more of us Kennedys at the Justice Department in an hour or so. My sister-in-law Ethel is coming over to hear Cox take the oath. General Richardson here has been thoughtful enough to schedule the ceremony in the office Archie used to occupy when he served under my brother Bob."

Nixon's hand, through with shaking Kennedy's, went back into his pocket and visibly clenched into a fist. "Good, good!" he exclaimed, as if the chosen location at Justice were a capital idea and the more Kennedys the merrier. The rictus opened again and Richardson noted how a cap on one of the president's front teeth seemed infinitesimally whiter, and curiously more sincere, than the rest of his smile.

Cox of course pushed every irritating button on Nixon's thin, ever-crawling skin: Harvard, the Kennedys, all of it. But who, Richardson had asked himself, was better credentialed? And what choice, really, did the president have? *I'm not sure you need a special prosecutor . . . But whatever you want.*

Kennedy withdrew, leaving Richardson just enough time and space for the briefest private word with Nixon.

"I can only repeat what I said weeks ago, when you honored me with this appointment, Mr. President. There's no 'they' out there. No one's out to destroy you, and we'll get to the truth."

Nixon smiled and took a second step down the stairs. "Will you be having a second reception over there?" he asked. "For Cox? You know, Martha redid the whole dining room at Justice. Her idea of Colonial Williamsburg, or something like that. Drove Mitchell crazy!"

With a last wave, he was off to Key Biscayne.

"How dare he make love to me and not be a married man!"

Julie Eisenhower looked up from her embroidery and laughed at Ingrid Bergman's reaction to this revelation about Cary Grant.

Pat joined in. She and her younger daughter were the only two people really paying attention to the movie. Eddie and Tricia had gone out to the patio; David was flipping through a magazine, and Rose was dozing. Dick, just in front of Julie, had his glasses far down his nose, eyes trained on a legal pad. They'd all been here in the Florida house since mid-afternoon, too exhausted from the celebration last night to do any more than they were doing now.

What an operation it had been! When she first recommended they use her strawberry mousse recipe for the dessert, she hadn't imagined its being prepared by the barrelful over at the Pentagon. For weeks in advance of the dinner, she and Lucy Winchester and the girls in the East Wing had had to scrounge china from every department of the government; the resulting mismatches hadn't been too bad, except for the awful stuff from Justice that looked like pewter.

Well, better Martha's china than Martha herself. It had been a real relief not to have her over at the State Department yesterday afternoon when the Cabinet wives gave a tea for the wives of the POWs. To think that not so very long ago she *would* have been there, sloshed and squawking, gobbling up all the attention. Not that the ladies of the press had themselves paid much attention to the purpose of the tea. Sure as shooting, all the questions had been about Watergate, until one of the POW wives interrupted to ask if the reporters wouldn't like to hear what the guests thought of the great president who'd managed to secure their husbands' release.

Did they ever find out who that gal was? Pat didn't want to wake Rose by asking, but she made a mental note to get the name and to handwrite the woman a thank-you letter.

The sight of Rose with her mouth half open provoked a feeling of tenderness. God, she had danced up a storm last night! For once there'd been no need for the younger staffers to go on "wallflower patrol" in search of the shy or unaccompanied. People were grabbing one another like it was Times Square on V-J Day.

For a week ahead of time, absolutely everybody, from the ushers' staff to the kitchen potato peelers to the volunteers in the correspondence office had been keyed up with an excitement she couldn't remember for any other event they'd hosted. Even a couple of secretaries who she bet secretly regarded the POW pilots as the worst "baby-killers" of all couldn't help but feel moved by their homecoming.

Turning her attention back to the movie, Pat felt that she could, in all seriousness, understand Ingrid Bergman's position here. If only Tom Garahan had been married! The whole affair (she still hated the word) would have been easier, because it would never have gotten started in the first place: it would have been beyond the pale. How odd that she should be the only one in this room, or in Washington, to know of his existence. Or was she? Had Hoover perhaps started a file back in '66? She wouldn't put it past his reach or his appetite.

Dick flipped a page of his legal pad more loudly than necessary—the kind of thing that had made her grind her teeth ever since the girls were babies. But she needed now to be much more than annoyed. She needed to get titanically, openly angry with him, as she'd been only two or three times in the past thirty years. She needed to do it, soon, if she was going to get through what they were facing. She couldn't fight his enemies, not to the finish, unless she first fought with him, got it out of her system, the way she had in '62, when he made things hellishly worse than they needed to be.

Last night they'd gone upstairs a little after midnight, and he'd kissed her before going off to the Lincoln Sitting Room. No *Victory at Sea*, thank God, so she'd been able to lie in bed a couple of doors down and hear, without interference, the strains of dance music from below. She'd felt almost peaceful.

But an explosion—one that she would detonate, between the two of them—was coming. She could feel the signs of it the way an Eskimo can smell the approaching snowstorm. Even today, at that swearing-in, she'd felt fury rising inside her when he made that joke about people with "matters pending before the courts"—right in front of Kennedy!— after laying it on so much thicker than he'd needed to about Richardson. A "man of character" and all the rest. The weakness of it, the *placating*, had disgusted her.

She was too restless to stick with this movie. She'd be better off going back to her book in the bedroom. But as she got up to do that, she saw Julie trying to catch her eye, motioning for the two of them to go out to the kitchen. Okay, she nodded, picking up an empty bowl of potato chips that could use refilling. What a pleasure to do such things, to make her own drink, whenever they were down here, the only place that wasn't staffed up to the eyeballs. Not being waited on was like— being waited on.

What did Julie want? Maybe there was baby news at last? When her daughter said nothing, Pat began the conversation by asking, "What's your father working on?"

"The yellow pad? Tallies. Which senators would vote to confirm Connally as secretary of state—if he finally lets Bill Rogers go."

"Well, *that* would freak out Dr. Kissinger, wouldn't it?" asked Pat, replacing the cap on a bottle of tonic.

"I haven't really had a chance to talk to you about last night," said Julie.

"I know." They'd both fallen asleep on the plane, and eaten dinner in a tired silence.

"Tricia and I went in and talked to Daddy in the Lincoln room last night. He was smoking his *pipe*," she said, nervously laughing. "With his feet up on the hassock."

Pat didn't know what to say. The pipe, the hassock—somehow it all brought to mind not Dick but Tom, whom she badly needed.

"Mother, he asked us if he should resign."

Pat shook her head in disgust, not at Dick's tormentors but at Dick himself. "What did you say?"

"We said, 'Don't you dare!' of course!"

She lit a cigarette. "He was just letting off steam, Julie." And, she thought, extracting testimonials to his worth and valor from his own daughters. She wanted to go back into the living room and tell him: *For God's sake, do that with Bebe; do it with Kissinger—but don't do it with the girls.*

Her anger was caged but flying, like the doves at the reception yesterday afternoon. One of them had nearly gotten out.

"What do I say the next time he asks?" wondered Julie.

Pat crumpled an empty bag of chips and threw it into the garbage pail.

"I'm going to bed," she said.

Hidden beneath the pitifully thin pillow with its volume turned low, Hunt's radio could make itself heard to his own ear without disturbing the snores of his cellmate or drawing attention from the lights-out guard. At ten p.m. the news announcer was still offering tidbits about last night's POW dinner, making Hunt wonder, not for the first time today, whether his own time in jail might eventually exceed the median figure served by men in Hanoi.

It was his first night here in Danbury. He'd been transferred up to Connecticut early this morning, in leg irons. The new prison promised to be a vast improvement over his D.C. dungeon. It had light and air and even a baseball diamond. But he'd been told to expect plenty of trips back to Washington, as a kind of commuter in chains, whenever the DOJ and Senate investigators needed to summon him. They'd have to rely on his memory, since his own papers were mostly destroyed or subpoenaed—whatever had been in the EOB safe; his desk in Potomac; his box at the bank; the file cabinet at Mullen.

Mullen! Bob Bennett's CIA-front consulting company, its offices one block from the White House and across the street from the CRP, suddenly came to mind. *Had* he taken everything out of there? Everything from his *own* filing cabinet, yes. But another, empty one there, which had belonged to nobody in particular, now formed a picture in Hunt's consciousness. He reached beneath the pillow and turned off the radio, trying to think back to the night of the *first* break-in.

He was soon remembering a small armload of stuff that Bernie had foisted upon him and that he had dumped, the following Monday, in the bottom drawer of this other file cabinet, which had contained nothing but some broken staplers and a bottle of aspirin. He'd intended, once he got the chance, to sift through the material for anything that might interest Liddy, and, ultimately, Mitchell. And now he realized: *it was still there.*

He'd forgotten all about it, the way that sometimes happened with him, with anyone. Not as some subconscious act of incrimination—*Pay to the Order of Lakewood Country Club, $6.36*—but authentic forgetting, pure and simple. They had soon after gotten so busy planning the

Watergate reentry that he had never thought of the stuff in the drawer, not until this moment. Now he found himself sweating with the prisoner's panic, the sudden bolt-upright, middle-of-the-night terror that something is out of place, that confiscation and punishment will arrive with the guard's next footsteps.

He fought down the surge of fear, tried to will the perspiration back into his body. Whatever Bernie had swept up was probably junk— "MOOT"? Hadn't that been the word on the envelope? Anyone who found it, two or three years from now, would toss it away after a moment's head-scratching.

Chapter Twenty-Eight

JUNE 29, 1973

2009 MASSACHUSETTS AVENUE; SENATE CAUCUS ROOM;

ROCK CREEK CEMETERY

"I haven't dictated in years!" said Mrs. Longworth. "It will be thrilling."

The girl had arrived at nine a.m. sharp to pick up the recipe Alice had agreed to contribute to the Kennedy Center's fundraising cookbook, which was overdue at the press. Mrs. Longworth had promised something suitable for the category "Tea After the Matinee" and sworn that she would have her typewritten submission ready to collect, but naturally she didn't. So she'd proposed dictation, handing the girl, who didn't know shorthand, a cracked pencil and a tablet of paper brittle with age.

"I used to dictate my *column*," she explained. This syndicated rival to Eleanor's "My Day" had not lasted long; the editors were always cutting and caviling and deciding she'd gone out of bounds. Of course, that was decades ago, and Alice realized that this girl, poised with ancient pencil over ancient paper, had a very sketchy idea of who she was. The thought displeased her.

Janie called from downstairs: "You're going to be late! Mr. Alsop's outside in a car, with a driver, and the motor's running!"

The housekeeper's order to hurry slowed Alice down further. "Read me Jackie's," she said to the girl, who pulled from her folder Mrs. Onassis's typewritten directions for "Risotto with Mushrooms," suitable for an "Early Dinner Before the Concert."

"And Mamie?" interrupted Alice, before the girl could even get to the beef marrow and onions in Jackie's list of ingredients.

Further rummaging of the folder revealed that President Eisenhower's widow had sent a dessert recipe for "Frosted Mint Delight." It called for a lot of pineapple juice and whipped cream.

"Revolting!" cried Alice. "Couldn't be worse if you topped it with a hair from one of her *bangs*. All right, I'm ready." She cleared her throat:

"Bread and butter," she said solemnly. The girl headed the paper with these words, and Alice continued: "Buy very good unsliced bread; cut it into very thin slices with a very sharp knife; then butter it with sweet butter."

The girl looked up.

"Did I go too fast for you?" asked Alice.

"Well, no, but—"

"Good, I'll telephone later if I think of anything else." She gave a little off-with-you-now wave, and picked up a page from Wednesday's *Post*, which lay open on the couch. So gripping was the drama being provided by young Mr. Dean that she had been reading—even underlining— Joanna's copies of Kay's rag, and hardly bothering to cover her tracks. She had, for example, put a large red circle around one transcribed exchange between the Ervin Committee's chief counsel, Mr. Dash, and the Tortoiseshelled Tattler, as she now liked to call the bespectacled young star witness:

> DASH: *Therefore, Mr. Dean, whatever doubts you may have had prior to September 15 about the President's involvement in the cover-up, did you have any doubts yourself about this after September 15?*
>
> DEAN: *No, I did not.*

She had put *two* red rings around a later bit of interrogation—Senator Talmadge asking the TST why he hadn't told Dick, right from the start, that everyone in his employ was trying to cover up the break-in:

> TALMADGE: *You mean you were counsel to the President of the United States and you could not get access to him if you wanted to, is that your testimony?*

And the reply!

> DEAN: *No, sir, I thought it would be presumptuous of me to try, because . . . my reporting channel was Mr. Haldeman and Mr. Ehrlichman. . . .*

He made it sound as if they were a battalion of ants in some skyscraper, not allowed to get on the same elevator with the boss. For heaven's sake, she could remember old John Hay, Father's secretary of state, *bursting* into the office to talk about his problems just after *she'd* burst in to discuss her own. There was no more barrier to his getting in than there'd been forty years earlier, when he was just little Johnny Hay and Lincoln's *private* secretary.

It was the *strangeness* of Dick's operation, not any misconduct, that had her shaking her head. When it came to accusations, she *preferred* not to believe Mr. Dean—but first she needed to see the Tattler in action, even if the opportunity for that depended on Joe trundling her in and out of the Senate Caucus Room.

"How long are you going to keep him waiting?" scolded Janie, who'd come upstairs after showing out the Kennedy Center girl.

Alice gave her housekeeper a hard look.

"It's twenty to ten," said Janie, whose patience with the old lady's nonsense went only so far. "And from what I hear on the radio, Senator Ervin likes to start on time."

Reluctantly, Alice accepted the other woman's help in getting out of her chair, into her hat, and down to the first floor. Once out the door, she called hello to the people at the bus stop, a few of whom recognized her. Joe's driver then assisted in getting her into the back of the big black car. "Thank you," said Alice, crisply, as if forgiving an imposition.

Alsop wouldn't even speak to his cousin while the car cleared Dupont Circle on its way east toward the Russell Building on Capitol Hill. In the space of two minutes Alice saw him take three nervous-Nellie looks at his watch. It was now a quarter to ten and he was worried, even with reserved seats in the Caucus Room, about their having to fight the crowd.

"I thought it was *thirty* transfusions that you'd supplied," said Alice, breaking the silence.

"It was," replied Alsop, confirming the number of blood donations he'd made to his still-dying brother. "It's been going on longer than a year now. Just like this goddamned thing." With the back of his hand he slapped the *Post*'s front page of Watergate news.

"Well, from the expression on your face, Joe, it looks more like *sixty* drainings."

"You should see Stew."

"Don't want to. Too depressing. And I'm sure he doesn't want to see me."

"You saw what he wrote? 'A dying man needs to die, as a sleepy man needs to sleep.' And the doctors say it could go on for *another* year."

Alice decided to change the subject. "Tell me, why am I not on the Enemies List?" The existence of an actual roster of the president's foes—people to be denied White House invitations and perhaps audited by the IRS—had come to light during Tuesday's questioning of Dean.

Alsop gave her a worried look. "Because you're his *friend*. You know, I'd be concerned that you're going through second childhood if it weren't fully apparent that you never left your first."

Alice ignored the insult. "I concede that it's a long shot, but not beyond possibility. Bobby was my friend, and if he'd gotten in in '68, I'm sure he'd have had such a list, and I'm sure I'd have done something to put myself on it by now. And we'd *still* be friends."

Alsop remained silent. He was weary of her monkeyshines.

But Alice plowed on. "Bella Abzug and Mary McGrory! Putting *them* on it. Could anything be more obvious? Aside from all else, I can't believe the *fuss* over this list—as if Dick isn't entitled to hate people." She paused briefly, before asking, "Why are you *so* gloomy? Apart from letting yourself be tapped like some maple tree?"

"There's this nephew of Susan Mary's who's coming for a long visit," said Alsop, with a sigh. "The two of them are great pals, and I can't stand him. He also can't stand me. They're going to chatter and whisper without letup, and I think he's going to convince her to leave me at last."

Mr. and Mrs. Alsop had held on so far—even gone to China together after the election, thanks to the *homme sérieux*—but Susan Mary still had the option on that apartment in the Watergate.

"And I'm gloomy about having to go look at *him*," Alsop added, meaning Dean, whom he'd described in print, even before his testimony began, as "a bottom-dwelling slug." A marathon "opening statement"—245 pages—and three days of questioning had not changed Joe's mind. He clung to a piece of logic he had put into his column a few weeks ago: "What is against one's interest is always credible. So they have to be believed if they say, 'The President knew nothing and ordered nothing.'" He was talking about Mitchell, Ehrlichman, Haldeman, and

Colson—all of them apparently ready to say just this, even if it made people believe that they'd been covering up at their own initiative— and were thus *more* guilty than if they'd just been carrying out orders. Dean, inconveniently, was saying something else, but Alsop hoped that its manifest self-interest (confession in exchange for leniency) would be obvious. And, in the absence of independent evidence, how exactly could Dean prove that he was *not* a bottom-dwelling slug?

The car drove past the courthouse at Third and Constitution, where the day before yesterday Fred LaRue had become the first figure in the cover-up to plead guilty. "You know," said Alsop, staring at the court-house and looking gloomier than ever, "I *tried* to get people to pay attention to Brezhnev's visit. But no soap." The Soviet leader had already come and gone, the Ervin Committee having agreed to postpone Dean's testimony while he was on U.S. soil. But the effect of the delay had been to heighten anticipation of Dean's appearance. "Like having to watch a documentary before the Beatles come on," Alsop now groused to his cousin.

They drove into the reserved-parking area beside the Russell Build-ing. Alice stuck her head out the car window, looking for Dean's "maroon-colored Porsche," by now a famous accoutrement of the scan-dal, even if it didn't have the evidentiary value of, say, the old protho-notary warbler. The crowd was making Joe nervous, and to irritate him further she pulled her head back in and leaned over him to read the newspaper on his lap.

But before she could get a rise out of him, she got one out of herself. The date on the paper: June twenty-ninth! It was Bill's birthday, and she hadn't realized it until this moment. She began counting on her fingers: he'd be a hundred and eight.

"Driver," she said sharply. "Take us to the Capitol Building."

Alsop looked at her. "You really have gone out of your mind."

"It is Senator Borah's birthday," she explained. The ancient open secret of Paulina's parentage was even now unacknowledged between her and Joe, and she uttered the fact of Bill's anniversary as if displaying a dispassionate regard for, say, Henry Clay. "I would like to put some flowers by his statue."

"You don't have any flowers," said Alsop, as the driver hesitated over what to do next.

"I can buy them at the cigar stand."

"There *is* no more cigar stand. And there's no time, either. If *you* want to skip the bottom-dwelling slug, that's fine by me. But I *have* to see him, and we can't do both. I'll get out here and have Mr. Ellis take you to the Capitol."

Alice briefly fell into a snit, then allowed herself to be led up to the Caucus Room, where she and Joe arrived less than three minutes before Senator Ervin's gavel was due to fall. She glared at a man who asked if she would remove her hat, then turned her eyes to the front of the enormous room. "I met that one in Florida," she said to Joe, pointing to handsome Senator Gurney. "Not the brightest orange in the crate."

"I know," Joe agreed, regretfully. Gurney had so far been Dean's only severe interrogator, but his mind wasn't quick enough to pursue any advantages he verged upon gaining. Alice had circled one or two bits of his questioning in the other day's paper. He'd asked Dean if it wasn't true that the cover-up "sort of grew like Topsy," and Dean had conceded the aptness of the image. The two of them would have the NAACP on their case if they kept it up.

As Ervin shuffled his papers and twitched his eyebrows, a television camera panned the audience. She rather hoped it would come to rest on her, so she could wave and mouth a hello to Dick, who was out in San Clemente, pretending not to watch the proceedings.

Joe readied pen and pad as the committee came to order with some questions for Dean from Senator Montoya. The precise little drone from the witness, like a fan being switched back on, reinforced Alice's dislike of him, which she'd felt ever since he began his opening statement with a Pecksniffian wish that Richard Nixon might be forgiven for whatever crimes he, John Dean, was about to charge him with.

Even so, the young man's memory and persistence had come to impress her. She'd given up hoping that anybody on the panel would break through some weak spot and make him falter; as it was, whenever they poked at him, he rebounded with some detailed, plausible explanation. Yes, he'd been fired from his first job with a law firm, but really only because he'd been about to quit. And yes, he'd borrowed a bundle of cash for his honeymoon from a White House safe, but he'd left an IOU and had long since put the money back.

One rumor—floated by Joe of all people!—held that he was inordinately fearful of being raped in prison. Seeing him at last in person, she decided that he was delicate, but not especially pretty; he had the mousey look of Nick's old Ohio cronies. He'd been on the make from the beginning, rooming with Goldwater's son at military school and making a first marriage to another senator's daughter. He couldn't have given that up easily, thought Alice, though the second wife, with her generous figure and blond hair pulled tightly back, was as beautiful as a maroon Porsche.

Gurney, who Alice believed would make a rather attractive cellmate, asked Dean to return his attention to a meeting he said he'd had with Herbert Kalmbach, Dick's California lawyer, at the Mayflower Hotel here in Washington, a couple of weeks after the break-in. They'd gone up to Kalmbach's room when the coffee shop proved too noisy for the conveyance of Dean's message. " 'I told him,' " Gurney now said, quoting Dean, " 'that Mitchell had suggested [Kalmbach] get his detailed instructions from Mr. LaRue . . .' "

Alice's mind started to drift. In her long life, the superior force of the here and now against the afterglow of the past had proved, by and large, a good thing, though at this moment, in this room, she found herself sinking into the softer hues of long ago. She had often come here in the late twenties, when Bill was chairing the Foreign Relations Committee. He would commandeer the great room in an attempt to attract attention to some place like Montenegro or Madagascar, but principally (and at her urging) to gain attention for himself. Nothing thrilling would ever happen—what hearings could compete with the ones for Teapot Dome a few years before?—but she would revel in being away from the baby's detestable crying and, after that, its monosyllabic gurgling, which provoked her revulsion instead of maternal rapture. Sometimes there would be so few people in the audience that she and Bill were practically having a tête-à-tête. No one ever asked why she wasn't over in the House chamber, watching Nick in his speaker's chair, because everyone knew.

She'd continued coming to see Bill even after he lost the chairmanship and Franklin went to the White House. By that point Nick was dead and Paulina sullen, beginning the long, slow-motion punishment of her mother. With Nick now buried in Cincinnati and Bill entombed in Idaho, only Paulina was right here, a few miles away in Rock Creek Cemetery, waiting for Alice to fill up the rest of the plot. How odd that she and her daughter would be spending eternity together! And yet Paulina—by now just bones and dust—remained the only commingling of herself and Bill that had ever existed. (She really would have named her Deborah—*de-Borah*—if Nick hadn't drawn the line at that.)

Joe was suddenly sitting up, rigid with attention, the business with Dean and Kalmbach having acquired some urgency. Today, as on Wednesday, the Tattler was insisting that he'd met Kalmbach in the coffee shop of the Mayflower. But Gurney had just produced hotel records, subpoenaed by the committee staff, which showed that Kalmbach had been staying not at the Mayflower but the Statler. Dean, for once flustered, suggested that Kalmbach had perhaps been registered at the Mayflower under a false name; the lawyer had after all always been jumpy enough to use code names for Mitchell ("the pipe") and Haldeman ("the brush") during their conversations. Yet even Gurney was sharp enough to realize that it made no sense for Kalmbach to have been at the Statler under his own name while at the Mayflower under an alias. Still, Dean felt sure it had been the Mayflower.

By now Alice had come to life with Joe and the rest of the audience. Perhaps this hotel coffee shop was the prothonotary warbler!—the item in the case that pops a stitch in the witness's story and unravels all his believability.

> GURNEY: *How long have you lived in Washington?*
> DEAN: *I have been here about ten years.*
> GURNEY: *And you don't know the difference between the Statler-Hilton and the Mayflower hotels?*
> DEAN: *I continually get them confused, I must confess. The point in substance here is that the meeting did occur. We met in the coffee shop. We went from the coffee shop to his room.*

Alice imagined Dick leaning forward over his bowl of Cheerios in San Clemente, talking to the TV, telling Gurney to hurry up and twist the knife he'd stuck into the little bastard.

Alas, thought Alice, handsome is as handsome doesn't. Gurney already seemed to be losing the thread, meandering into a series of unrelated questions about Dean's credit cards. Joe began twitching with exasperation, afraid the potentially fatal moment had passed. And then suddenly it was Dean, not Gurney, who was returning them to it, asking if he might impart a bit of information that someone had just helpfully conveyed to his lawyer: "The name of the coffee shop at the Statler is The Mayflower."

A burst of applause, loud enough to rattle the chandeliers, filled the room. Alice's gloved hands, ignoring which side she was supposed to be on, contributed to it. Joe shot her a glance, furious that she couldn't help herself: her love of smarts, her lifelong preference for winners over losers, trumped everything. If Iago was a species of "motiveless malignity," she was a creature of motiveless mischief. At this new low point in the president's fortunes, he felt only disgust toward her.

And yet it was Alice who now said, "I've seen enough."

"Good," replied Alsop. Remembering his manners, he gritted his teeth and reminded her of their plan to have lunch at the F Street Club. "I'm ready to go eat anytime you are."

"No, thank you," said Alice. "There's something else I'd rather do."

Alsop saw a chance to get rid of this petulant child. "If you want to go over to Borah's statue, I'll get a page to take you. And after that I'll have Mr. Ellis run you home."

"I want Mr. Ellis to drive me to Rock Creek."

Alsop looked at her painfully frail frame and shook his head. "You can *not* go to the cemetery. What are you going to eat?"

"Janie always puts a banana and peanuts in my purse. I'm starting to look like an ape, so she feeds me like one."

She was getting her way, thought Alsop. But he comforted himself with the thought that he would more or less be getting his, too. He headed for the rear exit of the Caucus Room; he would find Ellis and tell him to take her away.

Alice dozed during the drive to Petworth, the cemetery neighborhood near the District's northern tip. She guided Mr. Ellis, who had remained silent, through a gate on New Hampshire Avenue and then, at under five miles per hour, along the path to the graveyard's section A. "I'll get out here," she said.

Mr. Ellis at last spoke: "Mr. Alsop instructed me not to leave you by yourself."

"I am old enough to be Mr. Alsop's mother."

"I believe that's the point, ma'am."

"All right," said Alice, eager to escape. "I'll get out and let you follow at a reasonable distance. If I keel over, you'll see a black hat rolling across the lawn."

The afternoon was sweltering, and the old lady didn't even have a cane, but her catnap had revived her. So Mr. Ellis opened the door and helped her out of the car. She certainly looked as if she were dressed for a funeral.

Alice set off slowly through section A, wondering as she went whether Stew had gotten around to choosing where he wished to be buried. Perhaps he'd decided to send his carcass back to Connecticut, where it had been raised—a line of reasoning Alice always faulted for the way it made one's whole adult life seem a mere detour.

She passed the grave of Agnes Harvey Stone, widow of the chief justice, dead for fifteen years without ever having returned Alice's copy of *Ten North Frederick*. The mausoleums of Riggs and Heurich, the District's biggest banker and biggest brewer, soon came into view, each much nicer than that ridiculous "Grief" statue by Saint-Gaudens, a vulgar extravagance thrown up by Henry Adams to pay off the guilt he felt over his wife's suicide, just as another man might provide a diamond bracelet to the spouse he'd neglected for a chorus girl. Eleanor used to come out and sit on the bench across from this monstrosity, a fact Alice had turned into one of her party pieces. She would put a dish towel over her head to mimic the statue's veil, then raise her hand to her face, just like the sculpture, shutting her eyes to complete the imitation. And then, when her *tableau vivant* appeared fixed, she would buck out her teeth and say, in Eleanor's horribly untethered upper register, "I have just returned from surveying conditions in the afterlife!"

A circle of trees now shielded her eyes from the statue, so popular with visitors that it had become a *celebration* of suicide rather than a

caution. She preferred the plain lawn and modest headstones of section F—and there it was, her own eternal reward, the half-filled plot
beneath the granite marker for PAULINA STURM 1925–1957. Watching
Mr. Ellis watching her, Alice lowered herself onto the grass covering
HILDA WILHELMINA LUOMA, Paulina's preposterously named neighbor
since 1959.

From this seat, Alice recalled the expression on Dick's face as he
helped to carry her daughter's coffin to its open grave. She also again
remembered the night that had followed, her going to the Nixons' house
on Tilden Street, Pat remaining upstairs, the girls out of sight, watching
television somewhere. Alone with Dick in his study, she had forced herself to speak of suicide, the subject which all day had ruled everyone's
thoughts and stilled their tongues.

"She didn't do it, but I believe I shall," she'd told Dick, meaning it,
her voice quavering as it never had before or since. To her surprise, he'd
gone to one of his bookshelves, as if to fetch a *Physicians' Desk Reference*, and taken down a volume of Father's collected works. It took him
no time at all to find the passage he wanted: *And when my heart's dearest died, the light went from my life forever.* He read out loud, aston-
ishingly, what Father had written about her mother and, by extension,
about her, the child whose birth had brought on such a foul death and
such inordinate grieving.

She knew, right at that moment, why Dick had picked those lines,
and why she'd come to him. No, he had not yet protested the *Post*'s
libel about suicide, and not yet pressured the insurance company to pay
out. But she didn't need to see him do those things. She'd come to the
house that night because of the look on his face when he'd shouldered
the coffin—the creased, naked expression on this darkest of dark horses,
this misanthrope in a flesh-presser's profession, able to succeed from
cunning and a talent for denying reality at close range. She didn't share
his general dinginess: she smiled in delight, however viciously, whereas
he smiled only in a kind of animal desperation. But she shared the darkness beneath and the capacity for denial; she could sometimes change or
negate reality just with her contempt for it.

By the time she left his house that night, the two of them had effected
a little sorcery, succeeded in convincing her that Paulina had been *her*

own heart's dearest and that all the world knew it. She held on to this illusion long enough to get home to the empty house in Dupont Circle and throw away Bill's old straight razor with which she might have put an end to herself the way she'd imagined doing it, draining the blood as if she were her own taxidermist.

Dick's current illusions would evaporate soon enough. Fewer and fewer people shared them. Joe might be one of those, but he'd soon look a fool if his columns kept talking of resignation and impeachment as remote possibilities. Stew, who by now knew something about dying, rightly gauged Dick's prospects for survival as not much brighter than his own. She was still ashamed of her own early blitheness about the burglary; her dismissive remarks of a year ago now struck her not as the denial of reality, into which she'd successfully put so much of her life's energy, but a failure of imagination, a kind of laziness or, even worse, stupidity. She'd wised up soon enough, but shouldn't have been so dumb in the first place.

Would her kindred spirit at 1600 Pennsylvania Avenue—so shrewd and so deplorable—manage to hold on? The other afternoon, Janie, glued to the radio, had asked her the same question. "California, here he comes," Alice had replied, pleased with the remark as she made it, but rather miserable about it once she got back upstairs.

And yet, she now thought, closing her eyes against the afternoon sun: surely the Tattler had no *proof*. And if he didn't, could not the truth remain forever in abeyance, like Paulina's paternity if not her death? Could not Dick live on in the White House, known but not proved to be guilty, like Lizzie Borden in Fall River? Surely he could endure such a condition better than anyone. It was now the best he could hope for, and perhaps it would come to pass. After all, what *deus ex machina* could possibly provide corroboration for Mr. Dean?

The watchful Mr. Ellis, fearing she'd started to doze, honked the horn.

Chapter Twenty-Nine

JULY 18, 1973

NATIONAL NAVAL MEDICAL CENTER, BETHESDA, MARYLAND

"Just once more. Hard as you can stand it, sir."

Nixon braced himself before Miss Williams pounded both her hands against his chest, attempting to loosen more of the congestion. He moaned, but resisted complaint, enduring the blows of the inhalation therapist until she declared he'd had enough.

"Very good," said Miss Williams.

There were tears in the president's eyes, but he was breathing easier and hurting much less than he had been during the first awful hours of his hospitalization, for viral pneumonia, six days ago.

"You know," he said, offering a variant of their usual joke, "a lot of Democrats would love to have your job."

Miss Williams returned the serve. "A few Republicans, too."

Nixon, still clearly spent, managed a laugh.

"Dr. Tkach and Dr. Katz should be in soon," said Miss Williams. "I'll give them a good report in the meantime. And I'll see you again this afternoon."

Once she was gone, Nixon lay back on the bed and glanced into the sitting room of the hospital's presidential suite. Haig and Ziegler and Rose had been taking turns with it as an office. He could see the two tall metal boxes of important papers. They'd been brought over the day he arrived and were now, optimistically, packed up for a departure to Camp David, which he'd be permitted to make in a couple of days if he continued to improve.

He'd awoken last Thursday morning sicker than he'd ever been, with a roaring fever and a brutal pain in his right side. If it were a heart attack, he'd managed to tell himself, the pain would be on the left; but the deduction was more disappointing than consoling. As he'd sat up, his pajamas soaked with sweat, he'd allowed himself a wistful

moment to imagine history's gentle treatment of a president who'd
persevered in the duties of office until his enemies hounded him to
death.

Dr. Tkach knew it was pneumonia the minute the stethoscope
touched his chest. A few hours later the visiting German foreign minister told him he looked awful, but he'd toughed it out for the whole
day—foolishly, he now realized, since the fever had made him blow
his cool with Ervin over the telephone. Rather than making a calm
declaration of executive privilege against the Senate committee's document request, he'd disgorged all his pent-up fury against that cornpone
grandstander—who actually wanted him to come and testify in person!
In a voice so hoarse he barely recognized it as his own, he'd shouted
about its being perfectly clear that Ervin was out to get him. By lunchtime every staffer and intern on the Hill was hearing that Nixon had
gone crazy at last. He knew there was already talk among the Georgetown crowd that he'd landed here in the hospital not for pneumonia but
a nervous breakdown.

Well, if they were all so goddamned interested in seizing presidential
papers, let them ask for his medical records. They could have them—a
complete set of fever charts; the whole list of antibiotics; consultations
with Katz and pummelings from Nurse Williams.

He might be improving, but he was exhausted. Sometimes the fever
would flare up, and his breathing would once again become shallow and
fast. He'd been warned to expect a long recovery time.

At least he was unhooked from the monitor. After all its days of
blinking and beeping, he felt strange seeing it idle and unlit—you'd
think he'd died instead of gotten well. He now sat up a little, took in
more breath and felt a sharp twinge. Christ, was this what it had been
like to live as Harold and Arthur?

He clicked on the TV gizmo and got the Ervin show. Jesus, who was
this character testifying? With his girth and slicked-back hair he looked
like one of Colson's "ethnics," though from which "heritage group"
wasn't clear.

> He kind of looked at me and I said, "Well, it's definitely not your
> ballgame, Mr. Kalmbach."

Nixon realized that they were talking about the delivery of money to Hunt and the rest of them. Christ, what a system it must have entailed: you had Kalmbach, who always appeared as if he'd just gotten a manicure, having to work with this guy who looked like a loan shark. Where had they *gotten* the whole slew of goofballs like Segretti and Liddy, not to mention the Cubans? At its beginning, the administration had been full of crew-cut guys who could pass for astronauts.

He wanted to turn the thing off, but the remote control had decided to give him trouble, and he couldn't find the call button for the nurse. He'd have to wait until they came in with his hundredth glass of orange juice. Meanwhile he looked over at what he knew was a letter from Cox lying atop one of the metal boxes in the sitting room. Ziegler had brought it over an hour ago, and it was now the piece of paper that mattered most in the whole damned suite.

The special prosecutor was demanding eight tape recordings, whose existence had been let out of the bag, more like a lion than a cat, by one of Haldeman's boys, during testimony to the committee the day before yesterday:

> THOMPSON: *Mr. Butterfield, are you aware of the installation of any listening devices in the Oval Office of the President?*
> BUTTERFIELD: *I was aware of listening devices, yes, sir.*

Two years' worth of tape, a quantity of evidence you couldn't fit into a whole fucking farm's worth of pumpkins. Well, the tapes were now the nuclear football. In a way, revelation of their existence simplified the whole struggle. If these tapes were so goddamned important—the key to it all, as Cox and the rest of them now kept saying—then logic said they couldn't evict him from office without them. Awareness of the tapes was actually *weakening* all the testimony that had been shoveled into Ervin's lap the past six weeks; the tapes were turning it, by comparison, into a kind of second-rate inadmissible hearsay. And with any luck Cox and Ervin would wear each other out squabbling over who deserved to hear the recordings first. Ervin's letter asking for them, which had shown up yesterday, now sat beneath Cox's.

Haig came in and reached up toward the television when the president signaled for him to kill it. The chief of staff, as usual, was all cheer and charm. Nixon half-expected him to start dancing like Gene Kelly.

"Good news, Mr. President! The Chesapeake and Potomac Telephone Company says the penalty for a person's recording phone calls without telling the other party is limited to removal of the violator's equipment. And considering the importance of maintaining phone service at the White House, they've agreed to waive that."

Nixon let himself smile, feeling grateful he'd recovered the strength to brush his teeth.

"First the country, then the scandal," said Haig, setting his usual mind-over-matter priorities for what he knew would be a very short business meeting with the boss. "Bhutto will be happy to put off his visit until the fall. But we've yet to cancel the Shah, who's still supposed to be here next Tuesday. Dr. Tkach says you *might* be able to go through with it if you agree to an abbreviated schedule."

"Under no circumstances are we to postpone the Shah. Same with the Phase IV statement. Tell Shultz he's to go ahead." Nixon had no interest in this planned adjustment to wage-and-price controls, other than that the announcement take place on schedule. His instruction to Haig was reasonable enough, but even to himself it sounded stiff and artificial, as if he were playacting the role of president in one of those old Whittier amateur theatricals where he'd met Pat.

"Al, give me that yellow pad over on the cart."

Haig glanced at the writing on the pad's top page before handing it to its author:

YES	MAYBE	NO
Connally	Haig	Garment
Rocky	TCRN (?)	Haldeman
Agnew		
~~Richardson~~		

"If this is about who's for destroying the tapes, I'm not a maybe, I'm a yes," said the chief of staff. "I was trying to appear neutral yesterday so that I could moderate that rather lively discussion we had going on here."

"Goddamned Garment. He's the only real no. So worried about what his pals in the liberal press will say. Mitchell always knew we shouldn't have brought him with us from the law firm in New York."

"But you've got Haldeman down as a 'no,' too. Is he? I can't say I've spoken to my predecessor about this."

"He's a no, but for a different reason. He's certain the tapes can help. He listened to the one from March twenty-first and says he can hear me saying, 'It would be wrong'—you know, to do what Dean wanted me to do."

"What do you think about that?" asked Haig.

"I couldn't make out half of what's on the goddamned thing when I listened to it."

"Who's TCRN?"

"Pat. You know, Thelma Catherine Ryan."

"Oh. And Elliot? I see he's crossed out. Does that mean he's on his way out?" Haig laughed as he asked the question, but hoped to high heaven it wasn't true. That was all they needed, no matter how much he despised Richardson.

"He's crossed out in the sense of 'not applicable.' Hell of a thing having an attorney general you can't trust to ask for legal advice, isn't it? He'll want whatever Cox wants."

"And Agnew's a yes? Sure he's not trying to get you impeached?"

The president shrugged. "So that he can serve for two weeks before he goes to jail?" They both knew the case against the vice president was strong. Nixon now even wondered if Agnew had used the same lunkhead testifying on TV today to deliver *his* envelopes. "Connally and Rocky are both very strong, and neither of them has any special stake in things. Connally suggests a bonfire on the South Lawn."

Haig responded with more realism but no less urgency: "You could tell the Secret Service to just cart them away and get rid of them." As it was, Haig himself had already ordered the dismantling of the system and the end of any further taping.

"The hell of it is, Garment's right," said the president. "Just because there's no subpoena yet doesn't mean we wouldn't be in legal jeopardy by getting rid of them. I mean, Christ, those letters already demand them." He pointed to the metal boxes in the other room.

"Well," said Haig, "we can keep making the same executive-privilege argument we made when it was just documents. As Henry would say, 'It has the additional advantage of being true.' But, Mr. President, if you destroy the tapes you've got to do it right away, and not just to beat whatever process-server we see coming up the lawn. If you don't get rid of them within days, the public won't believe you really care about the principle of confidentiality. They'll just think you're sifting through them, weighing the pros and cons, maybe even tampering with them."

"Tomorrow morning," said Nixon, closing his eyes. "I'll decide by then." His energy had drained away in an instant. He was asleep before Haig could even step into the makeshift office. The chief of staff sighed, wondering how the president would keep his head from falling into the fruit cocktail when the Shah arrived next week.

Closing the door to the sitting room, Haig noticed that Rose was there, too, having come through the other entrance. She was casting a baleful look at the photographers three floors below, before briskly shutting the blue drapes.

" 'Viral pneumonia, no complications.' " Haig merrily quoted the recent, definitive diagnosis of the president's condition. "Finally, *something* around here without complications."

Rose handed him a cookie from one of the baskets still arriving from all over. He said he'd sit for just a minute.

The president's secretary took a bite from a macaroon and before she finished chewing lit into the latest group of her boss's critics: "I can't stand all these crybabies saying how *betrayed* they feel finding out their conversations were taped. Carl Albert!" She uttered the diminutive House speaker's name as scornfully as she could. "Maybe he's worried about how he sounds because he never draws a sober breath."

Haig playfully soothed her. "Jerry Ford insists he has no problem with having been recorded. Of course Jerry never has all that much to *say*."

A small piece of Rose liked the idea that her own voice would be on the tapes—her casual imprint on history, like lipstick on a napkin. She had nothing to hide either! But she always sided with the tough-guy position, because it was always right. If anyone asked, she would say that she was all for Connally's bonfire. She'd liked Garment well enough in the New York days, but if he couldn't see what the present moment demanded, he ought to pack his bags and go back up to the city.

Her general, as usual, was getting Rose through this latest storm: she hoped he'd get rid of the tapes as fast as he'd done away with the machinery that produced them.

"I knew they existed," said Rose. "This business that only Haldeman and his boys like Bull and Butterfield knew is ridiculous. I'd see the Secret Service changing the reels! And I knew how to work what was in the Oval Office desk."

"You know when *I* found out?" asked Haig. "Not until a month after I started—when I walked over to the EOB one morning, about six weeks ago, just after we'd gotten back from seeing Pompidou in Iceland. Steve Bull had set up a recorder for the boss, who was in there listening to a whole stack of tapes he'd requested. He never even took a lunch break, and I let him be."

"I'll tell you something," said Rose. "From the day our Mr. Butterfield walked into the White House, I wondered if he was some kind of Democrat plant. If he'd really wanted to, he could have danced around the committee's questions without letting on about the tapes—and without even perjuring himself."

"I know *you* could have, Colonel Woods."

"Well," she said, laughing, "I want a promotion when all this is over." She was struck by the words she'd chosen: *when all this is over.* Was she kidding herself? Would it ever be?

"I'll sleep on it, Rose. In the meantime, I've got to get back to the fort. Or is *this* the fort?"

"This is the *bunker*," said Rose.

Though it was usual for him to get the exit line, Haig decided he would steer clear of any Nazi jokes and settle for a wink. As he left the suite by the same door Rose had used, he reflected on that day in the EOB he'd just told her about: it only now occurred to him that there must be hours of tape filled with the sounds of Nixon listening to *earlier* tapes. Christ, these things had to go.

In the sitting room, Rose plucked and organized cards from the gift baskets and decided to put on the TV. She'd actually liked the palooka who'd been testifying an hour ago. There was a little of her brother Joe in him, and he'd been good for one or two laughs. But as the screen now came to life, she found Fred LaRue, whom she hadn't seen since that day in March, in the hall outside his apartment, occupying the witness chair.

He'd always looked a lot older than he was, but sort of stringy and appealing, too, like a cowboy. He was squinting at a chart and cupping his ear, and speaking so softly the committee could barely hear him.

> DASH: *And did you think that this money was being paid for humanitarian purposes?*
> LARUE: *Mr. Dash, my understanding of the payments to the defendants is that this money was paid to satisfy commitments that had been made to them by someone I do not know. Commitments had been made to them at some point in time, and—*

Rose grabbed a cookie and opened an orangeade, the only beverage she could find.

> DASH: *Now, when was your last payment to Mr. Bittman, counsel for Mr. Hunt? Do you recall?*
> LARUE: *Yes, sir, it would be in March.*
> DASH: *March of 1973?*
> LARUE: *Yes, sir.*
> DASH: *Can you tell us how much was involved in that payment?*
> LARUE: *As I recall, $75,000.*

Rose's nerves suddenly stood up. She had never actually imagined LaRue's testimony, and she hoped the boss would not choose this moment to walk into the room with some brainstorm. She leaned forward and crossed herself as the live, televised dialogue competed in her head with four-month-old echoes of her own voice and LaRue's.

> *Do you have what you need?*
> *Barely.*
> *You can add this to it.*

The televised LaRue had begun explaining to the majority counsel how, over the phone, John Mitchell had instructed him to go ahead and make the last payment.

> DASH: *And you followed the same method?*
> LaRUE: *Same method.*
> DASH: *That was a bigger packet, though, was it not?*
> LaRUE: *You would be surprised, Mr. Dash, how many $100 bills you can get in a small package.*
> DASH: *Good things come in small packages. By the way, was this $75,000 payment made just shortly before Mr. Hunt was sentenced on March 23?*
> LaRUE: *I think that is correct, yes, sir.*
> DASH: *Now, there came a time when you did go to the U.S. Attorney, is that true?*
> LaRUE: *Yes, sir.*
> DASH: *Would you tell us about when that was?*
> LaRUE: *As I recall, Mr. Dash, that would be approximately the middle of April—April 16 or 17.*

Rose felt the moment of danger pass like a bus that had come within inches of hitting her. She could feel her legs shaking, as if she had just stepped back onto the curb, astonished to find herself intact. While Dash questioned LaRue about the beginnings of his cooperation with investigators, she tried to calm herself, to use her head. If he had ever told the special prosecutor anything about her, she would surely have been summoned already.

As she sipped the orangeade with a trembling hand she thanked God LaRue was such a gent. Dabbing at her eyes, she looked over at the letters from Cox and Ervin. For everybody's sake, they had to get rid of those damned tapes. She now wished that the boss *would* wake up, would come in from the next room and ask for her two cents.

Pat Nixon didn't stop in until after dinner. "Hi, kiddo," she said, kissing her husband's freshly shaved cheek, before putting one dollar and three quarters onto his bedspread. "I'll spring for today," she declared. One of the newspapers had explained that $1.75 was the naval hospital's daily rate for commanders in chief.

"Have you recognized that yet?" She pointed to the painting of a New York City sunrise; she'd had it hung in here two days ago. "It's from the Fifth Avenue apartment. It used to be in that little hallway near the dining room, remember? It's been in the White House base-ment for the last four years. Julie and I dug it out so you'd feel more at home. But I guess it didn't work," she said with a laugh.

Nixon could feel himself tearing up; for the last couple of days his emotions had been breaking through his skin like his usual excess of perspiration. "You know, now that the pain is leaving"—he tapped his chest—"I realize more and more what Arthur and Harold went through. Christ, not to mention your father."

Pat instantly recalled the rages into which black lung had driven Tom Ryan. But she rejected any comparison. Like Dick's brothers, her father had lived with, and then died from, his disease. The illness that had put Dick in here was already cured, dissipating into the air. She could again feel anger rising inside her, this time over his dramatics; she raised her chin imperceptibly and narrowed her eyes. If anyone here had pulmo-nary worries, it was herself: the doctor had told her she was a prime candidate for emphysema. And it didn't help that right now she was dying for a cigarette.

"So how rough was Brünnhilde today? Did she crack any ribs?"

Nixon smiled. "She was in twice. She's a nice gal. Did you know she worked with a couple of POWs here? Ones who came back from Hanoi with crud in their lungs."

Pat took a chair near the window and looked out at the setting sun. "So," she asked after a couple of silent minutes, "do you want me to weigh in?" There was no need to say on which subject.

"Sure," answered Nixon.

"Get rid of them. Immediately." She'd been sick to her stomach with the thought of a hundred young Ivy League Democratic lawyers mock-ing every call Plastic Pat had ever made to the Oval Office. She could hear them mimicking her cheerfulness and twang as she conveyed to Dick the compliments of some African first lady, or told him how cute the Chinese pandas looked at the zoo.

He nodded, pleased that she was taking the hard line, but not really signaling his own intent.

"They will use whatever is on them, half a phrase, to finish you off," Pat argued. "And they'll eventually get *all* of them. Every reel, every syllable. They'll say it's all government property, created on the government clock." She was determined to avoid bringing up any personal stake she might have in the tapes' destruction, because she didn't want him granting her a favor and thereby giving her a reason to quell the anger still building inside her. Though tempted to note what embarrassment the tapes would cause the girls, she avoided that, too, since the girls would only seem to be proxies for herself.

She couldn't stand that her emotions were all over the place. Looking at the pill bottles, the now-silent respirator, all the dials and monitors, she became furious at the newspaper columnists and talk-show panelists who kept insinuating that Dick had barely been sick. And then, looking at Dick himself, she thought for just a second how much easier everything would be, for him and for her, if last Thursday night, with the fever still spiking, he'd run into some unexpected difficulty and died. *Viral pneumonia, with complications.*

"Well, I just thought I'd speak my piece. I know Al Haig's waiting to see you."

She rose from her chair, picked up her purse, kissed him lightly, and left the room.

By the time Haig entered, several minutes later, Nixon was out of bed and on his feet, wearing a robe with the presidential seal. The quarters that Pat had brought were jingling in his pocket.

"Welcome back to ambulation!" Haig cried in greeting.

"Well," said Nixon, moving slowly, "we'll see how far I get."

Plans had been made for a limited postprandial walk, and the two men now started down the corridor, shaking a few hands at a nurses' station before getting into the elevator.

"Feels good," said the president, stepping off on the sixteenth floor, close to the top of the hospital's tower. "Feels as if I'm getting the circulation back in my legs. Aside from everything else, *they've* been bothering me." He saluted the officer leading them to the floor's VIP suite. Once seated there, he pointed to his chest and told Haig, "Tkach says anybody can get this," meaning pneumonia. "It's just stuff in the air. I asked him if stress and overwork could have brought it on; he said doubtful. So I guess we can't put out the story that doing the nation's business is killing me."

Haig laughed, relieved by the conversation's tone. The two of them sat in catercornered club chairs, sort of the way things had been with Chairman Mao a year ago. As the navy steward poured coffee from an elaborate silver service, the chief of staff tried to figure out the best way to move Nixon toward a definitive decision about the tapes. After putting his spoon on his saucer, he observed casually: "You know, we're the ones who get called 'imperial,' but Cox has *eighty* people working on Watergate, while we've got a handful. If we complied with all the document requests, we couldn't find people to do the Xeroxing."

Nixon sipped his coffee, not ready to get into things, so Haig detoured from the business at hand. "There's another one of these suites upstairs," he told the president. "In fact, it's the one where Jackie Kennedy and the family waited out JFK's autopsy. Pretty grim. I suggested this one when I found out we had a choice."

"Oh, this one's much more interesting," said Nixon.

"How so?"

"Forrestal." The president made a swan-dive motion with his arm, refreshing Haig's memory of how Truman's just-fired defense secretary had jumped from the hospital's tower in 1948. A nervous breakdown? Probably; though there were darker suppositions, too.

The chief of staff knew that the Hiss era remained the principal frame of reference for most things on Nixon's mind, but it bothered him that the president should know the exact location of Forrestal's jump.

Noticing the look on Haig's face, Nixon changed the subject. "Johnson told me that Kennedy's autopsy was a botch, and that there wouldn't be half these crazy conspiracy theories if the doctors had done a better job." The president paused for a moment, waiting for a change in Haig's expression that didn't come. Then he shrugged. "I'm just surprised Kennedy didn't get up off the table. Years before, I lost count of how many times they gave him the last rites and he bounced back. Christ, I remember being over in the Senate Office Building in '54, while he was in New York getting his back operation. They didn't think he'd make it, and this was at a time when the majority kept going back and forth and I kept having to break ties. One geezer after another, theirs or ours, kept dying. Styles Bridges, a real bastard from New Hampshire, one of ours, organized a little cocktail party in a basement office when he heard that a priest had been called to Kennedy's hospital room. I managed to skip it." He took another sip of coffee. "I can imagine the glasses that are now being raised whenever my temperature rises half a point."

For a moment Nixon appeared almost comfortable, like somebody telling old football stories, and in this expansive instant Haig felt an urge to say: *Give it up. Don't force yourself through the hellish months ahead. Go home and write your memoirs. Take the tapes with you. If you resign, they'll let you have them.*

"Do you think the Secret Service have a second copy?" Nixon asked. "Of the tapes," he added, after seeing Haig's surprise.

"I doubt it, sir. There's barely enough room in the EOB to store the ones we have."

"You know, Al, when it comes to that March twenty-first tape, hell, somebody could *add*, if need be, a line that has me telling Dean not to pay any more money, or has me telling him to get to the bottom of things. I mean, they say some of Kennedy's autopsy photos are fakes."

Haig did not want to pursue this line of thought. "There's always the possibility you'll win in court with the executive-privilege argument," he replied instead.

"No," said Nixon. "Everybody on the Supreme Court, including our own appointees, will want to be lionized by the liberal press. 'Great victory for the rule of law,' et cetera. 'Courageous conservatives' and all that jazz."

Haig nodded.

"I never wanted the goddamned thing," Nixon said softly. "Johnson had a system, not quite as elaborate, and I had it ripped out, like the damned high-pressure shower nozzles he had. The water coming out of them could knock you back to California. *We* were going to preserve things by just asking everybody to submit memoranda of whatever meetings they were in—or whatever meetings they were assigned to witness between me and somebody else. And you should see what we used to get, if they remembered to turn in anything at all. Showboating, incoherent crap. So Haldeman came up with this instead—creating a record automatically."

"Well, it's gone now, and—"

"There's so damned much that's *not* Watergate on those tapes. Anyone who listens can hear that it was one percent of this presidency. Which ought to be reason enough to save them."

Haig murmured agreement, though he knew that for the past several months the figure was nearer one hundred percent than one.

Nixon closed his eyes and continued speaking. "I've been remembering a record my brother Harold made for my mother, not a month before he died, in Los Angeles. There was a place on Sunset Boulevard that you could go into, step up to a microphone, and come out with a hard waxy record you could play on any Victrola. Harold made one singing 'Street of Dreams,' and he was going to give it to Mother for her birthday. He died before he could. So when Mother's birthday came around, I went to get it from the closet shelf where we'd hidden the thing, and found out that my old man had gotten rid of it. 'Morbid,' he called it. And there went the last trace of Harold."

"You're tired, Mr. President." It was the only thing Haig could think of to say.

"Yes," said Nixon, opening his eyes. His thoughts had begun chasing, overriding, and recycling themselves—probably an effect of the medication. But when he looked through the window, at the deepening nighttime darkness, he knew with finality that he would keep the tapes. Inertia would win: he would fight for them in court, however hopelessly, rather than trigger a vast convulsion—and maybe impeachment—by their destruction. He himself had always loved the big play, the bold move, but he didn't have the crazy courage to light Connally's bonfire.

He looked at the window ledge and thought of Forrestal in *his* pajamas. With a surprising sadness, he realized that he also lacked, at least for now, whatever strange bravery it would take to leap from the window.

"Al, I'll let you know in the morning."

Chapter Thirty

SEPTEMBER 11, 1973
WATERGATE WEST 310; MONTGOMERY COUNTY
DETENTION CENTER, ROCKVILLE, MARYLAND

Out on the balcony with her second cup of coffee, Clarine was reading *The Optimist's Daughter*. Over her first cup, she had told LaRue
that the book's author, Miss Welty, had once years ago stopped into the
Jackson law firm in order to have something notarized.

LaRue had only nodded. He and Clarine weren't due at the Montgomery County Detention Center for a couple of hours, but he was considerably more nervous than she about the visit they'd be making there
in order to pursue a scheme of Clarine's devising.

A scam was actually more like it, and as its execution approached,
LaRue could feel the need for a couple of strong pops. But he resisted: it
was only eleven a.m. and he had to do the driving. In her thirty-eight
years, Clarine had experienced little trouble navigating the world, but
she had never managed to obtain a license.

Her plan had been formulated a few weeks ago, while LaRue was
back in Jackson. She had clipped a review of Howard Hunt's latest novel
from the Books section of the *Washington Post* and then written to the
novelist in prison, saying that she, unlike the reviewer, did not regard
Hunt as "a loser with a humid fantasy life who was subsidized by the
American taxpayer." In addition to expressing her enjoyment of *The
Berlin Ending*, Clarine's letter mentioned a longstanding and entirely
untrue interest in the life of King Zog, the Albanian monarch whose
exile Hunt and the CIA had long ago tried to manage. In fact, she'd
told Hunt that, after years of working among lawyers and politicians,
she was writing a biography of the late king, who she understood from
recent press reports may long ago have commanded his attention. She
included a picture of herself and signed the letter with her full, real, and
almost-never-used name, Helen C. Lander.

Clarine had told LaRue all of this over the phone, while he was in

Jackson trying to make a first round of repairs on his family life. That work was difficult, since he was also contemplating what roles prison and Clarine Lander might play in the life ahead of him. During his time at home, the television had provided a steadily unsettling background music: Jeb Magruder had taken his turn pleading guilty to obstruction of justice; and on a trip to New Orleans, Nixon had succumbed to accumulated frustrations by giving his press secretary a hard shove in full view of the cameras.

Considered against everything else, Larrie's caper seemed fraught with unnecessary peril. Her hope was to wangle a prison visit with Hunt, and to explore—delicately, she promised—whether the MOOT envelope might have gotten scooped up during the first burglary of the DNC. She had reminded LaRue that, if it had, there was probably no way Hunt could connect him to it: an initial letter from their Canadian contact—she distinctly remembered its arrival, along with Ike LaRue's bird gun—had promised that the investigators would communicate about the "incident" without mentioning any names or any identifiable circumstances.

The whole idea was mildly crazy, thought LaRue, but Larrie would not be deterred.

And then she'd gotten a reply from Hunt, the envelope from Danbury sporting a new "Progress in Electronics" stamp that some wit in the prison PO had sold to the convicted wiretapper. The letter said that Hunt would enjoy meeting her at the Montgomery County Detention Center outside Washington, his prison home away from home, where they had him stay whenever he was needed in the capital for testimony before a grand jury or committee. He was pleased to say that Miss Lander, as a reader and fellow writer, was permitted to visit him. Only journalists were not allowed, and even that restriction was breachable: *Time*'s David Beckwith had gotten in by saying he was a lawyer— which he was.

So that's where they were due, at the "MCDC," at one o'clock. LaRue wished they were already on the road, and his nervousness only increased when the phone rang. But as soon as he recognized the caller to be John Mitchell, gloom replaced his jitters.

"I've got a new telephone number to give you," said the former attorney general.

LaRue wrote it down.

"I'm at the Essex House, but it's a private line," Mitchell explained.

"Does that mean what I think it does?"

"Yes," said Mitchell.

While Clarine continued to read and smoke out on the balcony, Mitchell informed LaRue that he had finally left 1030 Fifth Avenue, and Martha, after she'd smashed a mirror in the apartment and brushed Ajax onto his oil portrait. If her drinking got any worse, he could expect to have his actual face assaulted.

"Okay, pal," was all LaRue could manage to say. He was touched—and god-awfully sorrowful—that Mitchell should want to maintain a thread of connection to him, a man making things worse for his old boss with every visit to the special prosecutor's office.

LaRue hung up thinking yet again that he himself might have kept Watergate from ever happening—if down in Key Biscayne a year and a half ago he'd just raised his voice of protest a couple of decibels and said they would be nuts to give Gordon Liddy one thin dime.

Clarine stayed calm as could be all the way to the Detention Center. LaRue sensed folly in what they were doing, but he was soothed by the spell of her confidence. There was also this to consider: Risky as her retrieval operation might be, was it any worse than allowing that old investigative report to float free in the world? And, aside from all else: however peculiar Clarine's scheme, participation in it kept him from the kind of brooding he had done back home in Jackson.

"You got your alibi?" he asked her. He was worried about the warden and the guards, no matter that the visit had been approved.

"I've even got my lipstick," she replied, putting on a fresh coat of it once he parked the car.

As it happened, no one asked her a single inconvenient question. The guard in the visitors' room stayed mostly out of earshot and let her sit across a small table from Hunt, without even a wire mesh between them. The inmate was permitted to bring a folder of papers with him. Even so, despite such leniencies, Clarine could now say she under-stood what prison pallor is. Hunt was even thinner than she had imagined; he bore no resemblance to any of his fictional heroes and fantasy projections.

"It's very good of you to see me, Mr. Hunt."

"I was delighted to get your letter. I thought it discerning and very generous."

"How are you getting on here—and up in Connecticut?"

Hunt laughed, hoarsely. "It's a long commute, and I'm not exactly on the Eastern Shuttle. Handcuffed in the back of a van, you know. I'm more or less a professional witness these days, like one of those doctors whose career consists of testifying for the insurance companies."

"Are you writing another novel?"

"Kind of you to ask," said Hunt. "But no. Not at the moment. I'm at work on two pieces of *non*fiction. The lesser of them is my opening statement for the Ervin Committee. I'll be testifying the week after next." He extracted several sheets of paper from his folder, as if they actually were the pages of a novel-in-progress and he was asking an admirer if she'd like to hear any of it. When Clarine indicated she would, he recited the following passage from the statement he was preparing: *"I have been incarcerated for six months. For a time I was in solitary confinement. I have been physically attacked and robbed in jail. I have suffered a stroke. I have been transferred from place to place, manacled and chained, hand and foot. I am isolated from my four motherless children. The funds provided me and others who participated in the break-in have long since been exhausted."*

Clarine shook her head sadly, without overdoing it, the kind of gesture that had once made a drama coach at Bailey Junior High School tell her she could go far. "And your reviewers accuse *you* of having no sense of proportion," she said.

Hunt took another set of stapled papers from the folder, a draft of the motion to vacate his conviction.

"Please," said Clarine. "Go ahead."

He scanned it and selected the crux of his argument: *"Whether or not the evidence, unexposed because of now notorious corruption by government officials, would have established the defendant's innocence, such misconduct so gravely violated his constitutional rights as to require dismissal of the proceedings."*

Clarine nodded. To make sure she understood, Hunt offered some extemporaneous explanation: "They burned the notebooks I kept in my White House safe. John Dean let the acting head of the FBI do it."

Clarine again nodded, wondering if the MOOT envelope had gone up in the same blaze.

"A thirty-five-year sentence for abetting a burglary," Hunt intoned, with the Ancient Mariner's practiced repetition. "Given to a man with no prior criminal record."

"How do you pass your time?" Clarine asked. "Aside from working on your statements."

"Here I more or less just go to court. In Danbury I'm one of the prison librarians."

Clarine wondered if LaRue's poor vision would doom him to manual labor once *he* went away. If so, maybe he could help to maintain the tennis courts she'd heard Danbury had. He might like that; Fred played a surprisingly aggressive game, tracking the ball with an animal instinct beyond the weak powers of his eyes and ears. Her curiously durable feeling for him now made her get down to business with Hunt. She removed her lime-green jacket with its three-quarter-length sleeves, revealing Dorothy Hunt's jade brooch clipped to her white blouse. She noted Hunt's immediate recognition of it.

"You're not a writer," he said, with equal flashes of anger and confusion. But he was too intrigued to alarm the guard by raising his voice.

Clarine repressed a sarcastic urge to say "Neither are you." She silently removed the pin and passed it across the table. The guard remained engrossed in his magazine.

"I don't understand," said Hunt. "Who gave you this? Somebody in the Chicago morgue?"

"I've never been to Chicago in my life," replied Clarine, who had decided it made sense to cultivate an air of maximum mystery.

"Why are you giving this to me?" asked Hunt.

"Because I want something in return." She paused. "Did you ever possess an envelope with the word 'MOOT' written across it?"

Hunt peered at Clarine, trying to figure out who might have sent her here. Not Justice or the White House—neither would dare—but the Agency? For reasons swathed in a dozen different layers of camouflage?

A decided possibility. But could she also be some mysterious friend of his wife's, one of several he suspected Dorothy had made, during those six months of stress, without telling him?

Clarine could tell from the look in Hunt's eyes that the MOOT envelope had not gone up in smoke with his notebooks, that it still existed. She decided to challenge him directly: "Wherever you put that envelope, it's still there, isn't it?"

"Suppose I could get it for you," said Hunt. "Why give me the pin now, instead of after I've delivered?"

"The pin is lovely, but it's not very expensive, or important. You're not going to do anything for me because of it."

"So then why *would* I? Do anything for you, that is."

Clarine made an effort to sound like a character in *The Berlin Ending*. "Don't think about this little jade pin," she said. "Think of the Rosetta Stone." However preposterous, she wanted him to believe that's what *she* was.

And he was regarding her—this sudden apparition, beautiful and duplicitous—as if she might indeed, somehow, be what would deliver him from the whole fifteen-month nightmare of shame, embarrassment, and death. Could she be the person able to demonstrate that no one—from Richard Nixon to the special prosecutor to himself—had ever known what this affair was *really* about?

"I think I know where to find what you want," he said at last.

"Good," said Clarine. "Think about it."

Eager not to overplay her hand, hoping to retain her aura, she got up and put her jacket on, then signaled to the drowsy guard that she was ready to be let out.

"How can I contact you?" asked Hunt.

"You have an address and phone number. Use one of them when you figure out how to get the envelope."

She saw him look at her with a reasonable certainty that she had nothing to do with the authorities currently oppressing him. In return, she knew that he would not talk, that he was seeing fine possibilities in her that must not be put at risk.

Once she was in the car, LaRue, who had imagined her running a gauntlet of thugs, asked, "Wolf whistles?"

"Not a one. Not even from him."

"Really? Even when he must have realized that the picture you sent doesn't do you justice?"

"He doesn't have the strength to whistle," Clarine explained, with unexpected sadness.

Chapter Thirty-One

SEPTEMBER 30, 1973
CAMP DAVID, MARYLAND

Kissinger had at last become secretary of state, and Rose had a new title, too—Executive Assistant to the President. She was thoroughly indifferent to it. "Personal secretary" had been fine, and this new moniker wasn't saving her from some of the worst scut work she'd ever been asked to perform. Here it was, past five o'clock on a Sunday, and here *she* was, amidst the mosquitoes of Camp David, a place she couldn't stand, trying to transcribe eight of the "White House tapes" so that their side would know exactly what it was arguing about with Sirica.

She had been at it for two days on a Sony 800B with no pedal. She'd yet to complete a single reel and she had a splitting headache. Three aspirin hadn't killed it, and she didn't think she could wait another fifteen minutes for cocktails. She had the TV on in the background, and the one station they got up here in Hooterville was broadcasting some week-in-review program. Agnew, filmed yesterday out in Los Angeles, was bellowing to a Republican women's luncheon—"*I will not resign if indicted! I will not resign if indicted!*"—and by the time he finished, some of the gals were standing on the tables, roaring approval and waving napkins.

Agnew was sleek as a seal in a circus, comfortable in his body and expensive suit, and always beautifully groomed. From the moment Rose first saw him in '68, she'd spotted him for an excellent dancer, and she'd not been disappointed the couple of times they'd been out on the floor together. She remained sympathetic to this bluff, manly character, even if he'd turned out to be a little crooked. Right now he was being killed, deliberately, by leaks from Richardson and all the career Democrats at Justice, and even if she didn't rise to her feet here inside Dogwood Cottage, Rose liked the sound of him fighting back.

Howard Hunt, whose testimony the TV was now showing, did nothing for her: a real oddball, like some disappointed professor or severe, scholarly priest. Liddy was supposed to be even stranger, but *he* still refused to testify, period, and that, in Rose's book, made him the most stand-up guy of all.

God, these tapes. The other day, when the boss approached her with the project, he'd made it sound like a piece of cake. "Rose, you're such a fast typist. I'll bet you have all eight of them done before we head back to Washington Monday morning." Fat chance! It was *agony:* listening to a few inches at a time; pressing the PAUSE button; each squeaky rewinding like a dentist's drill. She had to strain to make out one voice from another when everybody talked at once, and it was impossible to hear anybody's words over the rattle of coffee cups, the tapping of pencils, or an airplane passing overhead. The whole thing made her despair. And having to do it here only made it worse. She'd give anything to be home inside the cozy hive of Watergate West, ready to spend Sunday night by herself.

"How's it coming?" asked Richard Nixon.

"Jesus, you scared me," said Rose, before laughing.

The president had just come back from the pool. He was wearing a short-sleeved madras shirt above his still-wet swim trunks. Tufts of chest hair, more black than gray, sprouted from his open collar, showing off a virility he usually took pains to hide. Rose had always thought his visits to the barber bordered on the compulsive; he'd been afraid of his own five o'clock shadow long before people said it had cost him the debates with Kennedy.

"Sorry," said Nixon. "And sorry this is turning out to be such awful work." He put a towel over one of the chair cushions and sat down.

She smiled. "You're always talking about 'three yards and a cloud of dust.' Well, this is six inches of tape and a bunch of static."

"You mind?" asked the president, putting his finger on the PLAY button.

"Be my guest."

A cacophony of cross talk emerged from the speaker. After about twenty seconds Nixon shut it off.

"Three voices?" he asked.

"Yes," answered Rose. "You, Bob, and John. As soon as I'm sure John has left the room, I can stop transcribing this one. Al called back a couple of hours ago, after double-checking: the subpoena only calls for the part of this conversation that's between you and John."

Nixon nodded. "When is this one from?"

"Three days after the break-in. Just before lunch on a Tuesday." She pressed the button to play a little more.

"Who just whistled?" asked the president.

"I haven't a clue."

But both could now hear Nixon mentioning Ely, Nevada, the first lady's birthplace. He was responding to Haldeman, who'd just brought up a campaign trip Pat had finished making to South Dakota. Nixon was noting that her parents had been married in that state before moving to Ely.

He pressed the STOP button. "Take a break. Let's go have a drink and dinner."

"No arguments from me," said Rose.

Everyone at the table was so sympathetic to her ordeal that they practically sang "For She's a Jolly Good Fellow." But what really cheered her up, along with a third glass of Riesling, was a change in plans: they'd be going back to Washington late tonight instead of early tomorrow morning. The helicopter would leave around nine-thirty, after a movie. Refreshed by the prospect of sleeping in her own bed, she decided to go back to work and complete at least this first bear of a tape while the rest of them watched the film.

She took her coffee back to Dogwood, switched on the IBM Selectric, and hit PLAY on the Sony. She somehow hoped to *hear* Ehrlichman's absence, if not his actual exit, but it was like proving a negative. Was he still there while HRH and the president remarked on how the EOB ought to be checked for *Democrat* bugs? Or when they expressed disbelief that anybody could equate this bit of campaign hijinx with the leaking of the Pentagon Papers? As she listened to this portion of the conversation, she actually hoped Ehrlichman *was* still in the room: what was being said, if under subpoena, could actually help. The boss and Haldeman sounded surprised about the burglary, and their remarks showed a sense of proportion that the other side had long since lost.

Even so, Rose did not enjoy having to hear HRH's voice for the first time in months. She'd not even watched his Ervin testimony, and as she listened to more of this tape—not transcribing now, just searching for a hint of Ehrlichman's whereabouts—it was to Richard Nixon's voice that she more naturally inclined:

> RN: *Pat was telling me about the fundraiser at Taft Schreiber's place. Reagan was a big hit, but our own guys were acting sort of odd.*
> HRH: *Well, they'd gotten word of this break-in thing just before.*

The boss clearly didn't want to pursue the subject:

> RN: *She told me about looking down the hill from Schreiber's mansion. How it got her remembering the streetcar from Whittier into L.A. Well, she hasn't done badly for a girl from Ely. "You've come a long way, baby!"*

HRH, who didn't smoke, drink, go to doctors, or watch much TV, didn't seem to get the reference to the advertising catchphrase. The boss let it pass:

> RN: *Jesus, you know, I keep thinking about us in California ten years ago—one awful day after another on that campaign, everything ending at the Beverly Hilton.*

Rose, too, remembered every day of '62's horrible grind, right through the "last press conference."

> RN: *And now we've got Lew Wasserman and the rest of Hollywood eating out of our hands—if we don't screw things up! Jesus, back in '62 I think we had Adolphe Menjou and Irene Dunne.*

He laughed at the antiquity of these celluloid names, but Haldeman still said nothing, as if not wanting to revisit ten-year-old emotions he probably hadn't felt in the first place. Nixon was left to monologize:

RN: *You know, I'm not sure I want to go back to San Clemente in '77. Even with all we've done on the house. I'll be sixty-four, and I think I'd rather write the book and do everything else from New York. I certainly wouldn't have any trouble selling Pat on that idea.*

Even now no response:

RN: *Where do you see yourself, Bob?*

Startled to be asked, Haldeman finally came to verbal life:

HRH: *Back at J. Walter Thompson, I guess. Back in L.A.*
RN: *Really? You don't want to write your own book? Or lecture? Christ, you've got a lot more to teach in the way of political science than a bunch of professors at Harvard and Yale.*
HRH: *I never really saw this as my life's work. It was a chance to serve you—*
RN: *And I've put you through some long hauls: '60, '62. Even '56 couldn't have been that much fun.*
HRH: *Well, those were just intervals between everything else. I never wanted to solder myself to you like Rose.*

The boss said nothing for a moment. She waited for words in her defense, but they never came.

RN: *Well, it takes its toll, this life. The one I really worry about, because of Martha's drinking, is Mitchell. I mean, how the hell did he let this break-in happen? He's not himself, and it's because of her. She's taken over his whole attention span.*
HRH: *Oh, for sure.*

Rose hated the idea of Nixon being led to thoughts of Martha Mitchell by HRH's mention of *her.* Above all, she hated the idea of Haldeman as the standard of mental health: *I never wanted to solder myself to you like Rose.*

Looking down at the turning reels and fearing whatever she might hear next, she experienced a sudden fury, a desire to get rid of this tape, or at least this portion of it, which she realized she could do, since the continuing absence of Ehrlichman's voice by now *did* prove a negative. He couldn't possibly still be in that room.

Pushing her coffee cup to one side, and feeling the effects of the wine, she rewound the tape to the point at which they began talking of Ely, Nevada, and then she struck the RECORD button, a gesture more satisfying than popping a balloon. She let the button up but then pressed it back down, five more times, until this whole personal, irrelevant conversation was finished and the two men, the president and his chief of staff, began to discuss the Democrats' convention, which in the frozen world of the tapes was still approaching.

Ninety minutes later she was buckling herself into a seat on the helicopter next to Pat.

"How was the movie?" she asked the first lady.

"Horse manure in the living room."

Rose laughed, knowing Pat put up with all the westerns only for her husband's sake. "Which one?"

"*Lonely Are the Brave*."

Rose sighed. "Ain't it the truth?"

The helicopter rose above Catoctin Mountain. The air was already crisp with fall, and the leaves would be blazing in another week or two.

"We've got to get you some help with this awful transcription job," said Pat. "But who else can we trust?"

"Oh, I don't mind."

Pat touched Rose's hand. "It's going to be a terrible few months for everybody. Will you come for Thanksgiving?"

"Here?"

"No," said Pat, with a laugh, well aware that Rose disliked Camp David. "At the White House."

"Oh, absolutely. That'd be swell. Thank you."

"Do you want to bring Bob Gray?"

Lately, the PR man had been filling Don Carnevale's old role.

"No," said Rose, after a moment's thought, "but it's sweet of you to ask."

"I teased him about you at some reception last week."

"I'll brain you," said Rose, laughing.

"I asked him, 'Has she cooked for you yet?' "

"Yeah?"

"And he said, 'She's great with ice cubes.' "

The two women laughed, playing out the fiction that Gray, another confirmed bachelor, was a serious suitor. The pretense was designed to build Rose up, to make it appear she was playing the field, and to keep the lilac dust of spinsterhood from settling on her.

"It would be nice," said Pat, "to have Thanksgiving at a restaurant some year. Of course it'd be way too much bother. And if we commandeer the whole place to ourselves—well, what's the point? Besides, the only restaurant Dick ever wants to go to, whatever the city, is Trader Vic's."

"Where would *you* go?" asked Rose. "If you could pick any place."

"Oh, somewhere simple and festive. Like Gino's, up in New York, over on Lexington Avenue." She seemed to catch herself. "You know," she said. "We've lunched there."

"I don't think so," said Rose.

"Oh, sure we did," insisted Pat, a bit too brightly. Rose could see she was afraid to show she'd been thinking of some happy memory that involved another person entirely.

"Anyway," Pat went on, eager to finish with the subject, "it's an idle fantasy." She closed her eyes, as if needing to doze.

Rose gave no more thought to Thanksgiving. She leaned back in her seat and felt a cold draft of air coming through some microscopic space between a window and the helicopter's fuselage. The last of the Riesling's glow had worn off. She was stone sober and beginning to feel a terrible unease. Looking toward the metal strongbox with the tapes, which rested at the feet of the military aide, she wondered about what she had done. She tried to nap, but it was no use. Her eyes went back to the metal box, and her mind rehearsed the same anxious thoughts until the helicopter landed on the South Lawn.

Eleven sleepless hours later, she was back in the office, working off a different tape recorder—one with a pedal—that Steve Bull had gotten hold of. With this fancy Uher 5000, she was determined to see the

whole job, all eight tapes, through to completion. But she could not concentrate. She had already, twice, deliberately re-erased the erasure, as
if it were telltale. Angry over last night's loss of control, she had vowed
not to have so much as a glass of wine between now and New Year's.

But nothing could get rid of the guilty, apprehensive feeling. When
she could stand it no longer, she got up from her chair and walked to the
Oval Office, slipping in between appointments the president had with
Ziegler and Haig.

"I've made a terrible mistake," she confessed.

Nixon looked at her blankly, prompting her to explain that she'd just
been reviewing the last part of the June twentieth tape—to make absolutely certain Ehrlichman had left the room and it was safe to stop transcribing. "You know, just to be *triple*-sure. And then I got distracted by
a phone call. I think I hit the RECORD button instead of STOP, and I must
have kept my foot on the pedal. I now realize the tape kept running and
erasing itself. Oh God."

"For how long?" Nixon asked calmly.

"Four or five minutes."

This was a stupid, dangerous fib. She hadn't timed it, but she knew
the gap was considerably longer than that. Still, five minutes sounded
more believable and less embarrassing than fifteen or twenty, and thus
she decided to place one lie atop another. "I feel like such a fool," she
said, with real distress. "This is awful. In all my years of working with
your Dictabelts, I've *never* done something like this."

"Rose," said Nixon, "don't be hard on yourself. You're exhausted,
and you're doing a tremendous job. This is a mistake of no consequence.
They don't even want that part of the tape."

She looked at him with heartfelt gratitude, if not exactly relief. He
was always this way when face-to-face with a subordinate who'd let him
down. It might just be part of that loathing for confrontation he shared
with Pat, but if you were the subordinate, it felt like genuine tenderness,
even nobility.

"Thank you," said Rose, her voice catching. "I know you're right. But
they always want more and more. I mean Cox and Sirica and Ervin. I'm
afraid that eventually they'll ask for everything—including the part of
the conversation with just Bob."

"Well," said Nixon, with the reassurance of an older brother, "we're going to fight not to give 'em anything. And we're gonna win, Rose."

She reached over and patted his arm. "Thank you, Mr. President." She left without another word, and with no trace of last night's disappointment that he hadn't defended her to Haldeman.

A half hour later, Haig was walking the halls of the West Wing, as he always did, pepping people up, stoking their morale. Rose could imagine him as the department-store floorwalker he'd been long ago, before entering the army. She sometimes teased him about it and had once stuck a boutonnière in his lapel. When he entered her office, she smiled, but her hands were still trembling.

"The boss tells me you're upset," he said.

"I'm very, very peeved with myself. I don't usually burst in there like I did. I like to let you know." Even HRH had never been allowed to keep her out, but dropping in on the president was a privilege she rarely exercised. That she'd used it this morning to lie about something so stupid only added to her shame.

"Well," said Haig. "I just talked to Buzhardt in our little legal shop, and he says they've definitely asked for only the Ehrlichman stuff on that one. He checked the subpoena same as I did, so stop worrying that strawberry-blond head about it."

"Thank you, sir." She executed their Colonel Woods–General Haig routine as cheerfully as she could, but when he left the room she began to cry.

If anyone later claimed to have seen her in tears, she would deny that, too.

Chapter Thirty-Two

OCTOBER 12, 1973
1100 CREST DRIVE, McLEAN, VIRGINIA;
EAST ROOM OF THE WHITE HOUSE

At 6:50 p.m., while the television murmured from the other side of his large study, Elliot Richardson continued painting his watercolor of a buff-breasted sandpiper. The brown dots he was applying to the bird's head briefly brought to mind the crew cut of Bob Haldeman, who now seemed to belong to a remote political era.

Richardson rinsed his brush and looked up to read the inscription on a new plaque hanging in this same section of the study where he kept his easel. The engraved quotation came from his August speech to the American Bar Association:

Finding myself a citizen of the Watergate era, I have decided that one direct contribution I can make to countering suspicion of political influence in the Department of Justice is not only to forswear politics for myself but to ask my principal colleagues to do the same.

The editorials that had followed the speech—"A strong man has brought a new day"—were, he'd modestly remarked as they came out, "extremely gratifying."

Anne poked her head in. "Guess what? The White House operator just called. They want us in the East Room *tonight*—eight forty-five the absolute latest."

Both of them looked at Richardson's third martini, which stood not far from the paint box.

"A driver's coming at eight-fifteen," said Anne, before she rushed off to put herself together.

Nixon's announcement of a new vice president—surely the event prompting this Friday-night summons—had been necessitated by the resignation of Spiro T. Agnew, which Richardson had personally overseen on Wednesday. He'd traveled up to Baltimore to represent the government in the courtroom where Agnew pleaded no contest to a tax-evasion charge. As late as Monday, the attorney general had been hoping to send him to prison, but he'd finally had to settle for the resignation, thanks to a growing fear of "double impeachment." As Haig had liked putting it, Nixon needed to "outlast" his own VP; otherwise, if the Democrats forced Nixon out first, Agnew would succeed to the presidency and then have to be removed as well.

Richardson had argued for jail because the crimes merited it—taking cash right inside the White House! Maryland contractors had gone on paying Agnew for business he'd steered their way years before while governor. The gravity of a jail term would also diminish any appearance that Richardson's real goal was to sweep aside a rival for the '76 presidential nomination. As it was, some clever local law professor had filed a conflict-of-interest brief on Agnew's behalf.

But "double impeachment" had remained a formidable specter, and so on Wednesday Richardson had stood before the judge in Baltimore to offer three reasons why Spiro Agnew should be disgraced but not imprisoned: respect for the office of the vice presidency; human compassion; appreciation for Agnew's taking the deal and sparing the nation a lengthy trial on the charges at hand.

Three reasons; three lies. Richardson had no more respect for the vice presidency than he had for Spiro Agnew. Rarely in fact had a man and an office been so well matched. And the only person the bastard was sparing was himself, from certain conviction.

When Richardson had spoken with the president on Wednesday evening, reporting to him on the resignation arrangements, he'd tried to lighten things by saying he hoped the deal wasn't an example of "permissiveness," one of Agnew's great themes during his glory days on the stump. The joke had fallen flat. "Thank you for doing your job" was all Nixon said, quite solemnly, as if having to remove Agnew, rather than showing him leniency, had been the distasteful task.

As it was, this tepid "thank you" exceeded any presidential praise Richardson had received after that ABA speech. Things between him and Nixon had been frosty to the point of incivility ever since he'd suggested that the time might have arrived for the president to be using a personal attorney, and not the White House counsel, to handle his Watergate defense.

And so now it was time to learn the identity of Agnew's successor. Over the last two days, whenever reporters asked, Richardson had professed indifference to the prospect of being named vice president himself. The indifference, alas, stemmed mostly from the impossibility of its occurring. There would be a kind of banana-republican preposterousness in having one man serve as secretary of HEW, secretary of defense, attorney general, and then vice president in the space of ten months. And Agnew would be able to complain of a certain unseemliness should he be replaced by the man who'd removed him.

But Richardson was not indifferent to whoever *would* be the president's choice. In fact, he had fervent hopes that this lackluster office would go to one lackluster man in particular. It simply *had* to be Ford, he now thought, as he painted one of the sandpiper's wing tips. Was his hand, he wondered, shaking with the intensity of his hopes for dumb, affable Jerry? Or was it the martini? He decided he would stop for the night; he needed to be on his game.

Nixon wanted everyone caught up in the suspense he'd been creating about the choice, as if all the improvised hoopla would make people forget that he was having to choose at all only because he'd picked so badly the first time. Connally of course would be his heart's desire now, but the Democratic convert was simply not confirmable, and the other "big" men, Reagan and Rockefeller, presented ideological problems. Rogers? wondered Richardson. High-minded (up to a point), but too much of a crony. No, if his own long-term strategy was to bear fruit, it had to be Ford, who would be acceptable, as the law demanded, to both the Senate and the House. Members of that lower chamber would see themselves in Jerry, and thus feel worthy and enhanced—just as Nixon had tried to make the state party chairmen feel "included" during the past forty-eight hours, conducting a pseudo-survey of their preferences on the VP question.

The television now showed little Carl Albert, the Democratic speaker from Bugtussle, Oklahoma, who would remain next in line for the presidency until Agnew's replacement could be sworn in. This was a matter of genuine worry. With the Israelis and Arabs at war again, one could at least count on Nixon to keep the combatants straight; Albert might be too sloshed to tell them apart. Rumors even had him in treatment.

"Are you going to shave?" asked Anne, again at the door.

"In a minute, dear."

Richardson was closing the paint box as the TV turned its attention to Rockefeller's afternoon press conference. The governor spoke sorrowfully of Agnew—who had tried to get him into the presidential race in '68—before commenting on his own vice-presidential prospects. They were nil, he claimed, since he didn't want the job. "There's an old South American saying that nobody climbs to the top on the dead bodies of his friends."

Really? thought Richardson. The quotation seemed too cumbersome to be a "saying." Perhaps it sounded different in the original Spanish; or perhaps Nelson had concocted the line himself.

The attorney general rose from his chair, turned off the television, and went up to the bathroom to shave, humming "Climb Every Mountain" as he ascended the stairs.

Richardson and his wife entered the East Room at 8:45, passing under TV lights that stood on the edges of the room like giant flamingoes. Outside, on the White House lawn, the network reporters vamped and speculated through their live feeds, repeating the word "unprecedented" until it seemed a synonym for "routine."

As the Richardsons reached their seats, the attorney general looked at the Joint Chiefs and tried to remember the Marine Corps commandant's name; he hadn't, he realized, been secretary of defense long enough for it to register fully. He sat down next to his silver-haired successor in that post, Jim Schlesinger.

"How goes Armageddon?" Richardson asked.

Schlesinger frowned. Word had gotten out that he was on the carpet for not getting the Israelis resupplied fast enough against the Arabs, who looked as if they might succeed in driving the Jews straight into the Mediterranean. "Every hour I get a call from him telling me to hurry, move faster, get everything that can fly into the air. Well, if he doesn't think this is going to provoke his pal Brezhnev, he's kidding himself."

Richardson shook his head sympathetically as tiny Bryce Harlow, two inches shorter than Carl Albert, waved hello. The White House's liaison to the Hill, another throwback to the Eisenhower years, had been part of the operation that pushed Agnew out, and there was an element of mutual congratulation in the smiles he and Richardson now exchanged.

But the attorney general's face fell when he noticed Jerry and Betty Ford sitting here in the room with the rest of the House delegation. Would it after all be someone else who came through the doors by Richard Nixon's side? With a dismayed tilt of his head, Richardson pointed the Fords out to Anne. "Oh, dear," she whispered.

The Marine Band started in on "Hail to the Chief" just before 9:05 p.m. They might as well, thought Richardson, be playing it for whoever *would* enter with Nixon, so sure was that man's eventual ascent to the presidency.

But only Pat Nixon came down the center aisle with her husband.

Richardson looked over at Ford and for one last time ran through the personal possibilities that depended on Jerry's selection: Yes, Nixon had outlasted Agnew, but Nixon was going, too. And once he was gone, then it would be Ford who needed a vice president. And since he'd have come in under a cloud—owing his elevation to a man in disgrace—he would pick Elliot Richardson, the man who had brought Richard Nixon to justice via Archibald Cox. Elliot Richardson, the very perfume of probity, would take enough stink off Ford so that he could at least govern as a caretaker. But enough stink would cling to him to make his nomination in '76 out of the question—at which point the penitential party would nominate Vice President Elliot Richardson for president.

Nixon, now at the podium, looked less like a president than the host of an awards show, milking the suspense. After talking about all the qualities he had looked for in a new vice president, he announced that he had selected "a man who has served for twenty-five years in the House of Representatives with great distinction."

The applause swelled and all eyes, including Richardson's, went to Ford. Anne grasped his hand in relief.

"Ladies and gentlemen," said Nixon, just like Ralph Edwards on *This Is Your Life*, "please don't be premature! There are several men here who have served twenty-five years in the House." Pleased with his joke, he flashed that madly dissociative smile. Richardson had long suspected that Haig was lying, and that there'd been more than pneumonia to Nixon's July hospitalization. The sight of this mirthless mechanical grin was doing nothing to change his mind. But his own relief was right now too enormous for him to dwell on the president's mental condition.

"I proudly present to you the man whose name I will submit to the Congress of the United States for confirmation as the next vice president of the United States, Congressman Gerald Ford of Michigan!"

Well, thank goodness, thought Richardson, returning Anne's squeeze.

The Fords moved from the audience to the front of the room, acknowledging the cheers like victors in a ballroom-dance contest. There would be, needless to say, no mention of Agnew, whose liquidation already included the removal, from the White House entrance hall, of any pictures he'd been in. Before long, Richardson mused, it would be the same for Nixon, whose name would not be uttered in this room, or this house, or on any GOP convention rostrum, for years to come.

For the moment all was jolly. Even Ford was smart enough to understand the importance of his honest-Joe, regular-guy credentials. He reassured everyone in the great American viewing public that tomorrow morning would find him in Cedar Springs, Michigan, marching in the town's Red Flannel Day Parade, same as he had for the past twenty-five years.

As everyone laughed, Richardson could see at least three senators—Baker, Percy, and Hatfield—who would want the '76 nomination for themselves. But that wouldn't stop them from first having to vote him into the front runner's position, before very long, as Ford's VP.

He returned his eyes to the front of the room for an appraisal of Mrs. Ford's proud, glazed expression. He knew that Anne, always over-vigilant about him, would be appraising it, too. He'd bet that at the reception starting a few minutes from now, the nominee's spouse would limit herself to a glass of tonic water and then, once home in Alexandria, make herself a couple of stiff ones. He'd also wager that she'd be sleeping in tomorrow while Jerry flew off to Red Flannel Day.

At least Nixon was willing to attend *this* reception, unlike the one for his new attorney general back in May. The Blue Room was full to bursting by the time the Richardsons made their way into it.

Haig was chatting with Rose Mary Woods, who pointedly moved away when Richardson drew near.

"That was a long day, Wednesday," observed the chief of staff. "While you were taking care of things in Baltimore, over here we had first Mobutu and then the National Medal of Science winners. The witch doctor and the wizards."

Richardson smiled before saying, with a kind of pained wistfulness, "Agnew didn't seem willing to shake my hand once it was over. I would have preferred things to end a little more civilly than they did."

"Elliot, he didn't like shaking your hand *before* all that started."

It was true, of course. The two of them had fought on the Domestic Council, and even before that, Agnew had been furious with Richardson for leading a doomed little rebellion against his selection at the '68 convention, when Richardson helped persuade a couple hundred delegates to vote against the race-baiting parvenu Nixon had chosen. Still, it didn't have to be personal.

"In fact," said Haig, "Agnew used to do a mean imitation of you." The implication seemed clear that the chief of staff had enjoyed watching it.

Richardson and Haig had made useful common cause since July, when the attorney general had shown him the whole range of evidence against Agnew. For months after that, Haig had maintained a tough approach whenever Agnew complained—even to Nixon, on those rare occasions when he was granted a meeting—about the leaks coming from Justice. Through it all, both of them had tried to scare the vice president into quitting, jail or no jail, though if Agnew had known as much about Nixon's guilt as Richardson now did, he might have held out longer, kept fighting even after Justice began threatening plump little Mrs. Agnew. Tough tactics, but the tax fraud at issue *had* been committed on a joint return—something Haig had noted as well.

At this moment, however, in the Blue Room's good-humored hubbub, it was clear that any alliance between Haig and Richardson was finished. For lack of another thing to say, the attorney general remarked: "Jim Schlesinger tells me he's under a lot of pressure from the president about the airlift."

Haig replied with speed and spirit: "What the president is doing is bigger than Berlin in '48, and just as important. It's why Henry's already left this party. Believe it or not, there's still a Free World to lead."

Richard Nixon, who presumably should be allowed to continue leading it, locked eyes with Richardson from several feet away, but then
pretended he didn't see him. Haig also turned to someone else, leaving the attorney general stranded between two other conversations.
Dobrynin, the Soviet ambassador, was telling John Scali, the administration's man at the UN, that the Fords would be "the first truly normal
people to live in this house since the Trumans." Dobrynin then, diplo-
matically, caught himself: "If it comes to that." Not far away, Richardson could also overhear Betty Ford telling Mrs. George Shultz about
Jerry's promise to her to retire in '77.

She really didn't get it, Richardson thought. She didn't realize that
between now and then there would occur a brief presidency that hadn't
yet started; that after tomorrow, for the next couple of years, there
would be no more Red Flannel Days for Jerry to march in and for her to
sleep through. Within months, maybe even weeks, she and her husband
would be moving their things upstairs.

The Court of Appeals had, after all, just ordered that the eight tapes
be surrendered. The White House had seven days to turn them over,
one desperate week in which they would have to seek a compromise
with the special prosecutor and the Ervin Committee. If they defied the
order, there would be chaos, and if they took the matter to the Supreme
Court, they would lose.

Haig, taking leave of the Blue Room, found himself forced into
exchanging a few words of goodbye with Richardson.

"Well," said the chief of staff, "at least we can now get back to the
main business."

"Yes," said Richardson, "the main business."

One of them meant the business of saving Richard Nixon; the other
meant the business of finishing him off.

Chapter Thirty-Three

OCTOBER 19–23, 1973
THE WHITE HOUSE; THE McLEAN TENNIS CLUB;
THE DEPARTMENT OF JUSTICE

"I'm feeling like a goddamned president again!" Nixon told Kissinger over Friday-evening cocktails in the Residence.

"You have never failed to function, through all of this, at a supremely high level," replied the secretary of state.

Ignoring the auto-flattery, Nixon asked, "When do you actually leave?"

"A little after midnight."

"Play it hard with them, Henry. Don't hesitate to let Brezhnev know there's been considerable improvement in my position over here."

"That will be an enormous factor, Mr. President."

In a matter of days, thanks to the airlift, the Israelis had bounced back. It was the Arabs who were now on the run and the Russians who were calling, preposterously, for a cease-fire at the pre-1967 borders. Well, Kissinger would go to Moscow and get them to drop that. Then, once a more realistic cease-fire was in place and Congress had voted the two billion dollars in aid he'd just requested for Israel, the president would tilt to the Arabs and get them to turn the oil back on. The Israelis would be unable to resist his pressures for a real peace settlement, and pressure them he would. They had no choice: he'd saved their country! Golda Meir said there'd be statues of him dotting the landscape someday.

After twenty-five years, he would get this goddamned thing solved, and the solution would be bigger than China, Vietnam, and arms control put together. Watergate would at last, to anyone but a lunatic, seem a shameful obsession.

"You know," he told Kissinger, "Ervin admitted he's actually *relieved.*"

The committee chairman had been in the Oval Office an hour ago with Howard Baker and had agreed to a compromise: the White House would turn over *summaries* of the eight tapes after John Stennis—a Democrat, it should be remembered—had listened to them and verified the accuracy of the synopses. And Stennis would do just that: not because he was hard of hearing, but because he had a sense of proportion. He would understand that the cover-up had essentially been Dean's doing, and that the president's little verbal flights of complicity had been more apparent than real.

"Mr. President, we are *all* relieved," said Kissinger.

"Hell, once Ervin agreed, I even apologized for chewing him out over the phone this summer."

"That was just the pneumonia talking."

"Talking pneumonia!" said Nixon, with a laugh. He hadn't been this cheerful in months. "You know, Taft Schreiber was in this afternoon. He brought in some movie they haven't even released yet—not like those moth-eaten old reels up at Camp David. We're going to run it tonight, right after Ziegler announces the compromise."

"Will they go 'live' with Ron?" asked Kissinger. "If they do, Professor Cox will be switching to *Sanford and Son* to cheer himself up."

"That son of a bitch is on his way out. Christ, he's been into my taxes, the San Clemente deal, Bebe's businesses! Richardson says he even wanted in on Agnew."

"He was foolish to reject this compromise."

"Well, he's going to be canned for it. Richardson was over here with Al and Garment and Buzhardt this morning, and he agreed to get rid of him."

"He's been conducting a persecution, not a prosecution," observed the secretary of state.

Abruptly, as if Kissinger had been forcing him to discuss the petty business of Watergate, the president changed the subject. "Henry, you're to make it clear to Brezhnev that everything you say comes from me personally, and that I'll now be strong enough to follow through on it."

"Yes, Mr. President."

"Good. And by the way, did you notice Dean pleaded guilty this morning? I don't give a damn if it *was* to just one count and he's been immunized up to his eyeballs on the rest. The history books can now say the president's accuser was a convicted felon."

"Mr. President, the history books will not be mentioning John Dean at all."

Two hours later, as Taft Schreiber's movie, *The Sting*, was being readied in the projection room, Haig called the Residence. "The bastard stiffed us," he informed the president.

"Which bastard?" asked Nixon.

"Richardson. I called him a minute ago, after Ziegler's announcement. I don't know if I did it to celebrate or because my instincts told me he needed checking on, but he said, 'I can't fire Cox.' No, actually, he said, 'I cannot fire Cox.' Contractions are beneath Elliot."

"Son of a bitch," said Nixon, with a sigh.

"I told him we had his word—not to mention *witnesses:* me, Buzhardt, Garment."

In a voice that was even, but hollowed out, Nixon asked, "What exactly was his explanation?"

"That he couldn't possibly have agreed to Cox's firing. That it would break a promise he'd made to the Judiciary Committee during his confirmation hearings—not to get rid of the special prosecutor except for 'extraordinary improprieties.' He could barely get the two words out tonight; they kept slurring over each other. He admitted to me that he was tired and had had 'a' drink."

As if nostalgic for the actual goddamned president he'd gotten to be a few hours ago, Nixon asked, "What is Brezhnev going to say if he sees my own attorney general defying me?"

Instead of answering, Haig beat the dead horse of the tapes compromise: "I told him, 'You *first* agreed, Elliot, days ago, to a two-step plan. To tell Cox the Stennis deal was a *fait accompli* and see if he'd resign. Then, if he refused, to fire him.'"

Nixon squeezed the coils of the telephone cord. "Well, I'm not surprised that pious cocksucker cares more for his ass than his country. Get him in to see me tomorrow morning. It'll probably be the first Saturday he's ever worked in his life."

———

The following evening, across the river at the McLean Tennis Club, Alice Longworth reassured a young waiter nervously guiding her to a courtside table: "If I get beaned, it will probably knock some sense into me."

Art Buchwald, the humor columnist, was throwing himself a birthday celebration that had taken over the entire place. Most of the invited guests, when not at the tables or bar, were taking turns playing mixed doubles.

Tom and Joan Braden had invited Joe Alsop to tag along here with them. This attempt to cheer him up now that Susan Mary had finally decamped had been seized upon by Alice, who insisted that she herself needed cheering up, too. In truth, she didn't, but she was enjoying this trip out of the house, an increasing rarity, more than Joe seemed to be.

"Brighten up," she commanded him. "You can at least be happy that the Tortoiseshelled Tattler is going to jail."

"Yes," said Alsop, with no hint of a smile. "Probably for about six months."

"At this point I would consider six months a prognosis of longevity." She was looking more birdlike than ever, but the remark was greeted by protests from everyone seated and hovering around her.

Lyndon's little poodle, Jack Valenti—now a miniature, silver-haired version of the MGM lion, cheerleading for the movie business on Capitol Hill—complimented her same old black straw hat as if it were some fabulous new piece of plumage. David Brinkley, the NBC man, sidled up to shake her hand, and then came Ben Bradlee with an attractive, sharp-eyed girlfriend, apparently a reporter, who wanted to know if she could write a profile of Mrs. Longworth on the occasion of her birthday— "your ninetieth, I believe"—which would be coming up in February.

Alice glared at her. Of course she would eventually say yes, but there was no point in making the girl's evening.

"So," she asked Joe about the gaggle of admirers, "is this what they call a full court press? Is that a tennis term?"

"Basketball," he informed her.

"Short answers make you fat," she responded. She waved a handkerchief for the waiter, who rushed toward her. "Bring Mr. Alsop a whiskey sour, very strong, immediately." The drink's intended recipient looked skeptical, but she insisted. "You don't need to be siphoned for Stew for another week. You told me yourself."

Pert Mrs. Braden now raved about Professor Cox's afternoon news conference, during which he'd explained his rejection of the Stennis compromise. "It really *was* like watching your favorite professor, just as someone said."

Alice imagined that Mrs. Braden had had a *lot* of favorite professors and that her grades had been very good.

Buchwald arrived at the table with an extremely pretty blonde and Edward Bennett Williams, the biggest Democratic lawyer in town.

"Happy birthday," said Alice, extending her hand to the humorist. "If I'd ever read your column, I'd quote you a line or two from it."

Alsop wearily offered something like an apology: "She pretends not to read the *Post* but a minute ago she didn't give Bradlee's girlfriend a definite no about doing an interview."

"That has nothing to do with whether or not I read the paper. I don't. But I do watch television. You look familiar," she said to the blonde.

Lovely Rene Carpenter, now divorced from the astronaut, explained that she hosted a show on topics of interest to women.

"You may have seen one of her more *advanced* programs," said Williams, who retained a good deal of primness beneath his courtroom bluster. "She showed"—he decided he couldn't say it—"well, it was the most disgusting thing I ever saw."

Mrs. Carpenter smiled brightly. "It was a diaphragm, Mrs. Longworth. And a tube of gel."

"I saw it!" cried Alice, with an enormous grin. "I thought you were frosting a cupcake! And then I put on my glasses."

"ROGER MUDD, PLEASE CALL YOUR OFFICE," boomed a loudspeaker. "MR. MUDD, PLEASE CALL YOUR OFFICE."

Alice noted that Bradlee had already gone off in a rush. She looked at the television above the distant bar and thought she could make out a man with a beard and mustache who looked like a villain out of Sherlock Holmes. People began moving quickly back and forth between the bar and the tables, ferrying fact and rumor. The mixed-doubles players on the courts had been reduced to a solitary pair who wondered if they should carry on with a singles match.

It was first a set of facts that reached Alice and her group: Elliot Richardson and his deputy had both resigned after refusing to fire Professor Cox. The bearded man on the television was the department's number three, who had agreed to do the deed.

Then the rumors arrived: that the FBI had gone to the special prosecutor's office on K Street—perhaps to seize files; perhaps to protect them. Or the files had already been *hidden* by the special prosecutor's staff, who—rumor also had it—were rushing from their homes to the office.

Alice found the present moment to be one of a handful in her long life when she could not command an audience. Joe had left her for the TV, and Tom Braden had left with him. "You should go, too, dear," she said to Mrs. Braden. "You never know what spry luminary is likely to be there wanting to buy you a cocktail. Averell Harriman. U Thant . . ."

Someone had turned the television up so loud that even Alice could now hear it without getting up from the table. John Chancellor of NBC was speculating that this might be "the most serious constitutional crisis in history."

Oh, please, thought Alice, who could remember legless Civil War veterans begging in the streets. And yet, the palace *did* seem to be firing back on the peasants. As a student and theorist of the scandal—who wasn't?—she believed that Hunt had somehow been the one who'd managed to pull back the curtain on all that might have remained hidden. But who had really *started* everything? And did that matter now?

Joe had returned to the table with Braden, two old pundits wishing they were once again young reporters.

"Watch them forget about confirming Ford and go straight to impeaching Nixon," Braden predicted.

"No," said Joe. "Not with Carl Albert more oiled than the drunkest man here. Almost as well-oiled as a Soviet missile." He shook his gloomy head. Even now he couldn't stand the thought of his *homme sérieux* ceding the presidency to somebody less substantial, let alone that boozing homunculus out of Bugtussle.

"What are you doing?" he asked, when he looked over and saw Alice scribbling.

She was making a record on the Page-A-Day pad she'd extracted from her purse. With a large fountain pen, she wrote: *The clock is dick-dick-dicking.*

On Tuesday morning, waiting for his cue, Elliot Richardson reflected on how wise he had been to stay off the Sunday interview shows. Veterans Day—on the newfangled federal calendar—had shut the DOJ on Monday, so almost seventy-two hours had now passed since his resignation, long enough really to whet the public's appetite for an appearance by him. It was time that he and Bill Ruckelshaus and Archie Cox, the slaughtered of the "Saturday Night Massacre," rose up, covered with principle and glory.

By late Friday night, after the phone call from Haig and most of a pot of coffee, he had regained his nerve. The following morning, when the chief of staff asked if he would hold off on resigning until things settled down with the Russians and the Arabs, he'd informed Haig that that was simply not possible—and managed to refrain from suggesting that surely the president could hold off on firing Cox until the same such tranquility descended upon the Middle East?

By the time he saw Nixon on late Saturday afternoon, it was the president whose speech seemed a bit slurred; his own had been as crisp as he could ever recall it. "I'm sorry that you insist on putting your personal commitments ahead of the public interest," Nixon had more or less recited. And he himself had replied, politely, that they each seemed to have a different view of the latter.

So here he was, three days later, ready to tell the assembled Justice Department employees—he could hear them buzzing out there in the auditorium—that he'd just cleaned out his desk.

When he stepped onto the stage, one would have thought the Boston Red Sox had just beaten the Yankees for the American League pennant—and that he was the winning pitcher.

He looked around sheepishly, as if all this were really unnecessary. He promised to be brief, and he was: praising Nixon's overall policies; making it appear that sorrow was trumping anger, let alone pleasure. "I have been compelled to conclude that I could better serve my country by resigning from public office than by continuing in it."

He could picture the plaque onto which this sentence would soon be engraved. It would hang next to the one from the ABA, not far from the easel.

And that was it. No hamming it up and botching things the way MacArthur had. Within minutes he was being driven west toward home, past the White House, where a protester's HONK FOR IMPEACH-MENT sign was being met with deafening, almost universal compliance. Oh, the temptation to roll down the tinted window and show them who was here! But he resisted.

At three o'clock, back in McLean and alone in the study, he mixed himself a cocktail, took out his paint box, and put on the radio. Archie was having a press conference, declaring that he'd decided to stay in town for a bit, in case the Ervin or Judiciary committee wanted testimony from *him*. Richardson supposed he, too, should be prepared for that, though he rather wished Archie had resisted going before the press so soon after he had. He felt a bit as if the batter who'd merely driven in the winning run were crowding the pitcher out of the locker room photo.

Now, though numberless fates of death beset us which no mortal can escape or avoid, let us go forward together, and either we shall give honor to one another, or another to us.

Over the weekend he'd quoted this, from the *Iliad*, to Archie. It was inscribed—correctly, he wondered?—on a photo here in his study, a gift from Judge Learned Hand, for whom, in addition to Frankfurter, Richardson had once clerked. Only now did it occur to him that Cox, too, had clerked for Judge Hand; perhaps he had the same photo with the same inscription.

Well, whatever the case, there was really no *us* about it anymore. He was now on his own—an odd position for a perpetual appointee—and he must wait until the brief Ford presidency, when he would get himself appointed anew and be carried by another man for the last time, across the ultimate threshold.

He dipped into the darkest brown paint in the box and applied some last touches to the tail feathers of the buff-breasted sandpiper.

The radio said that Kissinger was already back from Moscow with a cease-fire, but that there would be no press conference by the secretary of state in view of all the commotion on Capitol Hill and at the federal courthouse, where Charles Alan Wright, Richard Nixon's new lawyer, had said that his client would surrender the tapes after all, because, of course, "this president does not defy the law."

Richardson rinsed his brush and thought he could almost hear the sandpiper singing.

Chapter Thirty-Four

NOVEMBER 22, 1973
THE WHITE HOUSE AND CAMP DAVID

"Mr. President, I have Mrs. Onassis."

"Thank you, Operator. Happy Thanksgiving, Jackie."

"They found me here in Peapack!"

The breathy, Marilyn Monroe voice was unchanged—and he knew it was for real. He could recall the first time he'd heard her, twenty years ago, before he'd ever even seen Monroe in a movie.

"When we lived in the White House," she now told him, "the operators used to amaze me. They once found my sister when she was shopping for shoes in Marrakech! And here I am in my little gray house in New Jersey."

Nixon laughed. He didn't imagine the house was all that small. "Well, I just wanted to wish you a wonderful day."

"Oh, you beat me to it, Mr. President! I wanted to thank you for your wonderful *words*. I heard them on the radio this morning."

He himself had seen the Thanksgiving proclamation on his desk only a couple of hours ago. At first he'd been annoyed by what he guessed was a Ray Price flourish, about the coincidence of today and the tenth anniversary of Dallas: *As we give thanks for the goodness of the land, therefore, let us also pause to reflect on President Kennedy's contributions to the life of this nation we love so dearly.* But he'd decided it was probably all right, especially with the commentators still going on about how he'd really canned Cox for being a Kennedy man.

"Well, we all miss Jack," he told Mrs. Onassis.

"You're so kind to say that, and to *do* this. You and Lyndon have both been so good to me. I should call Lady Bird, shouldn't I? It just occurred to me that this must be her first Thanksgiving without him. You know," she added, as if fearing any pause in the conversation, "the children just treasure the letters you wrote them after we came to see the portraits."

She laid it on thick, but she always had a way of making you believe it. "Well, you know we'd love to have you back anytime," he responded.

"Are you and Mrs. Nixon having Thanksgiving in the White House?"

He noticed her artful deflection of his open invitation. "We're going up to Camp David a little later."

"Oh, that's lovely. I don't think we ever made enough use of it."

Why would they have, once Papa Joe got them that place in the Virginia horse country?

"Are the children with you today?" he asked. There was no point inquiring about Onassis, who apparently was never around. Having gotten what he wanted, he didn't need to gaze upon it.

"Oh, yes," said Kennedy's widow. "We went to mass this morning, and we'll go riding later."

"I saw some of the family at the president's grave this morning. The television had a picture. I think it was Mrs. Lawford standing in the middle."

"I didn't see it."

Had he been wrong to bring this up—as if implying she were derelict by her absence? He wished he had a talking-points card, the little series of cues and compliments and personal facts that Rose would have prepared for a call to any national committeewoman having a birthday. No gaffes that way.

"It's been such a wonderful and terrible week," said Mrs. Onassis.

He knew the terrible part: Teddy's boy losing a leg to bone cancer. But the wonderful part? Had one of Bobby's kids gotten married? Fortunately, she kept talking. "I heard from my sister-in-law that you sent Teddy Jr. the most wonderful letter—handwritten! I don't know where you find the time."

"I saw my brothers go through so much at his age," said Nixon.

"Yes."

It was clear she knew nothing about all that, whereas of course everyone was expected to absorb every bit of the Kennedy legend. Still, he'd never disliked her. She was a lot nicer than the gene pool she'd dived into by marrying Jack. Johnson thought the same thing.

But this call was a mistake. All the stiff overstatement was depressing him. He'd had them ring her on impulse, always a bad idea, after

Connally had called him this morning. Mostly with political advice: accuse the Democrats of delaying on Ford to steal the presidency and put in Albert. But the two of them had of course wound up talking of how Connally had gotten shot up that day, nearly bleeding to death while all the doctors worked on the already-dead JFK.

"Well, Jackie, I do hope you have a wonderful day in spite of this terrible anniversary."

"Oh, thank you, Mr. President!" Once she realized he was ready to wind up the conversation, she couldn't keep her relief from being audible. "You enjoy it, too! And please give my best to your family."

He sat at the desk for a couple of minutes, thinking how strange it had been for *him* to wake up at the old Baker Hotel in Dallas that same morning. He'd been eager to get out of the city ever since the previous day's luncheon, when the Pepsi-Cola bottlers made it politely clear that they were more excited by Joan Crawford's presence on the dais than his own. Friday morning, on the way to the airport, he'd seen all the flags set up along the motorcade route, and he'd been painfully aware that he was on the wrong side of the divide, traveling in the opposite direction from the one Kennedy would soon be taking. Late that night, up alone in the New York apartment, he'd written to Jackie, and her oddly sloppy reply, in ballpoint ink and full of dashes, had come in the mail a few weeks later. He still had it by heart: *I know how you must feel—so long on the path—so closely missing the greatest prize—and now for you all the question comes up again . . . Just one thing I would say to you—if it does not work out as you have hoped for so long—please be consoled by what you already have—your life and your family.*

Would they have been consolation enough had he not tried again, or had he lost in '68? He swiveled in his chair to regard the faces in the framed photographs on the shelf behind the desk. They were positioned for the TV cameras to pick up whenever he spoke from here. Would they be consolation enough *now*, if he had to give up what he'd sought, and sought again, and finally won?

Well, thought Pat, this is a new record: worst Thanksgiving ever. Dinner consumed, start to finish, in thirty-five minutes flat.

"A stupendous meal," said Bebe Rebozo to the navy steward bringing him a second cup of coffee. Ed and Tricia Cox nodded their agreement, as did the president and, finally, the first lady.

Rebozo turned to Nixon. "There's only one thing you could have improved upon."

The president smiled and asked, "What would that be?" Feeding Bebe straight lines was one of his few forms of relaxation.

"You should have brought Richardson up here to mix the cocktails. They'd have been a little stronger."

Word had gotten around Washington of Haig's phone call to the well-lit attorney general the night before the so-called Massacre.

Nixon laughed. "You know, Elliot's crowd are now saying we've deliberately been spreading the word about his boozy run-ins with the law. Not true."

"I've only been around him a couple of times," said Rebozo. "But let me tell you, he was so marinated, I thought, If this guy opts for cremation over burial, the body's going to burn for six months."

Pat looked at Tricia, the crueler of her daughters, who was laughing. She herself liked Bebe just fine; it was better for Dick to have one friend than no friends, as had been the case when they married, but she didn't want this—the two of them joking as if they still had the upper hand. Black humor she could understand; this was just stupid.

"I tell you, though," said Nixon. "Haig's made no bones about calling Elliot a liar, and I'm all for getting that out. He was *there*. He welshed on an agreement that he'd made himself."

Pat imagined what would be happening if Richardson had kept his word. John Stennis would be spending Thanksgiving with his hand cupped to his ear, leaning in to listen to all those half-audible tapes and going out of his mind.

"What have you got for us tonight?" the president asked the steward, who would know what movie they were rigging up.

"*The Snows of Kilimanjaro*, sir."

Pat laughed, sardonically. "Gregory Peck."

Nixon looked puzzled.

"He's on your enemies list."

The president smirked. "*My* list. I never even heard of the thing until Dean mentioned it. If it belonged to anybody, it was Colson's list."

Pat rose from the table and, without excusing herself, walked off to her bedroom. To her considerable surprise, Dick followed to see what was the matter. For a moment she was touched, but she knew the flash of gratitude would not be enough to cap the gusher of rage that seemed at last ready to escape. It had been building for months, and had nearly burst forth during the helicopter ride up here.

"Anything wrong, honey?" her husband asked. "I thought we'd call Rose and say hello. I was sort of hoping you'd get on the line."

"Do you know why Rose isn't here?"

Nixon laughed, effortfully. "Well, Rose has become a city girl."

"Don't talk to me like I'm a reporter," Pat snapped. "I told her months ago that we'd have Thanksgiving in the White House, but then the horns started honking and we had to come here so we didn't go out of our minds like three years ago. And Rose *would* have come here—not liking Camp David is just something she says—but she didn't want to come because she's too nervous. Do you know where she *is* spending Thanksgiving?"

Nixon looked down at his wing-tipped shoes. "With one of her brothers, I assumed."

Pat threw a balled-up tissue into the wastebasket. "She's with the family of her *lawyer*. It's the first time she's ever *had* a lawyer. After dinner they're going to work on getting her ready for court on Monday."

The attorney had been retained several days ago, when Fred Buzhardt had discovered—*Oh, by the way*—that Sirica's subpoena for the tape Rose messed up *did* in fact cover the conversation with Haldeman as well as Ehrlichman. He'd also discovered that the gap—he called it a "phenomenon"—went on for eighteen and a half minutes, not four or five. The story of the blank stretch had broken yesterday, just after the president had assured a meeting of Republican governors that there would be no more nasty Watergate surprises. And Rose had been ordered to court for a fact-finding session about the maimed recording.

"Well," said Nixon, still regarding his shoes, "Rhyne is a good man. A good lawyer, too." They'd gotten Rose his old Duke classmate who'd served a year as president of the American Bar Association.

"She was lucky to get *anyone*," said Pat. "Every lawyer in town is booked up with Watergate clients, from John Mitchell to John Dean!"

"Pat, calm down." As he spoke the words, Nixon realized that he'd never before had to use them in thirty-three years of married life.

She was realizing the same thing. It was all too much, and it was killing her. Five days ago, in front of the press, who were now spreading lies about their tax returns, he'd let slip the phrase "I'm not a crook." He'd said it more in desperation than defiance—but the awful vulgarity of it! Like some line in a gangster picture being made on the Warner Brothers lot. She could feel the winds beginning to shred the starched curtains she had managed to keep over the windows of the miner's shack for the past fifty years. Her whole life was giving way.

At a loss for anything more to say about Rose, Nixon remarked, almost airily: "I called Jackie Kennedy this morning."

With her back to him, looking out the window and down the mountain, furious at the change of subject and disgusted by the simple sound of his voice, Pat responded: "Why don't you call her on Jack's *birthday* sometime?" She whirled around and showed him an expression he'd never seen, a strange but discernible mixture of deep sympathy and high-octane rage.

"You don't understand," she said, even now not raising her voice. "I *know* they're to blame." She didn't have to tell him who they were: the Kennedys and everyone else who'd made him into the archfiend since the days of Jerry Voorhis and Helen Douglas, and who'd flung five times the mud and brimstone he had. "I would have made an enemies list twice as long as yours and Colson's, and I would have done something to *get* the people on it. *Anything* to be rid of them forever—the way I thought they were gone from our lives after '60, and then '62, and then—surely!—at this time last year. I *hate* your enemies, but you *love* them. You love their existence; they're what gives you your own. *That's* why I'm sick with anger at you: for bringing us to the top of this awful mountain. We're never going to get back down without being devoured!"

The slightest narrowing of her eyes was usually enough to drive him from a room. But he just stood there, for one more long moment, as if looking into an atomic blast. Finally, he turned to leave.

"I want to go *home*," said Pat.

He turned back to face her, aware that his own eyes were glistening with tears the same as hers. "Where's home?" he asked, hoping to ingratiate himself with a sheepish shrug, to gain forgiveness by reminding her of how they'd held on together for the whole long, improbable ride, from one coast to the other and back, and then back again.

"I know exactly where home is!" cried Pat, before turning back to the window, turning her back on *him*, willing him out of the room. She was shaking, and wouldn't be able to breathe until she'd had a cigarette. If he *didn't* leave right now, she feared she would tell him everything, that home was a widower's apartment on upper Madison Avenue and that she hadn't seen it in six years.

But doing that would only add Tom Garahan to the stack of victims who were piling up like a cord of wood.

Once Dick was gone, she sat on the bed and smoked three cigarettes in the dark room. Half an hour went by before she came out and quietly took a seat with everyone else, Dick included, beneath the snows of Kilimanjaro. She watched the gangrene eat away at Gregory Peck's leg, and she watched the vultures circle.

She felt calm returning. The storm that had gathered inside her for months had, in the space of an hour, spent itself. She knew that she would be with him to the end.

Chapter Thirty-Five

NOVEMBER 27, 1973
WATERGATE WEST

"Cheer up, Rose," said Charles Rhyne, the following Tuesday after-noon. "Tomorrow should be only half a day, and that ought to do it. At least for a while."

She smiled as gamely as she could.

"And just promise me you'll *think* about it," her lawyer importuned.

Rose shook her head sternly; what they'd been discussing was out of the question. "Charlie, there's about as much chance of that happen-ing as of me making that peach cobbler recipe your wife gave me on Thanksgiving. But thanks anyway, to both of you."

Rhyne smiled, but tried to indicate with a tilt of his head that he would at some point again be bringing up the subject. "Are you all right?" he asked.

"Yes. Now let me out of here," she said, managing a laugh as she fumbled with the passenger-door handle inside the lawyer's big sedan. Instead of leaving her at the clam-shelled entrance to Watergate West, he'd driven into the complex's underground garage, private prop-erty, where the press, who had already today given chase at the court-house, wouldn't be allowed.

Rose's day and a half on the witness stand—in combat with that miniskirted bitch from the prosecutor's office—had been humiliating enough, but before long the legal principals would have to reassem-ble in her White House office, in front of some still cameras, so that she could reenact her explanation of how the tape had gotten erased. She had already pantomimed it in the courtroom, maintaining that she'd pushed RECORD instead of STOP—and then held the pedal with her foot—when she leaned over to answer the phone. "But you just now took your foot off the pedal, didn't you?" asked snide Mrs. Volner. And Rose realized, horribly enough, that she'd in fact done exactly that.

At last out of Rhyne's car, she waved goodbye and watched the attorney pull away. She was left to look around the garage in confusion. Her own car, which she'd not taken today, was in a far-off spot on the other side. While searching for the exit, she recognized only one other automobile: Ed Brooke's blue Mercedes, which he was immensely proud of, though he always took care to tell people that the dealer had given him a good break on a demonstration model. He'd once given Rose a spin in it; the two of them lived on the same floor here, and he'd shouted "Hop in!" one Saturday after spotting her walking on Virginia Avenue.

In the garage's half-light, her admiration of the beautiful car quickly curdled into anger at its owner. The anger then accelerated with a speed that stunned her—like the "zero to sixty" they cited in the car commercials. On a recent Sunday afternoon, Brooke had called for the boss's resignation on *Issues and Answers*, and he'd repeated his suggestion to Richard Nixon's face at one of the little cocktail gatherings the president had started to have for Republican senators, buttering them up in case things came to an impeachment trial.

Al Haig had called to tell her about the incident—that was the only word for it—the night it happened. She'd been so steamed she nearly marched down the hall, from her apartment to Ed's, to give her favorite dancing partner a piece of her mind. There was no risk of having his wife open the door—they'd been separated for years—but his TV-reporter girlfriend might be there, and Rose had finally decided she didn't want to risk having her witness a little altercation.

Up from the parking garage, safe inside her apartment, she took off her coat and mixed a drink. She'd decided she was off the wagon until Sirica's court finished with her; but nothing was going to help her relax tonight. She'd had a horrible moment leaving the courthouse, when somebody shouted, "Hey, Stretch!" And here she was now, personal secretary to the president of the United States and afraid to put on the television news! She was likewise dreading next week's newsmagazines: God knows what the pictures they'll be taking at her desk will turn out like. The outfit she had on today was a mistake: the colors were too loud and the fabric too clingy, and she'd been worried about midriff bulge all through the reenactment.

She sat on her sofa, fiddling with the Harry Winston ring that Don had given her, a small ruby set inside the sharp-edged gold petals of a rose, and she wondered how long this would go on. A panel of scientists was now supposed to study the "integrity" of the tape, and no one expected their report for at least a month.

Tomorrow, once court finished and she got back to the office, she would again have to confront all the telegrams that had been piling up like yellow sand dunes ever since Cox's firing. No instruction had been given about when they could be destroyed, or what sort of sampling had to be saved and sent to the Archives.

She looked at the light now coming through the crack beneath the apartment's front door, as if it were beckoning her into the hallway that could still take her to Ed Brooke. She was drinking her cocktail too fast, swirling the ice cubes and wondering what it *was* with these supposed Republicans from Massachusetts like him and Richardson. The boss had campaigned for Brooke when he won his seat in '66; he'd encouraged him to run for it in the first place. In fact, Ed had once told her that Martin Luther King voted for Ike in '56 because Richard Nixon, solid on civil rights, was on the ticket. And here was Ed's gratitude!

Before she even realized it—in almost the same way she had struck the RECORD button up at Camp David—she was on her feet and out the apartment door. She heard it shut behind her, with its modern metal thud, as she strode the carpeted hallway to Brooke's residence. Ignoring the little push-button doorbell, she rapped on the painted surface with Don's sharp-edged ring.

Brooke opened it almost immediately, in his shirtsleeves, with a drink in his hand. "Terpsichore!" he cried, in delighted surprise. "I was just watching you on TV!" She could see him noticing that she had yet to change her dress, and, much worse, she could feel the horrible words that were rising to her lips: *You black bastard.* She thanked God they didn't escape, and hated herself for even thinking them. But she hated *him* more. She was so purple with rage that she couldn't get *any* words out.

Brooke, slow to register her agitation, tried to mollify her. "Rose, come in for a glass of wine. I know you've had an awful day."

"You ought to drink *alone*! That way you can't stab anybody in the back."

"I haven't done that to anyone, Rose."

"Oh, no?"

"Rose, Jim Buckley—not exactly a liberal inside the party—*agrees* with me, and he told the president so at that same meeting."

"Then you're *both* backstabbers!"

"Come inside, Rose. Please."

His fastidious aversion to a scene only swelled her contempt for him. But in the midst of her own extreme upset, she could still appreciate how bad it would be for the boss if someone were to overhear all this and go to the press.

She stepped into Brooke's apartment, but declined the offer of a drink. She also refused to sit.

"You—and Elliot! The biggest backstabber of all! Why don't you just get off your high horses and admit you're no better than the rest of the human race? Did you *hear* him the other day, when somebody pointed out that it was his word against Haig's? He came back with 'I haven't told a lie since I was thirteen.' Anybody who says such a thing is the biggest liar you'll ever meet!"

Brooke smiled, indulgently. "It's funny that you should think of me and Elliot as two such peas in a pod. We've been rivals nearly forever."

"Oh, please."

"Please nothing. Go back to 1962."

"Not my favorite year," Rose replied.

"Well, it was certainly mine! I won the state attorney general's race in Massachusetts that fall. But only after knocking Elliot Richardson's block off in the Republican primary."

Rose laughed straight into his face, imagining this primary battle to have been about as fierce as a game of bridge at the club.

"There's very little he and I ever really agreed on," Brooke explained, softly. "Unless you count that," he added, pointing to a Boston newspaper that lay open on the couch. "When I went to the Senate in '67 and he at last got the state AG's job, I handed *that* little problem over to him." Albert DeSalvo, the Boston Strangler, had been killed inside a Massachusetts prison two nights before. Rose now saw his face staring up from the *Globe*.

"They stabbed him in the heart, six times," Brooke said matter-of-factly.

The shift in subject proved strangely calming, as if Rose were a restive child being soothed with a scary story beside the campfire.

"Neither Richardson nor I was ever sure he did it," said Brooke, as he and Rose both regarded DeSalvo's old mug shot. "We finally put him away on another charge entirely. But I can tell you one thing for sure. The stranglings ended once he was arrested."

Rose could remember reading about each one of them in the *Daily News* during the law-firm years in New York. Every time she did, no matter that she was two hundred miles from Boston, she would get up to check the deadbolt on her front door, before scolding herself for acting like an idiot.

"At least he got stabbed in the *front*," she said, recovering her anger.

Exasperated now, Brooke sighed. "I'd like you to tell the president—whom I still like, and still admire—"

"Oh, spare me, Ed."

"I'd like you to pass on to him a piece of advice. He ought to get Lee Bailey to replace Charles Alan Wright."

Rose could not believe her ears. The president of the United States should hire the lawyer for the Boston Strangler!

"The president says he's not a crook," Brooke explained. "I'd still like to believe him. But if being a crook is now the issue, then he needs a powerhouse criminal lawyer like Bailey instead of a constitutional scholar like Wright."

As evenly as she could, through her fury, Rose responded, "I'm sure the president will speak to you again. He'll have to, on some occasion or other. But I never will."

She stormed out, wishing the door were the old-fashioned wooden kind that could still be slammed. With the blood pounding in her ears, she marched toward the elevators instead of her apartment. As she went, Charlie Rhyne's words repeated themselves inside her head: *Promise me you'll think about it.*

She would *not* think about it, even for her own protection. Rhyne wanted her to tell the press that "certain people" were bent on making her a scapegoat. Yes, that would throw dust in the eyes of the prosecutors, would cast further doubt on the whole sorry erasure "phenomenon," and help to set up "reasonable doubt" if she were ever charged. But it would also increase suspicion of Richard Nixon himself.

She pressed the button for the parking-garage level, and her stomach dropped along with the elevator while she remembered the worst moment of all in court. One of the other prosecutors, not bitchy Mrs. Volner, had pointed out that anything she said could be used in later proceedings against her. She was being read her rights.

She was the one who needed Bailey. If they'd been ready to go after Judy Agnew over the veep's taxes, they would certainly go after the president's secretary.

For a moment, after the elevator doors opened, she just stood still and thought: she would never be able to bear a prosecution; she would rather be strangled by an intruder in her bedroom. Hesitating to step into the dark underground space, she wondered, staring, if she should go back to Ohio, as if she might somehow be safe there. No; even if it were possible, *that would be the cowardly thing to do.* According to Al Haig, those had been the boss's words to Brooke in reply to the suggestion that he quit.

Finally, she walked forward. Her own heels sounded terrifyingly loud and seemed to belong to someone else. She kept expecting Albert DeSalvo to come out from behind one of the concrete pillars, holding a necktie or a rope in his hands. But she pressed on, moved ahead, until she reached Senator Edward Brooke's blue Mercedes.

She looked around—no one was in sight—and then she took Don's sharp-edged ring to the driver's door, raking it as deeply as she could, leaving a gash that no one would ever fully be able to erase.

Chapter Thirty-Six

JANUARY 27, 1974
POTOMAC, MARYLAND, AND WASHINGTON, D.C.

Inside his second-floor study, Howard Hunt put down the glass of milk he was drinking for his ulcer and rubbed the bursitis in his elbow. He told himself, in the deliberate inner voice he'd learned from Transcendental Meditation, that he was enjoying "a normal Sunday morning at home." And yet, despite the calm insistence with which he thought the words, he could not, a mere three weeks since his release from prison, fully believe that they were true. Still, the comforting facts remained: a higher court than the Wop's had deemed his motion for appeal worthy of consideration, and, moreover, declared him entitled to his freedom until a final decision about a new trial could be rendered.

He was all alone here in Potomac. His daughter Kevan had returned to Smith and his two other grown children, Lisa and St. John, were sharing an apartment over in Kensington. They'd been moved there before Christmas by William Snyder, the new young lawyer Bill Buckley had secured for him. The plan at that point was to sell the Potomac house, since nobody, least of all Hunt himself, had been anticipating his sudden release.

David, his youngest son, would remain in Miami with Manuel Artime—almost squaring a circle, given that a decade ago, after his release from a Cuban prison for participation in the Bay of Pigs, Artime had spent time with the Hunts. David would be better off around Manuel's young children than inside this big gloomy house with his mother's ghost—not to mention the likelihood of his father's reimprisonment: Leon Jaworski, Cox's replacement as special prosecutor, had called the appeal "frivolous" and would probably get his way before long.

Thinking about all this, Hunt realized that he'd forgotten to put the business of Manuel's long-ago stay with his family into the proposal for an autobiography that he would soon be shopping. Ed Chase at Putnam had told him the book might command six figures, leaving politely unspoken his hope that a memoir by Hunt would recoup some of what the publisher had lost on *The Berlin Ending*.

He was hard at the book each day, either here in the study or down in the basement, where he'd set up a work table near the giant imperial flag brought home as a souvenir of his Agency posting to Japan. He was determined that these memoirs would outperform the ones being written by Jeb Magruder and Mitchell's wife, let alone the book Elliot Richardson was under contract to produce, a surefire snorer on the American political system.

He left off rubbing his elbow and finished the glass of milk. Unfortunately, the silence of the study seemed even worse than what surrounded him in the basement. The Afghan hound, glad to have him back, occasionally wandered in but didn't say much. Hunt had put away almost all tangible reminders of Dorothy, including the jade pin from Helen C. Lander, which he'd managed to keep hidden in prison until he got one of his daughters to take it home. He'd explained that the piece of jewelry had only lately been discovered by an honest attendant in the Chicago morgue.

Since his release he'd wondered almost continually about what Miss Lander had told him. And because the terms of his release allowed him unsupervised movement within the District of Columbia, he had decided that today would be the day to do a little investigation of what she had suggested.

He rose and went into the bathroom and lightly powdered his hair, adding five years to the five that prison had already etched into him. The powder certainly provided a more subtle transformation than the wig he'd used in the ITT operation a couple of years back—another fiasco that you could lay at the feet of Chuck Colson.

Putting on a pair of dark glasses, he exited the front door of 11120 River Road and made the long walk to his car. He was soon driving east, past Potomac's split-rail fences and toward Washington. The fences, alas, reminded him of the five thousand cows whose pastures he had recently had to tend at Allenwood federal prison, a miserable job performed at five a.m., with the flimsiest of coats to protect him from the cold.

His period as a commuter witness from Danbury had ended when the government decided it was more convenient to park him for a couple of months at Fort Holabird, here in Maryland, where a dozen or so Mafia canaries had proved more appealing company than Jeb Magruder. Holabird's best feature had been a typewriter that the government provided. He'd at last been able to answer the more rational and interesting of the letters that still came his way, including two additional cryptic communications from Miss Lander.

But as winter approached he'd been uprooted once more, dispatched to Allenwood, where he might have died from the misery and cold—a "country club," the journalists called it—had his work detail not eventually been changed from the pastures to a clerical job inside a barn. And then on January 2, twenty-five days ago, he'd been recalled to life, like Dickens's Dr. Manette, and hustled off to Washington, D.C., whose downtown he was now approaching in a spirit of contentment, actually taking pleasure in the cold air hitting his face through the open car window.

Although the streets were deserted on this Sunday afternoon, he parked more than two blocks from his destination and purposely left his overcoat in the front seat. Walking south, he looked across Seventeenth Street to the EOB and could almost imagine it was early '72 and that he was ready to do his mental hopscotch over the black-and-white floor tiles of the building's corridors, on his way to an afternoon of b.s. and bombast with Gordon Liddy.

He had to remind himself that his current destination was neither the EOB nor the CRP, which had occupied a third corner at this intersection. He was headed for 1700 Pennsylvania, the site of his old cover job at Robert R. Mullen Company.

Once inside the lobby, he had no trouble getting past the bored security guard, who left him a bit crestfallen by not asking for the pictureless ID card he'd recently forged, with someone else's name, at his basement work table. He was soon entering the Mullen offices with the same key he'd used from '70 through '72, and which no one had ever thought to ask him to return.

The premises, where he'd never spent much time, contained not a soul this afternoon, a development that relieved him but also renewed his disappointment. He would have no chance to use the dialogue he'd rehearsed in the bathroom mirror at home, no need to tell anyone that he, Harvey Leonard, had just now come down from the firm a floor above, hoping to use the Mullen Company Xerox machine, which Bob Bennett had told him he was welcome to whenever their own was on the fritz. If he ran into someone he actually knew, someone who saw through the powdered hair, his plan was to say that he'd come back, after all this time, simply to return his key, an action just strange enough to comport with the odd personality the newspapers now attributed to him.

Atop a desk not far from where his own had been, he thought he recognized a few framed pictures of somebody's children, the color drained from their faces by the photos' exposure to sunlight, the way his own complexion had faded last year from a lack of the same element. The two buff-colored file cabinets he was seeking were not in the exact place he remembered, but he soon spotted them. He opened the bottom drawer of the nearest one and found inside it a broken stapler, a fold-up umbrella, and—yes, just as it had reappeared to his memory in prison—an interoffice-mail envelope that was secured with a little red string.

He undid the fastener, reached in, and found another envelope, white and legal-sized and quite thick, which bore a 1957 Canadian postmark. It was addressed to a law firm in Jackson, Mississippi, and had the word "MOOT" written boldly across it, front and back. Too big for the breast pocket of his suit, it fit more comfortably into the right-hand one where he had his keys. He now replaced the outer envelope inside the drawer, slid it shut, and prepared to exit the premises—though not before feeling the old Kilroy-was-here temptation to leave his mark. Not the self-destructive calling card of that personal check left behind in the Watergate Hotel; just some small sign of an improbable job well accomplished. He hated the reputation as a bumbler that he'd acquired in the press.

But he couldn't think of anything that would be intelligible. So he shut the single light he'd put on and made his way down to the lobby, past the guard who was now actually dozing, and out onto the street, wondering as he went if he now had the Rosetta Stone to the whole

Watergate affair in his jacket pocket. Walking up Seventeenth Street, he passed a magazine store that still had Sirica's Man of the Year *Time* cover in its window. The issue might be weeks old, but there would still be some tourist wanting to bring it home as a memento of time spent in the edgy, scandalized capital.

On November 9, the Man of the Year had given him a final sentence of eight years in prison and a ten-thousand-dollar fine. During the proceedings, Hunt had refused to shake hands with McCord—a good piece of playacting that made him appear as angry as Liddy over the way McCord's March letter to Sirica had broken open the case. Whereas, of course, Hunt remained happy that McCord had written it, just the way Hunt knew he would after receiving that other letter in his mailbox: *The WH will try to use even the plane crash in order to shift blame for Watergate over to the agency . . .*

Crossing the street now, he pulled the lapels of his jacket a little closer, even as he continued to enjoy the cold air. In fact, he wondered at this moment how he could ever have been angry enough at the White House, or even at the Wop, to pull that ruse and thus tip over the whole china cabinet. Right now he was suffused with goodwill toward everyone—Jim McCord, Chuck Colson, and Richard Nixon included!

Was it perhaps time to jump back onto the black squares?

He stood still on the sidewalk for several seconds: How *had* it all begun? Why had Liddy asked them to go into the DNC? The radio had this morning mentioned that Brezhnev would be visiting Cuba this week. Détente or no détente, the fundamentals still applied. Maybe there *had* been Cuban money going to the DNC. For the first time, standing here by a curb, Hunt asked himself: Had Manuel Artime—wasn't he a friend of Rebozo's?—somehow been connected to the burglary? Perhaps even been its prime mover? Had Manuel *asked* him to do it?

He was certain of nothing. While outlining his memoirs, he had noticed how speculations kept getting tangled in actualities, how he sometimes disappeared into several narratives concurrently and ended up unsure of which one he'd really lived.

He resumed walking.

"You've never before thought it might be Manuel, have you?"

He moved along without answering. The questioner was Dorothy, and until he reached his car he felt quite sure she was actually there.

An hour later, Fred LaRue was sitting in the courtyard of the Old French House in Biloxi, his bulky knit sweater more than enough protection against the Gulf Coast's January weather. Mary Mahoney, the restaurant's proprietor, had just brought him a plate of fried catfish to go along with his glass of bourbon.

"Thanks, darlin'," said LaRue.

"That bottle back there's got your name on it. So don't drink it all up, or there'll be nothin' left when you come out."

She meant out of jail, and LaRue laughed softly. He was still more at home with this kind of humor, directed at oneself and one's friends, than he was with the sort that prevailed in Washington, where jokes generally required the vivisection of people one disliked or didn't even know.

"Mary," said Fred, pointing to his food, "with all the testifyin' I've got to do first, by the time they even send me away this catfish is gonna have evolved into a dolphin." The grand jury hadn't yet even indicted Mitchell, and nobody knew exactly when the former AG and the rest of the higher-ups would come to trial.

Mary retreated inside, laughing as she went, and as LaRue watched her he felt the desire to come home for good from his long, peculiar sojourn in the District of Columbia. His love of the political game had long since faded, though he sometimes toyed with the notion that once he'd done his prison stint Eastland might find something for him to do down here.

He took a bite of the catfish and sat back in his chair, letting the oak tree that dominated this eighteenth-century courtyard shield his sparse head of hair from the sun. In some ways, he'd come to realize, his reinvolvement with Clarine was connected with this wish to turn back the clock and come home; it was, he suspected, the same with Clarine herself, notwithstanding her sympathies for the Negro race and George McGovern. Of course, if he truly wanted to be home he'd be back in Jackson, not here in Biloxi, trying to do an oil deal; and Clarine's nature, more restless than his, would again soon enough lead her away from both him *and* home, should she even come back at all. But right now he had a sharp desire to be down here *with* her, to take more complete advantage of whatever in her had decided, after ten feckless years, to find safe harbor in his hangdog face.

Neither one of them was on a normal timeline or path in life. He was forty-five and looked sixty, running on another clock and compass altogether from the ones he should be using. And yet these peculiar instruments of his somehow synchronized with Larrie's, by way of an old magnetism he was disinclined to question. Something in her was newly drawn to his burden of doubt, which he carried like original sin, no matter that it had fallen upon him seventeen years ago and not at birth. And something in *him* was once again beseeching her for absolution, or damnation. Or just asking to be held in a kind of wild abeyance, what the two of them had always floated through during their nights of lovemaking—amidst the old breezes of Gulf Hills and, more lately, inside the small, curved perimeter of his Watergate apartment.

The Watergate centrifuge—the swirling building and the churning scandal—would soon enough stop spinning. Both he and Larrie would be thrown from it, and they would land in different places. She would get right to her feet, and he, bruised and broken, would rise more slowly, or not at all.

One of Mary's pretty waitresses now came out to the courtyard carrying some tartar sauce. "I'm so sorry! I should've brought this out before!" She put down the little dish as if it were a more urgent matter than the message she was also bearing. "And, Mr. LaRue, there's a telephone call for you at the bar—long distance, I think."

"Thank you, sweetheart."

LaRue left the catfish to cool and carried his bourbon inside, passing under the high old ceiling on his way toward a stool near the phone. Had somebody on Jaworski's staff found him here? To summon him back, earlier than planned, for yet one more session in front of the grand jurors?

But it was someone else entirely.

"I just had a call," said Clarine.

"Oh?" asked LaRue, suddenly alert and uncomfortable. "Who

from?" Aside from the people in Eastland's office, there wasn't a single acquaintance the two of them shared.

"An old client of yours."

LaRue knew she was not teasing him into a game of twenty questions. Clarine was smart enough not to trust the phone.

"Oh?" he asked.

"The client found that envelope I thought he might have."

LaRue let out a long low whistle and said, "Jesus Christ Almighty." He picked up a short pencil from the bar and nervously wrote "MOOT" on a cocktail napkin.

"Has he got any plans to get this envelope to you?" he asked Clarine.

"We didn't get that far," she answered.

LaRue laughed. "Well, he's got a history of askin' for lots of money. Did he ask for any in exchange for this?"

"No," said Clarine. "He doesn't know *what* he wants. So, Hound, you've got to stay in limbo for at least a little while more."

"Where exactly is he?" asked LaRue.

"He's fallen into one of his own books. But someone's shuffled the chapters. He doesn't know where he is—let alone who."

Chapter Thirty-Seven

FEBRUARY 12, 1974
2009 MASSACHUSETTS AVENUE, WASHINGTON, D.C.

Mrs. Longworth had instructed the waiters and Janie that no one was to be admitted without a present—not even Richard Nixon, who arrived at 5:20 p.m. to help Alice celebrate her ninetieth birthday with about two hundred other guests.

The president, in fact, showed up with two presents. The first one that he handed Mrs. L was a tiny music box sporting an enamel presidential seal, one of several choice items the Nixons had acquired for special gift giving from Don Carnevale, before the jeweler's death fourteen months ago. Mrs. Longworth opened the little mechanism and was relieved to hear it begin playing a Strauss waltz instead of "Alice Blue Gown," which she'd been putting up with for too many decades. Still, there seemed something cruel, not just crass, in having that presidential seal affixed to the box's tiny lid—like a jewel embedded into the shell of a turtle.

"Our other present," said Nixon, as the crowd in the entrance hall pressed close to hear him, "is from the Shah to Pat and from Pat to you." He handed Alice a big silver spoon with a ribbon on it and, after taking them from the Secret Service, placed two large jars of caviar atop the hall table. "Use that spoon with these—not one of those little forks!"

"How thoughtful," said Alice, giving Pat a kiss before the president and first lady ascended to the second-floor drawing room. Once they were gone, she lifted the jars one by one and handed them to Janie, as if they were Christmas fruitcakes. "Passalongs," she said.

Senator Percy, next in line to shake her hand, informed Mrs. Longworth that he'd passed up a home-state Lincoln's Birthday celebration in Springfield in order to be with her. Having to share February 12 with the Railsplitter had always rather annoyed Alice. "When *I* reach one hundred and sixty-five, you can ignore me and go to Illinois," she responded.

Margaret Truman Daniel gave her a very gentle hug and pointed to the press photographer who wanted a picture of the two presidential daughters. "Shall we oblige him?"

"Yes, right away, otherwise he'll ask us to wait while he goes off to find Tricia and Lynda Bird, and I don't know which of them is worse. Do you?"

Standing in the crowded hallway, Mrs. Daniel, the wife of a news-paperman, declined to comment. After the momentary silence, Alice mused upon the way no one ever seemed to ask *children* to do much when their politician fathers suddenly died; it was another story with the wives. "When Nick croaked, a lot of people wanted me to take his seat in Congress."

Mary McGrory, the liberal columnist who'd watched Nixon pass through the hallway as if he were a bad smell, asked, "Why didn't you?"

"An awful idea," said Mrs. Longworth.

"Margaret Chase Smith?" offered Miss McGrory, by way of gentle contradiction.

"I rest my case," said Alice.

She pointed Mrs. Daniel's attention toward Julie and David Eisen-hower. "*More* progeny. Not a very exclusive club we're in."

Janie then reminded her that it was time to go upstairs, according to the schedule that Alice herself, generally punctual, had drawn up. The butler took Mrs. L's arm and led her to the second floor, where she again saw Pat, who looked both tense and peculiarly exhilarated.

The first lady was talking with Susan Mary Alsop, now separated from Joe by a whole neighborhood within the city and at least twenty-five feet within this room.

"I've been decorating an apartment," said Mrs. Alsop, though she didn't say it was her own.

"Oh, that's loads of fun," responded Pat.

"It's tricky figuring out what to do with a curved wall."

"Hmm," said the first lady. "Let me guess where it is."

"Oh, dear," said Mrs. Alsop, with a slightly horrified look. "I—"

Mrs. Nixon laughed. "It's all right."

Strange, Pat thought, that she herself had never been in the Watergate, not to see the Mitchells' place, or even Rose's, though Rose of course understood the three-ring circus of presidential logistics and didn't feel slighted; Martha had always held it against her.

While Mrs. Alsop said some things about bamboo and chintz, the first lady gripped her purse a little tighter, thinking about the stapled, three-page schedule inside it, wondering what logistical finesse might be required to accomplish one item on the itinerary. A lot more than going to the Watergate would entail.

Alice was busy ignoring a foreign-service officer peppering her with questions. She allowed her eyes to move back and forth between a picture of Bill Borah and the preoccupied first lady. Suddenly, thanks to Bill, it occurred to her: Could Pat—no, surely not; but *why* not?—have a lover? Or could she have *had* one, somewhere? All at once Alice left her interlocutor—"You won't excuse me, will you?"—to go over to Mrs. Nixon and Susan Mary. "Congratulations," she said to the latter.

"Congratulations? *You're* the birthday girl."

"On being rid of Joe. He's impossible."

She turned to Pat. "How are you, my dear? I didn't really get a chance to say hello when you came in with all that fish." She looked at the first lady's powder-blue suit and noted her extreme slenderness. "Are they feeding you enough in that awful house?"

Mrs. Alsop gently touched Alice's sparrow-like frame. "That's the pot calling the kettle thin," she said, protectively.

"Oh, I'm fine," said the first lady. Even these days she never told anyone anything different. "*Dick's* the one going in for a physical tomorrow. And he'll be fine, too. After that we're off to Key Biscayne."

Her current anxiety had nothing to do with health, or even politics. It centered, as did a furtive happiness, on that item in her purse, the draft itinerary for next month's trip to South America, where without Dick she would lead a U.S. delegation to two different presidential inaugurations. There on the third page, "Brasília Events," beside "Hospital/ Charity Visit—Location TBD," she had inked in a suggestion: the Tom Thumb Home for children of tubercular parents. The choice would catch Dick's approving eye and allow her to hide in plain sight: she knew, if the little American-funded facility got on the schedule, that news of its designation would draw Tom Garahan, the charity's mainstay, down to the Brazilian capital.

She hadn't yet given her suggestion to the staff. So far, full of excitement, and ambivalence, she was just carrying around the list like an unsent love letter. Would she have the nerve to act on her own idea? She was lost in thoughts of the possibility when the pop of a guest's flashbulb reminded her that she was still in conversation with Mrs. Alsop and Alice, who was now giving the offending picture-taker an especially hard look.

"My dear," she then said to Pat, "there's a bathroom upstairs where you can take a break from this and puff away unseen to your heart's content."

Pat laughed. "You know me too well, don't you?"

"The cat's probably hiding in there. I forget his name, but you'll like him."

Alice decided to toddle over—destestable expression—toward Joe, who was sitting on the velvet mulberry-colored sofa, next to his *Post* colleague Buchwald and still far away from Susan Mary. She noticed that he had tossed her well-known lettered pillow—IF YOU CAN'T SAY SOMETHING GOOD ABOUT SOMEONE, SIT RIGHT HERE BY ME—from the sofa to the floor.

"I guess that's why they call it a throw pillow," she told him.

Buchwald stood up to kiss Mrs. Longworth's gloved hand and to offer her his seat. He recalled her presence at his own birthday party on the night of the Saturday Night Massacre and wondered what extramural event could top that tonight.

"Martial law, I should think," suggested Alice. "The president could get the ball rolling by firing *him*," she said, pointing to Henry Kissinger, who had slid into earshot.

"Kim!" she cried, to her nephew a few feet away. She tilted her head toward Nixon and gave her relative a what-are-you-waiting-for look.

As commanded, Kermit Roosevelt moved toward the president, who was discussing Maryland politics, pre- and post-Agnew, with Senator Scott and some friends of Mrs. Longworth's granddaughter.

"A word?" said Roosevelt, with the family's usual lack of shyness.

Nixon could hardly refuse the grandson of TR and the nephew of his hostess. "Certainly," he said to Roosevelt, as two Secret Service men created a small, nearly private space beside some bookshelves. The human wall the agents provided was not exactly soundproof, but it seemed forbidding enough to other guests. As it was, the president and Roosevelt spoke to each other in low tones.

"I hope you know how much fervent support you still have left," declared the retired CIA agent.

"That's very kind of you to say." Nixon tried to remember what Mrs. L had told him about Roosevelt and Hunt—all of it wrapped up with King Zog—at that dinner more than a year ago. It had been too convoluted to remember, let alone follow up on. And yet, sure enough, Hunt was Roosevelt's subject. "My old colleague," he was soon saying, "has always been a very malleable man. That made him 'fungible,' to use the Agency's terminology."

Christ, it was like talking to Foster Dulles's brother. "Tell me what you mean," said the president, politely.

"Well, the life of Hunt's imagination sometimes blends, conveniently, into his actual cognitive existence."

No, this was worse than Allen Dulles. It was like those ridiculous psy-ops briefings they'd given him in Vietnam in '65 and '67, when he'd come calling as both Elder Statesman and Man in the Wings. He was no less malleable than Hunt, if you came down to it; he only wished that Roosevelt would come to his point.

"With all due respect, sir, I know that there are those who say you paid blackmail to Howard Hunt."

Nixon replied crisply: "Hunt himself says he never blackmailed me."

"Yes," said Roosevelt. "It would be helpful for him to emphasize that."

"It would." The president was losing interest; there was nothing new here.

"It would be even more helpful," said Roosevelt, "to have him recant his testimony, to indicate that the Watergate burglary was begun and carried out at his own insistence, because of connections he believed to exist between the Democratic Party and Castro's Cuba. And because he believed the operation to be consistent with the Agency's longtime overall objectives. The Agency itself would remain blameless for the particular act."

Nixon looked back toward the party while wondering what the proportion of craziness to genius might be in Roosevelt, let alone Hunt. With a lot of the old OSS types, it ran about eighty–twenty.

"He would be contradicting no one," Roosevelt continued. "No one else has owned up to it, and Mr. Liddy continues to say nothing. If Hunt were to take all responsibility, there would be an enormous shift in the situation—seismic, one might say. Yes, he could concede that there had been a Gemstone plan; and, yes, people had covered up when they shouldn't have. But the actual, specific event that caused the catastrophe would have been his doing, not something done at the direction of anyone high up in the campaign or White House."

"Do you know something I don't?" asked Nixon.

"Only about the possibility of Mr. Hunt's saying something different from what he's said so far. Of his deciding to come forward and assume, through his recantation, a heroic status with your defenders."

"A coerced recantation?" asked Nixon, almost in a whisper, with one eyebrow raised. He knew what Colby, his own CIA director, had been capable of in the Vietnamese jungles.

"Not coerced. Not even persuaded. Mr. Hunt was always *suggestible*— and is even more so at this point."

Nixon said nothing. Why would Hunt step forward when Mitchell hadn't been willing to?

"Just something for you to consider," said Roosevelt, as if he'd been passing along a stock tip to some fellow commuter on the B&O. "And very good of you to listen. I should let you get back to my aunt's celebration."

As the Secret Service reimmersed Nixon into the crowd, Roosevelt looked at his aunt and indicated with a nod that he had done his duty. Alice, who guessed it was too late to save Dick by the sort of spooky shenanigans Kim had described to her, gave her nephew a weary wave of acknowledgment before turning to notice Averell Harriman standing before two framed cartoons of Franklin and Eleanor. Appearing to take fresh offense at their irreverence, he transferred his regard to a small picture of the Chinese Dowager Empress, who Alice supposed must be striking him as yet another contemporary.

She next noticed sad Joan Kennedy, standing on her long, unsteady legs and clutching the arm of that other in-law, Mr. Shriver. She looked around for Stew: not here. Nearing the end? she wondered. Dick was giving her a little goodbye salute and Pat was blowing a kiss. Once he was gone from the room, she went over to its front window and waited for him to descend the stairs and depart the house. As the president, he was entitled to a showy goodbye wave from his hostess, and so, at her direction, one of the waiters opened the window, ushering in a marvelous blast of winter air.

Along with it came the staler sound of Dick's presidential voice. There on her front walk he was talking to a few of the reporters who had trespassed onto her property.

"Mrs. Longworth's secret to a long life?" he asked, repeating the question that had been put to him. "Not being obsessed by the Washington scene," he replied. "Applying her excellent mind to more than political scandal or the obsession of the moment. You know, I spoke at the Lincoln Memorial today—one of Washington's *other* monuments," he added, pointing back at Alice's house. "I talked about how vilified Lincoln was in his time, and how he never let himself show he was being hurt by it." The comparison—between the apelike caricatures of Lincoln and the mad-hunchback ones of himself—was invited but unspoken.

Russell Baker, the *Times* columnist standing next to Alice at the window, asked her about what they'd just heard. "Is that true? Is that how you've kept yourself so young?"

"If I had the strength of an actual young person, I should rear my head back and roar with laughter. Not wallow in Watergate? I can't wait to see what happens next!"

Despite her semblance of good cheer, she had had enough. She felt suddenly sick of it all—the party, everything. If Dick could even pretend not to know that the essential fact of her life had been a failure to apply her fine mind to anything useful, he was too daft even for politics. She looked around for Janie and began moving toward the stairs. She wanted to get up to the third-floor bedroom and resume her vampire existence. After a nap she would get up and read the Latin grammar that had been taking her through the last several nights. She found a certain symmetry in being the dead student of a dead language, and by the time she opened the book tonight, it would be pitch dark outside. On a normal day, which she now wished this was, Janie would already have drawn the curtains, at sunset, the way she'd done ever since coming to work here in 1957, just after Paulina's death.

Sweet Joan Kennedy was all at once standing over her, tremulously trying to kiss her goodbye. Alice flinched, shook her head, and snapped, "That's why I usually wear a wide-brimmed hat."

Mrs. Kennedy looked childlike and stricken. Janie whispered to her: "It's okay, honey. She just hates being touched."

Chapter Thirty-Eight

MARCH 15, 1974
THE TOM THUMB HOUSE; BRASÍLIA

Pat Nixon consulted the mirror in her compact as the limousine pulled away from the Alvorada Palace. The scattered, unobtrusive highlights that Rita had put into her hair made it look almost windblown. The effect was rejuvenating, and she was glad she'd let Rita talk her into doing it just before the start of the trip down here.

She turned around in the backseat for a last look at the clean white lines of the palace, which resembled a world's fair pavilion and for a moment made her remember the day in 1959 that she and Dick had opened the monorail at Disneyland. All the oblongs and ziggurats of this new capital looked as if they'd been dropped onto the Brazilian jungle from the sky. No, not Disneyland: what it really made her recall were the big modern towers of midtown Manhattan—her walks with Tom past the Seagram and Pan Am buildings.

It was a good thing their meeting would come on this last day of the trip. The anticipation had pulled her through the two countries and the long schedules: Venezuela before Brazil; two swearings-in and two parades; four embassy receptions; a half dozen schools and hospitals amidst everything else.

The inauguration here was faintly ridiculous: they were installing an unelected general who'd already been ruling with the rest of a junta for ten years. But Venezuela had been different: an honest-to-God election, and the new man, Pérez, couldn't have been nicer. Same with the crowds, who this time, unlike sixteen years ago, had pelted her with flowers instead of rocks. Comments on the improved mood had been almost continual, even if some of the Venezuelan politicians thought Jerry Ford, at the least, should have been the American designated to make the trip. But there'd been more press for her than there would have been for him; the papers couldn't resist running side-by-side photos of now versus '58. Even Dick had sent word that he was pleased with the coverage.

Of course nothing really lifted, for very long, the sense that they were free-falling toward doom. Pérez had accepted her invitation to visit the White House, but she had to wonder if she'd be there to greet him by the time he showed up.

Another sign of final disaster seemed to lurk in the way everything new these days only reminded her of something old, as if she and Dick and Rose and all the rest of them had spent their full allowance of life and could now only bounce checks against the past. A couple of evenings ago at the American embassy reception she'd looked down the hill toward the lights of Caracas and thought of that party at Taft Schreiber's mansion. Only later did she remember that that had been the night it all began.

No one seemed to know how the Tom Thumb House, which they were now approaching, had gotten its name. The gingerbread building was festooned with flowers, and the smallest of the kids who lived there were lined up, waving American and Brazilian flags.

"*Estas são para si,*" said the little girl handing her a big bunch of gloxinias.

"'These are for you,'" said Mrs. Carvalho, Tom Thumb's English-speaking director.

"Thank you! They're so pretty. And so are all of you!"

When the Portuguese translation produced some giggles, the first lady added: "I probably should say 'handsome' for the boys."

"*Bonitos,*" said Mrs. Carvalho.

The scrubbed, smooth-skinned children all applauded. There was nothing wrong with them; it was their parents who were sick, isolated somewhere in treatment for TB. The boys and girls—she could remember Tom explaining this to her years ago—would be cared for here until their mothers and fathers were either cured or dead. She felt relief that the girls and boys were so pretty, or handsome. She had consciously begun taking comfort in one fringe benefit of the doom that might be approaching: once Dick left politics, she would never again have to let her heart be assaulted by a malnourished or cleft-palated child being thrust toward her in his Sunday best.

"I hope you'll study hard and not give your teachers a tough time. I used to be a schoolteacher myself, so I know! And I hope your parents will be surprised by how much you've learned and how tall you've gotten when they next see you!"

The children clapped their hands like fifty butterflies, going on long enough for her to see the man in the doorway. He was joining in the applause and smiling as if to say, "Well done, Victoria."

Mrs. Carvalho escorted her inside and showed her the clean, sunny bedrooms, the dining hall, the backyard garden and the soccer field beyond it. Mr. Garahan—"our man at Catholic Charities in New York," Mrs. Carvalho explained—followed along a couple of steps behind, until he and Mrs. Nixon were ushered into a little office where a private consultation between them had been scheduled. The first lady was offered a chair beside a vase of yellow flowers.

"Do you want a notetaker?" asked Helen Smith, who'd become her press secretary since Connie Stuart's departure.

"No, I can handle Mr. Garahan myself. He's an old acquaintance."

Mrs. Smith nodded. "Ten minutes? Press picture afterwards?"

"Ten minutes. No picture."

As soon as Mrs. Smith left with Mrs. Carvalho, Tom said, "I felt a little like Prince Philip out there. Walking two steps behind."

"Welcome to *my* world, pal. This isn't typical, believe me."

"I heard one of the little boys say '*dama bonita*.' I agree."

Pat laughed. "Clever man. You know, I *do* remember you telling me about this project—ages ago, when I had to pry tales of your good works out of you."

"I didn't know at the time that this one would come in so handy."

"It did—for me. I'm the one who put it on the list."

"I figured. I'm glad."

"So what can we do for the Tom Thumb House? It's lovely."

"Oh, Mrs. Smith already has a manila folder full of things. Three grant applications and two appropriations bills that you could nudge."

"Okay, sir, I'll nudge."

"Good, we've done our business and still have eight minutes."

"We're hitting a museum after this. Very much our old speed, you and me. Want to come along?"

"Nope. I already share you enough as it is."

The way he used the present tense for what was supposed to be a thing of the past—them—excited her. She waited to see if he would apologize, the way people do when they find themselves saying "was" instead of "is" about the dying. But he didn't, and it made her happy. She could see him looking through the pane of glass in the door, checking the space beyond, taking note of the Brazilian soldier having a chat with a Secret Service agent.

"I want to know if you're coming home," he finally said.

She was unsure of what he meant and could feel her emotions too near the surface. She would rein them in by continuing to banter: "I don't even get to go home from *here*. The plane flies to Nashville, not Washington." Dick was going to open the Grand Ole Opry's new auditorium, where he would look sillier than Coolidge in an Indian headdress. But his poll numbers in Tennessee were a little higher than elsewhere, so he'd try to rouse his supporters by sitting down at the piano to play "God Bless America" the way he played everything else, in the key of G.

"By 'home' I mean New York," said Tom.

He now did look like the head of a charity who had only eight minutes in which to make his pitch. The good cause was himself, was *them*, and she could see that he was going to go for broke.

"Let's forget talking about minutes," he said. "Let's talk about months. I give him six, at best."

There was no need to identify whom he meant. She said nothing, but thought back to January, to the State of the Union message: *I want you to know that I have no intention whatever of walking away from the job that the people elected me to do for the people of the United States.* There had actually been hissing in the House chamber.

"Which means," Tom continued, "that you're going to be moving. Have you talked with him about where?"

"No," Pat answered, as guarded as if she were talking to one of the ladies of the press.

He persisted: "Don't let him take you back to California. Make him come back to New York. It's better for him. He can write serious books and see serious people. And you can see me sometimes. With a little more subterfuge than we used to have to use. But we'll manage. And we'll keep each other alive."

His eyes were no longer twinkling and merry. They blazed with urgency—and then embarrassment, as if he'd gotten a glimpse of himself. But he couldn't return to humor, and he couldn't stop looking at the clock. "I feel like Bogart at the airport gate in *Casablanca*. Except his advice doesn't apply. You know why, Victoria? Because I can't help feeling that it's Watergate that doesn't amount to a hill of beans compared to the lives of three little people. Or make that two. You and me. I know I'm the only one involved here who feels that, but there you are. Just tell me that when it's over you'll come home—whether that's in six months or, if he hangs on, for the whole three years. Tell me you'll come home."

"You don't want it to be six months," she replied.

"For your sake, no. For mine, yes."

"No, not for your sake, either. Because if it's six months, it may not be New York *or* California."

"Where, then? *Florida?* 'The Key Biscayne Compound'?" He dripped a comical contempt over the words. "You'd rather live next door to Bebe Rebozo than ten blocks from me?"

To his surprise, she didn't laugh. "No," she responded at last. "We wouldn't be going to Florida. Maybe Pennsylvania. Maybe Arkansas."

She was talking about jail, he realized, and he was all at once a little sick with guilt about the conversation, this pressing of his needs upon her.

"Let's go," she said, softly. She got up from her chair, and like Prince Philip he followed suit and rose. They walked toward the spot outside the door where Helen Smith now waited with Mrs. Carvalho and the security men—and thank God no press.

She stopped him several steps away with a gentle, intimate press of her hand against his arm. She whispered, "For the past ten minutes I've *been* home. Thank you."

She smiled at Helen and Mrs. Carvalho. "Mr. Garahan is a very persuasive man. The Tom Thumb House is lucky to have him!"

"Oh, we know that!" replied Mrs. Carvalho. "And we're lucky to have *you* with us. We have a little surprise before you go. We know it's a little early, but still." She led everyone into the garden, where the girls in white dresses and the boys in blue serge pants broke into "Happy Birthday to You," in English.

She was glad there was no cake. She felt older than Alice Longworth and would have been too weak to blow out the candles. She looked up at a particular blue roof tile that was catching the sun. She made herself concentrate on it, and she did not cry.

Chapter Thirty-Nine

APRIL 17, 1974
ATLANTA, GEORGIA

At 8:20 a.m., Elliot Richardson took his first-class seat on Eastern Airlines Flight 905, Washington to Atlanta, and politely declined the stewardess's offer of a cup of coffee. Along with the literary agent who'd sold his book proposal, he now had a lecture agent, too. Harry Walker might take twenty-five percent, but he was getting Richardson $2,500 for each appearance and doing a fine job with all the arrangements door-to-door. From the moment the former attorney general leaves his house in McLean until he returns that night or a day later, a steady stream of drivers, airport lounges, and hotel fruit baskets keeps him buoyant and appreciated.

He'd given Harry four different talks to offer groups interested in booking him. "A Constitution for All Seasons" is probably the best of them, but of course every appearance is really about Watergate. Audiences can never wait to get to the question-and-answer period, when they ask for new details about Saturday, October 20, or for some dark insight into the real Richard Milhous Nixon.

Harry has gotten him even more than his usual fee for the customized version of "Can the Center Hold?" that he will be delivering at lunchtime today to the American Society of Newspaper Editors, an especially choice group. But even the lesser hosts are helpful long-term. Over the past three weeks Richardson has been to Des Moines for Supreme Court Day; to Yale for that Chubb Fellowship business; then on to Providence and, just two days ago, Philadelphia, to deliver "Education and the Community" at Penn. One could fill a doctor's waiting room with the magazines that have recently run profiles of him or have them in progress. The interviews and photo shoots—for *Esquire*, *Harper's*, *The Atlantic*, and *Parade*—are squeezed in between trips like this one.

And then there are the job offers—made and declined or still being floated: professorships at Boston University and Kent State (a nice touch, that one); the presidencies of Northeastern and URI. Better not to take anything right now, advises his bright young aide, Dick Darman, who warns that the Richardson résumé already looks like a species of time-lapse photography. Much preferable for the moment just to write the book, accept applause for these speeches, and let the Judiciary Committee go about its work. This is his official public position: the constitutional process is preferable to resignation.

No one can deny that that process is under way. Jaworski had only yesterday asked Sirica to subpoena sixty-four tapes. And for all that Richardson is *hors de combat* and biding his time, he has learned from his sources at Justice a stupendous fact of which Richard Nixon himself is not yet aware: the March 1 indictment of Mitchell and Haldeman and the rest of the "Watergate Seven" has named the president an unindicted co-conspirator. Disclosure of this still-secret status, which would lock Nixon into a kind of halfway house, is a card that Jaworski—actually a much sharper character than Cox—can play how and when he wants.

Richardson fends off the Saran-Wrapped breakfast and snoozes for most of the flight. Arriving at the Hyatt Regency on Peachtree Street, he's brought to a suite where he can freshen up, until a young man very like Dick Darman comes to take him to the dais in the hotel's Phoenix Room. His mere entrance provokes the editors' applause, which reaches a volume nearly as high as the one attained during that "Man of Conscience" dinner he'd been honored at in New York. Which foundation had given it? He can't quite remember.

As the introduction begins, he casts his eyes modestly downward and doodles a great horned owl, the same bird he's drawn for his local YWCA's recent auction of jottings from the corridors of power. The introducer soon reaches a description of his Normandy heroics, leavening the story with a newspaperman's joke about some famous typographical errors: the "battle-scarred veteran" who wound up both "battle-scared" and "bottle-scarred" in print.

Are the editors laughing a bit too pointedly, as if the story were not a mere digression but had some direct relevance to *him*? Should he allude to the rumors with his own joke? Something that shows his fearlessness of scurrility and innuendo, the kind being practiced by very powerful men who are increasingly desperate? He'll decide when he gets to the rostrum.

How much talking he's already done about Watergate! He's been speaking of it for as many months as he actually *dealt* with it at Justice. He imagines that all the memoir-writing felons are experiencing this same sense of disproportion. If the saga leads where he hopes—*Do your job, my boy. It may take you all the way*—will he look back on this strange in-between period the way Nixon regards his own "wilderness years" in New York?

There is no denying that the applause he receives *before* a speech, what he is receiving just now—"Thank you, you're much too kind"— tends to exceed what comes after. Dick Darman still wants him to hire a coach, but he's decided that he is getting better enough on his own. Also, the tendency to mumble and shamble a bit—the way Cox does with those scratchy, casual inflections—adds a certain charm and authenticity to the picture.

"About those 'battle-scared' and 'bottle-scarred' heroics. Gentlemen, if I'm a hero at all, I would have to agree that 'battle-scared' was true. But 'bottle-scarred'? Well, the Knight newspapers say that is also true."

The laughter is loud enough that Haig and Nixon will get wind of it—which is the idea. Let them go ahead with their whisper campaign and see how far they get.

"I know that my speech-making has been likened to a riot-control weapon"—more laughter, of a healthier kind—"and it's true that as a New Englander, or, even worse, a Bostonian, I inherited some of the unpleasant characteristics of the preacher and reformer, or even the common scold."

Smiles; they'll be happy with whatever sermon he gives.

He is soon embarked upon it, drawing his parable from a case of graft he prosecuted during the late fifties in Massachusetts, when the work of a corrupt contractor caused the collapse of a bridge and the deaths of two innocent people. Well, his home state is quite a bit cleaner these days, but he tells his listeners that they may be interested to know how "the description of corruption in Maryland in Richard Cohen and Jules

Witcover's book *A Heartbeat Away* compares almost point for point with the pattern uncovered by those investigations in Massachusetts fifteen years ago."

That is the way—without ever mentioning his name—to remind them of how he saved the country from Agnew. Which now brings him to Watergate and the must-be-faced fact that "free representative self-government is not possible where people cannot trust the truth of what they are told. Imagine walking on an English moor not knowing whether that nice green area just up ahead is grass or pond scum, not knowing whether you're going to remain on your feet or sink toward oblivion."

He looks over the lectern and sees a slight perplexity on the editors' faces. Is the analogy a bit too patrician—English moors—or just plain confusing? Perhaps Darman can clean it up a bit before he gives this speech in Detroit.

He's ready to perorate, to offer his solution to the mess they are all in: "I submit that the only buffer to cynical acid is truth. The only restorer of confidence is scrupulous honesty." It is time for "a politics of openness," and time for those who decry "wallowing in Watergate" to realize that, in the investigation of this transcendent scandal, it has been "in the public interest to subordinate considerations of fairness to individuals that should otherwise and in ordinary circumstances have had greater weight." He cannot of course get into particular cases, cannot tell them who may have been leaned on a bit hard, but, yes, that's how tough this battle-scarred veteran has been in their service.

Questions?

"Gene Patterson of the *St. Petersburg Times*, sir. If nominated for the presidency, would you accept? And if elected, would you serve?

The question itself is applauded, and Richardson's answer—"Yes"—provokes cheers. "Of course, you understand," he adds, "that doesn't make me a candidate."

That evening, after drinks with the *Boston Globe*'s Tom Winship—shoring up his favorite-son status—a limousine took Richardson to the airport for a flight to Richmond. He would spend the night at a Holiday Inn in Ashburn, talk to the students at Randolph-Macon tomorrow afternoon, and hit the University of Virginia Law School tomorrow night, before heading home.

He leaned back in his seat and sighed. Unemployment was, in its way, more tiring than most of his jobs had been. The backlog of portraits alone! He'd not yet even posed for the one that HEW required, and once he'd done that, there'd still be sittings for Defense and Justice. They couldn't very well all hang the same canvas. But all those hours behind someone else's easel would take time from the relentless if inchoate business—there was so much guesswork involved—of positioning himself for '76.

He flipped through his calendar as the driver approached the Atlanta Municipal Airport. On Friday he'd be in Chicago for the Bar Association. The Detroit speech, to the local NAACP, came on Sunday. Fordham University, the Cleveland Park Synagogue, and *Meet the Press* followed in the days after that. If he taped the show on Saturday, he could still get out to Anaheim for the National Association of Elementary School Principals on Sunday, the twenty-eighth.

Some initiatives required little decision-making. There was, for instance, hardly an argument to be made against doing the Georgetown commencement on May 19. Other requests were trickier, like the two he'd been carrying inside the front flap of his briefcase the past several days. Perhaps he could dispose of them now. He looked at his watch before entering the first-class passengers' lounge. There was time to find a pay phone and call Darman.

"Dick, I'm hoping you're through with your dinner by now."

"Yes, sir! How did it go? Did you wow the newsmen?"

"Oh, it was fine. I just thought that with three or four idle minutes in front of me, I'd try to take care of one or two things hanging fire."

"Fire away, sir."

"One of them is this Bernstein and Woodward thing."

"Yes," said Darman.

"Give me the case for going."

Darman explained why, all things considered, the former attorney general should indeed show up at the publication party, on June 13, for a book the *Post*'s reporters were calling *All the President's Men*. "This is *not* the same as the book about Agnew. You're not one of the principal subjects in this one—I gather, I'm afraid, that only about three pages of it concern you. So you won't appear to be gloating if you go. Your appearance will solidify your 'clean' image, and it probably won't be covered in Peoria. Those are the 'pro' arguments. And there's only one 'con' argument I can think of—also concerning Peoria."

"What's that?" asked Richardson.

"Well, it *might* be covered out there, and that might antagonize the diehard Nixon voters a bit more than you need to—or might, I should say, antagonize them a bit *prematurely*."

"Mm-hmmm," Richardson replied.

"What's the other matter?" asked the highly organized Darman.

"The ABC thing."

"Yes," said Darman. "Frank Reynolds. Their evening news is doing segments on the '76 field. It's desirable—no, essential, sir—to be on the list. At this point you need to seem 'maximally mentioned' and 'minimally seeking.' A three-minute interview, which is what they want, won't have you exceeding the limits of the latter category. You should do it, sir, and we should rehearse it. I'll play Reynolds."

Richardson sighed. "All right, Dick. You've persuaded me."

As Richardson hung up the phone, he noticed a member of the plane crew coming through the lounge with his rollaway suitcase, approaching him for an autograph. Richardson reached for his pen and the calendar that was still open on his lap dropped to the floor. Its pages flipped to July. The destinations "U.S.S.R." and "JAPAN" were spread, in his secretary's bold hand, across the grid of dates. He'd be burnishing his foreign-policy credentials in those two nations before a spot of rest in Hawaii, early in August, when even Watergate should be enjoying a summer lull.

Chapter Forty

APRIL 25, 1974
JACKSON, MISSISSIPPI

Nixon stood in a holding room off the main stage of the Mississippi Coliseum. A Democratic congressman was telling him, with only slight exaggeration, that twelve thousand people were waiting out front.

The Democratic governor had met the president's plane, which Senator Eastland had proudly been aboard. If it came to impeachment, the southern states and their Democratic congressional delegations would be Nixon's firewall. When color-coded onto the strategic diagram he had sketched with Haig and Bryce Harlow, these friendly territories resembled the pacified circles on the old Vietnam map in the Situation Room.

Back in the White House, Rose's most trustworthy girls were this week typing up conversations from the forty-two tapes the Judiciary Committee had subpoenaed on April 11. Jaworski could go fuck himself when it came to his latest request for sixty-four more, but Nixon had decided that four days from now he would release a stack of transcripts that Rose said would exceed a thousand pages. And he would do it on TV, too—in an act of prolonged nakedness, the kind he'd not put himself through since the Checkers speech. It was a long ball, just like the one he'd thrown twenty-two years ago, and his biggest worry didn't involve any of the supposed evidence he'd be handing the impeachment mob. What bothered him was this phrase "expletive deleted"—a coinage they'd come up with to take care of the curses on the tapes. All the white-gloved churchgoing ladies who'd lined the motorcade route twenty minutes ago, the ones he's depending on to save his political life, are going to imagine words a lot worse than most of the ones he actually said. But there's probably no alternative: the ladies wouldn't like "goddammit" any better than they'd like "cocksucker."

Christ, this is what it was coming down to.

The event here, nominally an address to the Mississippi Economic Council, is really a giant rally put together by the old Democrats for Nixon organization from '72—men as conservative as they could reasonably be without bolting their party altogether. He might have gotten them do just that by '76 if all this chickenshit hadn't intervened. As it is, he can hear them roaring and stamping their feet out front.

Eastland came up to present his granddaughter to the president, and to observe: "It's been more than a year since we had lovely Miss Tricia down here."

"Well, Jim, she sends her best."

"You say hello to her and to that fine-looking son-in-law you've got."

Nixon snapped off a little farewell salute, and Eastland turned his attention to the excited young aide who'd just approached him. The walls of the room were beginning to shake while the Democratic governor, doing the introduction, fired up the crowd:

"Do you believe the president's in a friendly place right now?"

"YES!"

Steve Bull and the Secret Service were ready to get him onstage, but the governor was really stretching out the hog-hollering praise. Strange, thought Nixon, that these southerners, among whom he'd always felt so odd at Duke, should be giving him refuge. Last month at the Grand Ole Opry he'd made a fool of himself playing with Roy Acuff's yo-yo, but he'd felt the tears come to his eyes when they all started singing "Stay a Little Longer." The crowd had loved seeing him sit down at the piano to play "Happy Birthday" and "My Wild Irish Rose" to Pat, who'd sat there smiling and clutching some little birthday present, a piece of jewelry she'd been given on the Brazil trip. He'd joked with her later that she looked like an Arab with a string of worry beads, and she'd laughed. "It was in a little box, waiting for me in my cabin, when we took off from Brasília to Nashville."

"Mr. President?" asked Eastland, who'd just come back over to him. "One more quick word?"

Standing at the back of the vast hall, Fred LaRue squinted toward the stage filled with those "regular Democrats" Clarine and her kind had started opposing way back in the "Freedom Summer" of '64. What his poor eyesight beheld was what he'd spent ten years building, from Goldwater on: a kind of Republican Party right inside the Democratic one.

The Old Man reached the first applause line in his speech. As the cheering swelled, Clarine, standing beside LaRue, started to hum the theme from *Gone with the Wind* into the better of his two ears. Whether she meant it to apply to Richard Nixon or to this whole political edifice of Fred LaRue's construction was not clear. A foot or two away from them a NIXON NOW MORE THAN EVER sign began bobbing furiously, as if someone had detected her treacherous sentiments.

Clarine had come down to Jackson a few days ago and was staying with an aunt. After this rally LaRue planned to sneak off with her to the Gulf Hills Hotel, down near the old dude ranch that had burned down three Christmases ago. The two of them, here in Mississippi together for the first time since the old days, would see if they could re-create the powerful feeling of room 205.

While Nixon announced a plan to help increase housing starts, LaRue tried to shut his weak eyes and anticipate tonight's rendezvous. But the Old Man wouldn't leave his thoughts. Soon enough he will have to tell the Judiciary Committee the same largely true story he told Ervin's gang last summer, but this time it will feel like testifying against Nixon in a court of law, since the House committee will be working up to a vote on the president's removal from office. It will feel as bad in its way as having to testify at Mitchell's trial, which will also be coming soon.

In the meantime, Clarine has been continuing her game of cat-and-mouse with Hunt, trying to make him give up the MOOT envelope, tantalizing the old spy with hints of something she "knows," never letting him realize that she is acquainted with only one minor combatant in the whole Watergate war. For a cat, she has told LaRue, she doesn't have much power. She is all bluff, and there are even moments when she thinks she might herself be a mouse. She cannot shake the sensation that somebody, maybe one of Hunt's old paymasters, has become aware of her cryptic dance with him, and taken to watching her.

Nixon was launching into a list of "America's great goals," when a man LaRue recognized as Billy Pope tugged at his sleeve and said, "I *thought* I saw you." Billy had been a college kid working for Goldwater in '64 and had ever since floated between the Republicans and the old-style Democrats. "Can you stay put a minute?" he now asked LaRue. "I've got somebody who'd like to see you. I told him I thought I'd seen old Fred LaRue out in the crowd!"

Clarine, pretending to be a stranger, looked on with amusement.

"I got nowhere else to go," said LaRue. "Leastways not for a while."

Billy clasped his forearm; he understood that LaRue meant prison. "Stay right here. I'm gonna fetch him." He hightailed it back toward the front of the Coliseum.

Clarine asked, "Is this another of those professional sons you're not even old enough to have sired?" She had come to understand the way so many of the administration's young men, like Magruder, had made a father of this man who spent his own life wondering if he'd killed his daddy. "Who's he on his way to fetch, Hound?"

"No idea," said LaRue. "Could be any of a dozen guys I had beatin' the bushes here in '64 and '68."

Clarine lit a cigarette. "Oh, they beat on more than the bushes."

She was back to Freedom Summer, talking about politics in their usual oblique, hit-and-run way. To this day a part of him suspected the killing of those three "civil rights workers" had been a hoax. Who knew for sure whose bodies had really been buried inside that dam?

Soon enough, as the Old Man went on about "prosperity without war," LaRue saw Billy Pope striding back up the leftmost aisle of the Coliseum, ahead of two policemen and the round, bespectacled head of Senator James O. Eastland.

Under the circumstances LaRue would almost have preferred seeing his wife come toward him.

Clarine took in the situation, drew on her cigarette, and laughed. She retreated several feet to hide from Eastland, the task of making herself inconspicuous complicated by the red cocktail dress she'd chosen to wear, as well as by her long, fashionable hair amidst all the beehives and permanent waves.

"Mr. President," LaRue said with a smile, using Eastland's Senate title, the "president pro tempore" he had gotten from thirty years' worth of seniority.

Eastland tilted back his soccer ball of a head and laughed. A silver filling inside his open mouth caught the beam from a ceiling spotlight, as did his Rhodesian tie clasp. He asked one of the policemen to take him and his "old friend Freddy LaRue" someplace quiet for a minute or two. Once they'd been escorted down one of the Coliseum's ramps, to a corridor with some utility closets, the senator said, "Freddy, I was backstage with the *real* Mr. President when Billy told me he thought he'd seen you. I figured it would be a little awkward for Mohammed to come to the mountain, so here I am, comin' to Mohammed."

"I suppose that makes Richard Nixon into Allah," said LaRue with the same soft laugh Eastland had always appreciated.

"I suppose it does, Freddy." The senator raised his voice over yet another burst of applause, dulled by distance but strong enough to travel even down here.

"Deafenin', ain't it?"

LaRue shook his head and smiled, acknowledging the political improbability of it all.

"If he goes to trial in the Senate," said Eastland, "we're going to hold the line."

"Can you do it?"

"Today? Yes. Tomorrow? Could get complicated. I'm not talkin' about these transcripts we hear are comin'. I'm talkin' about whatever other surprises still might be out there. Anything you know I don't?"

"No, sir. But what I don't know was always more than what I did."

"Freddy," said Eastland, solemnly, "you know how bad I feel about everything that's happened."

"Yes, sir."

The senator took his elbow. Drawing him further away from Billy Pope and the cops, he practically whispered in his ear: "Freddy, Mr. President knows you're here. I told him so back in the holdin' room once Billy said he thought he'd spotted you."

LaRue raised an interested eyebrow.

"He said to tell you hello." Eastland imparted the greeting as if it were a secret message smuggled out of an occupied country. "This whole political fortification he's now countin' on is The House That Freddy LaRue Built—his exact words, or nearly so."

"Nice of him."

"He said more. Said that you should 'keep the faith.'" Eastland laughed at the phrase. "Sounds like a nigger preacher, but that's what he said. And it's what you ought to do, Freddy. Keep the faith. Get your lawyer to string things out for as long as he's able. See if he can keep you out of jail through '76, because Mr. President will go out of office issuin' a bunch of pardons. He said this, Freddy."

LaRue said nothing. He didn't see how he could go on playing Scheherazade for another two years. The committees and the prosecutors would soon have their fill; the tale would exhaust itself, and he would be locked up.

"He knows that you've never asked for anything, Freddy. And he gave me this assurance very privately, without a hundred special prosecutors buzzin' around."

"And no hidden microphones."

Eastland laughed.

"Well," said LaRue, "I appreciate even moral support."

"Oh, we can do a lot better than *moral* support. Freddy, I'm not goin' to be staying up in Washington, D.C., forever. I'm planning to retire in '78 and come back to my cotton and soybeans. Yes, sir, this is my terminal term. And when I'm home, you can help me out runnin' those six thousand acres."

LaRue laughed. "Do you know how much money I've lost in one business and another? I'm better at counting votes than dollars."

Eastland gave him a serious look. "There'll always be a place for you, Freddy. You just need to keep your head high and think about comin' home. Everybody *does* come home, you know—at least everybody who comes from here." He extended both his short arms, as if to take in the whole state of Mississippi.

"Everybody?" LaRue asked with a smile.

"They sure do. In fact, do you know who my Elizabeth saw shoppin' in McRae's yesterday?"

"Who?"

"Miss Clarine Lander! Standin' in front of the makeup counter, tryin' on the fiercest lipstick in the store."

"You don't say."

"I do say. *Everybody* comes home, Freddy."

The senator nodded to Billy and the policemen, ready for their escort. "I'd best be gettin' back to say my goodbyes to Allah. You keep well, Freddy. And you remember all I told you."

LaRue shook Eastland's hand and returned to the ocean of stand-ees at the back of the Coliseum, squeezing his way through dozens of folks until he reached Clarine. As he murmured "excuse me" to them all, Nixon was winding up: *I say today that 1976, the two-hundredth-anniversary year for America, will be the best year in its history, the most prosperous, the most free!*

Watching the crowd whoop themselves silly, LaRue saw a small cluster of blacks, curiosity-seekers, he supposed, politely withholding their applause. Larrie withheld hers, as impolitely as she could, staring balefully through her dark glasses.

LaRue thought about 1976 and decided he didn't want to wait. He wanted to go to jail and get it over with. If he did it soon enough, with a little bit of luck and leniency he might be home free before '76 was even through.

Everybody does come home, you know.

Maybe so. But as he looked at Clarine, he knew that she wouldn't stay for long.

Chapter Forty-One

MAY 29, 1974
ST. JOHN'S CHURCH; THE OVAL OFFICE

Nick had always said she'd be late for her own funeral, and at ninety Alice supposed she already was. She was indisputably late for Stew's this morning, but she didn't like being rushed by Janie or the driver, and she had decided to take her time—now that Stew had all the time in the world.

When she arrived at the church, one of Stew's sons—what was his name?—led her down the aisle that she had never walked as a bride. Roland Smith, the rector of St. John's in 1906, had been annoyed when it was announced that the Episcopal bishop of Washington would perform her wedding to Nick in the East Room. Strange that she could recall Smith's name and not this boy's, but she was not going to believe that her inability to come up with it presented evidence of some mental decline to go along with the physical one she'd been feeling, markedly, since the birthday party.

Strange, too, on this lovely morning, to be thirty years older than the corpse. She's been told, thank goodness, that there will be no eulogy, so she won't have to sit in this second-row pew and listen to tales of how brave Stew had been while being poked by the doctors and infused with Joe's vinegary blood. He *had* been brave, of course, and had written of his ordeal better than any preacher could talk of it; the mourners might now show a little bravery by not yammering on about all the lessons that suffering can teach us and all the comforts we can offer one another. There *is* no comfort, and there is no "we"; death is omnipotent, and it will go on performing its extinguishments, one by one.

I know that my redeemer liveth, and that he shall stand at the latter day upon the earth: and though this body be destroyed, yet shall I see God, whom I shall see for myself, and mine eyes shall behold, and not as a stranger.

Fiddlesticks. Stew was as likely to meet up with the stuffed tiger whose paw had come off in his hand as he was to meet his Maker. She looked toward the coffin. It was ready, once the service finished, to be loaded into a hearse for burial up in Connecticut. Why not burn it? And, honestly, why not now consider whether she really wants her own carcass to spend eternity next to Paulina's? Could she perhaps split the difference? Would Rock Creek accept a can of her ashes to go into the ground instead of her bones?

What Stew's death would do to Joe was anyone's guess. He'd told her on the phone last night that he felt amputated from the brother with whom he'd shared his byline and blood. He'd yet to get over his *mother's* departure, now three full years ago. Alice leaned forward and tapped him on the shoulder, and when he turned around in the front pew, she saw how ashen and distressed he really was. For one awful moment she thought he would lean over and kiss her, but he instead just surveyed the congregation stretched out behind him.

Here in "the church of presidents," Alsop could not keep his gaze from returning to the president's pew, number 54, from which the behind of Richard M. Nixon was lamentably absent. Up until a minute ago, Joe had been hoping for the sudden murmur of excitement that would indicate the arrival of his *homme sérieux*. But it was not to be. The White House had commented on the "sad loss" but sent no human offering, not even so modest a one as Jerry Ford. Joe could spot Shultz and Bryce Harlow and—amazingly enough—Kleindienst, Mitchell's successor and his equal in disgrace as attorney general; he'd filed his own guilty plea two weeks ago. Had Stew once written something sympathetic about him? Joe couldn't recall. Another craning of his head revealed Arthur Schlesinger and Mrs. Dean Acheson. God, what a back number the very mourners were making him feel! But he did notice one more or less up-to-the-minute touch in the presence of Larry O'Brien, presumed target of the Watergate burglary and thus, in his way, prime mover of the current apocalypse.

A scolding look from Alice warned him to put an end to his fidgets and face the altar.

Thou anointest my head with oil . . .

His mind went back to Stew as a little boy destined to be handsome but then beset with eczema. They'd had to swathe him in gauze and slather him in cocoa butter. The memory now filled Joe's eyes with tears, which persisted in falling for the rest of the service, all the way through "Abide with Me" and "The Strife Is O'er." Oh, how he wished it were! And oh, how he'd come to loathe this city where he'd outlived himself.

The honorary pallbearers—Tom Braden and Kermit Roosevelt among them—walked beside the casket as it rolled back up the aisle on a platform with casters. Joe helped Alice to shuffle along behind it, something she accomplished with such difficulty that, once she reached the vestibule, he got one of the vestrymen to set out a chair for her right there.

Alice accepted the offer reluctantly. The throng who now had to pass her looked slightly startled. Some were afraid to approach, and others were excessively eager. Jack Valenti and George Bush came over as if she were the wallflower at a dance, in need of their high spirits and loud voices. Then came Ben Bradlee and Kay, marching together like Watergate, Inc.

"How are you, my dear?" asked Mrs. Graham.

Alice said nothing.

"I loved Stew," said Bradlee, his voice sounding as if it were grinding rocks. "The *indignation* that the man could display. Just gorgeous."

"Yes," said Alice. "I've never been capable of it myself." Nor, she thought, could she ever approximate the sorrowful expression on Kay's puss. She decided to speak to her. "You did get the obituary right this time. Leukemia. So often your paper gets the cause of death *wrong*."

Kay looked mystified; she just smiled weakly and moved on. Alice knew the penny would drop later, that she would realize the reference had been to Paulina.

The Shrivers said a brief, solemn hello. At least they acted like people at a religious service, which wasn't the case with Teddy and Ethel, now following them through the vestibule. Alice was polite to her, for Bobby's sake, even while the silly woman jabbered on about everything she'd put into her sympathy letter to Joe—a boatload of nonsense about how Jack and Joe Jr. and Kick and Stew and Bobby would now all be talking to one another in heaven, as if earthly life were just a matter of packing for some eternal picnic. "You know," said Ethel, "Teddy and I are heading over to Arlington from here. It's Jack's birthday. He'd be fifty-seven! Can you imagine?"

Well, yes, she could.

Stewart Alsop's mourners lingered to chat outside the church, whose simple stucco walls could belong to almost any house of worship in any American small town—which is what Washington, D.C., had always seemed to Joe, before the 1960s unleashed their detestable passions. For a brief, genuine moment, Lady Bird Johnson put her arms around him.

But then a peculiarly excited young man introduced himself as Richard Darman and conveyed to Joe the regrets of Elliot Richardson, who would love to have been here this morning but couldn't break his commitment to give this year's Shattuck Lecture to the Massachusetts Medical Society. "He trusts that you'll understand," said Darman. "If anything is going to make progress against this dreaded disease from which your brother suffered, that of course will be medical research."

Joe looked at him as if he were mad. Alice, now positioned on a lawn chair near her cousin, watched the encounter with a certain fascination until her nephew Kermit, whom she hadn't seen since the birthday party, approached to tell her that after much dithering the Central Intelligence Agency had decided to work on Hunt.

Alice looked at Kim in the same way Joe had regarded the boy named Darman. "I would suggest that they stop," she advised him.

"I'm afraid it doesn't work that way," replied Roosevelt. The CIA, it seemed, was a sort of submarine, unable to retract its torpedoes once they were launched.

Lady Bird was now walking over to Alice with Margaret Truman Daniel in tow. Oh God, the whole presidential-family business, yet again. She didn't think she could stand it. Fortunately, Joe interrupted.

"Are you coming back?" he asked, meaning to the buffet lunch he would be giving in his wifeless house.

"No," said Alice. "But somebody can drop me at home on their way. I dismissed the driver."

Joe gave her an exasperated look. Lady Bird, smoothing things over, said that her driver could do it.

"When did I last see you, dear?" Alice asked Lyndon Johnson's widow.

"I believe it was 1968—that terrible year! Dr. King, Senator Kennedy, the riots." She looked over at the White House, where she'd once lived, just blocks from the still-charred stretches of downtown. "My son-in-law was the lucky one. He got to be in Vietnam that year!"

Alice closed her eyes and tried for a moment to think of Watergate as the comic denouement of all that, bringing war and riot to a close with Richard Nixon, like Malvolio, locked up in the cellar. But, then again, didn't Malvolio escape at the end?

The church's bell, cast in Boston by Paul Revere's son, began to ring; not a mournful tolling but a joyous series of loud clangs.

Nixon heard the ringing on the way back from the barber shop to the Oval Office. He would be appearing on television at one p.m., and as part of his regular trim he'd asked the barber to clip a little tuft of chest hair emerging above his collar.

Once at his desk, the president looked over toward a shelf holding the "Blue Book," the transcripts still stacked up from the night of his last TV address, a month ago. What a fiasco! Their release had made things much worse, with—sure enough—every "goddamn" taken to be a "fuck," every "inaudible" or "unintelligible" assumed to be him ordering the assassination of McGovern or, on the later reels, John Dean. There was no need to wonder how it was playing in Peoria: it had bombed. Even the *Omaha World-Herald* was gunning for him now, while Jaworski still clamored for the other sixty-four tapes.

He took out a pad of yellow paper in order to draft a letter of condolence, nothing fancy, to Joe Alsop:

> *We know that Stewart's death is a great personal loss to you as well as to all the members of your family. Mrs. Nixon and I just wanted you to know that we are keeping you in our thoughts and prayers.*

He made an annotation indicating that this should go out, typewritten, on regular White House letterhead. It was strange, he knew, that the recipient would never get the much more desirable handwritten draft, but that was how he liked it. His holography remained nearly as concealed as his chest hair; he felt better reserving it for the most personal special occasions, like notes to the girls when they'd gotten married, or that assassination exchange he'd had with Jackie a decade ago and which he still kept in his desk.

Now, on May 29, he all at once remembered Pat's angry November suggestion—*Why don't you call her on Jack's birthday sometime?*— but no, he wouldn't telephone the widow, not when he'd spoken to her only six months ago. He wondered, in fact, if he'd ever speak to Jackie again: if he's forced to leave office, the shame will be too great.

The church bell had stopped pealing, and hardly a sound now penetrated this huge egg of an office. At times these days he felt completely alone, robbed of all his former associates. He might as well be Martha in her fourteen-room apartment up in New York. Mitchell said that she was still there, by herself, the maid terrified to go home at night lest Martha burn the place down with some cigarette she'd left going someplace. It amazed him that Mitchell was still in love with her—you could hear it in his voice—when she was the reason everything, all of it, had happened. She was what had distracted her husband from the campaign and allowed him to let Hunt and Liddy run wild. He'd almost said as much when he called Mitchell a month ago, after his acquittal in the Vesco trial. Christ, some *good* news for once!—made even better by the fact that Dean had testified and the jury didn't seem to believe the little ferret.

He had long wondered about Mitchell's health; lately he wondered and worried about his own, too. There were even bullshit rumors going around that the president had had a stroke. The truth that no one, not even Haig, knows is how bad his *leg* has gotten—worse than when he went to Japan twenty years ago.

The leg isn't the only secret putting an uncomfortable distance between him and his chief of staff. Three weeks ago—four days before the Judiciary Committee started its hearings—Jaworski had come over to the White House and told Haig that he'd settle for *eighteen* of the sixty-four tapes, but that if he didn't get those he'd reveal to the press what he was now telling the chief of staff: that Richard Nixon had been named an "unindicted co-conspirator" in the big indictment of Haldeman and Mitchell and everyone else.

Unindicted co-conspirator. In a way he *did* remain among his former associates, at some weird remove, like Eichmann in a glass cage.

Haig had suggested that he listen to the eighteen tapes before he let Jaworski blackmail him as badly as Howard Hunt had. So he'd gone to his EOB hideaway, where he was now almost able to operate the recorder without assistance from Steve Bull. And that's when he'd heard what he knew he would: himself talking to Haldeman. Even so, he'd played it a second time, and then a third, hoping to hear something else:

> . . . *just say this is a sort of comedy of errors, bizarre, without getting into it: "The President believes that it is going to open the whole Bay of Pigs thing up again"* . . . *they should call the FBI in and say that we wish, for the country, don't go any further into this case—period!*

There it was. Jaworski and Rodino might now find—practically by accident—what Cox and Ervin had never managed to get to: the daisy chain of Nixon telling Haldeman to tell the CIA to tell the FBI to ignore the break-in.

Christ, why couldn't this be the stretch of tape Rose had erased? Never mind that he and Bob had more or less been bullshitting—or that as soon as Gray mentioned being uncomfortable about CIA pressure, the president had told him to go full-steam-ahead with the FBI investigation. And could anybody seriously claim that the thing had been *under*investigated since? But it didn't matter. They would hang him with this tape as surely as if it were rope.

In one way, hearing it, knowing it was there, had made for a certain relief, or at least clarity. He'd come back from the EOB and told Haig to tell Jaworski: Not sixty-four tapes, not eighteen tapes, not another goddamn six inches of tape. The loser's game of cooperation and compliance was over.

Still, he had not told Haig what was *on* the tape, just instructed him to keep this reel and the rest of them locked up, even though the one he'd heard could just about burn its way through any strongbox. And who knew what was on the rest of them? Keeping his discovery to himself had given him his first sensations of real guilt since the whole thing had started, two years ago. He now felt like the poor bastard of a client who's lying to his own lawyer. But Jim St. Clair didn't *need* to know what was on the tapes in order to defend the principle of their confidentiality in the Supreme Court, where—it was now certain—a loss would send him back to California, and maybe to jail.

Haig now entered the office. "Terrific, top-notch," he said, in his usual clipped, peppy voice. He was talking about the statement the president would read for the TV cameras, in the press room, at one o'clock: the announcement of an agreement between the Syrians and the Israelis to disengage their forces in the Golan Heights.

"Goddámmit, Al, we can *still* get things done in the world—even now."

The Middle East situation was astonishing on every level. Richard Nixon, domestic archfiend, had become, abroad, the brave honest broker, the man who'd saved Israel but was also pressuring her to make concessions. *Everyone* wanted him to take the lead.

"We're going to go ahead with this trip, Al. Israel, Egypt, Saudi Arabia, Jordan—*Syria*, for Christ's sake! Every one of them has got the red carpet out." The region was suddenly a casino, and he was running the table.

"There are still risks, of course," said Haig.

"What have we got to fear? That the Arabs will turn fickle and we'll come home empty-handed? What's going to happen? We'll drop in the polls?" Knowing there was nowhere left to drop, the two of them shared a moment of the West Wing's new gallows humor. "Whatever the case," Nixon continued, "going there is better than sitting here being tarred and feathered with these goddamned subpoenas."

Haig nodded as he did a last scan of the one o'clock text. Nixon looked out the window, imagining a triumphal progress through Cairo, Tel Aviv, and Damascus. Before he left he should get some suits with wider trousers, so that the swollen left leg didn't show so much when he sat down. But, Christ, where would he even find the money for new clothes? They were determined to drive him not just to jail but the poorhouse, too. The IRS now wanted four hundred thousand in back taxes, after disallowing the deduction he'd taken for donating his vice-presidential papers to the Archives—all because his tax attorney had wound up having to backdate some form he'd overlooked. For Christ's sake, the boxes of papers had been *delivered* to the Archives before the donation was even due! He was being pauperized because somebody forgot to do a piece of paperwork.

Pat found release of their financial records more mortifying than publication of the tape transcripts. Here they were, the nation's "first family," subjected to more green-eye-shaded scrutiny than they'd had when they were still the church mice of the Checkers speech.

And so now, what I am going to do—and, incidentally, this is unprecedented in the history of American politics—I am going at this time to give to this television and radio audience a complete financial history, everything I've earned, everything I've spent, everything I own.

He had watched her sit through every live televised minute of that—my God, the self-control!—listening to his recitation of every cheeseparing fact:

I have just four thousand dollars in life insurance, plus my GI policy, which I've never been able to convert, and which will run out in two years. I have no life insurance whatever on Pat. I have no life insurance on our two youngsters, Tricia and Julie. I own a 1950 Oldsmobile car. We have our furniture. We have no stocks and bonds of any type.

She'd sat on the couch on that stage, her jaw slightly lifted, and he'd never admired her more. It was the moment when he'd realized that admiration was his highest form of love, and the only kind he wanted for himself.

Was he losing her, too? He was suddenly thinking of another stage, the one in Nashville, where she'd clutched that little present in her hand, almost daring him to ask whom it was from.

"You know," he finally said to Haig, who'd finished checking the statement, "Pat's stopped reading the papers. She can't stand it anymore. They just send a copy of the daily news summary over to the East Wing and she reads that."

"Get Rose to do the same," Haig suggested. More gallows humor.

"We already did. She's now given up even that."

He had come to realize that Pat had been right about everything: don't release the tax returns; don't release the tapes. If the tapes had been burned, these idiotic sanitized Blue Books would never have been created. What had been the point of making the tapes in the first place? Whatever they contained about his grand policy designs, Kissinger would still get all the credit, just as he would for whatever they accomplished in the Middle East next month.

"Christ, Al," he said, as a crushing weariness descended. "I've got more congressmen to entertain on the *Sequoia* tonight, trying to keep these jackasses loyal with hors d'oeuvres and souvenir tie pins."

"Bring a few of them to the Middle East with you."

It wasn't a bad idea; maybe they could take a senator or two as well.

"Come on," Nixon said, hiding a wince as he stood up on his bad leg. "Let's get this done."

The two men walked to the press room, where the president bypassed Ziegler and went straight to the podium. Three different red dots stared him in the face, tiny portals through which he would now walk into fifty million different living rooms. He wondered if the man from the Omaha paper was here and willing to consider returning to the fold. And then he began to read the statement, not even hearing his own words, just thinking how the game might *still* be won, even if St. Clair lost in the Supreme Court. Could he win it *himself* with a miracle performed in the desert, where water had been turned into wine and Lazarus raised from the dead?

Chapter Forty-Two

JULY 3, 1974

RAYBURN HOUSE OFFICE BUILDING; WATERGATE WEST 310;

ABOARD AIR FORCE ONE; LORING AFB, CARIBOU, MAINE

"Are you a married man?" asked Albert Jenner, majority counsel to the Judiciary Committee.

"Yes, sir," answered Fred LaRue.

"Do you have a family?"

"Yes, sir. A wife and five children."

From the back of the hearing room Clarine could see that even Fred's lawyer was having trouble staying interested. He knew the committee really just wanted to hear the same song that had been sung last summer. If anything, its members were hoping Hound could sing it a little faster: they had only just now, in the middle of the afternoon, gotten him sworn in, and if they couldn't finish with him today, they'd have to resume on Monday, after the holiday weekend.

But the narrative could be speeded up only so much. It required its high points and also its groundwork, the pre-Watergate movements Clarine had heard about or followed from afar: LaRue's work on the GOP campaigns of '64 and '68; his recruitment of southerners to the Nixon administration; his absence from the White House directory, and his EOB office with no name on the door.

And then, of course, came the fateful Thursday, March 30, 1972, in Key Biscayne:

"My only recollection is that Mr. Mitchell read this paper, asked my opinion of it, and I gave him my opinion. And Mr. Mitchell, as I recall, commented that this was not a decision that needed to be made at this time."

There was lately talk in the papers of a movie being made from the Woodward and Bernstein book, but Fred had told her he felt as if he'd already sat through six showings of it. Jenner now said he was having trouble hearing the witness's soft voice, and it seemed to Clarine as if the majority counsel were asking someone to turn up the sound on the projector.

Fred did his best to stay audible through his latest reconstruction of the Monday, June 19, meeting at the Mitchells' apartment:

"As I recall, Mr. Mitchell asked Mr. Magruder if he had a fireplace in his home. He stated he did, and Mr. Mitchell said, 'Well, it might be a good idea if you had a fire tonight.' "

The hour grew late and Jenner never made it to March 21, 1973, the day when—the committee would have to decide—the president either did or did not order that a final payment be made to Howard Hunt. The chairman declared adjournment at 5:48 p.m., but the words of that March conversation between Nixon and Dean, so familiar to everyone by now, would keep playing in everyone's head over the holiday week-end, as if the movie's soundtrack were continuing through the picture's interruption: *You could get a million dollars . . . The question is, who the hell would handle it . . . Mitchell's got Fred LaRue doing it . . .*

In fact, the hearing's resumption would have to wait until Monday *afternoon:* Nixon's lawyer needed to be present, and on Monday morning he would be tied up arguing the president's case in the Supreme Court. Watergate, Clarine realized, could no longer keep up with itself: on Monday, in addition to what went on at the Court and here in the Rayburn Building, Hunt would be testifying against Ehrlichman at the Plumbers' trial in another part of town.

Fred rose from the witness table and squinted in an effort to catch sight of her. When he did, he seemed, as always, surprised—as if he'd been expecting her already to have bolted, for Biloxi, or Bora-Bora. He shook hands with his lawyer, who pretended not to know that his client would be departing room 2141 with the woman who'd been hidden, all year, at the center of his life.

Back at Watergate West, Clarine watched Fred make himself a drink, one finger of water atop two inches of bourbon, before he sat down behind the coffee table. The books on it were starting to pile up. LaRue had told her he had no desire to read *All the President's Men*—he'd had a two-year-long bellyful of Woodward and Bernstein in the *Post*—and the arrival of a book by Jeb Magruder (courtesy of the publisher!) had produced, he insisted, even stronger revulsion.

Jeb was fun, dumb, good-looking, and, until recently, lucky. That he should write a book at all seemed pretty ridiculous. For it to carry the fancy-ass title *An American Life* was enough to make you upchuck. The book even offered analysis by the Reverend William Sloane Coffin, the antiwar Yale chaplain who'd had the same job at Williams when Jeb was smiling his way through there in the fifties. Coffin was now happy to recommend Jeb's American life as a study in the country's warped values, blah blah blah.

But Clarine kept irritating LaRue with the book, urging it upon him like a feather being tickled against his nose.

She picked it up yet again as she sat down beside him on the couch.

"It takes a man with a powerful lack of vanity," she said, "to resist even looking for his name in the index."

LaRue took a swallow of his drink and gave her the kind of smile he did when she tried to bait him with progressive pronouncements about the war or the races, like a recent lecture she'd enjoyed giving him on how Elvis had really stolen his music from the blacks who lived around Tupelo.

"LaRue, comma, Frederick C.," she read from Magruder's index. "Pages 183 to 184, 236, 251, 278—"

"What's he say on 184?" asked LaRue. He picked the number at random, hoping she'd toss him a sentence or two and get the book out of her system.

"*If Fred LaRue came into a room,*" she read, "*you'd hardly know he was there.*"

"Well," said LaRue, "there's no arguin' with that."

"*Mitchell had the highest regard for LaRue, and around the first of the year he sent him over to CRP 'to help out,' with no clear-cut title or assignment.*"

Clarine saw LaRue glance in the direction of John and Martha's old apartment. He was, she knew, remembering the weekday suppers, the storytelling, his first meeting with each of them. *I hope you'll never LaRue it, honey.*

He gave her a look: that's enough.

But she continued reading: *"LaRue was no threat to me. He had no desire to be a manager, only to advise. We became so close, both professionally and personally, that people in the office used to refer to us jointly as 'Magrue.'"*

LaRue took more of his drink. "Yeah, Larrie, you should have seen the shit-eating grins the two of us and everybody else wore at the beginning of '72." He'd told it all to her during evenings after he'd returned from the prosecutor's office: how everybody at the committee had been awash in a constant stream of money and good news. Liddy might occasionally alarm them, like some village idiot who'd just acquired a car and a gun, but "Magrue" had had plenty of untroubled time to go off and drink together, early in the evenings, avoiding their families—in Hound's own case by a thousand miles and for weeks at a time.

"You know," she said, "page 183 is actually more interesting than page 184. In fact, the index has an entry for LaRue, comma, Ike, page 183."

LaRue said nothing, and she went to the page.

"Fred LaRue . . . was an introverted soft-spoken Mississippian whose life had been haunted by tragedy. Fred's father, Ike LaRue, was an oil man and a cousin of the Texas oil millionaire Sid Richardson. Ike LaRue was sent to prison in Texas for banking violations, and upon his release started over in the oil business in Mississippi. In 1954 he and his sons, Fred and Ike Jr., struck oil in the Bolton field, twenty miles from Jackson, and made a fortune. Then, three years later, in 1957, during a duckhunting trip in Canada, Fred LaRue accidentally shot and killed his father."

LaRue's mood and expression changed considerably. The passage was registering as Clarine had hoped it would: as something disgustingly impersonal, scientific, something that turned LaRue into a swab of blood on a slide. Here was the other side of Jeb, the user.

"I guess," said Fred, "that adds a little chunk of somethin' to Jeb's thin gruel." He took the book from her hands and shut it hard. At the sound, he added, "I'm tryin' to remember, from my visits to Daddy, whether prison doors clanged or thudded."

Jeb had gotten his own sentence from Sirica in May, and he'd been locked up for the last few weeks.

Clarine got up to start dinner, knowing that she looked pleased. The feather, pushed against Hound's nose, had at last gotten him to sneeze.

"You know," said LaRue, "I really like Jeb. And I really dislike him, too."

"That's not uncommon," she said, coaxingly, from the kitchen. "Are you going to visit him, since he keeps askin'?"

LaRue ignored her question. "I loved my daddy twenty times as much—and hated him twenty times more, too."

Clarine poured herself some bourbon and came back to the couch. "So, Hound, what are you saying?"

LaRue murmured more faintly than usual. "I'm sayin' that anything could have happened in those woods. We were drinking too much of this"—he wiggled his glass—"and we'd all been arguin' way too much."

She looked at the wall. He had always forced himself to keep his daddy's bird gun out in the open, mounted in everybody's full view, to risk its becoming a conversation piece and not just a private, penitential reminder of what he had done, by accident or a moment's lunacy, with his own gun.

"Yes, I imagine anything could have happened," said Clarine.

"I feel like I don't know much of anything anymore, but I ought to at least know that."

She put her hand on the back of his neck and scratched it. "You will, Hound."

She was still doing her best to make sure of it. The other day she'd been paid a call by some horn-rimmed ex-CIA man who wanted to ask questions about her "friendship" with his old colleague Howard Hunt—whose own two trips to her apartment had been, it would seem, surveilled. Clarine had no exact idea who the horn-rimmed man might be, and his references to the wisdom of some ancient aunt gave her no clue. Would she, he wished to know, use her "influence" with Hunt, get him to recant his previous testimony and say that the Watergate burglary had been conducted entirely at his own initiative, because of what he'd heard about Cuban money and the Democrats?

The CIA, it would appear, had decided this late in the game that Nixon was indispensable: he might be pursuing détente, but he had also gotten the Russians kicked out of Egypt.

She had deflected his suggestion that winning Hunt's cooperation might prove advantageous to herself. There was only one thing she wanted from Hunt, and her instincts—not about politics, but about men—had lately convinced her that, after some delay and discouragement, she was soon going to get it.

She now looked at LaRue, who no longer seemed to be thinking of the woods, or even of the MOOT letter. His eyes were looking straight at the wall with the bird gun; his foot was on the coffee table, planted on top of Jeb's book. He was seething with a sense of betrayal, and she was glad to see it. If she could get the letter, and if she could keep him angry, he'd be strong enough for her to move on.

At this same hour, the plane Nixon had rechristened *The Spirit of '76* was flying over the North Atlantic, returning to the United States from Moscow. Pat Nixon, who had come out of her cabin to take a seat beside Rose, had her feet up. Both women, exhausted from the trip, were alternately dozing and then waking with a start. Ollie Atkins, the White House photographer now coming up the aisle, occasioned Rose's latest resumption of consciousness.

"Are we landing a.m. or p.m.?" she asked him. "All I remember is that it's supposed to be around eight." She couldn't even recall whether it would be July third or fourth.

"P.M.," answered Atkins. "July three."

"Thanks," said Rose, managing to laugh. Even so, her heart was fluttering with the thought that she'd dropped the ball and somehow lost herself and everybody else a whole day.

Seeing that she was awake, Marje Acker now handed Rose a fact sheet about the arrival ceremony planned for an air force base in Maine. Rose saw that Ford would be there to greet the plane, accompanied by his daughter but not his wife.

"Julie will be there, too," she told Pat, who was emerging from her own nap.

The first lady brightened. "Oh, that's swell." After a pause that took away her happy expression, she added, "God, she's done so much more than her share."

Rose didn't have to ask what she meant. Week after week the president's younger daughter valiantly sought out the press in order to defend her father. Tricia? Well, that was another story.

"I felt you go bolt upright a minute ago," Pat said to Rose. "I did the same thing this morning in my bedroom in the Kremlin. I thought we were in Cairo!"

It was as if they'd been on one big trip; Russia had followed the Middle East with only six at-home days in between. The Soviet part of the journey, just finished, had produced no big arms-control treaty, only a few minor agreements, like the small potatoes in a babushka's market basket. Well, they could blame Dick for that, too. Having brought off three summits in three years, he'd made them look routine.

But, dear Lord, Cairo, a couple of weeks ago: *anything* but routine. The cheering from the sidewalks and balconies had been a kind of tornado. In almost thirty years of campaigning and traveling the world, she'd never seen or heard anything remotely like it. And they were cheering for him.

All this travel—twenty-five thousand miles in about twenty days— made her feel as if they were already living a life in exile. And all these hours in the air made her think of those nuclear-war movies that have the president taking to the skies to keep himself and the government alive while everything falls to smithereens below.

Propped against a wall inside her cabin was a painting of Moscow by night that Brezhnev had given them. The other present, amber jewelry, would of course go to the Archives, but she wondered if, without creating another impeachment count, they might actually be able to keep the painting. She could imagine hanging it beside the Manhattan sunrise she'd brought to the hospital last summer. What she couldn't yet visualize was where both paintings would end up. *Don't let him take you back to California . . . We'll manage. And we'll keep each other alive.*

Haig was coming up the aisle, cheering the troops, and Pat decided she would pretend to be sleeping.

Rose had noticed the chief of staff's underlying weariness, as well as his new distance from the president. Even so, at one of the banquets yesterday, Haig had told her that their boss—despite the diagnoses of amateur headshrinkers in the press—was actually the sanest of men.

Anybody else would have cracked in two while half the world called him a devil and the other half proclaimed him a Christ. Jaworski had proved as good as his word, telling the press about the "unindicted co-conspirator" designation as soon as he didn't get his way on the tapes. Every cartoonist had immediately put the president into stripes—and then six days later the Egyptians were screaming their approval of the man who was saving them from the Russians and maybe leading them toward peace.

Rose had yet again resolved: if *he* could keep from going crazy when caught between such fires of scorn and adulation, then she and everybody else could for damn sure hold themselves together. She was hardly in the clear over the tape erasure—the panel of scientists had declared that five separate manual operations had been required to produce it—but "the eighteen-and-a-half-minute gap" was just one clod of dirt in Richard Nixon's mountain of troubles. She would continue to live with her feelings of guilt, continue diminishing them with a constant penance of fear that she could be charged at any time.

Haig reached her seat on the aisle. "You ought to start reading the papers again, Rose. There's occasionally good news in them."

"You think?" she said, playfully frowning. "I sometimes sneak a look just to punish myself. And speaking of punishment: What's the penalty for strangling a committee chairman?" She meant Rodino, who last Thursday had told reporters that all the Democrats would be voting for impeachment—never mind that there had as yet been no public hearings and no presentation from the defense.

"Joe Waggoner counts seventy votes for us on his side of the House," said Haig.

Rose looked skeptical. Waggoner was one of the boss's mint-julep Democrats. God love 'em, but they wouldn't be enough.

"Ford and Harlow agree with him," Haig insisted.

Rose passed him a caramel. "Don't try to cheer me up. It's better if I stay inconsolable. That way I don't get knocked back down again."

She'd been struggling to recover her equilibrium ever since the fall, when she'd lost control with the Sony 800B and then with Ed Brooke. She had to keep herself steady, especially if the end really was approaching. She was glad the Muslims hadn't made a single drop of alcohol available on that long Victorian train ride from Cairo to Alexandria.

Haig walked toward the press at the rear of the plane, leaving Rose and the first lady more or less alone. Pat, now fully awake, seemed reflective. "Dick's been playing the piano a lot before bed. Or at least he was before we left. Sometimes he seems less depressed by everything than David is. I often worry about David the most. You know, Mamie wants me to go up to Gettysburg, just to hide out for a while, have a rest, gossip."

"You should go," said Rose.

"Julie should go. She's the one who deserves a rest. I can make do just lying in my bathtub."

Rose laughed, knowing what she referred to: the room the first lady had had, with a half dozen chandeliers, in the Saudi queen's palace, cooled to what the queen's major domo thought were American tastes, which is to say freezing. Lest she offend her hosts, Pat had actually slept in the tub for a couple of hours in the middle of the night with every blanket she could find, since the bathroom at least had a little heater. "Starlight sees it through," she said, mocking herself with her Secret Service code name.

Pat grew a little nervous when they saw Dr. Tkach heading up to the president's cabin. One night in Salzburg, on the way to Cairo, Dick had finally shown her, along with Haig and Rose, his leg—unveiling it more like a secret weapon than a potentially fatal vulnerability. Over the next days it had been awful to watch him standing up in the limousines that drove them through those tornadoes of cheering, even if the adrenaline probably did more to help than all the hours spent keeping the leg elevated in whatever palace they repaired to later. He'd insisted his condition remain a secret among the small group who knew from Salzburg.

"He's probably just getting his throat sprayed," Rose now guessed, as Dr. Tkach disappeared into the cabin. "He sounded awfully hoarse at that last luncheon."

"Yes," said Pat, thinking of the twenty-five thousand miles' worth of recycled airplane air. Part of her husband, she felt certain, had hoped he would die in Cairo—in a more heroic version of what could have happened at the naval hospital last summer. That time history might have said he'd been hounded to death by his enemies; this time, if he'd collapsed in the limousine inside the tornado of sound—the clot having traveled from his leg to his heart—history would be forced to say he'd died pursuing peace for the world.

At 7:50 p.m., a few minutes after the plane touched down in Caribou, Maine, Pat felt the shock of the cool summer air against her face. She breathed it deeply, ridding her lungs of the plane's stale oxygen and the Kremlin's opulent stink. Jerry Ford kissed her on the cheek a moment after Julie did, and then he stepped to the microphones to lay it on pretty thick for the returning boss: "What better way could the American people celebrate our one-hundred-ninety-eighth Fourth of July than with the assurance that you bring of a world that's a little safer and a little saner tonight than it was when you left. Your strategy for peace, Mr. President, has been bold but never rash, courageous but never foolhardy, tough but never rude, gentle but never soft."

Pat looked at Ford's daughter, Susan, a big, athletic, uncomplicated-looking girl, so unlike her own daughters, each of them intense in a different way. She was sufficiently absorbed in the comparisons that she almost missed Ford's compliments to the boss's wife: "Mrs. Nixon has charmed and captivated both the officials and the citizens of every country she has visited as first lady." Well, maybe; maybe not. She never felt she'd gotten anywhere with DeGaulle or Prince Philip. But it was sweet of Jerry to say anything at all, which you could bet was more than she'd be hearing any minute from Dick. And yet that was fine, too. In fact, knowing there would be nothing made her feel a funny surge of affection for him, for the way he'd be keeping faith with the shared reserve that still bound them.

Or was that only what she told herself? It was the truth—and it wasn't. Just like with everything else. Watergate was enormous, colossal; and it was nothing.

She watched Ziegler and Haig nod with pleasure to each other about the serious-looking military backdrop that viewers must now be seeing on their television screens. She knew what they were thinking: the images would help to placate Dick's critics on the right, the ones who thought détente was too soft. They were, of course, forgetting the far greater number of people who would just be annoyed by the interruption of their favorite television shows.

Glad to be out of camera range, she drank in the cool—almost cold!—breeze and wondered why, as soon as they refueled, they had to go straight from here, in July, to Key Biscayne. Dr. Tkach had ordered Dick to swim and to walk the beach, even if he did it in his wing-tips, but surely they could find someplace else for him to get the exercise.

She could see him favoring the bad leg, almost imperceptibly, as he took the microphone from Ford. "To each and every one of you," he told the welcoming party, "and to perhaps millions who are listening on television and radio, I can assure you of one thing, and that is, it is always good to come home to America."

He spoke of the last several weeks as if they had indeed been one long trip—"all of these visits were directed toward the same purpose, and they are all interconnected"—and he implicitly pleaded to be kept on the job, reminding the audience of the need to negotiate another arms-control agreement before the current one expired in 1977.

Even at this distance, and from a side angle, Pat could see in his eyes what she had seen in Cairo, as he stood in the limousine amidst the Cecil B. DeMille throngs. *He's hiding something,* she thought. Something quite specific; and he was hiding it even from her. And whatever it was, he'd been hiding it since early May.

She looked far to her left and saw Rose clutching a rosary, the way she'd been doing on and off for months. The sight made her squeeze more tightly the small, solid-gold shamrock that had been waiting for her on this same plane before it took off from Brasília—months and continents and humiliations ago.

Chapter Forty-Three

JULY 24, 1974
CAPITOL HILL AND 1200 EIGHTEENTH STREET,
WASHINGTON, D.C.

Clarine stared at the flag. Flying at half staff over the Supreme Court, it had all morning puzzled people in the crowd outside, as if the decision they were awaiting had already been rendered—to official disapproval. Then someone would explain, as a man now did to Clarine, that the flag was still flying low out of respect for Earl Warren, who had died two weeks before.

"Ah, of course," she said.

She had been with LaRue when each of them heard the news. *Go on, say something*, she'd told him. *De mortuis nil nisi bonum*, he'd replied—the only Latin he remembered from school. But he was the sort of fellow who could say it and mean it. Her own daddy, were he still alive, would have been dancing a jig over the great desegregationist's demise.

KEEP FAITH WITH MADISON—AND MARTHA! read the sign closest to her. Most of the others were a good deal graver.

The Court, perhaps within minutes, would hand down its decision about the tapes, and then tonight the Judiciary Committee, over in the Rayburn Building, would start deliberating the impeachment counts. Yes, it was all dramatic, but she was uncertain why she'd come, and still unsure whether a quick departure by Nixon would make things better or worse for LaRue. Before long, whatever curiosity had brought her here felt idle, and she remembered her appointment with the travel agent arranging her tickets to Europe. She would allow herself one more fast survey of the scene, this time from the nearby steps of the Capitol, but that would be it.

A few hundred people—the quietest, politest protesters she'd ever been among—were keeping vigil there. An odd mixture, Clarine thought: lots of Asians and what seemed to be Jews. Then she noted the signs identifying them with the Reverend Moon and that rabbi who'd gone everywhere defending Nixon for months. Support for the president was now a fringe position. Back home her mother's minister might not be leading any prayers for the late chief justice, but according to Mamma the sheer *meanness* of the White House tapes, never mind the cuss words, had shocked him.

A pimply white country boy, almost as skinny as his tie, was now telling Clarine that he and his pro-Nixon compatriots had been there all night and would stay until someone from the Unification Church told them to leave. The general feeling of strangeness in the air was being heightened by the president's absence from the capital. It seemed as if he might already be gone for good, that he might just stay in San Clemente, where he'd been for more than a week, and never come back to resign or face trial in the Senate.

Clarine finally turned away from all the different vigils, so that she could proceed with her errands. More than three hours passed before she arrived home at her apartment, carrying a one-way ticket for a flight to Madrid. It would leave Dulles the morning after Labor Day.

Walking and thinking had tired her, and the humidity had made things worse: there was no sweetness to the liquid air, the way there would be back home. She thought of the May breezes at the Gulf Hills Hotel, where she'd tried playing Hound's game and nearly succeeded—pretending they were really at the old dude ranch; that the sliding synthetic curtains were still the old fluttering muslin ones; that the garment she tossed on the floor was a shirtwaist dress hemmed an inch below the knee instead of a miniskirt whose Pop Art circles were themselves passé.

Now, standing in her own apartment after a long nap, she poured herself some sweet tea and considered the reasons she had reentered the life of Fred LaRue. Yes, she'd needed to tell him what befell the envelope that had been so long in her custody, but she knew she'd really come back to ease his way toward the prison that awaited him. She remembered the way he'd held on to her during his panic seventeen years ago, when whatever had happened in the duck blind was still anything but MOOT. She remembered how powerful his clinging had made her feel. It was a sensation that she had been seeking ever since, and the likelihood of Hound's imprisonment, two decades later for something so different, had drawn her to him.

If she was easing him toward jail, he was easing her out of Washington, now that she had decided she was definitively done with both her second husband and the hapless Democrats—maybe even with miniskirts. Madrid might just as well be Manchuria. It didn't matter. In fact, thanks to Nixon, she now reflected, Manchuria itself would soon be a bookable destination.

She probably loved LaRue, but had not imagined that her visit to him in April of last year would turn into a fifteen-month adventure. She'd been held by the soft voice and the squint; by the gentleness he'd evidently sustained amidst all the pseudo-rough characters he'd worked with; and by the way he was always more alive in the dark than the light. She was held, as it were, by the clinging.

She wanted to see him through, to get him the envelope and then fortify him for jail. But her capacity for doing either seemed to be waning.

Not only Hound's fate, but maybe even Nixon's, continued to depend on Howard Hunt. The town's pundits and mandarins now regarded the president's March 21 meeting with Dean—*You could get a million dollars*—as the most crucial one of all: Had the President authorized blackmail? On this score LaRue had done one last favor for the Old Man (Clarine detested the epithet) before wrapping up his testimony to the Judiciary Committee a couple of weeks ago: he'd said that Dean had called him on the twenty-first, with instructions to advance the last big payment to Hunt, *before* Dean had talked with Nixon, which meant that the blackmail had gone ahead without the president's specific authorization. When he'd testified to Sam Ervin a year before, Hound hadn't been so sure of the chronology.

Clarine put some Mozart on the stereo and sipped her sweet tea for twenty peaceful minutes, until the intercom sounded.

"Robert Dietrich," said the voice from the lobby.

She should have been excited, yet Clarine couldn't keep from rolling her eyes: Hunt's pseudonyms had begun to seem silly. But she went ahead and buzzed him in, and flipped over the LP as he came up in the elevator.

He had driven in from Potomac wearing a white suit that looked as if it might be left over from his Cuban days. She poured him a drink and pitched her affect, as she had during his two or three other visits, toward something Ava Gardner–ish. She knew from his novels that this would speak to his idealized sense of himself, what he projected through all those chiseled cold-warring protagonists.

He sat down on her couch and explained how peculiar it felt to be out of jail, if only pending appeal, now that Colson and Magruder had been put away like Liddy. Ehrlichman, too, would soon be going: he'd been convicted twelve days ago, partly through Hunt's testimony.

Clarine listened, acting the way Ava might when the script called for a "Sphinx-like" expression.

Hunt informed her, solemnly: "The decision made me come over this afternoon."

"The decision?"

"Eight to zero. Against Nixon. Didn't you hear it on the radio?"

Clarine calmly explained that the Mozart was coming from a record player. This *was* the first she'd heard of it. The end was approaching and she ought to be calling Hound. But then she noticed the bent, legal-sized envelope sticking out of Hunt's torn suit pocket.

She pointed to the tear in his jacket and did what any southern girl, even Ava Gardner, would do: she offered to mend it.

Hunt declined, but added, "I do miss a woman's touch."

Clarine knew he meant it in the domestic sense, but she still cringed. "Your wife took good care of you."

"Yes," said Hunt. "She had exceptionally good judgment. Same as Jacobo Arbenz's wife. A much smarter character than her husband."

Clarine had become familiar with the odd frame of reference he wobbled inside. He had told her twice before, apropos of nothing, about the Guatemalan coup he'd once engineered against Arbenz.

"We wound up living two streets from them, the Arbenzes, in Montevideo, some years after the event, while he was in exile. I was under cover at the embassy."

"Yes, I've seen the picture of you shaking hands with Eisenhower when he came through Uruguay. Strange, the things that connect people. I wonder what old Ike would make of all that's going on with his former protégé these days?"

Hunt showed no interest in talking about Eisenhower; his mind was still on his wife. "Dorothy was a very strong woman. She knew how to keep things to herself. She never even told me the dollar figures she was dealing with during those months. And I never asked."

Clarine nodded, recalling Dean on the tapes—*Mrs. Hunt was the savviest woman in the world.* She also remembered what LaRue said Dorothy had told him at the airport: *If the plane crashes, I'll still be thirty grand behind.*

"The figures must have been awfully high," said Clarine. *You could get a million dollars.*

"There were others' needs involved besides our own," Hunt replied.

"Yes."

"Lawyers' fees. Living expenses. Even bills for a child psychiatrist." He was talking about his youngest boy.

"They say it will all come down to March twenty-first," Clarine ventured.

"Unless," said Hunt, "there's something big on these new tapes that they've just forced out of him."

"Yes," replied Clarine, who assumed there must be—otherwise Nixon's team wouldn't have fought so hard to keep them secret. "Either way, nothing can save him now."

"Nothing?" Hunt protested. "I could come forward and say I *told* Richard Nixon the break-in was my idea. And that he covered up to protect the Agency and national security—the same way he fought to protect presidential privacy by not surrendering the tapes."

The CIA man who'd followed her a few weeks ago, whose name she still didn't know, had clearly started talking to Hunt once it was clear she had no interest in cooperating with whatever he and his friends in the Agency wanted.

"Why would you do that?" she asked. She didn't give him a chance to answer before adding, "This morning I *did* have the radio on, and it said that this president you worked for is about to sign a bill creating a new legal services corporation, a pet project of all the left-wingers you despise. He'll do *anything* for the votes in Congress that can save him."

"It's all part of the game," said Hunt, as if she were now some naïf instead of Ava Gardner.

"Richard Nixon called you a blackmailer on national television."

"I never blackmailed the president."

She had been noting his swings between literalness and grandiosity, wondering how wide they had been before Dorothy Hunt's flight to Chicago, before Watergate itself. "He says that you did," she retorted. "That you threatened to expose Ehrlichman's 'seamy' activities."

"I only *mentioned* such activities to Dean. He's the one who drew a conclusion from that."

"I heard another thing on the radio this morning," said Clarine. "Elliot Richardson is in Moscow telling them that détente will continue even after Nixon is ousted."

Hunt shrugged.

"Didn't you want *victory* over the Soviets? Instead of this truce that Nixon has more or less brought about?"

"I didn't want George McGovern. Or Teddy Kennedy."

"Richard Nixon calls you an idiot on the tapes."

" 'Idiot' is Dean's word, actually."

"Nixon doesn't disagree when he hears it."

"The idiocy referred to," Hunt retorted, "could be the botched operation itself, not the *idea* for it. Bill Buckley has suggested just such an interpretation."

Clarine went over to the stereo and lifted the needle from the Mozart record. From the table next to it she picked up a paperback copy of *The White House Transcripts*. She brought it back to the couch and read from page 118:

> NIXON: *That was such a stupid thing!*
> DEAN: *It was incredible—that's right. That was Hunt.*
> NIXON: *To think that Mitchell and Bob would have allowed— would have allowed—this kind of operation to be in the campaign committee!*

"I think that refutes Mr. Buckley's interpretation," said Clarine.

She could see that Hunt was upset, and she decided to let up on him, for reasons both human and strategic. "What were you doing before you came here today?" she asked.

"I was working on my book," said Hunt, with an effort at dignity. "We'll probably call it *The Road to Watergate*."

"Don't," Clarine advised. "It will make you and Liddy sound like Hope and Crosby."

He laughed, but Clarine could see that the dignity he'd summoned a few seconds ago was making him consider a change of title.

"Why did you break into the DNC?" she asked.

"Foreign money. We heard that they'd been getting secret contributions from Castro."

"But who told you to?"

"Jeb Magruder. He told Liddy, and Liddy told me."

Clarine could see it rankled him that Liddy, younger than himself and stranger—at least on the surface—had been the operation's head man.

"Who told Magruder?" she asked.

"People were always pushing him."

"Which people?"

Clarine could see Hunt trying to look as if he shouldn't tell. But it was evident that he simply didn't know, and that the question baffled, even scared, him. His expression again showed a sudden change. He now looked as if he were coming up for air, finding himself in a different place from where he'd last disappeared below the surface. "How did you get my wife's pin?" he asked.

This was the question Clarine had anticipated since she'd given it to him last September. On that day, he'd never persisted in asking it— probably because not asking seemed to restore an appearance of being in control. And maybe, up until this moment, he'd preferred whatever scenarios and explanations he thought up himself.

She began to tell the story she had prepared. "Your wife gave it to me."

"That's not possible. She was wearing it the day she died. She had it on when I drove her to the airport."

"Your memory is playing tricks on you. I got in touch with her, met her on one of her trips into the District that fall. That's when I got the pin."

She knew he would believe the sentences she'd just spoken. She could see his awareness of his own mental fragility; he could scarcely doubt that he was sometimes imagining things. And as for her knowing Dorothy? Well, Clarine reasoned, if he'd not asked his wife to tell him the size of the payments, he would certainly believe that Dorothy had kept this little secret, too.

"Why did you contact her?" asked Hunt.

"For the same reason I later approached you. I wanted to get that envelope back." She pointed to his pocket. "Have you read what's inside it?"

"Yes."

Fear—the least familiar of Clarine's emotions—now clutched her. Suddenly she was not ready to hear what the letter contained.

"It's a report about some shooting from the 1950s," explained Hunt, obviously frustrated by its irrelevance to himself. "People are referred to by letters instead of names. 'Mr. X' and so forth. Doesn't even mention a place."

"Yes," Clarine said evenly, hoping he would go no further.

"It has nothing to do with Watergate."

"I never said it did."

Hunt bristled. "You tried to suggest otherwise in every possible way." *Think of the Rosetta Stone.*

Clarine pointed to the envelope. "What's in there is only about someone's old private torment."

"You deceived me."

"Of course I did. I didn't think you'd help me any other way."

Hunt said nothing.

"I tried to act as intelligently as she would have," Clarine added.

"Who?" asked Hunt.

"Your wife."

From the time she was a girl, long before LaRue ever walked into the law office in Jackson, Clarine could always spot heartbreak. She knew that she was looking at it now.

"Why did she give you the pin?" Hunt asked.

"I admired it."

"And she just gave it to you."

"Yes, she was touched by the story I told her, about that person's private agony. You already know what it was about if you've read the contents."

Hunt's eyes moistened. He was imagining this conversation that she and Dorothy had never had. Dorothy would have listened to Miss Lander's tale of a lover's woe and given her the little piece of jewelry she'd remarked upon a moment earlier. He could see it happening.

He handed Clarine the envelope, as if under the circumstances he himself could do no less.

"Did my wife speak of me?" he asked.

"Yes."

"Did she love me?"

"Very much."

Lie upon lie upon lie. But Clarine felt even less guilty than she imagined Richard Nixon had while piling up the stack of falsehoods now toppling over on him.

Hunt picked up his sunglasses and rose to leave. Clarine quietly followed him to the front door. "Thank you," she said at last, simply, as if he were a neighbor who'd dropped in to bring her a piece of mail that had been delivered to the wrong apartment.

He nodded and headed off toward the elevator. She could hear him murmuring, as if talking to someone he imagined walking beside him. She realized that he would drift among three or four different realities in the time it took him to get down to the lobby.

Chapter Forty-Four

AUGUST 8–9, 1974
THE WEST WING; 2009 MASSACHUSETTS AVENUE;
WATERGATE WEST; LINCOLN SITTING ROOM

Too busy to indulge in disbelief, Rose continued packing her office. Two cardboard boxes were filling up with items she would take home to the Watergate, among them a pretty enamel strawberry that Don Carnevale had had made to match her Secret Service code name.

Steve Bull had asked her to watch the resignation speech with him in the East Wing theater, but she'd said no, just as she'd declined Len Garment's invitation to join him and Buzhardt and Safire for dinner at the Sans Souci. She'd given the same excuse Ray Price had made: she needed to stick around in case the boss needed any last-minute changes to the speech. But things had not been good between her and Garment since last fall, when the gap on the tape was discovered and he brusquely told her it was time she got a lawyer. On top of everything else—the Sans Souci! Were they kidding? With Edward Bennett Williams and the whole Democratic crowd sure to be on the premises, crowing their lungs out?

Well, thank God she no longer needed Charlie Rhyne or any other lawyer. Jaworski had sent word three weeks ago that she wouldn't be prosecuted—a small bone flung toward the crumbling White House, probably to show how fair and gallant the special prosecutor could be. What she *did* need tonight, badly, was a drink, but she'd allowed herself no more than a glass of what somebody in the speechwriters' office told her was a "light beer," something new. She'd been working on the president's remarks for two days, and if Price or the boss wanted one more comma, or one less adjective, she was prepared to retype the whole thing yet again.

But there would be, of course, no further draft. In less than ten minutes, Richard Nixon would deliver what he had on the desk, and it would all—the whole last twenty-three years—be finished.

When she'd sat down at the large-type machine two nights ago, she'd been unable to stop thinking of '52. The Fund story had broken, the Checkers speech had been made, and Eisenhower still couldn't decide what to do—how the hell had he ever handled D-Day? The boss, sick with frustration, had asked her to send a telegram with his resignation from the ticket. She took down the message in shorthand and gave it to Murray Chotiner, the toughest guy on the campaign, God rest his soul, knowing that he would rip it up. Which he did. And if he hadn't, she would have snatched it back and ripped it up herself.

But there was no way to stop tonight's broadcast.

She couldn't bear the thought of going to the West Hall to watch with Pat and the girls and Bebe. She would sit in front of the television here. She wouldn't hover outside the Oval Office, either. She would leave that to Kissinger, who was already there, ready to walk the boss back to the Residence after it was done. Henry had been making a huge show of telling everyone he would resign as secretary of state if the president were ever put on trial. Big deal! Though for sheer lack of manliness nothing topped the calls HRH had been making to the White House all day—angling for a pardon, Rose felt sure. She only hoped Haig would stand firm and not put him through tonight.

Jesus, Mary, Joseph.

She reached for her rosary as the boss came onscreen in the same blue suit he'd worn on Soviet TV two years ago. She fingered one of the beads and whispered a fast "Hail, Mary," praying that he would make it all the way through the pages she'd typed and retyped so many times.

I have never been a quitter. To leave office before my term is completed is abhorrent to every instinct in my body. But as president I must put the interest of America first . . .

She felt a hand on her shoulder and nearly jumped out of her skin. "Don't worry," said Haig. "He won't cry. But you go ahead."

And then the general left her alone, even though he was the only one with whom she could bear sharing this moment.

———

I shall resign the presidency effective at noon tomorrow. Vice Pres-
ident Ford will be sworn in as president at that hour in this office.

———

Alice awoke after midnight. Horns continued to honk in Dupont Circle, where she imagined that the young people were even now boogalooing in the fountain. She had slept through Dick's speech but hadn't really needed to hear it. She'd known it was coming ever since Joe called late last night, very excited and self-important, to tell her that the White House switchboard had earlier rung him up in order to locate Kissinger, who, sure enough, had been sitting right at Joe's deadly-dull dinner table. The secretary had then rushed back to 1600 Pennsylvania Avenue for a long, maudlin, slightly premature farewell to his boss. They'd toasted each other with the bottle of brandy they'd opened after receiving the China invitation three years before. Joe was *thrilled*, positively rejuvenated as a journalist, to have gotten these details from Kissinger just afterwards—even if he had to agree not to put the tale of Dick's rambling, tearful behavior into print. But he'd told her. Dick asking Kissinger to pray with him! Could anything be more revolting?

Alice managed to shuffle—you couldn't call it walking anymore—to the open window. She stuck her head out. It was cool for August and the drizzle refreshed her. Once she retracted her noggin, she turned on the television, which was still covering the evening as if it were election night, the reporters piling trivia upon trivia.

One of the networks was now replaying the speech itself, for what she supposed was the fifth time:

To those who have stood with me during these past difficult months,
to my family, my friends, to many others who joined in support-
ing my cause because they believed it was right, I will be eternally
grateful for your support.

She could read his face, even through the fuzzy screen of her aging TV, could see the darkness coming up through the creases—what she'd noticed all those years ago in Rock Creek as he'd helped to shoulder Paulina's coffin.

> *Sometimes I have succeeded and sometimes I have failed, but always I have taken heart from what Theodore Roosevelt once said about the man in the arena, "whose face is marred by dust and sweat and blood . . ."*

Of course. Father had muscled his way into one more historical event.

She turned off the television and went looking for a box of White House ephemera that not long ago had been organized by her grand-daughter: *recent* items, menus and place cards and such from the last thirty or forty years. Rooting around in what she found, she came up with the invitation to last year's inaugural events, all of which the flu had kept her from. There on an attached sheet were telephone numbers for Miss Woods's office, as well as her home—which Alice was welcome to use for any and all assistance with arrangements.

She dialed the home number.

Rose had been in the apartment for fifteen minutes—sitting in the dark, TV off, no drink in her hand—when the phone rang. She ignored it after making sure it wasn't the special White House line, which would be disconnected tomorrow. No, it was her own phone in the bedroom, probably her brother calling, or one of her nieces or nephews, checking to see how she was holding up. Or maybe it was Bob Gray, hoping to cheer her with a dinner invitation—probably to the Sans Souci!

She needed to get out of her dress and into bed if she really intended to be back at her desk by eight a.m., but she was too exhausted to move. At least she could dispense with her nightly cold-cream application: her tears would only run right down it.

This caller wouldn't quit! The ringing persisted—probably a crank, though she of course wasn't in the book. The noise unnerved her, as if the Boston Strangler were keeping his finger on the doorbell. Unable to stand it any longer, she picked up the receiver, determined to let who-ever it was really have it.

"*Who is this?*"

"It's Mrs. Longworth. There's no need to shout."

Rose was on the verge of replying, "And I'm Marie of Rumania," but the voice was unmistakable, and she knew about the old lady's nocturnal habits. "You startled me" was all she said.

"It's only one o'clock, my dear. I've been watching television."

"What did you think of the speech?" Rose found herself asking, automatically. It was the question she put to everyone whenever the boss spoke on TV; she would ask it pointedly, making sure people knew there was only one right answer. But now it came out almost pleadingly, with a weird sort of feebleness.

"Passable," said Mrs. Longworth. "Are you still dressed?"

"Yes."

"Good. So am I. Do you run a car?"

"Yes," said Rose, surprised by the question and its antique formulation.

"Good," Mrs. Longworth said again. "Be here in ten minutes."

"What?"

"Honk the horn. Do *not* ring the bell. You'll wake Janie, who's the only one here besides me. My granddaughter is out celebrating with the rest of the city."

"Are you all right?" Rose asked.

"Of course I am," Alice snapped. "I suspect I'm in better shape than *you* are. Better than your boss, too."

"He'll be all right," replied Rose, prepared to scold even this old waxwork if she, too, deserted Richard Nixon.

"What do you suppose he's doing right now?" asked Alice.

"The same as he was half an hour ago: making calls, up in the Lincoln Sitting Room. That's where I said good night to him." She paused, wanting to disclose some of what she'd seen; needing to be, for once, the least bit indiscreet. "He keeps saying 'I hope I haven't let you down' to everyone on the other end of the line."

"Is Pat up?" asked Alice.

"She'll be up all night. Packing some of their things—with less help than you'd imagine."

"I won't disturb her. I want to see only him."

See? "But, Mrs. Longworth—"

"You said he was still up making calls. I suspect it's a long list."

"You may even be on it," said Rose, hoping to dissuade the old lady from this ridiculous idea that she'd apparently formed. "He knows how late you stay up."

"My dear, one doesn't sit around waiting for the telephone to ring. I imagine you've done too much of that in your life."

Being called an old maid by this gargoyle!

"Good," said Alice, when Rose didn't respond. "He won't mind a brief interruption. You'll take me to him. See you in ten. Fifteen at most. *Don't ring the bell.*"

Rose heard her hang up the phone.

At 1:15 a.m. Alice left her mansion, not bothering to lock the door, and proceeded with small, purposeful steps toward Rose's car. A young couple necking in the moonlit bus shelter by the curb looked up, startled at the sight of such an old lady in a hat, as they'd been startled a minute before by the sound of Rose's horn.

"So," said Alice, as soon as the president's secretary had helped her into the front passenger seat, "what's new?"

The heartless humor of the question prompted Rose to burst into tears. "He's in terrible shape," she now admitted as she pulled the car out into Massachusetts Avenue for the quick drive to the White House. "And I've been a basket case since Tuesday, ever since he picked *me* to tell Pat that he'd decided to quit." The tape they were now calling the "smoking gun"—*Don't go any further into this case—period!*— had come out the day before, and the skies had begun raining fire and ash.

"Was she for it or against?" asked Alice. "His quitting."

"Dead set against. Julie, too. They'd known about that tape since last Friday. The president sent up copies of the transcript to Pat and the girls and Bebe, to prepare them." She made it sound like an act of uncommon tenderness, but Alice snorted: "A little late to be letting them in on it, don't you think?"

Rose, who could still be angered by any hint of defection, pointed out that Jim St. Clair, the president's own lawyer, hadn't learned about the tape until last week. "And once he found out," she explained, contemptuously, "he got worried that *he* would be accused of obstructing justice unless he reported the contents to the special prosecutor. He could barely wait for a transcript."

Within a few minutes the car was nearing the White House. The crowd singing "Jail to the Chief" was smaller than an hour before, though even at its jeering height it had been somehow easier to take than the quiet along the Potomac three nights ago, when Rose and the rest of the presidential party aboard the *Sequoia* had sailed past silent clusters of spectators on the banks, all of them keeping a solemn death watch in the summertime twilight.

She held up her pass to the policeman on duty and drove to her parking spot on West Executive Drive.

Alice pointed out the exceptionally bright lights that appeared to be on in the East Room. Several of the people who'd attended her wedding there had filed past Lincoln's body in the same space forty years before that, but none of this was on her mind now; her attention and will were fully focused on the present moment.

"They're setting up television equipment in there," Rose explained. "He wants his farewell to the staff to be broadcast live."

She helped Mrs. L out of the car and onto the walkway leading to the West Wing. Only now, on the floodlit grounds, did Alice notice, and remark upon, Rose's pink dress and pink shoes.

"I was determined not to look as if I were at a funeral today," Rose said, stiffly.

"I *always* dress for one," Alice replied.

Rose took her past the Cabinet Room, where the boss had earlier tonight said goodbye to more than forty men, mostly longtime supporters from the Hill, many of whom had been in tears. Once the two women went inside her office, Rose saw Alice crinkle her nose: she was smelling smoke and assuming, correctly, that some papers had recently been burned in the room's fireplace. "Good for you," said Mrs. Longworth, who then admired a long feather boa hanging on an old clothes tree. Rose explained that she'd gotten it at a tango party at the Argentine embassy; Bob Gray had been her escort. "Take it," she said to the old lady, who did.

Rose then called the Residence to say that she was coming up. The

Secret Service man was surprised but accommodating. Yes, the president was still awake, still in the Lincoln Sitting Room.

"I want you to go home after you bring me up there," Alice instructed.

Rose hesitated. "Well, I could get a driver from the pool to take you home. The agent could bring you down to him when you're through."

"Yes, do that," said Alice, who was already back out in the hallway, trailing the boa behind her. The two women made their way toward the Residence and into the elevator, and when its doors closed, Mrs. Longworth remarked to Rose, "I really must get one of these installed in the house. You have no idea how cramped the dumbwaiter can be."

At 1:45 a.m., they walked into the sitting room. The president, in shirtsleeves, was startled to see Rose and unsure whether to believe his eyes at the sight of Alice.

"Mrs L!" he said, rising to his feet and wincing; he'd forgotten to favor his phlebitic leg.

How much thinner he looked than at her birthday party six months ago, thought Alice. She noticed a plate of bacon and eggs, and saw that the sofa had several books, some of them open, on one of its cushions.

"Memoirs by men who've lived in this house," Nixon said, rather oratorically, when he saw the books capture her attention. "None of them were written from prison, though. Mine may be the first."

One more club he was excluding himself from, thought Alice. She said nothing but peered at the face she had regarded an hour or two earlier on her television. Nixon was now wearing a pair of large, unfashionable reading glasses. The TV makeup, which he'd not removed, was streaky with tears. Lowering her eyes, Alice noticed the yellowness of his fingernails—a bad sign in a nonsmoker.

"I've been wondering how I'll support myself," he told her, without remembering to suggest she sit down. "It's not only the lawyers who need to be paid; there are my taxes. My debts exceed my assets," he confessed, flashing a smile, as if he'd just announced that he was double-jointed.

"I was once in the same position."

"How did you get out of it?"

"I did an advertisement for Lucky Strike."

Nixon said nothing, but then observed, "My watch has stopped. Honest."

"Simple coincidence," said Mrs. Longworth.

"I had a quote from your father in the speech, about being 'in the arena.' Did you hear it?"

He was still buttering her up, more than a quarter century after coming to town. "Yes, I heard it."

She moved closer to the couch and saw, amidst the presidential books, a copy of her father's diary. Beside it were Grant's memoirs, Lincoln's letters, someone's biography of Franklin. They were, she could see, not volumes from the White House library but rather Nixon's own copies, which he'd been reading for years. She noted that the back of his suit jacket, draped over an arm of the couch, was still soaked with sweat.

He at last gestured for her to sit down in a club chair across from the sofa. Returning to his own seat, he said, sighing, "I hope I haven't let you down."

"Don't be ridiculous." She was annoyed by this fishing for compliments. He was worse than Father.

"There's so much I still could have done in the Middle East—almost like TR, bringing the Russians and the Japanese together. Making peace when you're not one of the combatants."

"Yes," said Alice. "You've lost that chance."

Nixon looked surprised. This was not like the bromides he'd been hearing all night on the phone.

"I'm finished, Mrs. L."

"Politically? Yes, of course."

"Every which way. I may even be dying." He pointed to his leg, now much remarked upon in the press. "There are enough drugs in Dr. Tkach's black bag to finish me off fast."

Alice said nothing, just picked at the feathers of the boa, which might have been an ordinary raincoat for all the notice Nixon took of it.

"We'll be in San Clemente by this time tomorrow night," he said. "Then I'll be alone and it will really be over."

"I detest self-pity, and I find self-destruction absurd."

Nixon looked at her, knowing she hadn't always felt that way.

Alice could see what he was remembering. "Yes, that night in 1957," she said.

"When you came to the house on Tilden Street."

She leaned over and picked up her father's diary, quickly locating a passage from 1884. She read it aloud: *"She was beautiful in face and form, and lovelier still in spirit. As a flower she grew, and as a fair young flower she died . . . As a young wife; when she had just become a mother, when her life seemed to be just begun, and when the years seemed so bright before her—then, by a strange and terrible fate, death came to her. And when my heart's dearest died, the light went from my life forever."*

"Yes," said Nixon, neutrally.

"You read it to me that night."

"And you scolded me," the president reminded her.

"Yes. I thought it was preposterously inappropriate. Since I was the baby blamed for all the trouble and death in 1884, it could hardly be consoling. Especially when we were talking about the death of my *own* daughter more than seventy years later."

"I was trying whatever I could," said Nixon. "Trying to point out how your father had managed to go on, despite what he wrote."

"In its own way, the passage was, I suppose, weirdly pertinent. You reminded me of what *I'd* managed to survive before Paulina's death: the subconscious hatred of my father."

Nixon didn't say, "Oh, of course not," as he might have, had he not known what it was to survive the wrath of his own father. "You've done well," he said instead.

"Up to a point," said Alice. "I allowed my personality to swallow whatever real person I might have been. But you're correct: the strategy was not without a certain success."

"It's too late for strategy in my case. This is a tragedy."

"This is *not* a tragedy. It simply does not qualify as such."

Nixon said nothing. He was unsure, even now, *what* Watergate really was. He remained as baffled as he'd been when talking to Haldeman on June 23, 1972. He would forever be able to hear himself on the tape: confused; groping; taking the first approach that came to mind; dooming himself.

With difficulty, he turned away from his own story and back to Mrs. L's. "Why did you come to the house that night?"

"Because I saw the look on your face when you were carrying that wretched girl's coffin. You understood the ghastliness of it all, and you knew how to deny it, too. I realized that you could do that with almost anything, always find another layer of makeup to put over the tears."

"Is that a compliment?"

"No, it's a fact. If I let myself be swallowed by *one* personality, you hid yourself behind dozens of them, one 'new Nixon' after another." She paused for a second or two before asking, "Do you remember what else we talked about?"

"You told me about Senator Borah."

"That was hardly a secret," said Alice.

"Still, I don't suppose you told many people."

"That's true. I never told *her*. I let her know that Nick wasn't her father, but I didn't tell her who *was*. One more species of cruelty I visited upon that impossible, sullen, stuttering child. But by the time I left your house that night, we'd convinced ourselves that I had been a wonderful mother, and that the only cruelty to worry about was the article in Kay's paper. I went back to my own house and threw away Bill's razor, which I'd been looking at for days. The illusion we created sustained me for years. It still does from time to time."

"What else sustains you?" Nixon asked. He was by now too exhausted even to lift his drink.

"The truth, mostly. I was a *terrible* mother. In my deepest, swallowed self there was no denying it. But I eventually found my means of expiation."

"What was that?"

"I became a *marvelous* grandmother. None better."

Nixon offered her an atta-girl campaign smile. Alice realized he was too ravaged to see the point she was trying to make. So she would explain. "For a long time, like it or not, fair or unfair, you are going to be regarded as a terrible president."

"Not much I can do about that." A second grin, different from the first, but still automatic and false.

"You can rise above it the way I did. You can be a marvelous *ex-*president."

She could see another, deeper reflex now operating—his eyes were shifting, his inner wheels turning. He was responding to the mention of resurrection the way a plant does to light. But he was also dangerously riven. His immediate need was to get through the night and then tomorrow morning, and then to get out of the city.

"There's something I want you to do tomorrow," Mrs. Longworth said.

"Tomorrow?" asked Nixon.

"Yes, during whatever you have planned in the East Room. By the way, it's a terrible idea to put your wife through that on television, but I gather from Miss Woods that it's too late to call things off. Do you know what you're going to say?"

"No. I thought I'd just speak from the heart. Do it off the cuff."

Another terrible idea, thought Alice—as if he were some great ad-libbing wit. "I want you to send me a signal," she instructed. "A signal that you've understood what I've said and put away your morbid thoughts, as I once put away mine."

"What sort of signal?"

"Read that passage from Father's diary. Work it in. It will be our secret."

However bone-weary he might be, Nixon's internal meter made a quick measurement of the pros and cons. "They'll be ringing you up afterwards, you know. The press."

"I won't even be watching. I'll be asleep. And when they do get to me, I'll tell them that it was ridiculous, vulgar, whatever. It will be an intense pleasure to lie to the *Washington Post*. That's one more thing you and I share."

Nixon looked at her. Two tears were running down his makeup.

Alice rose from her chair. "I shall, I'm sure, never see you again." She extended her hand. "Take care of yourself. And go to bed." She motioned for him to summon the agent who would take her down to the car Miss Woods had promised.

As soon as someone in the hall opened the door, she walked toward it and did not look back. She flipped the Argentine boa over her right shoulder—and looked smaller than whatever red bird had supplied its feathers.

Chapter Forty-Five

AUGUST 9, 1974
HOTEL HANA, MAUI, HAWAII; AIR FORCE ONE

While he waited for the hotel operator to put through his call, Elliot Richardson sketched a Laysan duck, an endangered species native to the Hawaiian Islands. Richardson himself had been here in Hawaii only since Tuesday, but he was increasingly worried about his own extinction. Yesterday's *New York Times* lay on the bedspread, open to an article that put him at number three, behind Rockefeller and George Bush, on a list of vice-presidential choices available to President Gerald Ford.

It was 5:35 a.m., Hawaiian time, an hour after Nixon's mawkish East Room farewell—that Roosevelt quotation!—with about thirty minutes to go before Ford's swearing-in.

Richardson felt himself envying young Dick Darman, whom the hotel operator was trying to reach back in Washington. Dick had been with the Richardson family—indispensable, really—during their long just-concluded weeks of travel in the U.S.S.R. and Japan, but he'd gone straight home instead of on to Hawaii, where Richardson now found himself stuck, with Anne and the children, at this most inopportune time. The former attorney general didn't see how he could endure another week of it before the family's scheduled departure for San Francisco. He was supposed to address yet another ABA gathering in Honolulu on the fifteenth—but would he lose all chance of doing that as vice president designate by being trapped here in the meantime, so far from the decision-making in Washington? Rocky and Bush might both be at their summer places, but working the phones from Maine was a lot easier than working them from here.

At last, Darman.

"Dick," he said, with relief.

"Wasn't it *awful*?" Darman cackled. " 'When my heart's dearest died.' *Christ!*"

Richardson muttered something about dissociative personalities, and after a bit more laughter Darman got down to business. "Some good news. I hear that George Will is preparing a column that will run tomorrow saying it should be Rocky or you."

Prompted by a mental image of Will, Richardson began sketching an owl. The news wasn't cheering him much. "Even Sandman appears to be for Nelson," he said, gloomily. The New Jersey congressman, one of the Judiciary Committee's most conservative members and the kind of Nixon Republican who'd loathed Rockefeller for years, now seemed to find him acceptable.

"Well," said Darman, "Rocky looks a lot further to the right than he used to. With those drug laws up in New York, and the high body count at Attica."

Richardson understood the assessment but thought it indelicate to comment on the political dividends of a prison massacre.

Darman's own tone became a little gloomy. "What I hear from Woodward is not so good: Bob thinks Ford is pretty close to deciding on Bush."

Richardson sighed. Despite the idyllic weather and fruit-flavored cocktails, his nerves were raw; his body didn't know what time zone it was in.

Darman recommended patience. "The man who will be making this decision is extremely suggestible, not a leader. That's why we need a steady drumbeat from surrogates making the case for you over the next several days. In Jerry Ford we're dealing with a modest man who doesn't think for himself."

Trying to look on the bright side, Richardson murmured something like agreement. "As I've told you before, Richard, we all have the corresponding defects of our qualities."

"Maybe even you, sir!" Darman's pleasure in being called "Richard," something the boss did at his most fatherly and mentoring moments, was audible to Richardson even from five thousand miles away.

"So," he asked, "do I come home?"

"No," answered Darman. "Don't look overeager. No announcement is expected for at least ten days. And Bill Rogers agrees with what I've just laid out. That surrogates' drumbeat should reach a crescendo just as you arrive home *on schedule*."

Richardson, who'd hoped for a different answer, shifted the subject. "I've got interview requests in front of me from the *Boston Herald*, the *Honolulu Star-Bulletin*, and one of the local television stations. Do I do them?"

"Yes," said Darman. "They won't be picked up here."

Richardson silently wondered what then was the point.

"Sir," said Darman, "I'll make my calls and you make yours. Let's continue down the lists we drew up yesterday, and I'll check in with you again tonight at six o'clock my time."

"Okay, Dick."

Richardson looked at the column of names he'd created in his odd, swirling penmanship, whose little dots and horizontal scimitars looked more like Arabic than English. He considered the first several names:

CHAFEE
MATHIAS
McGREGOR
HARLOW

The very first one depressed him. Instinct convinced him that the navy secretary would soon be coming out for Bush, if he hadn't already. Was there really a point to calling him? Certainly not at the moment, when like everyone else Chafee would be watching Ford's swearing-in—or attending it in person!

Richardson went back to his doodling, stealing an occasional glance at a second list, the one he'd made of his rivals' liabilities:

ROCKY (too old, pushy)
BUSH (unseasoned)
BROOKE (too liberal, black)
GOLDWATER (too yesterday, too right-wing)

Alas, his own liabilities would now be getting talked about: his supposed lack of warmth; his ironically too-close association with Watergate. Never mind that he had been on the right side of that; Ford no doubt wanted to get away from the whole thing.

Well, the only way to do that would be to pardon Nixon. Otherwise the country would remain obsessed by a former president's efforts to stay out of jail. But once made—Richardson did the calculus—a pardon would be greeted with such outrage that Ford would need Elliot Richardson . . . *for* his association with Watergate, his record of cleanliness amidst all that chicanery.

Timing was everything here. *Recommend Pardon*, he now wrote on his pad. He must talk that up with whomever he discussed the miserable but necessary office he was seeking. Urge that the pardon be given *now*, before the choosing of the veep. *If it were done when 'tis done, then 'twere well it were done quickly.* Make clear that it will only be harder to do it later, and hammer home the point that the administration will otherwise never get off the ground. Even at this moment, with the new president about to take the oath, the television was mentioning Nixon's name two or three times more often than Ford's.

Bill Ruckelshaus, Richardson's fellow martyr of the Saturday Night Massacre, had advised him to call Ford even before Nixon resigned, so he'd done that yesterday. It was understandable, given all the commotion and the time difference, that the call had yet to be returned, but having to wait for a response was fraying Richardson's nerves ever further. He also had a call in to Kissinger. Henry would probably prefer as VP an old patron (Rocky) to an old semi-protégé (they'd gotten chummy when both attended NSC meetings during the administration's early days); but Henry might, if Rocky faded, go for Richardson over Bush.

It all made Richardson's head swim, and the sight of the call sheet was enough to induce indigestion. The sort of pleading it represented was worse than asking for campaign contributions, one of the repellent chores that had long ago made him give up elective life for the appointive kind.

Richardson turned off the television; there was nothing to be gained from any attempt to read Gerald Ford's blank face. He went back to his Laysan duck, but the phone rang almost as soon as he picked up the brush.

"I have the White House on the line," said the hotel operator.

"Thank you," said Richardson.

"Good morning, Elliot. Did I wake you?"

To Richardson's distress, his call was being returned by Al Haig, who he'd hoped had flown off into exile with Nixon. But, of course, good old suggestive Jerry had decided that Haig should stay on for a bit as chief of staff.

"Not at all," answered Richardson. "I was just watching a replay of the president's farewell. I've rarely been so moved."

"Really."

"Oh, yes," said Richardson, wondering how he and Darman were going to get past this enormous, unexpected stumbling block. Would Haig be around for another week? Through the whole VP selection?

"Well," said the general, "I've got to get into the East Room, but I saw that you'd called and just wanted to let you know that your name is certainly being very much mentioned around here."

"Is it? That's very flattering, Al."

"Yes, for ambassador to England. We'll be in touch."

Haig hung up the phone. Richardson looked out the window, regarding the sun on the coconuts, marooned in the paradise of his reputation.

"The flight plan says we'll be passing over Liberal, Kansas," Frank Gannon informed Diane Sawyer. "Should we waggle our wings?"

"We're also supposed to go over Gallup, New Mexico," she pointed out. "What do we do there? 'Experience a sudden loss of altitude'?"

As Air Force One flew west, the two weary young staffers kept up the gallows humor, no matter that the trapdoor had already dropped. It was the same with the president, who had come aboard shockingly tired but managed to observe that the back of the cabin "smelled a lot better than usual," now that it was free of the press. Ziegler had succeeded in keeping them off this final flight from Washington to San Clemente.

Only thirty-four passengers were traveling, and most of them remembered to look at their watches as twelve noon EDT arrived and, somewhere over Jefferson City, Missouri, Nixon ceased to be president. All chatter stopped for a long moment. "Air Force Once," someone finally muttered. No one had the heart to be wearing the flight jackets they used to don as status symbols. Nixon himself was in a sport coat, inside his cabin, taking the first sip of a martini with Ziegler.

The stewards began serving shrimp cocktail and prime rib a little ahead of schedule. Some people couldn't summon the energy, or stomach, for more than a couple of bites. In Haldeman's day, the plane's mood had been especially severe, but it hadn't lightened all that much with his departure. The blue-gray decor of the new aircraft, which became available after the '72 election, suggested a submarine traveling at a low, serious depth. One almost expected to hear the pinging of sonar.

When Ziegler emerged from the president's cabin, Steve Bull read his anxious expression, and asked, *"Another* call?"

The press secretary shook his head, knowing that Bull referred to Haldeman's continual pleas for a last-minute double pardon of the Watergate conspirators and Vietnam draft evaders. "No," he said, "I've got to talk to you about El Toro." A large crowd was apparently forming at the marine air base where they'd be landing. It was friendly, to be sure, but so big that the now former president might feel required to address it. "And I'm a little worried about *her*," said Ziegler, pointing to the first lady's small, private cabin.

Inside it, Pat sat behind a little writing table, knowing that Dick was on the other side of the thin wall. She wanted to lie down on the narrow bed but had decided she should use the time to write some thank-you notes. And yet, when she saw the two stacks of available stationery, she didn't have the heart to use either. One sported a letterhead saying "The White House," where they no longer lived, and the other was embossed with the words "Air Force One," which this plane hadn't been for twenty minutes. She decided she had her excuse not to work. She swept both piles of stationery into the trash basket—as wasteful a gesture as she'd allowed herself in the last five years—leaving only her untouched lunch and a pack of cigarettes on the desk.

Closing her eyes, she thought again of what she'd seen on the South Lawn after boarding the helicopter: three soldiers rolling up the red carpet and hanging on to their dress caps against the chop of the rotors. It looked as if they were wrapping up a corpse. She'd heard herself say, "It's so sad, it's so sad," as the helicopter rose above the Ellipse, and she had scarcely said a word since. She'd spent the whole flight in this tiny cabin.

It was comfortable enough, but she preferred the old plane, even with its assassination taint. It had had bright desert colors, and every time she stepped onto it she would remember the day in '68, just after the election, when they'd come aboard and Dick had twirled her in his arms, thinking no one was looking.

She regarded the blank, greenish screen of the little Sony TV in here and experienced a curious moment of joy, thinking that her own face might never again appear on any television, anywhere. She tried to prolong the thought, to comfort herself with it, but there was one more thing she had to do before she could even pretend to relax.

She opened the door and stuck her head into the aisle, catching the eye of Colonel Brennan, who came forward immediately.

"I'd like to place a call," she said, handing him a slip of paper with the number.

"Right away, ma'am."

She closed the door, sat back down, and waited for the phone to ring. Once she picked it up, she realized that the signal was terrible; the roar of white noise sounded like the crowds in Cairo.

"*What?*" she asked, louder than she liked. "What did you say?" She'd only caught a word or two.

Then Tom Garahan's voice again broke through, a little more clearly this time: "I said you're heading in the wrong direction!"

"Oh!" she cried, hoping he would hear her laugh. "For a long time now!"

"What?"

"—long time now—"

And then, suddenly, the signal cleared, as if the static had been turbulence and the pilot had just found a calm airstream.

"They're waiting for you," said Tom, sounding almost as if he were in the cabin.

"Who?" she asked.

"The crowd where you're going to land. There are thousands of them there already, singing 'God Bless America.' "

She took a cigarette from the pack. She could feel the tears and nausea coming. She could *not* do it, not after this morning's televised torture in the East Room. And not after this, which was killing her all over again.

"The screen keeps shifting back and forth between there and Washington," Tom explained.

"Turn it off, please."

She could hear the click, after he got up from the couch in the Madison Avenue apartment.

"I sent you something," she said, when Tom returned to the line.

"I already got it, this morning."

She'd written him Tuesday night, after Rose had told her there was no turning back.

"Good for the Post Office," she said.

"For delivering news like that?"

"Tom . . . you understand."

"I understand. In fact I've already carried out your instructions."

She had sent him back the gold shamrock. She'd told him not to keep it but to go to Schrafft's and leave it—a shiny, mysterious piece of luck, for someone else to find—on the table where they'd first sat together. *The gentleman said to tell you that he's an independent, but that everybody likes apple pie.*

"Schrafft's has seen better days," Tom informed her.

"So have I."

"I offered it up, Victoria."

He had once explained the phrase to her. It was what the Catholics do with any sorrows and trials that had to be borne: accept the burden; carry it; and make a gift of the labor to God. She'd asked Tom why they couldn't make an offering of joy, and he'd replied, "Are you sure you're really even half-Irish?"

"I offered up the joy," he now told her.

She could no longer walk between two fires, one steady and warm, the other a wild alternation of blaze-ups and gutterings that now looked on the verge of going out for good. But only the second truly needed her tending. She did not know what lay ahead—certainly not joy—and she doubted her strength to endure it, let alone offer it up, but she knew where she had to be.

"Thank you, Roger." She felt relief and sadness, a cold wave of each crashing into the other.

Oh, Tom!

She had gotten through this, too.

She realized from the funny blank buzz on the line that the connection had cut out, the way it sometimes did at this altitude. The communications man came on: "Mrs. Nixon, we're sorry; the call dropped. I'll try it again."

"That's okay. We were finished."

"You're sure?"

"Yes, thanks."

She hung up, safe in the knowledge that there was no recording of the conversation: Johnson had taped every call to and from Air Force One, but Dick had had the system removed after taking office and had left the jet unwired when, two years later, everything else got tapped. The mystery of this exception was one more thing she intended never to think about once they were back in their own house.

After the plane had traveled another ten minutes, another hundred miles west, she knocked on the door of Dick's cabin. Ziegler opened the door and cleared out instantly.

Her husband looked so hollowed out that the swivel chair he sat in seemed like some prescribed medical appliance. She spotted the Teddy Roosevelt book on the table, wondering who'd brought it along after Dick had used it in the East Room.

"Are you sure it's ours?" she asked, pointing to it. "Not the White House library's?"

"Yes. Don't you recognize it?"

"Sort of. I'm just afraid they'll accuse us of stealing that, too." She took the seat beside him. "How's the leg?"

"All right for the moment."

"It ought to be up." She pulled the hassock toward him, and as she leaned over to do so their faces came closer. Each could see how much the other had been crying.

"What'd you think of what I said?" he asked. "You couldn't really call it a speech."

She didn't answer.

"I know you didn't want the cameras there."

"No," she said softly. "But I realized once you started that it would have been just as hard without them. Did you see Herb Stein?"

"Yeah." The stolid economist's eyes had been gushing tears in the East Room. "I almost broke down watching him," said Nixon. He paused. "You know, that's why I mentioned my mother and my old man instead of you and the girls. I was afraid you'd break down, too."

"Oh, you don't need to tell *me* that!" She lightly touched his knee. "*They're* the only ones who wouldn't get it." She pointed in the direction of where the press used to be.

"I'm so . . . mystified!" He groped for this word she couldn't remember him ever using, and once he found it he started to sob. "I don't know how it happened, how it began. Half the time I hear myself on the tapes I realize that I'm barely remembering who works for who over at the Committee. I hear myself acting like I know *more* than I do—pretending to be on top of the thing so I don't embarrass myself with whoever's in the room—especially Ehrlichman. Christ, I can't now apologize for what I can barely understand! I mean, if Mitchell and Martha—"

"Dick," she interrupted, patting his swollen knee. "You're going to make yourself sick." Martha, the most ancient of history, headed the list of things she would never think about again.

He closed his eyes and the sobs let up, at least for a moment. The tears continued down his face, as copious as the sweat that had drenched his suit jacket last night.

She was worried, even with the engine noise, that someone would hear him, the way she'd worried when he wept on the train going through Oregon in '52. She was alarmed by how bad he looked, and didn't know how he could put himself out in front of another crowd an hour from now. She wanted him to stop crying, the way she'd made herself stop this morning.

"Dick," she whispered, taking his hand.

He was looking at her now, wanting to tell her that he loved her. She knew that he couldn't, no more than he could make himself ask if she loved him. For an awful second she feared he would say, "I hope I haven't let you down," as if she were one more congressman from Nebraska. But he knew better than to try that with her.

She rubbed her thumb back and forth across the top of his hand, soothing him, trying to change the subject. "You can't say this isn't a smooth ride. Remember that first one?"

He nodded, like a child subsiding from a tantrum. He knew what she was referring to: their first plane trip together, after the '48 election, flying east to west, the four of them, with both the girls in little bonnets. Six prop flights to get them from Washington to California. Julie's infant ears hurt each time they touched down; but the baby's mother never lost her temper, or so much as a pair of gloves, the whole trip.

She looked at him now, a sight so painful she couldn't conjure any image from the happier years behind them. She could only see the months ahead—the encouragements, the scoldings, the jokes and stratagems it would take to keep him alive, at home or in prison. That would be her work, and she would offer it up with whatever tenderness she had in her. It was the one thing left for her to do, and she would be worthy of it.

"Do you love me?"

Suddenly the words were out of him, making her flinch, like a firecracker thrown during a motorcade. He wanted her to answer a question he hadn't asked in more than thirty years, since before those propeller flights. She leaned over to kiss his forehead, trying to find words to use herself, and they came to her, from all the campaign banners they had walked under two years ago, on their way toward this moment, this ruin. "Now more than ever," she whispered.

Chapter Forty-Six

SEPTEMBER 8, 1974
WASHINGTON, D.C., AND FORT HOLABIRD, MARYLAND

Clarine had left Washington five days ago. "Gone to Spain, darlin' Hound," was all she'd written, near the word "MOOT" on the crinkled envelope she left with the doorman at Watergate West. LaRue suspected he would never see her again.

He had no idea whether she had read the envelope's contents; whether the original sealing was intact or if the flap had been reglued. He had still not opened it himself, let alone read whatever was inside, though he'd carried it around since Tuesday, sometimes thinking of it as his fate and sometimes as just a poor papery trace of Larrie.

He had it with him even now, at the counter in the waffle shop across from Ford's Theatre. He'd driven downtown, passing a Sunday-morning crowd outside St. John's. Word must have gotten out that the new president would be attending services. Well, he had plenty to pray about, thought LaRue.

Wishing he had some bourbon instead of maple syrup to pour over them, LaRue was fortifying himself with a large plate of waffles before he headed off to see Magruder for the first time since that hour in the neighbor's driveway a year and a half ago. Jeb had been asking for a visit ever since June, but Allenwood, the first place he'd been incarcerated, had said no: they didn't want two Watergate guys having the chance to align their stories, never mind that both of them had already pled guilty and testified in public to every part of the scandal's minutiae.

But at Holabird, where Jeb had just been transferred, things were different. The old fort up in Baltimore was getting ready to shut down, and fewer than eighteen prisoners remained on its grounds, doing their own cooking and wearing their own clothes. A whole little Watergate platoon was now stashed there in advance of the Mitchell trial: Kalmbach and Colson were in residence along with Magruder, and Dean himself had lately arrived. With all of them already living and talking together, the authorities hardly cared if LaRue came to shoot the Sunday breeze. One of the marshals had even told Jeb he'd be happy to take him to his son's birthday party when the boy's big day came—and then drive him back in time for lockdown.

Cozy as it all might sound, LaRue was not looking forward to the reunion. He lingered over his coffee and the *Post* before paying his check and hitting the road. He kept the envelope on the passenger seat as he drove. It traveled with him like a passport: if he feared opening it, he was also by now afraid to be without it. Next to it sat a box of peanut brittle, something Clarine had suggested as a present for Magruder's sweet tooth, before she took off.

LaRue had once told Jeb about Larrie—during the high-water bosom-buddy days of "Magrue." In the early spring of '72, he and Jeb had spent a long evening at a booth in Billy Martin's Georgetown tavern, the same wooden nook where John F. Kennedy was said to have popped the question to Jackie. LaRue had been sporting a double glow of booze and well-being, knowing the latter wouldn't last, that he would soon enough be remembering the dark spot at his center, the duck blind he carried inside. And yet, before all that took over, before he got as sweaty as the Old Man during a big speech, he'd let himself feel the bourbon and contentment and tell Jeb all about the affair with Clarine—almost the whole story, from the Jackson law office to the dude ranch and beyond. He'd told him he met her because he needed help with some legal technicalities after the hunting accident, not that there'd been an investigation; and he'd never mentioned this letter now beside him on the passenger seat. But he did tell him how the later flamingly liberal Larrie had gone to work for the DNC, which had gotten them laughing about life's ironies and tilted the conversation back to the usual campaign bullshit.

He'd wondered for days now whether Clarine had left because of something inside the envelope. Had she been repelled to find out for certain what she'd for so long been able to accept as mere possibility?

When would he open the damned thing? When the trial was over and he'd finished speaking his piece against Mitchell? Or maybe the night before he, too, went to prison? That way, if it was bad news, he could imagine he was being sentenced for something truly awful, not the little cloak-and-dagger foolishness of Watergate.

A breeze came through the car window. The clouds were scudding by fast in the direction of Chesapeake Bay. Thoughts of its marshes took him back, yet again, to the spot in Canada; to the two blinds they'd set up because he and Daddy weren't getting along; to the six snorts of bourbon he'd had while sitting by himself; to the gun that felt as heavy as his limbs felt light; to the moment he'd raised it to fire at the birds; and then to the weirdly long report that came back over the reeds; the cries of "Ike! Ike! Ike!"

Who knows what impulse the drink might have made him give in to?

He tried, as always, to banish the image, turning up the radio's volume to the point where Rosemary Clooney was singing "Tenderly" as loud as the kid in the next lane had Jimi Hendrix or whoever it was playing the guitar. And then the station interrupted the record for an unexpected piece of news, a recorded announcement that Jerry Ford had made sometime between going to church and teeing off at Burning Tree:

> . . . a decision which I felt I should tell you and all of my fellow American citizens . . .

LaRue knew what was coming, no matter that Ford had spent all spring assuring his fellow American citizens that the Old Man was innocent.

> . . . do grant a free, full, and absolute pardon unto Richard Nixon.

Did the Old Man make a deal for it—through Haig? Or was it simply that Ford couldn't get his presidency going with everyone still lined up outside the courthouse waiting for Nixon to arrive in shackles?

Or maybe it was honest-to-God pity. Eastland had called LaRue a week or so ago to say that the Old Man had been crying on the phone from San Clemente. He was in the worst shape imaginable and, according to the senator, both Jaworski and Jerry Ford needed to know it.

Well, Nixon was now off the hook, and that was fine with LaRue.

He tried to imagine the Old Man enjoying the moment, feeling the relief as he sat on the ash heap of his life beside the Pacific Ocean. He couldn't begrudge him the reprieve, and he wouldn't complain that he and Mitchell still had prison stretches ahead of them.

And yet, God Almighty, what would it be like to feel such relief after seventeen years of doubt as to what his subconscious *might* have made him do to Ike LaRue, to Daddy, who could be hell on wheels and whose money anyone would have enjoyed sooner rather than later?

Up ahead LaRue saw the sign for a rest stop. On impulse, he let himself turn into it. He shut off the engine, picked up the envelope, and tried to do what he'd resisted doing for five days—open it.

But he couldn't, even now, make himself do it. He stayed seated in the car, parked at the rest stop, letting his mind wander over his life—the last two years, the first twenty-eight, the fifteen that lay in between. He kept the radio low, listening to a Sunday gospel program, restarting the car not when he reached some moment of clarity, but only when he feared he'd otherwise drain the battery.

He arrived at Holabird an hour late. Magruder came toward him— fit, if a little pale—in a blue Ban-Lon shirt. His Dale Carnegie manner was undiminished: "Fred LaRue, you're looking fine!"

When the two of them sat down, Jeb seemed to sense his visitor's preoccupation and, with the instinct of a salesman, did enough chatting for two. "So I guess you heard about the Old Man," he began.

"Yeah," said LaRue.

"McGovern's already come out against it!" Magruder laughed, as if the joke were still on the sad sack they'd run against two years ago.

"So," he asked, when no laughter from LaRue met his own, "do you think we're next? For clemency? Colson does."

"I doubt it," LaRue replied. He hadn't given the matter any thought, whereas Jeb was now eyeing the possibility of a pardon the way he once would have looked at a promotion.

"I guess you're right," Magruder admitted, a little crestfallen. "I just hope they won't go *harder* on the rest of us now that the Old Man's gotten off scot-free."

"Is that how you see it?" LaRue asked, with a kind of wonderment that he could feel baking itself into hostility.

Magruder decided to change the subject, offering LaRue some reminiscences of his recent stay in Allenwood: "This place is a hell of an improvement over that one. We had fifty-four guys to a dorm there! I hadn't heard snoring like that since I was in Basic. They counted us six times a day—and forget this 'white-collar' stuff. There were plenty of ghetto guys up there, and the ones in for drugs blamed the Old Man—and us—for their stiff sentences."

To LaRue, Nixon's "war on drugs" now sounded as remote as the Vicksburg Campaign.

"Hey," said Magruder, cheerfully determined to keep the talk going, "you know who I played tennis with up there? Johnny Sample, that black guy from the Jets. He was in for passing bad checks."

LaRue nodded.

"But believe me, it wasn't all tennis. The first few weeks I did nothing but scrub pots and pans."

LaRue nodded again.

"This place is a lot easier on Gail," Magruder continued, speaking of his wife. "The shorter drive means she can do it as a day trip." LaRue still said nothing, while Jeb persevered in trying to jolly him out of his frozen state. "I guess even Allenwood had its pluses for her. She didn't have to worry about the Committee secretaries coming on to me, or about my drinking. But, boy, I'll tell you, there were a hell of a lot of tranquilizers up there—prescribed *and* bootleg. Half the guys stayed stoned all day."

"I guess you'll be at this place for a while," LaRue said finally, as if trying to nudge their meeting back toward some agenda it didn't have.

Magruder understood that he was referring to the postponement of the Mitchell trial, whose Washington venue was the reason for keeping the Watergate prisoners here. "Yeah," said Jeb. "It'll be a while. I feel sorry for Mitchell, with all the delays, but you won't hear me complaining as long as we get to work off our time down here instead of in Pennsylvania." His voice and expression turned somber for a moment. "You know, Gail always liked Mitchell, saw him as a father type."

"I thought *I* was the father figure," said LaRue, without a smile. He handed Magruder the box of peanut brittle. He declined a piece of the candy for himself, while Jeb described the courtly way one of Holabird's Mafia men always behaved when Gail visited.

When LaRue said nothing, Jeb chattered on, in search of a topic that might restore his visitor to his familiar old amiability. "They tell me the book is selling pretty well."

LaRue had been determined to keep the conversation away from Magruder's memoirs, and this was more than he could stand. "Jeb, your 'American Life' has about as much social significance as Dino's."

"Who's Dino?"

"The cocker spaniel in the apartment next door to mine. Barks all the time."

Magruder looked hurt.

LaRue, thinking of the letter out in his car, asked, "Where did you get off putting in that stuff about my father's hunting accident?"

Magruder appeared confused. "Did that wind up going in? I can't even remember, there were so many drafts. The ghostwriter must have decided—"

"You didn't read your own goddamned book?"

"Sure I did, but—"

"Hell, you couldn't resist whatever might make it a little more interesting, isn't that right?"

"Jeez, Fred, I've never seen you like this before."

"Well, fuck all, maybe I've never been in these circumstances before."

Jeb, not even wearing convict's clothes, looked like an organization man who'd just joined one more organization. Whereas, thought LaRue, prison would likely kill Mitchell. And maybe it would kill him, too—he could imagine getting shanked after thoughtlessly dropping some word like "coon."

He sat in silence, damned if he was going to tell Jeb what his own last year had been like; about all that he'd been through with Clarine; about the damned envelope out in the car.

Magruder, biting into a piece of the peanut brittle, took a philosophical turn: "You ever think how little it would have taken to keep things from ending up this way?"

"Yeah," said LaRue, indulgently.

Magruder warmed to the new subject. "I mean—if the security guard hadn't seen the tape on the door; if McCord had kept his mouth shut; if the president hadn't bugged his own office. So many variables."

LaRue gave a fatalistic shrug. "I'd dial it back to Key Biscayne myself." *Mr. Mitchell, to the best of my recollection, said something to the effect that, Well, this is not something that will have to be decided at this meeting.* Actually, he would rewind things all the way back to that meeting at Justice, where Liddy had presented his grand plans at the easel. Given a do-over, LaRue would have Mitchell throw Liddy out the window, just as the attorney general had fantasized about doing, "in hindsight," to Sam Ervin and Sam Dash.

LaRue didn't want to go any further with this pointless game, but Jeb persisted: "I should have been stronger, resisted the pressure I was always feeling from Haldeman and Colson. God, the day Chuck called me with Hunt right in his office! Asking when I planned on giving Hunt and Liddy something to *do*."

"Yeah," LaRue said, with rising anger. "Well, you sure picked the most useless target in fuck-all creation. I mean, Jesus, the damned DNC."

Magruder, believing the remark to be—at last!—a piece of the old Magrue insult humor, smiled. "Yeah, I could have picked a half dozen better places to tell them to go into. Even McGovern's headquarters would have been an improvement. But after Colson's call, the DNC was the first place that came to mind. You remember that night you and I had at Billy Martin's?"

"Yeah," said LaRue, recalling the occasion when he'd none too wisely poured out to Jeb his history with Clarine.

"When we were both pretty far gone," said Magruder, "I could hear you say, sort of muttering, 'Yeah, I'd love to know what's in Larry's desk.' Two or three times: 'Larry's desk.' You also said, sort of to yourself, 'Might make *no* difference; might make *all* the difference.' You kept repeating those two lines like they were from one of your country songs." He laughed.

LaRue looked into Magruder's blank, handsome face. He could almost hear the two of them speaking and slurring the way they did that night at Billy Martin's. He'd learned from the White House "Blue Book" and all the hearings what a difference there could be between what somebody said and what wound up getting transcribed, and all at once he realized what had happened when they stumbled from one personal and political topic to another that night.

I'd love to know what's in Larrie's desk.

"You dumb fuck," said LaRue, in a tone Magruder had never heard from him before. "We spent half that night talking about Clarine Lander—Larrie—L-A-R-R-I-E."

"Fred," said Jeb, still not getting it, "you look as if you're seeing a ghost."

I'd love to know what's in Larrie's desk: LaRue had mumbled the words to *himself*, since he'd told Jeb almost everything about Clarine *except* for the letter he knew was in her desk. Jeb had heard "Larry" instead of "Larrie," and days later he'd sent the burglars in search of whatever crap Larry O'Brien might have under his blotter or be talking about on his phone. And during their first entry—putting half-dead bugs onto the wrong lines, rifling the wrong desks, and photographing the wrong documents—Hunt's goons had swept up the MOOT letter.

Magruder seemed vaguely aware, at last, of what had happened. He sought to calm his old friend by laughing, and by telling him with a touch of pride, "You don't need to worry about this. I never told any of the investigators. I let them think Larry O'Brien was my idea!"

LaRue hadn't taken a swing at anyone in twenty years. He thought he might now, but reckoned that his fist would just sink, pointlessly, into Magruder's handsome custard pie of a face.

He got up, walked away, and said, over his shoulder, "Take care of yourself, Jeb."

Outside the visitors' room, he submitted to an examination of his pockets. His shaking hands excited a certain suspicion in the guard, but he forced himself to remain calm, even as he wondered about all that might not have happened if he'd not, while in his cups, mentioned Clarine by her nickname.

No, he wouldn't do it. Because if he started, he would never stop. He would have to wonder whether Watergate had really begun fifteen years before, in that Canadian duck blind, and whether it would have occurred if he'd never made a furtive visit to a lawyer's office in Jackson, Mississippi; if he'd never met a secretary named Clarine Lander. He would eventually rewind things to the point where he'd be asking if Watergate depended on Fred—or Ike—LaRue's having been born.

Once the guard nodded his okay and handed him back his wallet, LaRue walked out into the afternoon light, toward his car.

The letter lay on the passenger seat, the pre-electric typewriting on its envelope looking as official as all the green-covered transcripts of all the congressional hearings he'd recently testified at. But what good would it do him, he wondered, to know a truth that might be as untrue or as ludicrously incomplete as he now knew all those transcripts to be? Further knowledge would not save Mitchell from boozy decomposition, let alone prison. It wouldn't stop the Old Man's whirlings through his gray pardoned purgatory. It wouldn't bring back Clarine or, for that matter, Ike.

And so he put the envelope into the glove compartment and began his journey home, southwards, in the direction of Mississippi, where he would head for good and all, after one last night inside the Watergate's walls.

Each morning that she sat down behind Henriette's easel, Pat performed a bit of camouflage, putting both hands in her lap and placing the right one over the left, which even now, two years after the stroke, remained weak. As she posed, she would look out the window of the breakfast room, regarding the purple gazanias and occasionally catching sight of a hummingbird.

She'd lost track of the number of sittings and had long since run out of things to say to Henriette: she'd joked about how her garden was falling to ruin because of all the time she was spending in here, and asked if the picture was magically going to make her look a full, straight-backed five-feet-six again. Henriette was better at keeping up her end of the conversation, telling stories of the whole painting Wyeth family—her brother, Andrew; her nephew, Jamie—or about some of her recent sitters. Paulette Goddard and Helen Hayes!

Pat hadn't wanted to pose for a portrait at all. The girls had insisted on it for the past four years—for Dick's sake, or theirs, or just for history's. She had avoided argument about the first two sakes, but maintained that history would be better off without the picture. A missing portrait—the one never made of the only first lady evicted from the premises—would be more instructive than anything hanging on a wall.

"What's that lovely smell?" asked Henriette.

"Eucalyptus," Pat answered. "Manolo taught us to use the leaves for kindling. You can smell it long after the fire's gone."

Manolo, Dick's valet, was gone, too. He and Fina had retired and moved to Spain.

She'd agreed to the picture only this summer, when Julie at last gave them a grandchild. The baby was now three months old, and Henriette had been on the scene for three weeks.

An odd bond between painter and sitter had grown up around their hands. In Henriette's case the right, not the left, was twisted—from childhood polio. But she had taught herself to use it; she drew with her left hand and painted with her right. The division of labor, the self-discipline that must have been required to make it happen, fascinated Pat, though the two women had spoken of it only once.

She had lots of time to think while sitting here facing the blank back of the canvas. But her mind rarely traveled back to any past but the recent one, the four years that she and Dick had been together in this house. He had been the first one to approach death's door, just after they arrived here in '74. The blood clots nearly killed him, and the hemorrhaging during surgery was even worse. But he'd come home and rallied and written his book, and the two of them had fallen into a strange, anesthetized routine. She often felt that the ocean was not just on one side of the house but all around; that they were on an island, a little two-person leper colony. *Able was I 'ere I saw Elba.* She wondered if she would live long enough to teach Jennie, her new grandchild, about palindromes.

As for her Napoleon, his plots involved reclaiming not his throne but his reputation. He was now at work on another book—not another memoir, though she thought he'd gone too easy on his enemies in the one he'd written. This new project was a book about foreign affairs, how to handle the Russians. It would display the kind of expertise people were willing to concede him, the way they'd admit that the Bird Man of Alcatraz did have a way with canaries.

He was lately talking about returning to New York, where he could live amidst thinkers and editors and make himself available to any foreign minister checking in at the United Nations. Well, if he wanted to go, she would. She would give up the garden here for a window box there and be perfectly all right. She'd have little reason or desire to leave the apartment.

Dick never tired of saying that she'd had her stroke, in July of '76, because she'd made the mistake of looking into Woodward and Bernstein's second book, which spared not even her—tales of drinking and so forth. He had convinced himself of the connection, and he'd railed against the two authors throughout her recovery, every time he saw her struggling with the stair-steps of the exercise box, or trying to draw out the pulley they'd attached to a wall by the patio.

She *had* read some of the book, but it didn't make much of an impression, certainly not the kind made by the spring 1976 number of *The Tom Thumb House Newsletter*, which had noted with regret the passing of the charity's longtime friend and generous supporter, Mr. Thomas Garahan of New York. A heart attack at the age of sixty-six.

On February 20, 1980, eight days after her ninety-sixth birthday, Alice entered the last five minutes of her existence. The television in her bedroom showed Ronald Reagan fighting for his political life in New Hampshire and then, a moment later, the Russians marching through Afghanistan. Alice imagined that Father would soon be on his way to the Khyber Pass, forcing the combatants into peace talks.

Her mind, like the television, was sometimes on and sometimes off, but she felt certain, as did her granddaughter and Janie, that the end was quite near. Bronchial pneumonia, the doctor had said. When he told her, she'd experienced a slight disappointment that such an ordinary complaint would be what finally carried her off.

On the table by the bed lay the last piece of mail she would ever receive, a printed change-of-address announcement:

Mr. and Mrs. Richard M. Nixon are now residing at
142 East Sixty-fifth Street
New York, New York 10021

So far, she had to admit, he'd done rather well, and if he went on as long as she had, he'd be around for another thirty years. An advance copy of his latest book, sent a week ago "with the compliments of the author," sat on another table in the room. There would be no funeral for her, and no wake, but the dress she'd be buried in *was* laid out, at her insistence, across a chair near the foot of the bed. She had managed to place inside one of its pockets a little scrawl of Paulina's from fifty years ago: *Dear Mother, I love you very much. Love, "Kits."*

One piece of jewelry lay atop the dress: the wedding bracelet from the kaiser. The jewel thief who'd gotten hold of it in '66, when she was up in New York at Capote's party, had pried out all the diamonds, and they'd never been recovered, so there didn't seem any reason what was left of the thing shouldn't be buried with her—just those empty gold settings, like a mouthful of missing teeth. What could be a better memento mori?

Of course *she* wouldn't be needing any reminders, since she'd be dead, lying in Rock Creek Cemetery beside Paulina, with Hilda Wilhelmina Luoma as their neighbor a few grassy feet away. No Nick, no Bill, and no prospect of meeting up with either one in any sort of afterlife, let alone the big reunion bash that Bobby's widow continued to expect.

All at once she groaned, realizing that Joe was no doubt getting ready to write something about her for a newspaper or magazine. He'd repeat a half dozen of her hoariest remarks, at least three of which she would never actually have said.

Her mind again flickered off: she suddenly wasn't sure which of the brothers, Stew or Joe, remained alive, and which of them was dead. She looked out into the hall, toward the old stuffed tiger whose paw had once fallen off in Stew's hand.

As soon as she closed her eyes, for the last time, she saw it—the tiger, quite alive, coming toward her.

"We love you, Muggsy!"

The crowd in the hotel ballroom laughed and cheered, and Elliot Richardson acknowledged his self-bestowed nickname with a dignified, defeated smile.

"I'm proud of what I've done and what my conscience would not let me do," he declared, conceding his loss, by more than twenty-five points, in the Massachusetts Republican Senate primary.

The crowd applauded his sentiment, though not so loudly as it had applauded the nickname he'd assumed six months ago at a St. Patrick's Day luncheon roast hosted by Billy Bulger, the state senate's president, a man less famous for his legislative accomplishments than for his gangster brother, Whitey. When Bulger held up a mock-advertisement urging those who saw it to VOTE FOR ELLIOT, HE'S BETTER THAN YOU, Richardson had come back with a suggestion that the monicker "Muggsy" might serve to warm him up for an electorate either put off by his manner or unsure of who he was. He had, after all, been gone from Massachusetts for most of the last fifteen years.

Nineteen eighty-four hadn't looked completely hopeless back in March, but now, in mid-September, the smart money was moving to a Reagan reelection victory even here in Massachusetts. The fellow who'd just trounced Richardson in the primary was very much the president's sort of man—a self-made millionaire in what was now bewilderingly called "high tech."

"The Former Everything" had done his campaigning at Irish taverns and town dumps, flinging his Muggsy buttons like doubloons to whoever showed up. But once he began to speak it was usually of arms control (unlike Mr. Reagan, he was for it) or tax increases (with all due respect to the president, he saw their necessity). He was sorry to have to disavow so much of the Republican Party and its platform, but there you were. It wasn't the first time he'd had to, he would tell them. Some remembered what he was talking about; many didn't.

The jobs between Justice and now had gotten ever more rarefied and finally Ruritanian: ambassador to the Court of St. James's; secretary of commerce; chief negotiator for the Law of the Sea treaty. By the time he left Washington to make this Senate run, heading up to Massachusetts had felt almost like going off to Hawaii. Rather a lot of things were upside down now; he'd realized just how many when this May the American Society of Newspaper Editors—ten years after his own appearance—had chosen Richard Nixon for their speaker.

"I congratulate my opponent but hope he'll remain mindful of the kind of people and principles that have preceded him here in the Grand Old Party."

The applause had become decidedly weak, and he could tell from the camera lights that two of the local TV stations had cut away from the ballroom. It was time to wrap this up and have Muggsy bid everyone a fond good night.

Richardson imagined that from this point on—he was, after all, sixty-four—he'd be grazing in the pastures of the Kennedy School of Government just across the river, ruminating upon the Saturday

Night Massacre for the next dozen students writing a master's thesis on Watergate. Maybe Dick Darman would have some other ideas, but having found his way into the Reagan White House, Dick lately seemed uneasy taking his calls.

———

After reaching Geneva with the foreign minister's party, General Sobatkin summoned the KGB rezident from the Bern embassy and gave him private instructions to prevent a possible approach by agents of the People's Republic of China.

Howard Hunt was reading the final proofs for *Chinese Red* and watching the fifth Republican National Convention since the one that had renominated Nixon in '72, right here in Miami. He had been unmoved by the rhetoric of both George Bush and Pat Buchanan, each a very different veteran of Nixon's White House. The troubles of his own children, exacerbated by his time in prison, had deafened him to the culture-warring cries of the insurgent candidate; and it seemed to him, Gulf War aside, that Bush had done little these last four years but take the victory lap Reagan deserved for winning the Cold War. As for being a fellow "Company" man—well, how long exactly had Bush directed the CIA? About as long as Elliot Richardson had run the Department of Justice? Certainly less than the total of thirty-three months Hunt himself had spent shuffling from one prison to another—attaining, after the loss of his appeal, what must still stand as the longest sentence ever served for burglary by a first offender.

"Papa!" cried his youngest son. "Can I have money for the ice cream truck?"

Hunt found two quarters in his chinos and told the boy to be careful of the cars on Griffing Boulevard. He took a quick, protective look out the window, beyond the NO TRESPASSING sign, to see what the traffic looked like.

He and his wife had been married for fifteen years now. After his experience with Clarine Lander, he'd been wary of any out-of-the-blue prison visitor, but Laura had turned out to be the real thing. She was less dark and complicated than Dorothy, and while he still missed his first wife, he no longer found himself in conversation with her ghost. He traveled a straight and simple path these days, not preoccupied with stepping on the white squares or the black. Nearly seventy-four, he was too intent on supporting his new family to cultivate any instincts for self-destruction—that check he'd left in the hotel!—or even to engage in Transcendental Meditation. And he'd certainly lost his appetite for club memberships and housekeepers.

Along with the proofs and his bills, his desk was piled with letters prompted by recent twentieth-anniversary TV appearances. There would be another round of them two years from now, commemorating Nixon's resignation instead of the break-in, and in between he could count on a steady stream of inquiries and accusations from the Kennedy crazies, who were determined to put him on the Grassy Knoll back in '63. None of the anniversary interviews paid anything, but he liked to imagine they helped to move at least a few copies of novels like *Chinese Red*. He hoped his sales figures were better than Colson's. A copy of Chuck's latest born-again production, *Why America Doesn't Work*, inscribed with a nauseating "Yours in Christ," sat unacknowledged on a nearby shelf.

He read little about Watergate, but from time to time did discover some fact that was new to him. Only a few years ago he'd opened Magruder's memoir to check something before an interview and discovered—the story of LaRue's old man! So that was Mr. X, the person mentioned inside the envelope he'd carried throughout the maddest weeks of those mad two years. Even now he had to hand it to her: if he were still in the game, he'd probably try to recruit Miss Lander for the Agency.

But as he sometimes now said, "I don't do derring anymore." The long fever of his life, spiking even before the break-in, had thrown him into delirium and then it had broken, and he had no desire to exchange the improbable domestic contentments of old age for the excitements of his early and middle years. His novels, for as long as anyone wanted them, would be enough in the way of vicarious high flying.

He checked the cozy dedication of *Chinese Red*.

To Laura: through the tough times and the good.

The book, once printed, would take its place on a shelf next to *The*

Berlin Ending. For now, he replaced the dedication page in the stack of proofs under the old jade pin he used as a paperweight.

Nixon's head was throbbing, with such force and regularity that he could count the beats. This had been happening a lot in the past couple of weeks, and here in his pajamas, half a world away from home, he was trying to recall whether Pat had experienced this sort of thing before the stroke. But that was almost twenty years ago, and he couldn't remember. He closed his eyes and checked his lucidity by counting off his trips to Russia, one per throb, starting in '59 with Khrushchev and going all the way up to this current one, in March of '94.

Satisfied that he was not impaired, only overworked, he took his mind off his mind and began thinking about the substance of this latest trip. He had to prepare himself for the possibility that Yeltsin, usually inclined to roll out the red carpet, might this time stiff him, annoyed by his plans to meet with Rutskoi and Zyuganov, the opposition leaders.

Well, there was no way he could do that. In all his travels between '63 and '68 he had never failed, wherever he went, to sit down with both the head of the government and the heads of the opposing parties. If Yeltsin wanted to play in the big, respectable Western leagues, he still had to learn that that's how things go.

But there was nothing wrong with creating a little drama, making a little news. And Christ, he'd rather be rebuffed by Yeltsin than received by Gorbachev, who was in love with his own nobility and thought the approval of the *New York Times* made up for supervising the dissolution of his own goddamned country.

He'd also rather, once he got home, spend a half hour inside Clinton's chaotic White House, reporting back on the trip and attempting to be useful, than spend day after day on the golf course, or in some bullshit corporate boardroom, like Jerry Ford. The speaking fees that guy was pulling down to this day! With just one of them you could buy twenty of the old Truman crowd's mink coats.

He rubbed his head and almost wished whatever was throbbing would explode and be done with it, a fate preferable to wandering through a fog like Reagan—though with Reagan how could anyone tell the difference? Christ, the man had had more luck in his life than Ford, and that was saying something.

He massaged his left temple and reflected upon a tendency to see only bad luck, never good, operating in his own life. Bad luck was the source of his defeats, whereas his achievements had come from his own skill and nerve. This was, he knew, a lopsided, childish view, like LBJ talking to Kennedy on election night in '60: *I hear* you're *losing Ohio but* we're *doing fine in Pennsylvania.* He ought to get over it, even at this late date.

He looked out the hotel window at the big red star over one of those *Metropolis*-style towers Stalin had thrust into the Moscow skyline. He found his thoughts going back to Reagan, to the only thing that really bothered him about the man. Would the lucky actor be seen as the bigger visionary, the one who refused to settle for "a new relationship between the superpowers," deducing instead that one of them might be tipped over entirely? The "evil" empire. Every left-wing professor had recoiled at seeing the word used to describe the Soviet Union, but had no trouble applying it twice a week to Richard Nixon.

As he'd told Henry, it will depend on who writes the history. His own presidential library out in California is a joke, a Madame Tussaud's full of plaster statues and none of the records that matter. But as long as he lives, he will never settle with the Archives, who are more rapacious than Cox when it comes to the tapes. He will leave it to Julie to figure things out when he is gone for good, to see how he can be mainstreamed into history with the rest of the men, mostly unimpressive, who had preceded and followed him in office.

Too many goddamned funerals this past year. Connally and Norman Vincent Peale, Haldeman—and before any of those, Pat. When he buried his wife, he'd given the press what they'd always wanted from *her*—tears, sobs, a loss of control in front of the cameras. They'd said he wouldn't last a year without her, and maybe they were right. There was that bottle of 1913 Lafite-Rothschild in the basement in Park Ridge, awaiting his hundredth birthday. But nobody made it to a hundred, not even Mrs. L.

He was nervous alone in the house at night, but he had no regrets about giving up the office downtown, no more than Pat had had, years before, when they gave up the town house on East Sixty-fifth. She'd

THOMAS MALLON

told him once or twice that the city felt haunted, and her mood had lifted a little when they picked up stakes for Jersey.

Before long it wouldn't matter where one lived. Who needed an office in New York when you could have a fax at home in the suburbs? God, he loved that machine! He could have run the whole damned presidency from Camp David with it. For that matter, one would soon be able to run the world from Whittier.

But on the whole he felt pretty awful. He was sick, and so was the newly free city outside and below him. He reached over to the pad by the telephone—each sheet of it still as coarse as the old Soviet toilet paper—and wrote: *Russia—turning pessimistic—anti-American.* He would expand on this for Clinton, suggest a shift in tone.

He turned off the lamp, but by the night light he could still see well enough to reach for the Walkman Tricia's boy had gotten him for Christmas. He inserted the tiny padded earphones and fast-forwarded the tape of Mussorgsky to the part he liked, a point in the prelude to *Khovanshchina* where he imagined himself aboard the *Sequoia,* early in the first year, sailing down the Potomac. He listened. This wasn't the triumphal crashing of *Victory at Sea,* just something peaceful. His eyes were closing. The music, turned low, would eventually put him to sleep, but that was all right, because the tape would turn itself off.

On New Year's Day 2001, Rose's niece was helping to dismantle her aunt's little Christmas tree.

"You *love* Christmas," the niece said softly, trying to jog Rose out of a confused spell.

"Of course I do," Rose replied, harshly. "Everybody loves Christmas." But after a moment, her perplexity over the tree that had been in her apartment these last few weeks renewed itself. "Where did it *come* from?" she asked.

"Bob Gray," explained her niece. "An old Washington friend of yours. He always sends you one. Because he knows how *much* you love Christmas."

"But we're in Ohio," said Rose, with a suspicious tone, making it plain she wasn't about to be tricked.

"He has it delivered from a local man—yes, here in Ohio," said the niece, who got up to put on some old swing music, the kind her aunt had once loved dancing to. It soon put Rose into a better mood, where she would stay for a while, if the talk didn't turn, as it did from time to time, to McCrea Manor, the nursing home into which she had no intention of moving.

The apartment was neat as a pin, the niece had to concede as she got ready to lug the tree out the door and say goodbye. All of Rose's knick-knacks were dusted and in their usual places. Same with her two little shelves of books, which included her old boss's memoirs; Julie Eisenhower's book about her mother; and *The Haldeman Diaries*, a library-discard copy which a couple of years back a nephew had ill-advisedly given Aunt Rose as a present. He didn't know the history between those two, and Rose had given him a real earful. Still, she'd kept the book.

"Goodbye, Aunt Rose."

"So long, sweetie. You can bring back the tree whenever you're through with it."

Rose was relieved to be alone again. She scarcely ever left the apartment and had not traveled any considerable distance since the two California funerals, Pat's and the boss's, in '93 and '94. She was able to get along just fine with the help of the woman who shopped for her once a week. It was true that some mornings she woke up thinking she needed to get ready for work at the old Royal China Company, her first job, but that misapprehension did no one any harm, and it always lifted by the time she finished making coffee.

She still read the paper each morning, having resumed the habit a year or two after the coup—which is what it was and what she called it. Sometimes, to no particular purpose, she clipped items: six months ago they'd named a Boston courthouse for Ed Brooke! She'd thought he was dead. In truth, she wished he *were* dead, not out of any ill will, but from some sense that she'd once embarrassed herself in front of him. How exactly, she couldn't remember.

People occasionally found her—sent requests for her autograph or got in touch with arcane questions about Watergate. She never responded, and the people who wrote never had the wit to realize she couldn't remember half the things she *wanted* to, let alone stuff from that awful time.

"Bob Gray." She had tried to keep her niece from seeing she didn't really know the name, but it was on her mind now. For the life of her she couldn't remember who that was, and so she walked over to the bookshelves and did something she did very rarely and with the greatest reluctance: consulted Bob Haldeman's diaries. Yes, there was Bob Gray in the index. She fumbled with her arthritic fingers to get to page 21, where he figured in an entry made on January 25, 1969:

> *President received beautiful silver cigarette box from Bob Gray. Presidential seal and name on top, date on front, plays "Hail to the Chief" when lid lifted . . .*

She remembered it as a cigar box and would have sworn it had come from Don Carnevale. But maybe not. The real problem with the entry was that it didn't help her remember who Bob Gray was.

She never felt comfortable having this book open; she always imagined she would flip a page and find some nasty crack about herself or somebody she liked. But it was hard not to thumb through these entries from January of '69, the beginning of things, and sure enough, there she was, the night before the first inauguration:

> *Rose Woods said she cried all the way in from Andrews AFB, crowds along the streets, triumphal return vs. departure eight years ago.*

Nothing mean, but the lines excited such a powerful recollection that the tears were soon coming in a kind of relay—joyous ones, the kind she'd shed that day; and bitter ones, too, that it had all been taken away, so unfairly and so soon.

She felt a familiar rush of anger toward HRH, not for putting her through this now, but for having her there on the page in the first place, weeping with happiness; for putting on display that private moment she should never have told him about. He had no right to it.

She got up, steadied herself, and found the pair of scissors in the kitchen drawer. She brought them over to the book and carefully cut away the entry on pages 17 and 18, as if what it recorded had never happened.

———

"You know what he used to tell me?" asked one of the three men, buddies of Fred LaRue seated around a courtyard table at Mary Mahoney's. "That he gave the feds four months—and they gave him ten years."

The other men nodded. They'd heard LaRue say the same thing about the prison term he'd finally served in 1975. During his months at Maxwell, over in Alabama, he'd dried out and stopped smoking and played a lot of badminton, probably adding a decade to his life, which had now, on July 17, 2004, come to an end.

"He used to say it was more like bein' *overhauled* than rehabilitated."

The men laughed, more loudly than Fred ever had.

"Badminton! How the hell he played is beyond me. Take a look through these," said one of the men, passing the others a pair of eyeglasses they'd gathered up from a night table in Fred's room at the Sun Tan Motel, before the coroner came to collect the body.

"Christ," said another of the men, looking through the lenses. "These must be stronger than the Hubble telescope."

All three laughed and then fell silent, brooding again on the sad but likely fact that Fred had been dead for two or three days before the motel maid found him.

"He was never bitter, that's for sure."

"I never heard him say a word against Nixon or Mitchell."

"Only one I ever heard him talk against was, what's his name, Magruder."

"Oh, Christ," said the one closest to being a Watergate buff. "Even Colson never went and got himself *ordained*." He explained that in recent years Magruder had taken to giving interviews in his Presbyterian minister's surplice.

"Colson still alive?"

"Him and Dean. Couple of others." He pointed to the TV above the bar inside the restaurant. "The producers tended to forget about Fred whenever it came time to doin' another Watergate program."

"And that was fine with him."

With smiles they acknowledged their late friend's shyness, the way he never told them quite all there was to be told about anything. During his last years, his family up in Jackson had kept him on a long leash, and otherwise he was pretty much the same as he'd been before politics led him up to Washington, almost forty years ago.

The men called for another round, and while their empty glasses were being cleared from the table, they looked at the handful of LaRue's possessions, ready to be turned over to his family, sitting amidst the coasters and napkins.

"You seen this?" One of the men picked up an envelope. "It's the strangest goddamned thing." The stamps on it were Canadian; the postmark was from 1957; the addressee was a law firm in Jackson. And there was that word "MOOT."

"Never opened?"

"Doesn't look like it."

"Ever heard of the law firm?"

"Oh, open the goddamned thing."

The man holding it slit the envelope with a butter knife. He took out some thick stapled pages that were discolored where they'd been folded for forty-seven years. He flipped through the sheaf until he came to the fourth page, which had two paragraphs somebody had drawn a dark red box around. He positioned the paper so everyone could read it for himself under the sunlight filling the restaurant's courtyard.

Investigators conclude that Mr. X could not have been killed by Mr. X Jr.

When Mr. X Jr. stood up to fire at the birds, Mr. X, who had also been drinking alcohol (see medical appendix), reacted with startlement from his semi-upright position approximately 25 feet away. Mr. X's own weapon discharged itself into his upper-right torso, so quickly after the discharge from Mr. X Jr.'s that witnesses believed they had heard a single report.

"Jesus, they're talkin' about his daddy."

They all knew something of the story, most of it from people other than Fred.

The victim's intake of alcohol may have been a matter of contributory negligence—his own—but otherwise his death was indisputably accidental.

"And he kept this thing sealed up for fifty years? Never even opened it?"

"Fred had his own way of dealin' with the world."

"*Somebody* once opened it," said the waitress, who'd liked Fred and had been eavesdropping. She pointed to the box outlining the two paragraphs. "That was made with lipstick, sure as shootin'."

Acknowledgments

I am grateful, even more than usually, to my editor, Dan Frank, who guided me toward and through this book in innumerable ways.

I also appreciate the enthusiasm that my agent, Andrew Wylie, has shown toward this project over the past few years.

Thanks, too, to Ed Cohen, Altie Karper, and Jill Verrillo for all their skillful editorial and production help.

I owe a debt to all of the following people and institutions for archival resources and research help: Jeffrey M. Flannery at the Library of Congress; Susan Cooper and Marty McGann of the National Archives and Records Administration; Brian McLaughlin of the U.S. Senate Library; Margaret Zoller of the Smithsonian Archives of American Art; the Washingtoniana Division of the District of Columbia Public Library; Jonathan Movroydis at the Richard Nixon Foundation; the Hoover Institution Archives, Stanford, California; the Biloxi *Sun-Herald*, Biloxi, Mississippi.

For various kinds of encouragement and assistance I would like to thank: Michael Kaiser, president of the John F. Kennedy Center for the Performing Arts; Patricia Kenworthy; Dr. Joseph Abraham Levi; Priscilla McMillan; Charles Francis; Tom Duesterberg; Robert Nedelkoff; Michael Bishop.

For reminiscences of life within the Nixon administration and around Washington during the early 1970s, I am grateful to Robert Gray, Michael Balzano, and my dear friend Rene Carpenter.

James Rosen, author of *The Strong Man: John Mitchell and the Secrets of Watergate*, provided me with advice, Watergate lore, and research materials. Most of the latter pertained to Fred LaRue, and I am very much in his debt for them—though I should note here that, among the book's main characters, LaRue's life has undergone the greatest degree of fictionalization.

In this book, as in my previous novels, I have operated along the always sliding scale of historical fiction. The text contains deviations from fact that some readers will regard as unpardonable and others will deem unworthy of notice. But this remains a work of fiction, not history.

I owe thanks to John McConnell, who served in two presidential administrations, for a host of shrewd suggestions and free lunches in the White House Mess.

While writing this novel, my mind has often traveled back to conversations I had about Richard Nixon with my pal Kevin Morley when we were college freshmen during the tumultuous spring of 1970. I'm grateful for his friendship during that time and in all the years since.

Special thanks to Bob Wilson and Sudip Bose at *The American Scholar.*

But thanks, above all, to Bill Bodenschatz—for everything within, and outside, these pages.

WASHINGTON, D.C.
OCTOBER 15, 2011

ALSO BY THOMAS MALLON

YOURS EVER
People and Their Letters

A delightful investigation of the art of letter writing, *Yours Ever* explores masterpieces dispatched through the ages by messenger, postal service, and BlackBerry. Here are Madame de Sévigné's devastatingly sharp reports from the French court, F. Scott Fitzgerald's tormented advice to his young daughter, the casually brilliant musings of Flannery O'Connor, the lustful boastings of Lord Byron, and the prison cries of Sacco and Vanzetti, all accompanied by Thomas Mallon's own insightful commentary. From battlefield confessions to suicide notes, fan letters to hate mail, *Yours Ever* is an exuberant reintroduction to a vast and entertaining literature—a book that will help to revive, in the digital age, this glorious lost art.

Nonfiction/Letters

ALSO AVAILABLE
Fellow Travelers

VINTAGE BOOKS
Available wherever books are sold.
www.vintagebooks.com